Everyman, I will go with thee, and be thy guide,
In thy most need to go by thy side.

EVERYMAN'S LIBRARY

Founded 1906 by J. M. Dent (d. 1926)
Edited by Ernest Rhys (d. 1946)

POETRY & THE DRAMA

SELECTED COMEDIES
BY J.-B. POQUELIN MOLIÈRE · INTRO-
DUCTION BY FREDERICK C. GREEN
IN 2 VOLS.   VOL. 2

MOLIÈRE, the name assumed by Jean-Baptiste Poquelin, who was born in Paris in 1622. Studied law at University of Orléans. Attracted to theatre, formed a small troupe and toured the provinces acting plays written by himself, 1645–58. Died in 1673.

COMEDIES

VOLUME TWO

MOLIÈRE

WILDSIDE PRESS

CONTENTS OF VOL. II

DON JOHN, or THE FEAST OF THE STATUE

(A COMEDY)

Don John, *or* The Feast of the Statue, *a Comedy of Five Acts in Prose, acted at Paris at the Theatre of the Palace - Royal,* 15 *February,* 1665.

It was not by his own choice, that Molière wrote upon the subject of *Don John,* or *The Feast of the Statue.* The Italians, who borrowed it from the Spanish, had brought it upon their stage in France with vast success. A villain odious for his crimes and hypocrisy, the silly miracle of a moving and speaking statue, and the extravagant scene of Hell did not disgust the vulgar, who are always fond of wonders.

In 1660, De Villiers, a comedian of the Hôtel de Bourgogne, acted it in verse, and Molière performed it in prose in 1665. His company, who had set him upon this work, were sufficiently punished for their bad choice by the little success it met with; which might be occasioned, perhaps, either by the prejudice which reigned then against comedies of five acts written in prose, being stronger than the spirit of whim, which had drawn the public in crowds to the Italians, and to the Hôtel de Bourgogne; or else by their being offended with some hazardous passages in it, which the author suppressed the second time of its being acted.

A company which was formed in 1673, out of that of the Marais, and that of the Palace-Royal, which were both broke, acted Molière's *Feast of the Statue,* which Thomas Corneille had turned into verse at the Hôtel de Guénegaud in 1677, under which form it drew a prodigious concourse of spectators, and 'tis that alone which is played at present.

ACTORS

DON JOHN, *son to Don Lewis.*
ELVIRA, *wife to Don John.*
GUSMAN, *gentleman-usher to Elvira.*
DON CARLOS, } *brothers to Elvira.*
DON ALONZO, }
DON LEWIS, *father to Don John.*
FRANCISCO, *a poor man.*
CHARLOTTA, } *country-girls.*
MATHURINA, }
PIERROT, *a country-fellow.*
THE STATUE OF THE GOVERNOR.
SGANAREL, }
VIOLETTE, } *Lackeys to Don John.*
RAGOTIN, }
MR. DIMANCHE, *a tradesman.*
RAMÉE, *a bully.*
GHOST.

SCENE: *Sicily.*

ACT I

SCENE I

Sganarel, Gusman.

Sganarel. [*With a tobacco-box in his hand.*] Whatever Aristotle and the whole body of philosophers may say, there's nothing comparable to tobacco; 'tis the reigning passion of your better sort of people, and he who lives without tobacco, deserves not to live; it not only exhilarates and purges human brains; but it also trains the mind to virtue, and by this one learns to become well-bred. Don't you see plainly, from the time one takes it, in what an obliging manner one uses it with all the world, and how one is delighted to give it to right and left wherever one comes? one doesn't even stay to be asked for it, but prevents people's wishes: so true it is, that tobacco inspires all who take it with sentiments of honour and virtue. But enough of this matter; let us resume our discourse a little. So that, dear Gusman, Donna Elvira your mistress, being surprised at our departure, is come after us. And that heart of hers, which my master has touched a little too home, cannot subsist, you say, without coming here in search of him? Wouldst thou ha' me, under the rose, tell thee my thoughts? I fear she'll be ill-requited for her love, that her journey to this city will produce little fruit, and that you'd been just as much gainers had you never stirred off the spot.

Gusman. And prithee, Sganarel, tell me what reason can inspire thee with so ill-boding a fear? Has thy master opened to thee his heart upon this head; and did he tell thee his coldness to us had obliged him to depart?

Sganarel. Not at all, but upon view of the premises, I know pretty near the course of things; and without his having said a word to me, I durst almost lay a wager the matter tends that way. I may perhaps be mistaken, but upon such like subjects experience has given me great lights.

Gusman. What! should this unforeseen departure be a piece of infidelity in Don John? Could he do this injury to the chaste love of Elvira?

5

Sganarel. No, no, he's too young yet, and has not the heart——

Gusman. Can a man of his quality do so base an action?

Sganarel. O, yes, his quality! The reason is admirable; he would forbear on that account——

Gusman. But the sacred ties of marriage are an engagement upon him.

Sganarel. Ah! poor Gusman, my good friend, be' me, thou dost not yet know what sort of man Don John is.

Gusman. Truly I don't know what sort of man he may be, if he has been guilty of this perfidy towards us; and I don't comprehend how, after so much love, and such impatience expressed, such pressing homage, vows, sighs and tears, so many passionate letters, such ardent protestations and reiterated oaths, such transports in short, and ravings as he showed, so far as even to force the sacred obstacle of a convent in his passion, to get Donna Elvira within his power; I don't comprehend, I say, how after all this he should have the heart to fail of his word.

Sganarel. I have no great difficulty, for my part, to comprehend this, and did you know the wanderer, you would think the thing easy enough to him. I don't say he has changed his sentiments of Elvira, I have as yet no certainty of it; you know that by his order I set out before him, and since his arrival he has had no discourse with me; but by way of precaution, I give thee to know (*inter nos*) you see, in Don John my master, one of the greatest villains the earth ever bore; a madman, a dog, a demon, a Turk, a heretic, who neither believes in a heaven, a hell, or devil; who passes his life like a true brute beast, a hog of Epicurus, a true Sardanapalus; who shuts his ears against all remonstrances that can be made him, and treats our whole belief as an old wife's tale. You tell me he has married your mistress; believe me, he would have done more for his passion, and with her would have married even thee, his dog, or his cat. A marriage costs him nothing the contracting, 'tis his most usual snare to trepan the fair sex: and he marries at all adventures, lady, gentlewoman, citizen, country-woman, he thinks nothing too hot, or too cold for him; and should I tell thee the names of all those whom he has married in different places, the bead-roll would last till midnight. You seem surprised and change colour at this discourse; this is only a sketch of the man; and to finish the picture would require far stronger strokes of the pencil; let it suffice that the wrath of

Heaven must some of these days crush him; that I had much better be with the devil than with him, and that he makes me witness of such horrible things, that I could wish he were already I don't know where; but a great lord, a wicked man, is a terrible thing; I must be faithful to him in spite of me; fear in me does the office of zeal, bridles my sentiments, and forces me very often to applaud what my mind detests.   See there he comes to take a turn in the palace; let us part.   Harkee however, I have trusted you very frankly with this secret, and it has slipped me a little too quick; but should anything of it happen to reach his ears, I shall say flatly you lied.

SCENE II
Don John, Sganarel.

Don John.   What man was that there talking to thee?   He has a good deal of the air, I think, of honest Gusman who belongs to Elvira.

Sganarel.   'Tis something very like it.

Don John.   What! is it he?

Sganarel.   The very man.

Don John.   And how long has he been in this city?

Sganarel.   Since last night.

Don John.   And what subject brings him here?

Sganarel.   I fancy you can judge well enough what disturbs him.

Don John.   Our departure without doubt.

Sganarel.   The honest man is quite mortified, and asked me the reason of it.

Don John.   And what answer did you make him?

Sganarel.   That you had said nothing of it to me.

Don John.   But prithee, what dost think of it, what dost thee imagine of this affair?

Sganarel.   I?   I believe, without wronging you, that you have some new amour in your head.

Don John.   Dost think so?

Sganarel.   Yes.

Don John.   Faith, thou'rt not mistaken, and I must own to thee, that another object has chased Elvira from my thoughts.

Sganarel.   Oh! lack-a-day, I have Don John at fingers' ends, and know your heart to be the greatest rambler in the world; 'tis pleased to run from chains to chains, and never loves to rest in one place.

Don John. And tell me, dost not think I'm in the right to deal with it in this manner?

Sganarel. Oh! sir——

Don. John. What? speak.

Sganarel. Certainly you are in the right, if you have a mind to't. There's no saying against it; but had you not a mind to't, it might perhaps be another affair.

Don John. Well, I give thee liberty to speak, and to tell me thy sentiments.

Sganarel. In this case, sir, I shall frankly tell you, I don't approve of your method; and that I think it a base thing to fall in love on all hands, as you do.

Don John. What? would you have one tie one's self down to the first object that takes us; renounce the world for that, and be blind to every one else? A pretty thing to pique one's self upon the false honour of being faithful, of being buried for ever in one amour, and being dead from our youth to all other beauties that may strike us! No, no, constancy is only fit for fools; every fine woman has a right to charm us; and the advantage of being first met with, ought not to rob others of the just pretensions they all have to our hearts. For my part, beauty ravishes me wherever I find it, and I readily yield to that sweet violence with which it draws us; that I'm engaged signifies nothing, the love I have for one fair, does not engage my heart to do injustice to others; I have eyes to see the merit of 'em all, and to pay every one the homage and tribute that nature obliges us to. However it is, I can't refuse my heart to any lovely creature I see, and from the moment a handsome face demands it, had I a thousand hearts I'd give 'em all. The rising inclinations, after all, have inexplicable charms in 'em, and all the pleasure of love consists in the variety. One tastes an extreme delight in reducing, by a thousand submissions, the heart of a young beauty; to see the little progress one makes in it from day to day; to combat with transports, tears, and sighs, the innocent modesty of a mind which can hardly prevail upon itself to surrender; to force, inch by inch, through all the little obstacles she throws in our way, to conquer the scruples she values herself upon, and lead her gently whither we've a mind to bring her. But when one is once master of it, there's nothing more to wish; all the beauty of the passion is at an end, and we sleep in the tranquillity of such an amour, if some new object does not awake our desires, and present to us the attractive charms of a conquest still to make. In short, there's nothing so

delightful as to triumph over the resistance of a beauty. I
have the ambition of conquerors, in this case, who fly perpetually
from victory to victory, and never can resolve to set bounds
to their wishes. There's nothing can resist the impetuosity of
my desires; I find I've a heart to be in love with all the world,
and like Alexander, I could wish there were other worlds, that
I might carry my amorous conquests thither.

Sganarel. Od's my life, how you rattle! It seems as if you
had this by heart, and you talk for all the world as if 'twere
in print.

Don John. What hast thou to say to this?

Sganarel. Troth, I have to say——I don't know what to
say; you turn things in such a manner that you seem to be in
the right, and yet 'tis certain you are not. I had the finest
thoughts in the world, and your discourse has put 'em all out
o' my head; let me alone; another time I'll commit all my
reasons to writing, to dispute with you.

Don John. You'll do right.

Sganarel. But, sir, may it be within the permission you have
given me, if I should tell you that I am something scandalised
at the life you lead.

Don John. How? what life is't I lead?

Sganarel. A very good one. But, for example, to see you
marry every month, as you do.

Don John. Is there anything more agreeable?

Sganarel. 'Tis true, I conceive this is very agreeable, and
very diverting, and I should like it well enough, were there no
harm in it; but, sir, to trifle thus with marriage, which——

Don John. Go, go, 'tis an affair I shall easily rid myself of,
without thy giving thyself any trouble about it.

Sganarel. Troth, sir, this is scurvy jesting of yours.

Don John. Soho! Mr. Blockhead. You know I've told you,
I love none of your remonstrance-makers.

Sganarel. Therefore I don't speak to you, Heaven forbid
it. You know what you do; and if you are a libertine, you have
your reasons; but there are certain little impertinent fellows in
the world, who are so, without knowing why or wherefore, who
set up for free-thinkers, because they think it becomes them;
and had I a master of this kind, I'd tell him flatly to his face,
Does it become you, little earth-worm, little shrimp as you are
(I speak to the aforesaid master), does it become you, to set
yourself to ridicule what all mankind revere. Think ye, because
you are a man of quality, because you have a fair well-curled

peruke, a feather in your hat, a well-laced coat and flame-coloured ribbons ('tis not you I speak to, 'tis to the other), think ye, I say, that you're e'er the wiser man for this, that you should be allowed all liberties, and nobody should dare to give you your own for it? Learn from me who am your footman, that libertines never come to a good end, and that——

Don John. Peace.

Sganarel. Why, what's the matter?

Don John. The matter is to tell thee that a certain beauty has got my heart, and that captivated by her charms, I followed her to this city.

Sganarel. And are you under no apprehensions, sir, about the death of the governor you killed six months ago?

Don John. And why apprehensions? didn't I kill him fairly?

Sganarel. Oh! the fairest in the world, he'd be in the wrong to complain.

Don John. I had my pardon for this affair.

Sganarel. Yes, but this pardon does not perhaps stifle the resentments of relations and friends, and——

Don John. Poh! Let us not think of any ill that may happen to us, but think only of what can give us pleasure. The person I speak to you of, is a young creature promised in marriage, the most agreeable in the world, who was brought hither by the man she is to marry; and chance threw this pair of lovers in my way, three or four days before they set out on their journey. Never did I see people so satisfied with each other, and discover so much love. The visible tenderness of their mutual passion gave me emotion; I was struck to the heart, and my love commenced by jealousy. Yes, I could not at first view endure to see 'em so happy together, resentment kindled desire in me; and I conceived it an extreme pleasure to disturb their intelligence, and break that union, the delicacy of which was so offensive to my mind; but hitherto all my attempts have been in vain, and I have recourse to the last remedy; this intended spouse is to regale his mistress to-day, with the diversion of going upon the water. Without saying a word of it to thee, all things are prepared to gratify my passion, and I have a little vessel, and men, by whom I can easily carry off the fair.

Sganarel. Ah! sir——

Don John. What?

Sganarel. 'Tis mighty well done of you, and you take things in the right sense. There's nothing in this world like making one's self easy.

Don John. Prepare therefore to go along with me, and do you yourself take care to bring all my arms, that—— [*Sees Donna Elvira.*] Oh! most unlucky meeting. Traitor, thou didst not tell me she was here in person.

Sganarel. Sir, you did not so much as ask me.

Don John. Is she mad not to have changed her dress, and to come here in her riding habit?

SCENE III

Donna Elvira, Don John, Sganarel.

Donna Elvira. Will you do me the favour, Don John, to please to know me, and may I hope at least, you will deign to turn your eyes this way?

Don John. I confess t'ye, madam, that I am surprised, and that I did not expect you here.

Donna Elvira. Yes, I see plainly you did not expect me here, and that you are in truth surprised, but in a quite different way from what I expected, and the manner in which you appear so, gives me a full persuasion of what I refused to believe. I admire at my simplicity, and the weakness of my heart, in doubting of that treachery, which so many appearances might have confirmed me in. I was harmless enough, I confess, or rather foolish enough, to be willing to deceive myself, and to take pains to belie my eyes and my judgment. I sought for reasons to excuse to my passion that abatement of love I discovered in you; and I purposely forged a hundred just occasions for so hasty a departure, to justify the crime my reason accused you of. In vain was all that my just suspicions could daily say to me, I rejected their voice which represented you to me as a criminal, and I hearkened with pleasure to a thousand ridiculous chimeras, which painted you to my heart as innocent; but in short, this meeting permits me no longer to doubt, and the look you received me with, informs me of much more than I would ever have wished to have known. I shall be glad, nevertheless, to hear from your own mouth the reasons for your departure. Pray, speak, Don John, let us see with what an air you can justify yourself.

Don John. Madam, here is Sganarel knows why I came away.

Sganarel. [*Whispering Don John.*] I sir! with submission, I know nothing of it.

Donna Elvira. Well, Sganarel, speak. No matter from whose mouth I hear his reasons.

Don John. [*Making signs to Sganarel to come near him.*] Come tell the lady then.

Sganarel. [*Whispering Don John.*] What would you have me say?

Donna Elvira. Come hither, since he will have it so, and tell me a little the cause of so sudden a journey.

Don John. Won't you answer?

Sganarel. [*Whispering Don John.*] I have nothing to answer. You joke with your humble servant.

Don John. Will ye answer, I say?

Sganarel. Madam——

Donna Elvira. What?

Sganarel. [*Turning towards his master.*] Sir——

Don John. [*Threatening him.*] If——

Sganarel. Madam, the conquerors, Alexander and the other worlds, are the cause of our departure; that's all I can say, sir.

Donna Elvira. Will you be pleased, Don John, to clear up these pretty mysteries?

Don John. Madam, to say the truth——

Donna Elvira. Fie! How poorly do you go about to defend yourself for a man who is a courtier, and who should be accustomed to these sort of things! I really pity you, to see you in that confusion; why don't you arm your front with a noble impudence? Why don't you swear that you still entertain the same sentiments for me, that you love me eternally with an unparalleled affection, and that nothing but death is capable of rending you from me? Why don't you tell me that affairs of the last consequence obliged you to set out, without giving me notice of it, that, much against your will, you must stay here for some time, and that I need only to return from whence I came, assured that you will follow me as soon as possible? That 'tis certain you are impatient to be with me again, and that, separated from me, you suffer what the body does when separated from the soul? Thus it is you should defend yourself, and not stand thunderstruck as you do.

Don John. I own to you, madam, I have not the talent of dissimulation, and that I wear a sincere heart. I won't tell you that I have still the same sentiments for you, and that I am impatient to rejoin you, since 'tis certain, in reality, that I only came away to avoid you; not for the reasons that you may imagine, but through a pure motive of conscience, and because I could not think I could live any longer with you without sin. I have had some scruples, madam, and opened the eyes of my mind upon what I was a doing. I reflected that to marry you, I forced you from the cloister of a convent, that you have broke your vows which engaged you another way, and that Heaven is very jealous of these sort of things. I was seized with repentance, and dreaded the wrath of Heaven. I thought our marriage was only adultery in disguise, and that it would bring down some calamity upon us from above, and that, in short, I ought to endeavour to forget you, and to give you the opportunity of returning to your former bonds. Would you, madam, oppose so holy a resolution, and have me, by retaining you, expose myself to the vengeance of Heaven? That by——

Donna Elvira. Oh! abandoned villain; now do I know thee thoroughly, and to my misfortune I know thee when 'tis too late, and when this knowledge can only serve to make me desperate; but know, thy crime will not remain unpunished: and that that Heaven thou darest to mock, will revenge thy perfidy.

Don John. Madam——

Donna Elvira. 'Tis enough, I'll hear no more, and I even accuse myself for having heard too much already. 'Tis a meanness too far to explain what tends to our disgrace, and upon such subjects a noble spirit should fix its resolution at the first word. Don't expect I should exclaim against thee in reproaches and opprobrious language; no, no, I have no fury to spend in vain words, but all my heat is reserved for vengeance. I tell it thee once more, that Heaven will punish thee, perfidious man, for the wrong thou dost me; and if thou hast nothing to fear from Heaven, at least fear the anger of an injured woman.

Scene IV

Don John, Sganarel.

Sganarel. [*Aside.*] If ever remorse could seize him ——

Don John. [*After some pause.*] Come along, let us think of the execution of our amorous enterprise.

Sganarel. [*Alone.*] Oh! what an abominable master am I forced to serve!

ACT II

Scene I

Charlotta, Pierrot.

Charlotta. I'fakins, Pierrot, yau weer theer in the vara nick o' time.

Pierrot. S'bobs, they were within eams eace o' being drawnded, boath of 'um.

Charlotta. What it was the greit storm o' waind this morn, that o'orset 'um in the seea.

Pierrot. Eye, marry, Charlotta, I'se tell thee autright haw it fell aut; for, as the zaying iz, I spied 'um aut ferst, ferst I spied 'um aut. Soa in short, I was o' th' seea side, I and fat Lucas, and we were a-pleying the roague together, wi' clods o' yearth, that we threw at won another's heids, for yaw vara weell known, fat Lucas loves to pley the roague, and I sumtimes pley the roague too. Soa as we were pleying the roague, sens wee must e'en pley the roague, I parceaved a greit distance off, sumthing that sterred in the weter, and it came bobbing taw'rds us. I looked earnestly at it, and belive au' of a sudden I saa that I saa noathing moor. Whew! Lucas, says I, I think thear are two men a-swimming dawn thear. Pooa, says he, yaw eyn are not fellows, yaw eyn are dazzled. By th' mess, says I, my eyn are not dazzled, they are men. Noa, noa, says he to me, you're purblind. I hould a wager, says I, that I ben't purblind, says I, and that they are two men, says I, that are swimming streight hither, says I. By my trath, says he, I hould a wager they are not. Weell, cum on, says I, will yau hould tenpence on't? Marry will I, says he, and to show thee, thear's the muny dawn o' th' nail, says he. I was neather fool, nar foolhardy, dawn comes I bou'dly upo' th' graund, with fowr silver pennies, and six pen'orth o' ha'pence, as freely, by'r Lady, as if I'd drank a mug o' beer: for I'm vara ventersome, and go on helter-skelter. I knew what I dud, hawsomever, for au' my boudness! Soa we had but e'en just leayed the wager, but we saa the two men vara pleanly, who made signs to us to cum and fetch 'um, and I snatches up the stakes. Cum, Lucas, says I, yaw seen pleanly that they cawn us; let us goa off hand and seave 'um. Noa, says he, they made me loase. Then had we such a to-doo, that at last, to meak short on't, I preiched soa much to him, that we gat into a booat, and then I mead soa much wark, that I gat 'um aut o' weter, and then I carried 'um hoame to th' fire, and then they doffed 'umsels stark neaked to dry 'umsells, and soa then thear comes two moor o' th' seame cumpany, who weer seaved boath togither quite alone, and soa then comes Mathurina, and one of 'um had a sheep's eye taw'rds her. Just e'en soa, Charlotta, aw this happened.

Charlotta. Dadn't yaw say, Pierrot, that one of 'um was a great deal handsomer than t'others?

Pierrot. Eye, he's the master, he mun be some greit, greit mon to be suer, for he'as gould on his cloas, from top to bottom, and his sarvants are gentlefolkes 'umsells, and for aw his bein a greit mon, i'fakes he had bin drawned, if I'd not bin theer.

Charlotta. Consider a little.

Pierrot. Oh by'r Lakin, if't had not been for us, he'd a' gone to his last account.

Charlotta. Is he still at yaur hause stark neaked, Pierrot?

Pierrot. Noa, noa, they aw put on their cloas agean befoor us. Marcy o' me, I newr saw any o' these folks dress 'umsells before, what a parcel o' fiddle-faddle things these courtiers wear! I should loose mysel in 'um, for my part, and I was ameazed to see 'em. Marry, Charlotta, they han heare which doesn't stick to their heads, and they putt it on like a heuge cap of unspun flax. They han sarks wi' sleeves that thau and I might get into. Instead o' breeches they han a wardrobe as large as fro' this to Easter. Instead o' doublets, they han little tiny waistcoats that do nat reach to their breech; and instead o' bands, a greit neck-hankerchi', wi' four large tufts o' linnen hanging dawn o' their breasts. They han bands abaut their wrists too, and great raunds o' leace abaut their legs, and amung aw this so mony ribbons, so mony ribbons, that its borning shame. There's nought about 'um, e'en so much as their shoon but what is stuffed wi' um fro' one end to t'other, and they're made after such a fashion I should break my neck in 'um.

Charlotta. I'fakins, Pierrot, I mun go see 'um a little.

Pierrot. Oh! Hark thee, Charlotta, stay a little ferst, I have something elz to say to thee.

Charlotta. Weell, tell me, what is't?

Pierrot. Dost see, Charlotta, I mon, as the saying is, break my mind to thee. I'm i' love wi' ye, yaw known it vara weell, I am for us being married togither, but s'boddikins, I'm nat pleased wi' ye.

Charlotta. Haw? what is the matter then?

Pierrot. Th' matter is yau vexn my vara heart, in good deed.

Charlotta. Haw soa?

Pierrot. Feath yaw done not love me.

Charlotta. Hoh! hoh! Is that aw?

Pierrot. Eye, that's aw, and enough too, o' my conscience.

Charlotta. Lawd, Pierrot, yaw awlas sayn the seam thing to me.

Pierrot. I awlas say the seam thing because it awlas is the seam thing; an if it wern't awlas the seam thing, I would not awlas say the seam thing.

Charlotta. But what mun I doo, what would yaw ha?

Pierrot. Buddakins I'd ha ye love me.

Charlotta. Whya doan't I love thee?

Pierrot. Noa, yaw doan't love me, and for aw that I doo aw I con to meake ye. Noa offence, I buy ribbons for yaw of aw the pedlars that cum about; I break my neck to climb birds-nests for ye, I meak th' oud fidler play for yaw when your borthday cums; and aw this is noa moor than if I run my heid agean the wall. It is neather fear, nor honest, d'ye see, nat to love foulk that loven us.

Charlotta. Whya, weell-a-day, I love thee tew.

Pierrot. Eye, i'fakes, yaw loven me heugely.

Charlotta. Haw would yaw ha' one doo?

Pierrot. I would ha' ye doo as foulk doo, when foulk are in love to sum porpose.

Charlotta. Whya doan't I love thee to sum porpose?

Pierrot. Noa, when that's the cease, it's seen, and one dos a thousaud little apish tricks to foulk when one loves 'um in good earnest. Do but see fat Thomasine, haw hoo's in love like bewitched with young Robin; hoo's awlas about him to pleague him, and hoo newer lets him aloane, hoo's awlas a-playing him sum unlucky prank, or hits him a rap as hoo goas by him; an t'uther day as he was sitting on a joint-stool, hoo cums and whips it fro' under him, and dawn faws he at's foo length, upo' the graund. S'flesh, foulk don thus when they're i' love: but thau newer saist a word to me, for thy part; thau'rt awlas for aw the ward like a log o' wood, and I mu'd goa by thee twenty times, and thau newer sturr to gi' me the least thump, or say the least thing to me. Zooks, it's nat weel dun, after aw, and yaw're too could for foulks.

Charlotta. What wu'n yaw ha' me doo? It's my yumar, and I connot new-mak it mysel.

Pierrot. Yumar me noa yumar, when won loves foulk, won awlas gi's sum smaw inkling on't.

Charlotta. In short, I love thee as weell as I con, and if thau been't content with that, thau mun e'en love sumbody elz.

Pierrot. Why thear naw, didn't I say soa? i'fakes, if yau lov'd me, yau would not say that.

Charlotta. Why dun yaw pleague one so?

Pierrot. Ookers, what harm doo I doo ye? I no' but ask a little love o' ye.

Charlotta. Weell, let won aloan then, and do not teaz me soa, happen it may cum aw at wonce, withaut thinking on't.

Pierrot. Shak honds then, Charlotta.

Charlotta. Weell, thear.   [*Gives him her hand.*

Pierrot. Promise me then, that yau'll strive to love me moor.

Charlotta. I'll doo aw I con, but that mun cum of itsel. Pierrot, is that the gentilmon?

Pierrot. Yai, that's he.

Charlotta. Oh! lock-a-day, haw fine a is, and what pity't had bin, if a'd bin drawn'd!

Pierrot. I'se cum agean belive, I'se goa drink a mug to rease my spirits a little after my fatigue.

SCENE II

Don John, Sganarel, Charlotta, at the farther part of the stage.

Don John. We've missed our blow, Sganarel, and this sudden squall has o'er-set our sloop and our project; but to say the truth, the country-wench I have just parted with, repairs this misfortune, and I saw such charms in her, as have banished the vexation the ill success of our enterprise had given me. This heart must not escape me, and I have already made such a disposition that I shan't sigh long in vain.

Sganarel. I own, sir, you astonish me. We have scarce escaped the danger of death, and instead of thanking Heaven, for the compassion it has vouchsafed to have of us, you take pains afresh to draw down its vengeance by your usual whims, and your amours—[*Seeing Don John look angry.*] Peace, rascal as you are, you don't know what you talk of, and my master knows what he does. Come.

Don John. [*Spying Charlotta.*] Hah! whence comes this other country-girl? Did you ever see anything prettier, and tell me, dost not think this as handsome as t'other?

Sganarel. Certainly. [*Aside.*] Another new piece.

Don John. [*To Charlotta.*] What has blest me, my fair one, with this agreeable meeting? What, are there in these rural places, among these trees and rocks, persons of your make?

Charlotta. Just as you see, sir.

Don John. Are you of this village?

Charlotta. Yes, sir.

Don John. And do you live there?

Charlotta. Yes, sir.

Don John. Your name is?

Charlotta. Charlotta, at your service.

Don John. What a beautiful person is there! What piercing eyes are those!

Charlotta. You make me quite ashamed, sir.

Don John. Oh! Don't be ashamed to hear what's true. What d'ye say, Sganarel? Can anything be more agreeable? Turn about a little, pray. What a fine shape! Hold up your head a little, pray; what a pretty face is this! Open your eyes quite. How lovely they are! Pray, let me see your teeth. Oh! how amorous they are! And these inviting lips. For my part, I'm charmed, I never saw so fine a person.

Charlotta. Sir, you are pleased to say soa, and I doan't know whether you doan't banter me.

Don John. I, banter you? Heaven forbid, I love you too much for that, and I speak from the very bottom of my heart.

Charlotta. I am very much obliged to you, if it is soa.

Don John. Not at all, you're not obliged to me for anything I say, you are indebted only to your own beauty for it.

Charlotta. Sir, this all too finely said for me, and I have not wit enough to answer you.

Don John. Do but mind her hands, Sganarel.

Charlotta. Fie, sir, they're as dirty as I doan't know what.

Don John. Oh! Why do you say so? They are the prettiest in the world; pray, suffer me to kiss 'em.

Charlotta. You do me too much honour, sir, and if I'd known it just now, I'd not ha' failed to've washed 'em with bran.

Don John. Pray tell me, pretty Charlotta, are you married or no?

Charlotta. Noa, sir, but I am to be vara soon, to Pierrot, our neighbour Simonetta's son.

Don John. What, such a person as you, be married to a simple country-fellow? No, no, 'tis profaning so much beauty, and you are not born to live in a village; you plainly merit a better fortune; Heaven which very well knows this, has conducted me hither on purpose to prevent this match, and do justice to your charms: for in short, fair Charlotta, I love you with all my heart, and it shall be entirely your own fault if I don't carry you off from this miserable place, and put you in the condition you deserve. This passion is indeed very sudden; but what then, 'tis an effect, Charlotta, of your great beauty, and one loves you as much in a quarter of an hour, as another in six months.

Charlotta. In good truth, sir, I doan't know haw to behave when you talk. What you say pleases me, and I should have the highest desire in the world to believe you; but I've awlas been tould, that we must never believe the gentlemen, and that you courtiers are wheedlers, who mind nothing but to make fools of young women.

Don John. I am none of those people.

Sganarel. [*Aside.*] He scorns it.

Charlotta. Look ye, sir, there's noa pleasure in being imposed upon, I am a poor country-wench, but I value honour above everything; I'd sooner choose to die than to lose my honour.

Don John. Should I have a soul so wicked as to impose upon such a person as you, and be so base to debauch you? No, no, I'm too conscientious for that. I love you, Charlotta, in good earnest, and with honour: and to let you see I speak truth, assure yourself I have no other design but to marry you. Would you have a greater proof of it? Here am I ready, whenever you please, and I call this fellow to be witness of the promise I make you.

Sganarel. No, no, never fear. He'll marry you as much as you please.

Don John. Ah! Charlotta, I plainly perceive you don't as yet know me; you do me great wrong to judge of me by others; and if there are cheats in the world, people who mind nothing so much as to impose upon young women, you ought to take me out of the number, and never doubt the sincerity of my love; and besides, your beauty is a security for everything. Persons of your make are safe from all sort of fears; believe me, you have not the air of one who is to be imposed upon, and for my part, I protest I'd stab myself a thousand times to the heart, had I the least thought of betraying you.

Charlotta. Marry, I doan't know whether you speak truth or no; but you make one believe you.

Don John. You do me justice most certainly, when you

believe me, and I repeat to you again the promise I have made
you. Don't you accept it? Won't you consent to be my wife?
Charlotta. Yes, provided my aunt will have it so.
Don John. Give me your hand then upon it, Charlotta, since
you are pleased to agree on your part.
Charlotta. But however, sir, pray doan't deceive me, it
would be a sin; and you see I engage here, very honestly.
Don John. How! do you seem to doubt still of my sincerity?
Would you have me swear the most horrible oaths? May
Heaven——
Charlotta. Bless me, doan't swear, I believe you.
Don John. Give me one little kiss then, as a pledge of
your promise.
Charlotta. Nay, sir, stay till we are married, and after that,
I'll kiss you as much as you will.
Don John. Well, pretty Charlotta, just what you please,
only give me your hand, and let me, by a thousand kisses, express
the ecstasy I am in.

Scene III

Don John, Sganarel, Pierrot, Charlotta.

Pierrot. [*Pushing away Don John as he is kissing Charlotta's
hand.*] Sofly, sir, hou'd an yau please, yau're too hot, yau
mayn get a purisy.
Don John. [*Pushing Pierrot again very hard.*] What brings
this impertinent puppy here?
Pierrot. [*Placing himself between Don John and Charlotta.*]
I say yau mon hou'd, and yau monnat kiss our wives that are
to be.
Don John. [*Still pushing him.*] What a noise is here!
Pierrot. S'blews, yau monnat push foulk soa.
Charlotta. [*Catching Pierrot by the arm.*] Let him aloan,
Pierrot.
Pierrot. Haw, let him aloan? I'll nat let him aloan.
Don John. Hah!
Pierrot. Flesh, because yau're a gentilmon, yau cum heer
to kiss our wives under aur noazes, goa and kiss yaur own wife.
Don John. So, so.
Pierrot. And soa, soa, agein. [*Don John gives him a box
of the ear.*] Ookers, doan't straike me. [*Another.*] Ats fish!
[*Another.*] S'heart. [*Another.*] S'bud and guts, it isn't fair

to beat foulk; is this the racompense yau make me for saving yau from being drawn'd?

Charlotta. Doan't be angry, Pierrot.

Pierrot. I will be angry, and thau'rt a pitiful hussy, to let him wheedle thee.

Charlotta. Oh! Pierrot, it isn't as yau thinkn. This gentil-mon will marry me, and yau shouldn't be in a passion.

Pierrot. Haw? I'trath thaur't promised to me.

Charlotta. That makes noa matter, Pierrot, if yau lovn me, should ye nat be glad that I'm made a madam?

Pierrot. Wauns, noa, I'se as soon see thee hanged, as see thee gi'n to anuther.

Charlotta. Goa, goa, Pierrot, doan't fret thyself; if I'm a madam, I'se gi' thee sumthing, and thau shalt serve aur hause wi' butter and cheese.

Pierrot. S'blews, I'se newer sarve ye wi' anything an yau would pay me twice as much. What, don yau mind what he says then? Mess, an I'd known that just naw, I'se ha' ta'en greit ceare haw I had ta'en him aut o' th' weter, and I'd ha' gi'n him a good rap of th' heid wi' my oar.

Don John. [*Coming up to Pierrot, to strike him.*] What's that you say?

Pierrot. [*Getting behind Charlotta.*] Wawns, I'se afraid o' noa mon.

Don John. [*Coming towards him.*] Let me come up with you.

Pierrot. [*Steps on other side of Charlotta.*] I doan't care what yau doo.

Don John. [*Running after Pierrot.*] We shall try that.

Pierrot. [*Saving himself still behind Charlotta.*] I 'a seen mony a mon as good as yau.

Don John. Hey! Hey!

Sganarel. Fie, sir, let the poor rascal alone, 'tis pity to beat him. [*Placing himself between him and Don John.*] [*To Pierrot.*] Harkee my honest lad, move off, and don't talk to him.

Pierrot. [*Passing before Sganarel, and looking fierce at Don John.*] I will talk to him.

Don John. [*Lifts up his hand to give Pierrot a blow, who ducks down his head, and Sganarel receives it.*] Aye, I shall teach ye.

Sganarel. [*Looking at Pierrot.*] Plague take the booby.

Don John. [*To Sganarel.*] That's a reward for thy charity.

Pierrot. I'George, I'se goa tell her aunt aw theas fine dooings.

SCENE IV

Don John, Charlotta, Sganarel.

Don John. [*To Charlotta.*]   In short, I'm going to be the happiest of men, and I would not change my happiness for all the world could give me.   What pleasures shall we have, when you are my wife, and what——

SCENE V

Don John, Mathurina, Charlotta, Sganarel.

Sganarel. [*Seeing Mathurina.*]   So, so.

Mathurina. [*To Don John.*]   Sir, what are yau dooing thear wi' Charlotta, are yau coorting her too?

Don John. [*Aside to Mathurina.*]   No; on the contrary, she'd a mind to be my wife, and I told her I was engaged to you.

Charlotta. [*To Don John.*]   What is't Mathurina wants wi' ye?

Don John. [*Aside to Charlotta.*]   She's jealous at my talking with you, and wants me to marry her; but I tell her, that 'tis you I would have.

Mathurina.   What, Charlotta——

Don John. [*Aside to Mathurina.*]   All you can say to her will signify nothing, she has took this into her head.

Charlotta.   What then, Mathurina——

Don John. [*Aside to Charlotta.*]   'Tis in vain to talk to her, you'll ne'er get this whim out of her head.

Mathurina.   Would yau——

Don John. [*Aside to Mathurina.*]   There's no possibility of bringing her to reason.

Charlotta.   I should be——

Don John. [*Aside to Charlotta.*]   She's obstinate as the d—l.

Mathurina.   Truly——

Don John. [*Aside to Mathurina.*]   Don't talk to her, she's a fool.

Charlotta.   I think——

Don John. [*Aside to Charlotta.*]   Let her alone, she's a silly slut.

Mathurina.   No, no, I must talk to her.

Charlotta.   I will know some of her reasons.

Mathurina.   What——

Don John. [*Aside to Mathurina.*] I hold you a wager, she'll tell ye that I've promised her marriage.

Charlotta. I——

Don John. [*Aside to Charlotta.*] A wager with you that she stands to't, that I've given my word to take her for a wife.

Mathurina. Harkee, Charlotta, it's nat right to meddle with other foulk's bargains.

Charlotta. It isn't honest, Mathurina, to be jealous because the gentilmon talks to me.

Mathurina. The gentilmon saw me ferst.

Charlotta. If he saw thee ferst, he saw me second, and has promised to marry me.

Don John. [*Aside to Mathurina.*] Well, didn't I tell you so?

Mathurina. [*To Charlotta.*] Yer humble sarvant, it was me, and not yau he promised to marry.

Don John. [*Aside to Charlotta.*] Didn't I guess right?

Charlotta. Put yaur shams upon others, pray, not upon me, 'twas me, I tell you.

Mathurina. Yau joke with foulk; it was me, once more.

Charlotta. Here's the person can tell you, whether I'm in the right.

Mathurina. Here's the person can give me the lie, if I doan't say true.

Charlotta. Did yau really promise to marry her, sir?

Don John. [*Aside to Charlotta.*] You jest, sure.

Mathurina. Is't true, sir, that yau've promised to be her husband?

Don John. [*Aside to Mathurina.*] Could you have such a thought?

Charlotta. Yau see she affirms it.

Don John. [*Aside to Charlotta.*] Let her.

Mathurina. Yau are witness haw she avers it.

Don John. [*Aside to Mathurina.*] Let her aver it.

Charlotta. No, no, we must know the truth.

Mathurina. The matter mun be decided.

Charlotta. Yes, Mathurina, I'd have the gentilmon to show yau yaur mistake.

Mathurina. Yes, Charlotta, I'd have the gentilmon show haw yau're baulked.

Charlotta. Sir, please to decide the quarrel.

Mathurina. Adjust our difference, sir.

Charlotta. [*To Mathurina.*] Yau'll see.

Mathurina. [*To Charlotta.*] Yau'll see too.

Charlotta. [*To Don John.*] Say.
Mathurina. [*To Don John.*] Speak.
Don John. What would you have me say? You both maintain that I have promised to marry you. Don't each of you
know the whole of this affair, without any necessity for my
explaining further?   Why should you oblige me to a repetition
in this business? Has not the person I have really promised
myself to, reason sufficient within herself, to laugh at the discourse of the other; and should she give herself any uneasiness,
provided I make good my promise? Discourses don't at all
forward affairs, we must act and not talk, and facts decide
much better than words. Therefore that's the only way I shall
reconcile you, and you'll see, when I come to marry, which of
you has my heart. [*Aside to Mathurina.*] Let her believe
what she will. [*Aside to Charlotta.*] Let her flatter herself in
her own imagination. [*Aside to Mathurina.*] I adore you.
[*Aside to Charlotta.*] I am entirely yours. [*Aside to Mathurina.*]
All faces are ugly in sight of yours. [*Aside to Charlotta.*] When
one has once seen you, there's no enduring of others. [*Aloud
to both.*] I have a trifling order to deliver .I shall wait upon you
again in a quarter of an hour.

Scene VI

Charlotta, Mathurina, Sganarel.

Charlotta. [*To Mathurina.*] I am the person he loves, however.
Mathurina. [*To Charlotta.*] I'm the person he'll marry.
Sganarel. [*Stopping Charlotta and Mathurina.*] Ah! Poor
girls, I pity your innocence, and can't bear to see you run upon
your ruin. Believe me both, and don't be imposed upon by
the stories he tells you, but stay in your own village.

Scene VII

Don John, Charlotta, Mathurina, Sganarel.

Don John. [*At the farther part of the stage, aside.*] I would
fain know why Sganarel does not follow me.
Sganarel. My master is a knave, he only designs to debauch
you, and has debauched a good many others; he marries the
whole sex, and——[*Seeing Don John.*] 'Tis false, and whoever
may tell you this, you should tell him he lies. My master is

not one who marries the whole sex, he's no knave; he has no
design to deceive you, nor has he ever debauched any person.
Oh! stay, here he is, ask him rather.

Don John. [*Looking at Sganarel.*] Yes.

Sganarel. Sir, as the world is full of scandal, I do things by
way of prevention, and I was telling 'em that if anybody should
say any harm of you, they should be sure not to believe him,
and not fail to tell him he lied.

Don John. Sganarel.

Sganarel. [*To Charlotta and Mathurina.*] Yes, my master is
a man of honour, I warrant him such.

Don John. Hem!

Sganarel. They're impertinent rascals.

Scene VIII

Don John, Ramée, Charlotta, Mathurina, Sganarel.

Ramée. [*Whispering Don John.*] Sir, I come to give you
notice, that 'tis not proper for you to be here.

Don John. How so?

Ramée. Twelve men on horseback are in search of you, who
will be here in a moment; I don't know by what means they can
have followed you; but I've learnt this news from a country-
fellow of whom they inquired, and to whom they described you.
The affair presses, and the sooner you can go hence, the better
'twill be.

Don John. [*To Charlotta and Mathurina.*] A pressing affair
obliges me to leave this place, but I desire you would remember
the promise I made you, and depend upon't you shall hear from
me before to-morrow evening. As the match is not equal, we
must use stratagem; and dexterously to elude the mischief that
pursues me, I'll have Sganarel dress in my clothes, and I——

Sganarel. A pretty jest, sir, to expose me to be killed in
your clothes, and——

Don John. Come, quick, I do you too much honour, and
happy the servant who can arrive at the glory of dying for
his master.

Sganarel. Thank you for the honour. [*Alone.*] Since
death is in the case, Heaven grant me the favour not to be
taken for another.

ACT III

Scene I

Don John, in a country habit; Sganarel, dressed as a physician.

Sganarel. Troth, sir, confess me to be in the right, and that we are both disguised to a wonder. Your first design was by no means proper, and this conceals us much better than what you would have done.

Don John. 'Tis true thou art very well, and I can't imagine where thou hast been to unhoard this ridiculous equipage.

Sganarel. Yes; 'tis the habit of an old physician which had been left in pawn in the place where I got it, and it cost me money to have it. But d'ye know, sir, that this habit has already placed me in some degree of consideration, that I am saluted by the people I meet, and that they consult me as a man of skill?

Don John. How?

Sganarel. Five or six country-fellows and girls, seeing me pass by, came and asked my advice upon their different distempers.

Don John. You answered that you knew nothing of the matter.

Sganarel. By no means, I was willing to support the honour of my habit, I reasoned upon the disease, and gave each a prescription.

Don John. And prithee what remedies didst thou prescribe them?

Sganarel. I'troth, sir, I picked 'em up where I could get 'em; I prescribed at all adventures, and 'twould be a droll thing, if the distempers should be cured, and they should come to return me thanks for it.

Don John. And why not? Why should not you have the same privilege as all other physicians have? They've no more share in curing distempers than you have, and all their art is pure grimace. They only receive the honour of happy success, and you may take advantage as they do, of a patient's good luck, and find everything ascribed to your remedies that can proceed either from the favour of chance, or the force of nature.

Sganarel. How, sir, are you so impious in medicine?

Don John. 'Tis one of the greatest errors of mankind.

Sganarel. What, don't you believe in senna, nor cassia, nor emetic wine?

Don John. And why would you have me believe in 'em?

Sganarel. You are of a very unbelieving temper. Yet for all this you know the emetic wine has made a great bustle of late. Its miracles have converted the most incredulous minds; and 'tis but three weeks ago, that I myself, who speak t'ye, saw a marvellous effect of it.

Don John. What?

Sganarel. There was a man who had been in an agony for six days together, they knew not what more to prescribe to him, and none of the remedies took place; at last they took it into their heads to give him the emetic.

Don John. He recovered, did he not?

Sganarel. No, he died.

Don John. The effect is admirable.

Sganarel. Why, for six whole days he could not die, and that made him die at once. Would you have anything more efficacious?

Don John. You're right.

Sganarel. But let us drop physic, in which you've no belief, and talk of other things: for this habit gives me spirit, and I'm in the humour of disputing with you. You very well know that you allow me to dispute, and that you only forbid remonstrances.

Don John. Well?

Sganarel. I would know the bottom of your thoughts, and understand ye a little better than I do. Come, when will you put an end to your debaucheries, and lead the life of an honest man?

Don John. [*Lifts up his hand to strike him.*] Hey! Mr. Blockhead! you're immediately at your remonstrances.

Sganarel. [*Stepping back.*] S'heart, I am a blockhead indeed to concern myself about reasoning with you; do what you please, 'tis a mighty matter to me whether you undo yourself or not, and whether——

Don John. Peace. Let us mind our affair. Aren't we out of our way? Call that man there below us, and ask him the road.

Scene II

Don John, Sganarel, Francisco.

Sganarel. Soho, soho there, you man. Ho, gaffer. Ho, friend, a word with you, pray. Direct us in the way that leads to the town.

Francisco. You need only follow that path, gentlemen, and turn on your right hand when you come to the end of the forest. But I give you notice to be upon your guard, for there have been robbers hereabouts, for some time past.

Don John. I'm obliged to thee, friend, and thank thee, with all my heart, for thy good advice.

Scene III

Don John, Sganarel.

Sganarel. Ha! sir, what a noise, what a clashing is there?

Don John. [*Looking into the wood.*] What's that there, one man attacked by three? the match is too unequal, and I must not suffer this baseness. [*Draws his sword, and runs to the place of combat.*]

Scene IV

Sganarel. [*Alone.*] My master's a very madman, to throw himself into danger unsought for; but i'troth, the succour has succeeded, the two have put the three to flight.

Scene V

Don John, Don Carlos, Sganarel, at the farther part of the stage.

Don Carlos. I see by the scampering of these villains, how much I owe to your arm. Permit me, sir, to return you thanks for so generous an action, and to——

Don John. I have done nothing, sir, but what you would have done in my place. Our honour is concerned in such adventures, and the action of these rascals was so base, that 'twould have been taking their part, not to have opposed them. But by what accident fell you into their hands?

Don Carlos. I had wandered by chance from a brother of mine, and the rest of our company; and as I was endeavouring to join 'em again, I met with these robbers, who immediately killed my horse, and would have done as much for me, had it not been for your valour.

Don John. Is your design to go towards town?

Don Carlos. Yes, but without going into it; my brother and I are obliged to keep in the country, on account of one of those troublesome affairs which oblige gentlemen to sacrifice themselves and their families to the severity of their honour, since, in short, the most favourable success is always fatal, and if one doesn't lose one's life, one's forced to quit the kingdom; and this is what I think the rank of a gentleman unhappy in, not to be able to secure himself by all the prudence and justice of his own conduct, from being subject by the laws of honour, to the unruliness of another man's conduct, nor from having his life, repose and property depend on the freaks of the first audacious rascal who shall take it into his head to commit one of those injuries which an honest man must lose his life for.

Don John. One has this advantage, that we make those run the same risk, and pass their time as ill, who take the fancy of injuring us out of mere wantonness. But were it a piece of indiscretion to ask what your affair may be?

Don Carlos. The thing is not upon terms of making any longer a secret of it; and when an injury once breaks out, our honour does not oblige us to conceal our shame, but to blaze abroad our vengeance, and even to publish our intention. Therefore, sir, I shall not scruple telling you, that the offence we want to revenge is that of a sister seduced, and carried off from a convent, and that the author of this injury is Don John Tenorio, son of Don Lewis Tenorio. We've sought him for some days, and we pursued him this morning upon the report of a servant, who told us that he went out on horseback, and that he came along this way; but all our pains have been to no purpose, and we can't discover what's become of him.

Don John. D'ye know this Don John, sir, whom you speak of?

Don Carlos. No, I, for my part, don't. I never saw him, and I have only heard him described by my brother; but fame says no great good of him, he is a man whose life——

Don John. Hold, sir, if you please, he is something of a friend of mine, and 'twould be a kind of baseness in me, only to hear any ill spoken of him.

Don Carlos. Out of respect to you, sir, I shall say nothing of him; 'tis certainly the least thing I owe you, when you have saved my life, to forbear speaking before you of a person who is your acquaintance, when I can speak nothing but ill of him;

but be you ever so much his friend, I presume to hope you would not approve of this action of his, or think it strange that we should endeavour to revenge it.

Don John. On the contrary; I'll serve you in this affair, and spare you the fruitless trouble. I am Don John's friend, I can't help being so, but it is not reasonable that he should injure gentlemen with impunity, and I engage for him, he shall give you satisfaction.

Don Carlos. And what satisfaction can be given for these sort of injuries?

Don John. All that your honour can wish; and without giving you the trouble of inquiring further after Don John, I answer he shall be forthcoming wherever you please, and when you please.

Don Carlos. This expectation, sir, is very agreeable to injured minds; but after what I owe you, it would be a sensible grief to me, should you be of the party.

Don John. I am so far attached to Don John, that he can't fight but I must fight too: but in short, I answer for him as of myself, and you need only say when you would have him appear, and give you satisfaction.

Don Carlos. How cruel is my destiny! That I should owe my life to you, and Don John be one of your friends!

Scene VI

Don Alonzo, Don Carlos, Don John, Sganarel.

Don Alonzo. [*Speaking to his attendants, without seeing Don Carlos or Don John.*] Let my horses drink there, and then lead them after us, I'll walk a little. [*Seeing them both.*] Heavens! What do I see? What, brother, keep company with our mortal enemy?

Don Carlos. Our mortal enemy?

Don John. [*Clapping his hand to his sword.*] Yes, I am Don John himself, and your advantage as to number, shall not oblige me to disown my name.

Don Alonzo. [*Drawing his sword.*] Traitor, thou art a dead man, and——

Don Carlos. Ah! Hold, brother, I owe my life to him, and had not his arm relieved me, I had been killed by the robbers I met with.

Don Alonzo. Would you let this consideration prevent our

vengeance?   All the services the hand of an enemy may do us, are of no merit to engage our heart; and if we are to measure the obligation by the injury, your gratitude is in this case ridiculous; as honour is infinitely more precious than life, 'tis properly owing nothing, to owe one's life to him who takes away our honour.

Don Carlos.   I know the difference, brother, that a gentle-man should always make 'twixt one and the other; and gratitude for the obligation does not efface in me the resentment for the injury; but permit me here to restore to him what he has lent me, let me acquit myself immediately, for the life I owe him, by a delay of our vengeance, and allow him the liberty of enjoying a few days, the fruit of his good office.

Don Alonzo.   No, no, to defer is to hazard revenge, and an opportunity of taking it may never return; Heaven now makes an offer of it, and 'tis our part to improve it.   When honour is mortally wounded, one should not think of keeping any measures: and if you refuse to lend me your assistance in this action, you need only retire, and leave to my arm the glory of such a sacrifice.

Don Carlos.   Pray, brother——

Don Alonzo.   All this discourse is superfluous; he must die.

Don Carlos.   Hold, I say, brother, I won't suffer an attempt upon his life; and I swear by Heaven I'll defend him against any one whatsoever; I'll make that life he has saved to be his defence; and if you make a pass at him, it must be through me.

Don Alonzo.   What, d'ye side with our enemy against me? And so far from being seized with the same transports that I feel at sight of him, d'ye discover sentiments of compassion for him?

Don Carlos.   Brother, let us show moderation in a lawful action, and not revenge our honour with that fury which you show.   Let us wear a heart that we are masters of, and a valour that has nothing savage in it, and which proceeds by pure deliberation of our reason, not by the impulse of a blind rage. I won't be in debt, brother, to my enemy, and I have an obli-gation to him, which I must quit before everything else.   Our revenge will not be the less signal, for being deferred; on the contrary, it will receive advantage by it, and this opportunity we had of taking it, will make it appear more just in the eyes of all the world.

Don Alonzo.   O, the strange weakness and horrible blindness, to hazard in this manner the interests of our honour, for the ridiculous notion of a chimerical obligation!

Don Carlos. No, brother, give yourself no trouble about that; if I commit a fault, I shall make abundant amends for it, and I take upon me all the care of our honour, I know what it obliges us to, and this suspension for a day, which my gratitude demanded in favour of him, will only increase the ardour I have to do justice to it. You see, Don John, I am solicitous to return you the favour I have received, and by this you are to judge of the rest, to believe I acquit myself with the same warmth of everything I owe, and that I shall not be less exact in repaying you the injury than the favour. I won't oblige you to explain your sentiments now, and I give you the liberty to think at leisure what resolutions you are to take. You very well know the greatness of the injury you have done us, and I make you judge what reparation it demands. There are mild ways of giving us satisfaction; there are violent and bloody ones; but in short, whatever choice you may make, you have passed your word to me to give me satisfaction by Don John, pray mind to do so, and remember that, out of this place, I owe nothing more but to my honour.

Don John. I have asked nothing of you, and shall keep my word with you.

Don Carlos. Come, brother, a moment's mildness does no injury to the severity of our duty.

Scene VII

Don John, Sganarel.

Don John. Soho! Hey! Sganarel!

Sganarel. [*Coming out of a place where he had hid himself.*] Your pleasure, sir.

Don John. How, rascal, d'ye run away when I'm attacked?

Sganarel. Pardon me, sir, I only come from just there; I believe this habit is purgative, and that to wear it is taking physic.

Don John. Plague o' thy insolence! Wrap thy cowardice in a handsomer cover, at least. Dost know who he is, whose life I saved?

Sganarel. I? No.

Don John. 'Tis a brother of Elvira's.

Sganarel. A——

Don John. He's an honest fellow enough, he used me very handsomely, and I'm sorry I must quarrel with him.

Sganarel. It would be easy for you to make all things quiet.

Don John. Yes, but my passion for Elvira is worn out, and being engaged consists not with my humour; you know I love liberty in love, and can't resolve to immure my heart in a prison. I have told thee twenty times, that I've a natural propensity to give way to whatever attracts me. My heart is the property of the fair in general; and they must take it by turn, and keep it as long as they can.——But what stately edifice is that I spy in the grove there?

Sganarel. Don't you know it?

Don John. No, truly.

Sganarel. Good, 'tis the tomb which the governor ordered to be built, when you killed him.

Don John. Hoh! you're right, I did not know that it was hereabouts. Everybody tells me wonders of this piece of work, as well as of the statue of the governor, and I have a mind to go see it.

Sganarel. Don't go there, sir.

Don John. Why not?

Sganarel. 'Tis not civil to visit a man you have killed.

Don John. On the contrary, 'tis a visit I desire to pay him the compliment of, and which he ought to receive with a good grace, if he's anything of a gentleman. Come, let's go in.

[*The tomb opens, and discovers the Statue of the Governor.*

Sganarel. How fine that is! fine statues! fine marble! fine pillars! oh! how fine that is! What say you of it, sir?

Don John. That the ambition of a dead man cannot possibly reach further: and what I think wonderful, is that a man who during his lifetime dispensed with an habitation plain enough, would have one so magnificent, when he has no longer occasion for it.

Sganarel. Here's the statue of the governor.

Don John. Egad, he's admirably set out there in the habit of a Roman emperor.

Sganarel. Troth, sir, 'tis well made. He seems as if he were alive, and were going to speak. He casts such a look at us as would frighten me if I were quite alone, and I think he does not seem pleased at sight of us.

Don John. He would be in the wrong, and it would be an unhandsome reception of the honour I do him. Ask him if he'll come and sup with me.

Sganarel. That's a thing he has no occasion for, I believe.

Don John. Ask him, I say.

Sganarel. You jest sure! It would be foolish to speak to a statue.

Don John. Do what I bid you.

Sganarel. What a whim! Mr. Governor——*[Aside.]* I laugh at my folly; but 'tis my master makes me do it. Mr. Governor, my master Don John asks whether you'll do him the honour to come and sup with him. *[The Statue nods its head.]* Ah!

Don John. What's the matter? What ails thee? Tell me, will you speak?

Sganarel. *[Nodding his head like the Statue.]* The statue——

Don John. Well, what wouldst thou say, villain?

Sganarel. I say, the statue——

Don John. Well, what of the statue? Speak, or I'll beat out thy brains.

Sganarel. The statue made a sign to me.

Don John. Plague o' the rascal!

Sganarel. I tell you it made a sign to me, there's nothing more true. Try yourself, and see, perhaps——

Don John. Come, varlet, come; I'll make thee feel thy cowardice with thy finger's ends, observe. Will Mr. Governor come and sup with me?   *[The Statue nods its head again.*

Sganarel. I would not lay ten pistoles on't. Well, sir?

Don John. Come, let us be gone.

Sganarel. *[Alone.]* These are your free-thinkers, who will believe nothing.

ACT IV

Scene I

Don John, Sganarel, Ragotin.

Don John. *[To Sganarel.]* Let it be how it will, drop it. It is but a trifle, and we might be deceived by a false light, or surprised with some vapour that disturbed our sight.

Sganarel. Ah! sir, don't endeavour to give the lie to what we saw with our own eyes. There is nothing more real than that nod of the head, and I make no doubt but Heaven, offended at your way of life, has wrought this miracle to convince you, and reclaim you——

Don John. Harkee. If you tease me any more with your stupid morality, if you say the least word more upon that head, I'll call somebody to fetch a bull's pizzle, I'll have ye held by three or four people, and drub ye with a thousand bastinadoes. D'ye take me?

Sganarel. Oh! very right, sir, perfectly right; you explain yourself clearly: that's the good of you, that you affect no windings or turnings; you express things with an admirable plainness.

Don John. Come, let me have supper as soon as possible. A chair here, boy.

Scene II

Don John, Sganarel, Violette, Ragotin.

Violette. Sir, here's your tradesman, Mr. Dimanche, wants to speak with you.

Sganarel. Good, we want the compliments of a creditor, indeed. What's in his head, to come ask money of us? and why didn't you tell him that my master's not at home?

Violette. I have told him so any time this three-quarters of an hour, but he won't believe me, and is sat down there within to wait.

Sganarel. Let him wait as long as he will.

Don John. No, rather let him in; 'tis very bad policy to be denied to tradesmen. It's good to pay 'em with something, and I've the secret of sending them away satisfied, without giving 'em a halfpenny.

Scene III

Don John, Mr. Dimanche, Sganarel, Violetta, Ragotin.

Don John. Hah, Mr. Dimanche, come this way. How glad am I to see you, and how could I wish my fellows hanged for not bringing you in immediately! I had given orders not to be spoken with by anybody, but this order is not for you, you have a right never to have the door shut against you in my house.

Mr. Dimanche. Sir, I am very much obliged t'ye.

Don John. [*To Violetta and Ragotin.*] S'heart, rascals, I'll teach ye to leave Mr. Dimanche in the ante-chamber, and I'll make you know who is who.

Mr. Dimanche. Sir, 'tis no matter.

Don John. [*To Mr. Dimanche.*] What? To say I was not within, to Mr. Dimanche, to my very best friend?

Mr. Dimanche. Sir, I'm your servant. I was come——

Don John. Here, quick, a seat for Mr. Dimanche.

Mr. Dimanche. Sir, I'm very well as I am.

Don John. No, no, I'll have you sit as well as me.

Mr. Dimanche. 'Tis not necessary.

Don John. Take away this stool, and bring an elbow-chair.

Mr. Dimanche. Sir, you jest, and——

Don John. No, no, I know what I owe you; and I won't have 'em make any difference 'twixt us two.

Mr. Dimanche. Sir——

Don John. Come, sit down.

Mr. Dimanche. 'Tis needless, sir, I want only one word with you. I was——

Don John. Sit you down there, I say.

Mr. Dimanche. No, sir, I'm mighty well; I come to——

Don John. No, I won't hear you, if you don't sit down.

Mr. Dimanche. Sir, I do as you would have me. I——

Don John. Faith, Mr. Dimanche, you are brave and well.

Mr. Dimanche. Yes, sir, at your service. I came——

Don John. You've an admirable fund of health, ruby lips, vermeil complexion, and sparkling eyes.

Mr. Dimanche. I should be glad——

Don John. How does Mrs. Dimanche, your spouse do?

Mr. Dimanche. Very well, sir, thank Heaven.

Don John. She's a fine woman.

Mr. Dimanche. She's your humble servant, sir, I came——

Don John. And your little daughter, Claudina, how does she do?

Mr. Dimanche. Well as possible.

Don John. 'Tis a pretty little girl, I love her with all my heart.

Mr. Dimanche. You do her too much honour, sir. I desire——

Don John. And does little Colin make as much noise as ever with his drum?

Mr. Dimanche. Always the same, sir. I——

Don John. And your little dog Brusquet? Does he always growl so prodigiously, and does he bite people still as heartily by the heels, that come to your house?

Mr. Dimanche. More than ever, sir, and we can't quell him.

Don John. Don't be surprised, if I inform myself of all the news of your whole family; for I interest myself very much in it.

Mr. Dimanche. We are infinitely obliged to you, sir. I——

Don John. [*Holding out his hand.*] Shake hands then, Mr. Dimanche, are you really a friend of mine?

Mr. Dimanche. Sir, I am your servant.

Don John. Egad, I am yours with all my heart.

Mr. Dimanche. You do me too much honour. I——

Don John. There's nothing I would not do for you.

Mr. Dimanche. Sir, you are too good to me.

Don John. And that without interest, believe me.

Mr. Dimanche. I have not merited this favour, certainly; but, sir——

Don John. Hoh! Come, Mr. Dimanche, will you sup with me, without ceremony?

Mr. Dimanche. No, sir, I must return home immediately. I——

Don John. [*Rising up.*] Here, a flambeau quick, to light Mr. Dimanche, and let four or five of my fellows take musquetoons to escort him.

Mr. Dimanche. [*Rising also.*] Sir, 'tis needless, I can go very well alone. But——   [*Sganarel quickly removes the chairs.*

Don John. How? I will have 'em escort you, and I have too much interest in your person; I'm your humble servant, and your debtor to boot.

Mr. Dimanche. Ah! sir——

Don John. 'Tis a matter I don't conceal, and I tell it to all the world.

Mr. Dimanche. If——

Don John. Would you have me wait upon you back?

Mr. Dimanche. Oh! sir, you jest. Sir——

Don John. Embrace me then, pray; I desire you once more to rest persuaded that I am entirely yours, and that there's nothing in the world I would not do to serve you.

Scene IV

Mr. Dimanche, Sganarel.

Sganarel. It must be owned, my master is a man who loves you much.

Mr. Dimanche. 'Tis true; he pays me so many civilities, and so many compliments, that I can never ask him for money.

Sganarel.   I do assure you, all his family would die for you: and I wish something would happen to you, that somebody would take it into his head to cudgel you, you'd see in what manner——

Mr. Dimanche.   I believe it; but Sganarel, pray speak a word to him about my money.

Sganarel.   Oh! give yourself no trouble, his pay is as good as any in the world.

Mr. Dimanche.   But, you, Sganarel, you owe me something on your own account.

Sganarel.   Fie, don't speak of that.

Mr. Dimanche.   How? I——

Sganarel.   Don't I know very well that I'm in your debt?

Mr. Dimanche.   Yes, but——

Sganarel.   Come, Mr. Dimanche, I'll light you.

Mr. Dimanche.   But my money——

Sganarel.   [*Taking Mr. Dimanche by the arm.*]   You jest sure.

Mr. Dimanche.   I will——

Sganarel.   [*Pulling him.*]   Nay.

Mr. Dimanche.   I understand——

Sganarel.   [*Pushing him towards the door.*]   Trifles.

Mr. Dimanche.   But——

Sganarel.   [*Pushing him again.*]   Fie.

Mr. Dimanche.   I——

Sganarel.   [*Pushing him quite off the stage.*]   Fie, I say.

Scene V

Don John, Violette, Sganarel.

Violette.   [*To Don John.*]   Sir, here's your father.

Don John.   So, I'm finely fitted.   There wanted but this visit to make me mad.

Scene VI

Don Lewis, Don John, Sganarel.

Don Lewis.   I see plainly I disturb you, and that you could easily have dispensed with my coming.   To say the truth, we are each of us strangely troublesome to the other, and if you are tired with seeing me, I am likewise very much tired with your behaviour.   Alas! how little do we know what we do, when we leave not to Heaven the care of what we want, when we will be wiser than that, and importune it by our blind wishes, and

inconsiderate demands! I wished with unparalleled ardour
for a son, and incessantly prayed for one with incredible transports; and this son which I obtained by wearying Heaven with
my prayers, is the plague and punishment even of that life, of
which I thought he would be the joy and consolation. With
what eye, in your opinion, d'ye think I can look on the
multitude of unworthy actions whose scurvy appearance we
have much ado to palliate in the eyes of the world, that continued series of villainous affairs, which hourly reduce us to
weary the goodness of our sovereign, and which have exhausted
the merit of my services, and the credit of my friends? Oh!
what baseness is yours! don't you blush so little to deserve your
birth? Have you any right, pray tell me, to be vain of it?
And what have you done in the world to make you a gentleman?
D'ye think it sufficient to bear the name and the arms of one,
or that 'tis any honour to be sprung from noble blood when we
live infamously? No, no; birth is nothing, where there's no
virtue. Therefore we have no share in the glory of our ancestors,
any further than we exert ourselves to resemble them, and that
splendour of their actions, which they throw upon us, lays an
obligation upon us of doing the same honour to them, of following
their steps, and by no means degenerating from their virtues,
if we would be esteemed their true descendants. So that 'tis in
vain that you descend from the ancestors from whom you spring,
they disown you for their blood, and all the illustrious things
they have done, give you no advantage; on the contrary, their
lustre reflects upon you only to your dishonour and their glory
is a torch which shows the infamy of your actions in the most
glaring light to the eyes of the whole world. Know, in short,
that a gentleman who lives ill, is a monster in nature, that
virtue is the prime title to nobility, that I look much less upon
the name we subscribe, than the actions that we perform, and
that I should value more being the son of a porter, who was an
honest man, than the son of a monarch who lived as you do.

Don John. If you would sit down, sir, you'd talk more
at your ease.

Don Lewis. No, insolent wretch, I'll neither sit down nor
talk more, for I plainly see my words have no effect upon your
mind; but know, unworthy son, that the paternal tenderness
is by your actions driven to its last extremity, I shall, sooner
than you think of, put a stop to your irregularities, prevent
the vengeance of Heaven upon you, and by your punishment
wash off the shame of having given you life.

Scene VII

Don John, Sganarel.

Don John. Why, die as soon as you can, 'tis the best thing you can possibly do. Every one should have their turn, it makes me mad to see fathers live as long as their children.

[*Throws himself down in his elbow-chair.*

Sganarel. Oh! sir, you're to blame.

Don John. [*Rising up.*] I to blame?

Sganarel. [*Trembling.*] Sir——

Don John. Am I to blame?

Sganarel. Yes, sir, you're to blame for bearing what he said to you, and you should ha' turned him out by head and shoulders. Did ever anybody see anything more impertinent? a father to come and remonstrate to his son, bid him reform his actions, remind him of his birth, to live the life of an honest man, and a hundred other silly things of the like nature! Is it to be borne by such a man as you, who know how you ought to live? I wonder at your patience, and had I been in your place, I should ha' sent him a packing. [*Aside.*] Oh! cursed complaisance, whither dost thou reduce me?

Don John. Will you get supper ready presently?

Scene VIII

Don John, Sganarel, Ragotin.

Ragotin. Sir, here's a lady in a veil wants to speak with you.

Don John. Who can that be?

Sganarel. You must see.

Scene IX

Donna Elvira (veiled), Don John, Sganarel.

Donna Elvira. Don't be surprised, Don John, to see me at this hour, and in this equipage. 'Tis a pressing motive that obliges me to this visit, and what I have to say to you, will admit of no delay. I don't come here, full of that wrath which I discovered a little while ago, and you'll see me much altered from what I was this morning. 'Tis no more that Donna Elvira who uttered imprecations against you, whose irritated mind discharged nought but menaces, and breathed only

revenge. Heaven has banished from my mind all that unworthy passion I entertained for you, all those tumultuous
transports of a criminal attachment, all those shameful ravings
of a terrestrial and gross love; it has left nothing in my heart, in
respect to you, but a flame refined from all the commerce of
sense, a tenderness entirely sacred, a love detached from every
thing, which has no self-views, nor any concern but for your
interest.

Don John. [*Whispering Sganarel.*] Methinks you weep.

Sganarel. Pardon me.

Donna Elvira. 'Tis perfect and pure love which brings me
hither for your good, to impart to you a warning from Heaven,
and endeavour to recall you from the precipice upon which you
run. Yes, Don John, I know all the irregularities of your life,
and that same Heaven which touched my heart, and turned my
eyes upon the errors of my own conduct, has inspired me to
wait upon you, and to tell you from it, that your offences have
exhausted its mercy, that its dreadful anger is ready to fall upon
you, that it is in your choice to avoid it by a speedy repentance,
and that perhaps you have not another day to save yourself
from the greatest of all miseries. For my part, I am no longer
attached to you by any ties of this world. I am reclaimed,
thanks to Heaven, from all my foolish thoughts, my retreat is
resolved upon, and I desire only to live long enough to expiate
the crime I have committed, and to merit pardon by an austere
penance, for the blindness which the transports of a guilty
passion have plunged me into; but in this retreat, I should be
extremely grieved that a person I once tenderly loved should
be made a fatal example of the justice of Heaven, and 'twill
be an unspeakable joy to me, if I can prevail upon you, to ward
off the dreadful blow that threatens you. Pray, Don John,
grant me, for the last favour, this soothing consolation, refuse
me not your own happiness, which I ask with tears; and if you're
not moved by your own interest, be so, at least by my entreaties,
and spare me the cruel affliction of seeing you condemned to
eternal punishment.

Sganarel. [*Aside.*] Poor lady!

Donna Elvira. I once loved you with an extreme tenderness;
nothing in this world was so dear to me as yourself. I forgot
my duty for your sake. I have done everything for you: and
all the recompense I beg for it, is to reform your life, and prevent
your ruin. Save yourself, I beseech you, either for love of yourself, or for love of me. Once more, Don John, I ask it of you

with tears, and if the tears of a person you once loved are not sufficient, I conjure you to do it, by all that's most capable of moving you.

Sganarel. [*Aside.*]   Heart of tiger!

Donna Elvira.   After I've said this, I am gone; and this is all I had to say.

Don John.   Madam, 'tis late, stay here.   We shall lodge you in the best manner we can.

Donna Elvira.   No; Don John, detain me no longer.

Don John.   Madam, you'll oblige me in staying, I assure you.

Donna Elvira.   No, I tell you, let us not lose time in superfluous discourse, let me go immediately, don't insist upon waiting on me back, but only think of profiting by my advice.

Scene X

Don John, Sganarel.

Don John.   Dost know now, that I felt some little emotion for her once again, that I thought there was something agreeable in that whimsical novelty, and that her negligent dress, her languishing air, and her tears awaked in me some small remains of an extinguished flame?

Sganarel.   That's as much as to say, her discourse had no manner of effect upon you.

Don John.   Supper, quickly.

Sganarel.   Very well.

Scene XI

Don John, Sganarel, Violette, Ragotin.

Don John. [*Sitting down to table.*]   Sganarel, we must think of reforming nevertheless.

Sganarel.   Aye, marry must we.

Don John.   Yes, faith, we must reform; twenty or thirty years more of this life, and then we'll consider it.

Sganarel.   Ah!

Don John.   What sayest thou to't?

Sganarel.   Nothing.   Here comes supper. [*He takes a bit from one of the dishes that was brought, and puts it into his mouth.*

Don John.   Methinks thy cheek is swelled, what is the matter with it?   Speak, what hast thou there?

Sganarel. Nothing.

Don John. Let me see a little. Odso, 'tis an humour that's fallen upon his cheek; quick there, a lancet to open it. The poor fellow can't subsist long under it, and this imposthume may choke him; stay, see how ripe it is. How? rascal——

Sganarel. Troth, sir, I was willing to see whether your cook had not put in too much salt, or pepper.

Don John. Come, place thyself there and eat. I have business with thee, as soon as I have supped; you're hungry, I perceive by ye.

Sganarel. [*Sits down to table.*] I'm very apt to believe so, sir, I have not eaten since morning. Taste that, 'tis exceeding good. [*A footman takes Sganarel's plates away, as soon as he has got anything upon them to eat.*] My plate, my plate. Softly, if you please. S'blews, little gaffer, how nimble you are in giving one empty plates; and you, little Violette, how ready you are in giving one some drink! [*Whilst one footman gives Sganarel something to drink, the other still takes away his plate.*]

Don John. Who can it be that knocks in that manner.

Sganarel. Who the deuce comes to disturb us at our meal?

Don John. I would sup in quiet however, therefore let nobody come in.

Sganarel. Let me alone, I'll go to the door myself.

Don John. [*Seeing Sganarel return frightened.*] What ails you? What's the matter?

Sganarel. [*Nodding his head as the Statue did.*] The——who is there.

Don John. Let us go see, and show that nothing can stagger me.

Sganarel. Ah! poor Sganarel, where wilt thou hide thyself?

Scene XII

Don John, The Statue of the Governor, Sganarel, Violette, Ragotin.

Don John. [*To his servants.*] A chair and a plate here, quick. [*Don John and the Statue sit down at the table.*] Come, sit down.   [*To Sganarel.*

Sganarel. Sir, I'm not hungry now.

Don John. Sit down there, I say. Let us drink. The governor's health. I drink it to thee, Sganarel. Give him some wine.

Sganarel. Sir, I'm not thirsty.

Don John. Drink, and sing that catch of thine, to regale the governor.

Sganarel. I've got a cold, sir.

Don John. [*To his servants.*] No matter, come. You there, come and sing along with him.

The Statue. 'Tis enough, Don John; I invite you to come sup with me to-morrow. Will you be so bold?

Don John. Yes; I'll go with only Sganarel along with me.

Sganarel. I thank ye, to-morrow's fast-day with me.

Don John. [*To Sganarel.*] Take this flambeau.

The Statue. There's no need of light, when we are conducted by Heaven.

ACT V

SCENE I

Don Lewis, Don John, Sganarel.

Don Lewis. How, my son, is it possible that the mercy of Heaven should have heard my prayers? Is what you tell me really true? Don't you deceive me, with false hope? And may I rest assured of the surprising novelty of such a conversion?

Don John. Yes, you see me reclaimed from all my errors, I am no more the same since last night, and Heaven has wrought a change in me at once, which will surprise all the world. It has touched my heart, and opened my eyes, that I reflect with horror on the long blindness I was in, and the criminal disorders of the life I lead. I run over in my mind all my abominations, and am astonished that Heaven could bear with me so long, and that it has not twenty times discharged the thunder of its justice on my head. I see the favours its mercy has shown me, in not punishing my crimes, and I intend to make a due improvement of 'em, to discover to all the world a sudden change of life, to repair, by that means, the scandal of my past actions, and strive to obtain of Heaven a full remission. This is what I am now endeavouring; and I beg of you, sir, to contribute to this design, and to assist me in making choice of a person who may serve me as a guide, and under whose conduct I may walk safely in the way I'm entering upon.

Don Lewis. Ah! son, how easily is the tenderness of a father recalled, and the offences of a son instantly vanish, at the least mention of repentance! I have already lost all memory of all the sorrows you have occasioned me, and all is effaced by the words I have just now heard. I confess, I'm not myself, I shed tears of joy, all my prayers are answered, and henceforth I have nothing to ask of Heaven. Embrace me, my son, and persist I conjure you, in this laudable design. For my part, I fly immediately to carry the happy news to your mother; to share with her the sweet transports of delight I feel, and to return thanks to Heaven for the holy resolution it has vouchsafed to inspire you with.

Scene II

Don John, Sganarel.

Sganarel. Ah, sir, what joy does it give me to see you reformed! I have long been waiting for this, and now, thanks to Heaven, all my wishes are accomplished.

Don John. Plague o' the booby!

Sganarel. How, booby?

Don John. What, dost take all I've said for true sterling? And dost think my mouth acted in concert with my heart?

Sganarel. How, why isn't it——Don't you——your—— [*Aside.*] Oh! what a man! what a man! what a man is this!

Don John. No, no, I'm no changeling, my sentiments are always the same.

Sganarel. What, don't you yield to the surprising miracle of a moving and speaking statue?

Don John. Why really there is something in that which I don't comprehend; but be it as it will, it is not capable either of convincing my judgment, or staggering my mind; and if I said I would reform my conduct, and enter upon an exemplary life, 'twas a design I had formed out of pure policy, a useful stratagem, a necessary piece of grimace, to which I am willing to submit, to manage a father whom I have occasion for, and to screen myself, with respect to mankind, from a hundred troublesome adventures that may happen. I make thee my confidant in this business, Sganarel, being willing to have a witness of the true motives which oblige me to do these things.

Sganarel. What? Though still a libertine, and debauchee, d'ye pretend, at the same time, to set up yourself for a good man?

Don John. And why not? There are many others besides myself, who carry on this trade, and make use of the same mask to deceive the world.

Sganarel. [*Aside.*] Oh! what a man! what a man!

Don John. There's no manner of disgrace in this nowadays, hypocrisy is a modish vice, and all modish vices pass for virtues. The profession of hypocrisy has marvellous advantages. It is an art, the imposture of which always meets with respect, and though one discovers it, one dares not say a word against it. All the other vices of mankind are exposed to censure, and every one has the liberty of attacking 'em loudly; but hypocrisy is a privileged vice, that shuts everybody's mouth, and reigns quietly with a sovereign impunity. By dint of grimace one forms a strict alliance with all the partisans; whoever offends one, draws them all upon his back, and they who we are sure act in good earnest in the affair, and whom we know to be really touched: these people, I say, are most frequently the dupes of the others, they run innocently into the net of the hypocrites, and blindly support the apes of their actions. How many of these dost think I know, who by this stratagem have dexterously patched up the disorders of their youth, and under a respected outside have permission to be the most wicked fellows on earth? It signifies nothing that we are acquainted with their intrigues, and know 'em to be what they are, they have not, for all that, the less credit among people, and a certain downcast look, a mortified sigh, and two rolling eyes, set all to rights again, do what they will. 'Tis under this favourable shelter, that I design to secure my affairs. I won't quit my dear habits, but I shall take care to conceal myself, and divert myself with little, or no noise. But if I should come to be discovered, I shall have my whole cabal engage in my interests without my striking a stroke, and I shall be defended against, and in spite of all the world. In short, this is the true way to do whatever I please with impunity. I shall set up myself as a censor of other folks actions, shall judge ill of everybody, and have a good opinion of none but myself. When I am once, ever so little offended, I'll never forgive, and very calmly preserve an irreconcilable hatred. I'll act the avenger of oppressed virtue, and under this convenient pretext, I'll pursue my enemies, I'll accuse 'em of impiety, let loose the heady zealots upon 'em, who shall raise an outcry against them without knowing why or wherefore, who shall load 'em with opprobrious names, and roundly damn 'em by their private authority. 'Tis thus we must make our

ends of the foibles of mankind, and a wise man will accommodate
himself to the vices of the age.

Sganarel. O Heavens! What do I hear? You only wanted
to be a hypocrite to finish you in all respects, and that's the
height of abominations. Sir, this last puts me out of all patience,
and I can't forbear speaking. Do what you will with me, beat
me, knock me o' th' head, kill me, I must discharge my conscience, and like a faithful servant, tell you what I ought.
Know, sir, that the pitcher goes so oft to the well, that it comes
home broke at last: and as the author very well says, whose
name I've forgotten, man is in this world like a bird upon a bough,
the bough is fixed to the tree, he who is fixed to the tree follows
good precepts, good precepts are better than fine words, fine
words are found at court, at court are courtiers, courtiers
follow the mode, the mode comes from fancy, fancy is a faculty
of the mind, the mind is what gives life, life ends in death——
and—think what you will come to.

Don John. Excellent reasoning!

Sganarel. After this, if you don't yield, so much the worse
for you.

Scene III

Don Carlos, Don John, Sganarel.

Don Carlos. Don John, I meet you apropos, and am very
glad to speak with you here rather than at home, to ask what
are your resolutions. You know this is my concern, and that
in your presence I took this affair upon me. For my part, I
don't conceal it, I heartily wish things may be managed in an
amicable way, and there's nothing I would not do to prevail
upon your mind to take this method, and to see you publicly
confirm to my sister the title of your wife.

Don John. [*In a hypocritical tone.*] Alas! I would, with
all my heart, give you the satisfaction you desire, but Heaven
directly opposes it; it has inspired my soul with the design of
reforming my life, and I have now no other thoughts but of
entirely quitting all attachment to this world, of stripping myself
as soon as possible of all sorts of vanities, and of correcting henceforth, by an austere conduct, all the criminal disorders, into
which the heat of blind youth had hurried me.

Don Carlos. This design, Don John, clashes not at all with
what I say, and the company of a lawful wife may very well

consist with the laudable thoughts that Heaven has inspired you with.

Don John. Alas! By no means. The design is what your sister herself has formed; she has resolved to retire, and we were both touched at the same time.

Don Carlos. Her retreat can't give us satisfaction, since it might be imputed to the contempt you had thrown upon her and our family; and our honour requires her living with you.

Don John. I do assure you it can't be; I had for my part all the inclination in the world to it; and I even this day went to ask counsel of Heaven about it; but when I consulted it, I heard a voice which told me that I ought not to think of your sister, and that most certainly with her I could not be saved.

Don Carlos. D'ye think, Don John, to blind us with these fine excuses?

Don John. I obey the voice of Heaven.

Don Carlos. What? Would you have me be satisfied with such stories as these?

Don John. 'Tis Heaven will have it so.

Don Carlos. Have you taken my sister out of a convent to abandon her at last?

Don John. Heaven ordains it so to be.

Don Carlos. Shall we suffer such a blot upon our family?

Don John. Seek your redress from Heaven.

Don Carlos. Poh! why always Heaven?

Don John. Heaven desires it should be so.

Don Carlos. 'Tis enough, Don John, I understand you. I won't take you here, the place will not admit of it; but I shall find you before 'tis long.

Don John. You may do what you please. You know I don't want courage, and that I know how to use my sword when 'tis proper; I am going directly through the little by-street which leads to the great convent; but I declare to you, for my own part, I am not for fighting. Heaven forbid the thought, and if you attack me we shall see what will come of it.

Don Carlos. We shall see, true, we shall see.

Scene IV

Don John, Sganarel.

Sganarel. What the devil of a style are you got into! This is worse than all the rest, and I should like you much better as you were before; I had always some hopes of your being saved, but now I despair of it, and I believe Heaven which has bore with you hitherto, can never bear with this last abomination.

Don John. Poh! poh! Heaven is not so strict as you imagine; and, if at all times when men——

SCENE V

Don John, Sganarel, Ghost in the form of a woman veiled.

Sganarel. [*Seeing the Ghost.*] Ah! sir, 'tis Heaven that speaks to you, 'tis a warning it gives you.

Don John. If 'tis Heaven that gives me warning, it must speak plainer, if it would have me understand it.

Ghost. Don John has but one moment longer to lay hold on the mercy of Heaven, and if he repents not now, his destruction is determined.

Sganarel. D'ye hear, sir?

Don John. Who is it that dares talk so? Methinks I should know that voice.

Sganarel. Ah! sir, 'tis a ghost, I know it by its stalking.

Don John. Ghost, phantom, or devil, I'll see what it is. [*The Ghost changes shape and represents Time with his scythe in his hand.*]

Sganarel. Oh! Heavens, d'ye observe, sir, that change of shape?

Don John. No, no, nothing is capable of impressing a terror upon me, I'll try with my sword whether 'tis body or spirit. [*The Ghost vanishes the instant Don John pushes at it.*]

Sganarel. Ah! sir, yield to so many proofs, and repent immediately.

Don John. No, no, come what will, it shall never be said I was capable of repentance. Come, follow me.

SCENE VI

The Statue of the Governor, Don John, Sganarel.

The Statue. Hold, Don John, you gave me your word yesterday to come eat with me.

Don John. Yes; where shall we go?

The Statue. Give me your hand.

Don John. There 'tis.

The Statue.   Don John, obstinacy in wickedness brings on a fatal death; and rejecting the favours of Heaven opens a way to its thunder.

Don John. Oh Heavens! What do I feel? An invisible flame scorches me, I can bear it no longer, my whole body is a burning firebrand. Oh! [*Loud thunder and great flashes of lightning fall on Don John, the earth opens and swallows him : and flames burst out from the place where he descended.*]

Scene VII

Sganarel. [*Alone.*]   Ah! my wages! my wages! By his death, lo! all are satisfied. Offended Heaven, violated laws, seduced maids, dishonoured families, injured parents, wives reduced to misery, husbands to despair, all the world is satisfied; I am the only unhappy person, who, after so many years' service, have no other recompense than that of seeing my master's impiety punished before my eyes, by the most horrible of all punishments. My wages, my wages, my wages!

LOVE'S THE BEST DOCTOR

(A COMEDY)

LOVE'S THE BEST DOCTOR, *a Comedy of Three Acts in Prose, acted at Versailles, September 15, 1665, and at Paris at the Theatre of the Palace-Royal the 22nd of the same month.*

Love's the Best Doctor is one of those hasty pieces which we ought not to criticise upon with too much severity. The quarrel between Molière's wife, and the wife of a physician with whom she lodged, though never so well attested, appears too trifling a motive to determine Molière, as it is said it did, to bring the physicians so often afterwards on the stage. Being disgusted with the solemn countenance, studious appearances, and vain pomp of technical terms, which the physicians of his time affected, in order to impose on the public, he thought he could draw from thence a fund of comic humour, more entertaining indeed than instructive; for which reason the physicians and the marquises, whom he has often painted in different attitudes, are never the principal figures in the piece. Whenever he intended to reprove a more essential folly, or any vice that was injurious to society, he reserved the first place for one of those singular characters which deserved to have all the attention fixed on themselves.

ACTORS

SGANAREL, *Lucinda's father.*
LUCINDA, *daughter to Sganarel.*
CLITANDER, *in love with Lucinda.*
AMINTA, *neighbour to Sganarel.*
LUCRETIA, *niece to Sganarel.*
LYSETTA, *attendant of Lucinda.*
MR. WILLIAM, *a seller of tapestry.*
MR. JOSSE, *a goldsmith.*
MR. THOMÈS,
MR. FONANDRÈS,
MR. MACROTON, } *physicians.*
MR. BAHYS,
MR. FILLERIN,
A SCRIVENER.
CHAMPAGNE, *servant to Sganarel.*
THE OPERATOR.

SCENE: *Paris.*

ACT I

SCENE I

Sganarel, Aminta, Lucretia, Mr. William, Mr. Josse.

Sganarel. What a strange thing is life! And how well may I say with the great philosopher of antiquity, that "He who hath wealth hath warfare"; and that "One misfortune never comes without another." I had but one wife, and she is dead.

Mr. William. How many then would you have had?

Sganarel. She is dead, friend William; this loss is very grievous to me, and I can't think of it without weeping. I was not mighty well satisfied with her conduct, and we had very often disputes together, but in short death settles all things. She is dead, I lament her. If she was alive we should quarrel. Of all the children that Heaven has given me, it has only left me one daughter, and this daughter is all my trouble; for in short she is in the most dismal melancholy in the world, in a terrible sadness, out of which there is no way of getting her, and the cause of which I can't learn. For my part, I'm out of my wits about it, and have need of good advice on this matter. [*To Lucretia.*] You are my niece. [*To Aminta.*] You, my neighbour. [*To Mr. William and Mr. Josse.*] And you my companions and friends; advise me, pray, what I ought to do.

Mr. Josse. For my part, I look upon finery and dress to be the thing which delights young girls the most; and if I was as you, I'd immediately buy her a fine ornament of diamonds, or rubies, or emeralds.

Mr. William. And I, if I were in your place, would buy her a fine suit of hangings of landscape tapestry, or imagery, which I would have put up in her chamber to delight her mind and sight with.

Aminta. For my part, I would not do so, I would marry her well, and as soon as I could, to the person that they say asked her of you some time ago.

Lucretia. Now I think that your daughter is not at all fit for marriage; she's of a complexion too delicate and sickly, and 'tis wilfully sending her quickly into the other world to expose her, in the condition she is, to bring forth children. The world won't at all do for her, and I would advise you to put her in a nunnery, where she'll meet with diversions which will be more to her humour.

Sganarel. All these advices are certainly admirable. But I find a little too much of self-interest in 'em, and think that you advise mighty well——for yourselves. You are a goldsmith, Mr. Josse, and your advice smells of a man who has a mind to get rid of some of his wares. You sell tapestry, Mr. William, and you seem to have some hangings that incommode you. He whom you are in love with, neighbour, has some inclination they say for my daughter, and you would not be sorry to see her the wife of another. And as for you, my dear niece, 'tis not my design, as 'tis well known, to marry my daughter to any one at all, and I have my reasons for that; but the advice you give me to make her a nun, is the advice of one who could very charitably wish to be my sole heiress. Thus, gentlemen and ladies, though your advices are the best in the world, be pleased to give me leave to follow ne'er a one of 'em. [*Alone.*] These are your modish counsellors.

SCENE II

Lucinda, Sganarel.

Sganarel. Oh! here comes my daughter to take the air. She does not see me. She sighs. She lifts up her eyes to heaven. [*To Lucinda.*] Heaven keep thee! Good-morrow, my dear. Well, what's the matter? How d'ye do? What, always thus sad and melancholy; and won't you tell me what ails you? Come, discover thy little heart to me; come, my poor dear, tell, tell, tell thy little thoughts to thy dear little papa. Take courage. Shall I kiss thee? Come. [*Aside.*] I'm distracted to see her of this humour. [*To Lucinda.*] But tell me; wilt thou kill me with vexation, and can't I know whence this great languishment proceeds? Discover the cause of it to me, and I promise thee I'll do everything for thee. You need only tell me the reason of your melancholy, and I here assure thee, and swear to thee, that there's nothing which I'll not do to satisfy thee; that's saying everything. Art thou jealous of any of thy companions that thou seest finer than thyself? And is there any new-fashioned silk thou wouldst have a suit of? No. Dost not think thy chamber well enough furnished, and

dost thou long for any little cabinet out of St. Laurence's Fair?
'Tis not that. Hast a mind to learn anything, and wilt have
me get thee a master to teach thee to play on the spinet?
No. Dost love anybody, and dost wish to be married? [*Lucinda
makes a sign to him that 'tis that.*]

SCENE III

Sganarel, Lucinda, Lysetta.

Lysetta. Well, sir, you have been discoursing your daughter
Have you found out the cause of her melancholy?

Sganarel. No, the slut makes me mad.

Lysetta. Sir, let me alone, I'll sound her a little.

Sganarel. 'Tisn't necessary; since she will be of this humour,
I'm resolved to leave her in't.

Lysetta. Let me alone, I tell you; perhaps she'll discover
herself more freely to me than to you. What, madam, won't
you tell us what ails you? And will you grieve all the world
thus? There's nobody I think acts as you do, and if you have
any repugnance to explain yourself to your father, you ought
to have none to discover your heart to me. Tell me, do you
want anything of him? He has told us more than once that
he'll spare nothing to content you. Is it because he does not
give you all the liberty you could desire, and don't walks and
feasts tempt your fancy? Um? Have you been displeased
by anybody? Um? Have you no secret inclination for any one
whom you'd have your father marry you to? Ahah! I understand you. There's the thing. What the deuce! Why so
much ado? Sir, the mystery is discovered, and——

Sganarel. Go, ungrateful girl, I'll talk to thee no more, but
leave thee in thy obstinacy.

Lucinda. Since you will have me to tell you the thing,
sir——

Sganarel. Yes, I'll throw off all the affection I had for thee.

Lysetta. Her melancholy, sir——

Sganarel. The hussy would kill me.

Lucinda. Sir, I'll really——

Sganarel. This is not a fit recompense for bringing thee
up as I have done.

Lysetta. But sir——

Sganarel. No, I'm in a horrible passion with her.

Lucinda. But father——

II—C 831

Sganarel.   I have no longer any tenderness for thee.
Lysetta.   But——
Sganarel.   She's a baggage.
Lucinda.   But——
Sganarel.   An ungrateful hussy.
Lysetta.   But——
Sganarel.   A slut, that won't tell me what ails her.
Lysetta.   She wants a husband.
Sganarel.   [*Pretending not to hear.*]   I abandon her.
Lysetta.   A husband.
Sganarel.   I detest her.
Lysetta.   A husband.
Sganarel.   And disown her for my daughter.
Lysetta.   A husband.
Sganarel.   No, don't speak to me of her.
Lysetta.   A husband.
Sganarel.   Don't speak to me of her.
Lysetta.   A husband.
Sganarel.   Don't speak to me of her.
Lysetta.   A husband, a husband, a husband.

Scene IV

Lysetta, Lucinda.

Lysetta.   'Tis a true saying, "That none are so deaf as those that won't hear."

Lucinda.   Well, Lysetta, I was in the wrong to conceal my disquiet, and I had nothing to do but to speak, and to have all I wished from my father.   You see now.

Lysetta.   Faith, he's a villainous man; and I own that I should take a great deal of pleasure in playing him some trick.   But how comes it though, madam, that you hid your distemper till now from me too?

Lucinda.   Alas!   What service would it have done me to have discovered it to you sooner?   And should not I have got as much by concealing it all my lifetime?   Dost thou think I did not plainly foresee all that you now find?   That I did not thoroughly know all my father's notions, and that the refusal he sent to him who solicited for me by a friend, did not extinguish all hope in my breast?

Lysetta.   What, is it the stranger who asked you of your father, for whom you——

Lucinda. Perhaps 'tis not modest in a girl to explain herself so freely. But in short I must confess to thee, that if I was permitted to choose anything, it would be him that I should choose. We have had no conversation together, nor has his mouth declared the passion he has for me. But in every place where he has been able to get a sight of me, his looks and actions have always spoken so tenderly, and his demanding me from my father appears to me so very honourable, that my heart could not help being touched with his affection. And yet you see to what the harshness of my father reduces all this tenderness.

Lysetta. Come, let me alone; whatever reason I have to blame you for making a secret of it to me, I won't fail to assist your love, and, provided you have resolution enough——

Lucinda. But what would you have me do against the authority of a father? And if he's inexorable to my wishes——

Lysetta. Come, come, you must not suffer yourself to be led like a goose, and, provided honour be not offended by it, one may free one's self a little from a father's tyranny. What does he intend you shall do? Aren't you of age to be married, and does he think you are marble? Come, once more, I'll serve your passion; I from this present take upon me all the care of its concerns, and you shall see that I understand stratagem.—— But I see your father. Go in again, and leave me to act.

SCENE V

Sganarel. [*Alone.*] 'Tis good sometimes to pretend not to hear things which one hears but too well; and I did wisely to ward off the declaration of a desire which I don't mean to satisfy. Is there anything more tyrannical than this custom that people would subject parents to? Anything more impertinent and ridiculous than to heap up riches with great labour, and bring up a daughter with much care and tenderness, in order to strip one's self of both, and give 'em into the hands of a man whom we have no manner of concern with? No, no, that custom's a jest to me, and I'll keep my money and my daughter to myself.

SCENE VI

Sganarel, Lysetta.

Lysetta. [*Pretending not to see Sganarel.*] Oh! misfortune! O disgrace! O poor Mr. Sganarel! Where shall I find you?

Sganarel. [*Aside.*]   What does she say there?

Lysetta.   Ah, unhappy father!   What will you do when you know this news?

Sganarel. [*Aside.*]   What can it be?

Lysetta.   My poor mistress!

Sganarel. [*Aside.*]   I'm undone.

Lysetta.   Ah!

Sganarel. [*Running after Lysetta.*]   Lysetta.

Lysetta.   What a misfortune this is!

Sganarel.   Lysetta.

Lysetta.   What an accident!

Sganarel.   Lysetta.

Lysetta.   What a fatal mischance!

Sganarel.   Lysetta.

Lysetta.   Ah! sir.

Sganarel.   What's the matter.

Lysetta.   Sir!

Sganarel.   What is't?

Lysetta.   Your daughter.

Sganarel.   Oh! Oh!

Lysetta.   Sir, don't cry in that manner, for you'll make me laugh.

Sganarel.   Tell me then quickly.

Lysetta.   Your daughter, quite struck with the words you spoke to her, and with the terrible passion she saw you were in with her, went up immediately to her chamber, and, full of despair, opened the window which looks upon the river.

Sganarel.   Well?

Lysetta.   Then lifting up her eyes to heaven, No, said she, 'tis impossible for me to live under my father's anger; and since he disowns me for his daughter, I must die.

Sganarel.   So threw herself down?

Lysetta.   No, sir, she gently shut the window again, and laid her down on the bed; there she fell a-weeping bitterly, and all at once her face grew pale, her eyes rolled, her heart ceased to beat, and she remained in my arms.

Sganarel.   Oh! my daughter! she's dead then?

Lysetta.   No, sir, by pinching her I brought her to herself again; but this takes her again every moment, and I believe she'll not live out to-day.

Sganarel.   Champagne! Champagne! **Champagne!**

SCENE VII

Sganarel, Champagne, Lysetta.

Sganarel. Here quick, let physicians be got, and in abundance; one can't have too many upon such an accident. Ah, my girl! My poor girl!

ACT II

SCENE I

Sganarel, Lysetta.

Lysetta. What will you do, sir, with four physicians? Is not one enough to kill any one body?

Sganarel. Hold your tongue. Four advices are better than one.

Lysetta. Why, can't your daughter die well enough without the assistance of these gentlemen?

Sganarel. Do the physicians kill people?

Lysetta. Undoubtedly; and I knew a man who proved by good reasons that we should never say, such a one is dead of a fever, or a catarrh, but she is dead of four doctors and two apothecaries.

Sganarel. Hush! Don't offend these gentlemen.

Lysetta. Faith, sir, our cat is lately recovered of a fall she had from the top of the house into the street, and was three days without either eating or moving foot or paw; but 'tis very lucky for her that there are no cat-doctors, for 'twould have been over with her, and they would not have failed purging her and bleeding her.

Sganarel. Will you hold your tongue, I say? What impertinence is this! Here they come.

Lysetta. Take care. You are going to be greatly edified; they'll tell you in Latin that your daughter is sick.

SCENE II

Messrs. Thomès, Fonandrès, Macroton, Bahys, Sganarel, Lysetta.

Sganarel. Well, gentlemen!

Mr. Thomès. We have sufficiently viewed the patient, and there are certainly a great many impurities in her.

Sganarel. Is my daughter impure?

Mr. Thomès. I mean that there is much impurity in her body, an abundance of corrupt humours.

Sganarel. Oh! I understand you.

Mr. Thomès. But . . . We are going to consult together.

Sganarel. Come, let chairs be given.

Lysetta. [*To Mr. Thomès.*] Oh! sir, are you there?

Sganarel. [*To Lysetta.*] How do you know the gentleman?

Lysetta. By having seen him the other day at a friend of your niece's.

Mr. Thomès. How does her coachman do?

Lysetta. Very well. He's dead.

Mr. Thomès. Dead!

Lysetta. Yes.

Mr. Thomès. That can't be.

Lysetta. I don't know whether it can be or not; but I know well enough that so it is.

Mr. Thomès. He can't be dead, I tell you.

Lysetta. And I tell you that he is dead and buried.

Mr. Thomès. You are deceived.

Lysetta. I saw it.

Mr. Thomès. 'Tis impossible. Hippocrates says that these sort of distempers don't terminate till the fourteenth or twenty-first, and he fell sick but six days ago.

Lysetta. Hippocrates may say what he please; but the coachman is dead.

Sganarel. Silence, prate-apace, and let us go from hence. Gentlemen, I beg you to consult in the best manner. Though 'tis not the custom to pay beforehand, yet for fear I should forget it, and that the thing may be over, here——

[*He gives them money, and each in receiving it makes a different gesture*].

SCENE III

Messrs. Fonandrès, Thomès, Macroton, and Bahys.

[*They sit down and cough.*]

Mr. Fonandrès. Paris is wonderfully large, and one must make long jaunts when practice comes on a little.

Mr. Thomès. I must own that I have an admirable mule for that, and the way I make him go every day is scarce to be believed.

Mr. Fonandrès. I have a wonderful horse, and 'tis an indefatigable animal.

Mr. Thomès. Do you know the way my mule has gone to-day? I was first over against the arsenal, from the arsenal to the end of the suburb St. Germain, from the suburb St. Germain to the very end of the marshes, from the end of the marshes to the gate St. Honorius, from the gate St. Honorius to the suburb St. James's, from the suburb St. James's to the gate of Richelieu, from the gate of Richelieu hither, and from hence I must go yet to the Palace-Royal.

Mr. Fonandrès. My horse has done all that to-day, and besides I have been at Ruel to see a patient.

Mr. Thomès. But well thought on, what side do you take in the dispute betwixt the two physicians, Theophrastus and Artemius? for 'tis an affair which divides all our body.

Mr. Fonandrès. I am for Artemius.

Mr. Thomès. And I likewise; not but that his advice killed the patient, and that of Theophrastus was certainly much the better; but he was wrong in the circumstances, and he ought not to have been of a different opinion to his senior. What say you of it?

Mr. Fonandrès. Without doubt. The formalities should be always preserved whatever may happen.

Mr. Thomès. For my part I am as severe as a devil in that respect, unless it's amongst friends. And three of us were called in t'other day to a consultation with a strange physician, where I stopped the whole affair, and would not suffer 'em to go on unless things went in order. The people of the house did what they could, and the distemper increased; but I would not bate an inch, and the patient died bravely during this dispute.

Mr. Fonandrès. 'Twas well done to teach people how to behave, and to show 'em their mistake.

Mr. Thomès. A dead man is but a dead man, and of no consequence: but one formality neglected does a great prejudice to the whole body of physicians.

SCENE IV

Sganarel, Messrs. Thomès, Fonandrès, Macroton, and Bahys.

Sganarel. Gentlemen, my daughter's oppression increases, pray tell me quickly what you have resolved on.

Mr. Thomès. [*To Mr. Fonandrès.*] Come, sir.

Mr. Fonandrès. No, sir, do you be pleased to speak.

Mr. Thomès. You jest sure, sir.

Mr. Fonandrès. I'll not speak the first.

Mr. Thomès. Sir.

Mr. Fonandrès. Sir.

Sganarel. Nay, pray gentlemen, leave all these ceremonies, and consider that things are pressing.

Mr. Thomès. Your daughter's illness——

Mr. Fonandrès. The opinion of all these gentlemen together—

Mr. Macroton. Af-ter ha-ving well con-sult-ed——

Mr. Bahys. In order to reason——

[*They all four speak together.*

Sganarel. Nay, gentlemen, speak one after another, pray now.

Mr. Thomès. Sir, we have reasoned upon your daughter's distemper; and my opinion, as for my part, is that it proceeds from a great heat of blood: so I'd have you bleed her as soon as you can.

Mr. Fonandrès. And I say that her distemper is a putrefaction of humours, occasioned by too great a repletion, therefore I'd have you give her an emetic.

Mr. Thomès. I maintain that an emetic will kill her.

Mr. Fonandrès. And I, that bleeding will be the death of her.

Mr. Thomès. It belongs to you indeed to set up for a skilful man!

Mr. Fonandrès. Yes, it does belong to me; and I'll cope with you in all kinds of learning.

Mr. Thomès. Do you remember the man you killed a few days ago?

Mr. Fonandrès. Do you remember the lady you sent into the other world three days since.

Mr. Thomès. [*To Sganarel.*] I have told you my opinion.

Mr. Fonandrès. [*To Sganarel.*] I have told you my thoughts.

Mr. Thomès. If you don't bleed your daughter out of hand, she's a dead woman.   [*Goes out.*

Mr. Fonandrès. If you do bleed her, she'll not be alive a quarter of an hour hence.   [*Goes out.*

SCENE V

Sganarel, Messrs. Macroton and Bahys.

Sganarel. Which of the two am I to believe, and what resolution shall I take upon such opposite advices? Gentlemen, I conjure you to determine me, and to tell me without passion, what you think the most proper to give my daughter relief.

Mr. Macroton. [*Drawling out his words.*] Sir, in these mat-ters, we must pro-ceed with cir-cum-spec-ti-on, and do no-thing in-con-si-de-rate-ly, as they say; for-as-much as the faults which may be com-mit-ted in this case are, ac-cor-ding to our ma-ster Hip-po-cra-tes, of a dan-ge-rous con-se-quence.

Mr. Bahys. [*Sputtering out his words hastily.*] 'Tis true. We must really take care what we do; for this is not child's play; and when we have once faltered 'tis not easy to repair the slip, and to re-establish what we have spoilt. *Experimentum periculosum.* Wherefore we should reason first as we ought to do, weigh things seriously, consider the constitutions of people, examine the causes of the distemper, and see what remedies one ought to apply to it.

Sganarel. [*Aside.*] One creeps like a tortoise, and t'other rides post.

Mr. Macroton. For, sir, to come to fact, I find your daugh-ter has a chro-ni-cal dis-ease, and that she may be in jeo-par-dy if you don't give her some assis-tance; for-as-much as the symp-toms which she has are in-di-ca-tive of a fu-li-gi-nous and mor-di-cant va-pour, which pricks the mem-branes of the brain; for this va-pour, which we call in Greek *at-mos*, is caus-ed by pu-trid, te-na-ci-ous, and con-glu-ti-nous humours, which are con-tain-ed in the abdomen.

Mr. Bahys. And as these humours were engendered there by a long succession of time; they are over-baked there, and have acquired this malignity, which fumes towards the region of the brain.

Mr. Macroton. So that to draw a-way, loos-en, ex-pel, e-va-cu-ate the said hu-mours, there must be a vi-go-rous pur-ga-tion. But first of all, I think it proper, and it would not be in-con-ve-ni-ent to make use of some lit-tle a-no-dyne me-de-cines; that is to say, lit-tle e-mol-li-ent and de-ter-sive cly-sters, and re-fresh-ing ju-leps and sy-rups, which may be mix-ed in her bar-ley wa-ter.

Mr. Bahys. Afterwards we'll come to purgation and bleeding, which we'll reiterate if there be need of it.

Mr. Macroton. Not but for all this your daughter may die; but at least you'll have done some-thing, and you'll have the con-so-la-ti-on that she di-ed ac-cord-ing to form.

Mr. Bahys. It is better to die according to the rules than to recover contrary to 'em.

Mr. Macroton. We tell you our thoughts sin-cere-ly.

II—*C 831

Mr. Bahys. And have spoken to you as we would speak to our own brother.

Sganarel. [*To Mr. Macroton, drawling out his words.*] I ren-der you most hum-ble thanks. [*To Mr. Bahys, sputtering out his words.*] And am infinitely obliged to you for the pains you have taken.

Scene VI

Sganarel. [*Alone.*] So I'm just a little more uncertain than I was before. S'death, there's a fancy comes into my head, I'll go buy some orvietan, and make her take some of it. Orvietan is a remedy which many people have found good by. Soho!

Scene VII

Sganarel, The Operator.

Sganarel. Sir, pray give me a box of your orvietan, which I'll pay you for.

The Operator. [*Sings.*]
The gold in all lands which the sea doth surround,
Can ne'er pay the worth of my secret profound:
My remedy cures, by its excellence rare,
More maladies than you can count in a year.
          The scab,
          The itch,
          The scurf,
          The plague,
          The fever,
          The gout,
          The pox,
          The flux,
          And measles ever,
Of orvietan such is the excellence rare.

Sganarel. Sir, I believe all the gold in the world is not sufficient to pay for your medicine, but however here's a half crown-piece which you may take if you please.

The Operator. [*Sings.*]
Admire then my bounty, who for thirty poor pence,
Such a marvellous treasure do so freely dispense.

With this you may brave, quite devoid of all fear,
All the ills which poor mortals are subject to here.
                    The scab,
                    The itch,
                    The scurf,
                    The plague,
                    The fever,
                    The gout,
                    The pox,
                    The flux,
              And measles ever,
Of orvietan such is the excellence rare.

ACT III

Scene I

Messrs. Fillerin, Thomès, Fonandrès.

Mr. Fillerin. Are not you ashamed, gentlemen, to show so little prudence for men of your age, and to quarrel like young hair-brained simpletons? Don't you plainly see what mischief these sort of disputes do us in the world? And is it not enough that the learned see the contrarieties and dissensions which are between our authors and ancient masters, without our discovering the knavery of our art to the people too, by our disputes and quarrels? For my part, I don't at all comprehend this mischievous policy of some of our brethren, and it must be confessed that these contests have disparaged us lately in a strange manner; and that if we don't take care we shall ruin ourselves. I don't speak of this for my own interest, for thank God I have already established my small affairs. Let it blow, rain or hail, those that are dead are dead, and I have wherewith to pass amongst the living; but yet all these disputes do physic no good. Since Heaven does us the favour to let people for so many ages continue infatuated with us, let us not undeceive men by our extravagant cabals, but profit by their folly as quietly as we can. We are not the only people, you know, who try to take advantage of human weakness; the study of the greatest part of the world lies that way, and every one strives to take men on their blind side to get some profit from it. Flatterers, for example, seek to profit from the love men have of praise, by giving 'em all the vain incense they can wish; and 'tis an art that, we see, raises considerable fortunes. The alchymists endeavour to profit from the passion men have for riches, by promising mountains of gold to those that will hearken to 'em; and the conjurers by their deceitful predictions make a profit of the vanity and ambition of credulous minds. But the greatest weakness men have is the love they have for life; and we make a profit of that by our pompous jargon, and know how to make our advantages of the veneration which the fear of death gives 'em for our trade. Let us preserve ourselves then in the degree of esteem wherein their weakness has put us, and let us agree before our patients to attribute to ourselves the happy event of the distemper, and to throw all the blunders of our art upon nature. Let us not, I say, foolishly destroy the happy prepossessions of an error which gives bread to so many people, and by their money whom we have sent to the grave, has raised us up, on all sides, such fine estates.

Mr. Thomès. You have reason in all you say, but these are heats of blood, which sometimes we are not masters of.

Mr. Fillerin. Come then, gentlemen, lay aside all animosity, and let us bring you to a reconcilement here.

Mr. Fonandrès. I agree to it. Let him but admit of my emetic for the patient which is now in hand, and I'll admit of anything he shall please for the first patient he shall be concerned with.

Mr. Fillerin. Nothing could be said better; and this is being reasonable.

Mr. Fonandrès. 'Tis done.

Mr. Fillerin. Shake hands then. Farewell. Another time show more prudence.

SCENE II

Mr. Thomès, Mr. Fonandrès, Lysetta.

Lysetta. What, gentlemen, are you there? And don't you think of repairing the injury which they have done to physic?

Mr. Thomès. How? What's the matter?

Lysetta. There's an insolent fellow who has had the impudence to encroach upon your trade, and has, without your order, killed a man by running a sword through his body.

Mr. Thomès. Harkee, you make a jest of it now, but you'll come under our hands some day or other.

Lysetta. I'll give you leave to kill me when I have recourse to you.

SCENE III

Clitander (in the habit of a physician), Lysetta.

Clitander. Well, Lysetta, what say you of my equipage? Do you believe that I may gull the good man with this habit? Do you think I make a good figure thus?

Lysetta. The best in the world, and I impatiently waited for you. Heaven has made me of a nature the most humane in the world, and I can't see two lovers sigh for one another, without having a charitable tenderness, and an ardent desire to relieve the ills they suffer. I am resolved, cost what it will, to deliver Lucinda from the tyranny she is under, and put her in your power. You pleased me at first. I am skilful in men, and she could not have made a better choice. Love ventures upon extraordinary things, and we have concerted a kind of stratagem together, which may perhaps succeed for us. All our measures are already taken. The man we have to deal with is not the most crafty in the world; and if this adventure fails us, we shall find a thousand other ways to come at our end. Wait for me only a little here, and I'll return to fetch you.

[*Clitander retires to the farther part of the stage.*

SCENE IV

Sganarel, Lysetta.

Lysetta. Joy! sir, joy!

Sganarel. What's the matter?

Lysetta. Rejoice!

Sganarel. For what?

Lysetta. Rejoice, I say.

Sganarel. Tell me for what, and then perhaps I may rejoice.

Lysetta. No, I'll have you rejoice beforehand, dance and sing.

Sganarel. On what account?

Lysetta. Upon my word.

Sganarel. Come then. [*Sings and dances.*] La, la, la, lera, la. What the deuce!

Lysetta. Sir, your daughter's cured.

Sganarel. My daughter's cured!

Lysetta. Yes, I bring you a physician; but a physician of importance, who does marvellous cures, and who despises other physicians.

Sganarel. Who is he?

Lysetta. I'll bring him in.

Sganarel. [*Alone.*] I must see if this will do more than the others.

SCENE V

Clitander (in the habit of a physician), Sganarel, Lysetta.

Lysetta. Here he is.

Sganarel. This physician has but a young beard.

Lysetta. Knowledge is not measured by the beard; his skill doesn't lie in his chin.

Sganarel. Sir, I'm told you have wonderful recipes to make people go to stool.

Clitander. Sir, my remedies are different from those of others; they have emetics, bleedings, purges, clysters; but I cure by words, sounds, letters, talismans, and constellated rings.

Lysetta. Did not I tell you?

Sganarel. A great man this!

Lysetta. Sir, your daughter being yonder in her chair, dressed, I'll bring her to you.

Sganarel. Do so.

Clitander. [*Feeling Sganarel's pulse.*] Your daughter's very bad.

Sganarel. Can you tell that here?

Clitander. Yes, by the sympathy there is between father and daughter.

SCENE VI

Sganarel, Lucinda, Clitander, Lysetta.

Lysetta. [*To Clitander.*] Sir, here's a chair near her. [*To Sganarel.*] Come, let's leave 'em both here.

Sganarel. Why so? I'll stay here.

Lysetta. You jest sure! we must leave 'em; a physician has a hundred questions to ask which 'tisn't fit for a man to hear.

[*Sganarel and Lysetta retire.*

Clitander. [*Apart to Lucinda.*] Ah! madam, how great is my pleasure! and how little do I know in what manner to begin my discourse to you! Whilst I spoke to you only by my eyes, I thought I had a hundred things to say; and now I have the liberty to speak to you as I desired, I am silent, and my excess of joy stifles my words.

Lucinda. I may say the same, and, like you, I feel movements of joy which hinder me from speaking to you.

Clitander. Ah! madam, how happy should I be if you really felt all I feel, and if I were permitted to judge of your heart by my own! But, madam, may I believe that 'tis to you I owe the thought of this happy stratagem, which gives me the enjoyment of your presence?

Lucinda. If you don't owe the thought of it to me, you are at least obliged to me for having gladly approved the proposition.

Sganarel. [*To Lysetta.*] He talks mighty close to her.

Lysetta. [*To Sganarel.*] He's observing her physiognomy and the traces of her features.

Clitander. [*To Lucinda.*] Will you be constant, madam, in these favours you show me?

Lucinda. Will you be firm in the resolutions you have shown me?

Clitander. Till death, madam. I desire nothing so much as to be yours, and I'll show it in what I'm going to do.

Sganarel. [*To Clitander.*] Well, how does your patient? She looks a little brisker.

Clitander. 'Tis because I have already tried upon her one of the remedies my art teaches me. As the mind has a great influence over the body, and that being often the cause of diseases, my custom is first to cure the mind, before I come to the body. Therefore I observed her looks, her features, and the lines of her hands; and by my knowledge I find that her mind is the part she's sick in; and that all her disease proceeds only from an irregular imagination, from a depraved desire of being married. For my part, I think nothing more extravagant and ridiculous than that desire people have for matrimony.

Sganarel. [*Aside.*] A skilful man this!

Clitander. And I have, and always shall have a horrible aversion to it.

Sganarel. [*Aside.*] A great physician!

Clitander. But as we must flatter the imaginations of our patients, and seeing an alienation of mind in her, and even that 'twould prove dangerous without speedy succour, I took her on her blind side, and told her that I was come to demand her of you in marriage; suddenly her countenance changed, her complexion cleared up, her eyes were animated, and if you would but hold her in this error for some days, you'll see we shall entirely recover her.

Sganarel. Ay, I'll do it with all my heart.

Clitander. Afterwards we'll use other remedies to cure her wholly of this fancy.

Sganarel. Ay, that will do mighty well. Well, daughter, this gentleman has a mind to marry you, and I have told him that I am willing.

Lucinda. Alas! Is it possible?

Sganarel. Yes.

Lucinda. But really?

Sganarel. Yes, yes.

Lucinda. [*To Clitander.*] What, are you desirous to be my husband?

Clitander. Yes, madam.

Lucinda. And does my father consent to it?

Sganarel. Yes, daughter.

Lucinda. O how happy am I, if this be true!

Clitander. Don't doubt it, madam; 'tis not to-day that I began to love you, and burn to be your husband; I came hither for that alone; and if you'd have me tell you the thing just as 'tis, this habit is but a mere pretence, and I acted the physician only to get to you, and the more easily to obtain what I desire.

Lucinda. That's giving me marks of a very tender love; I am as sensible of it as I ought to be.

Sganarel. O poor silly girl! silly girl! silly girl!

Lucinda. Then, sir, do you give me the gentleman for a husband?

Sganarel. Yes; come, give me your hand; give me yours too a little.

Clitander. But, sir——   [*Holding back.*

Sganarel. No, no, 'tis only to——[*Stifling his laugh.*] to make her easy. Come, take hands. There, 'tis done.

Clitander. As a warrant of my fidelity, accept of this ring. [*Low to Sganarel.*] 'Tis a constellated ring which cures distractions of the mind.

Lucinda. Let the contract be made then, that nothing may be wanting.

Clitander. Lack-a-day! with all my heart, madam. [*Low to Sganarel.*] I'll call up the man that writes down my prescriptions, and make her believe 'tis a notary.

Sganarel. Very well.

Clitander. Soho! Call up the notary I brought with me.
Lucinda. What! did you bring a notary?
Clitander. Yes, madam.
Lucinda. I'm glad on't.
Sganarel. O poor silly girl! silly girl!

Scene VII

The Notary, Clitander, Sganarel, Lucinda, Lysetta.

[*Clitander whispers the Notary.*]

Sganarel. [*To the Notary.*] Yes, sir, you are to draw a contract for those two persons. Write. [*To Lucinda.*] The contract is making, girl. [*To the Notary.*] I give her twenty thousand crowns as a portion. Write.
Lucinda. I am obliged to you, father.
Notary. 'Tis done, you have nothing to do but to sign.
Sganarel. Here's a contract soon drawn.
Clitander. [*To Sganarel.*] But, however, sir——
Sganarel. Hey, no, no. Don't I know? [*To the Notary.*] Come, give him the pen to sign. [*To Lucinda.*] Come, sign, sign, sign. Well, I'll sign myself by and by.
Lucinda. No, no; I'll have the contract in my own hands.
Sganarel. Well, take it. [*After signing it.*] Are you satisfied?
Lucinda. More than you can imagine.
Sganarel. That's well, that's well.
Clitander. I have not only had the precaution to bring a notary, but I've brought several singers, musicians, and dancers, to celebrate the feast, and make merry. Call 'em in. These are people I brought with me, and which I make use of daily to pacify, by their harmony and dancing, the disturbances of the mind.

Scene VIII

Sganarel, Lucinda, Clitander, Lysetta.

Comedy, Music, Dancing, the Sports, the Smiles, and the Pleasures.

Comedy, Dancing, and Music together.
All humankind, without us three,
Would soon become diseased;
Their chief physicians sure are we
By whom their ills are eased.

Comedy.

> If you by pleasant means would aim
> To cure the vapoured head,
> Leave your Hippocrates, for shame,
> And come to us for aid.

All three.

> All humankind, without us three,
> Would soon become diseased;
> Their chief physicians sure are we
> By whom their ills are eased.

[*Whilst the Sports, the Smiles, and the Pleasures are dancing, Clitander carries off Lucinda.*]

SCENE IX

Sganarel, Lysetta.

Comedy, Music, Dancing, the Sports, the Smiles, and the Pleasures.

Sganarel. This is a pleasant manner of curing people. Where is my daughter and the physician?

Lysetta. They're gone to conclude the rest of the marriage.

Sganarel. What marriage?

Lysetta. Faith, sir, the woodcock's caught; you imagined you had been in jest, and it proves in earnest.

Sganarel. [*Endeavours to go after Clitander and Lucinda, but the dancers hold him.*] What the devil? Let me go; let me go, let me go, I say. Again? [*They endeavour to force him to dance.*] Pox take you all!

TARTUFFE, OR THE IMPOSTOR

(A COMEDY)

TARTUFFE, *or* THE IMPOSTOR, *a Comedy of Five Acts in Verse, acted at Paris at the Theatre of the Palace-Royal, August* 5, 1667.

The three first acts of the *Tartuffe* were performed at the feast of Versailles the 12th of May, 1664, before the king and the queens. The king afterwards forbade this comedy to be made public until it was finished and examined by persons capable of making a just discernment of it, adding, That he had nothing to say to this comedy. This, the hypocrites took an advantage of, in order to stir up Paris and the court both against the piece and the author; whereupon Molière was not only hated by the Tartuffes, but had likewise a great many Orgons for his enemies, those weak kind of people who are so easy to be seduced; whilst others that were truly religious were likewise alarmed, although the piece was scarce known to the one or the other of them. A certain curate affirmed, in a book which he presented to the king, that the author deserved to be burnt, and damned him by his own authority. In short, Molière had to bear everything of the most dangerous kind that could flow from revenge and ignorant zeal. The bishops and the Pope's legate, after having heard this work read, judged more favourably of it; and the king gave Molière a verbal permission for the playing of it. He softened several things in it, which 'twas plain they had required of him, and brought it out under the title of *The Impostor*; disguising that character by dressing him like a fine gentleman, and giving him a little hat, long hair, great cravat, a sword, and clothes richly trimmed; in which form he thought he might venture *Tartuffe* abroad on the 5th of August, 1667. But the order which was sent him the next day to suspend the acting of it made him less sensible of the applause it had met with. It was not till 1669 that the king gave him an authentic permission to bring that comedy again upon the stage, it being the 5th day of February in that year that it made its appearance again at Paris, when as soon as it was well known the truly religious were undeceived, the hypocrites confounded, and the poet justified. People found in the character and discourse of the virtuous Cleanthes, weapons to oppose the false and specious reasonings of hypocrisy.

It is not only for the singularity and boldness of the subject, or for the skill with which it is treated, that this piece merits applause. The first scene is as happy as new, as full of simplicity as of life. Instead of those mutual confidences which are so commonly made use of in this place, an old grandmother, offended at what she had seen amiss in her granddaughter, is brought on giving a severe lecture to those who belonged to the house, in which she draws the characters of them all; for we distinguish the truth even through the language of prejudice; from this moment everything is in motion, and the theatrical action gradually increases to the end. The fine raillery of Dorina in the scene between her and her master, gives us a plain idea of Orgon, and prepares us to know Tartuffe in the picture of the hypocrite, which Cleanthes opposes to that of the truly devout.   Tartuffe, who is only talked of in the two first acts, makes his appearance in the third, when the plot being then more animated receives equal vivacity from the new schemes which they employed against this villain, and from the address with which he turned everything which was attempted against him to his own advantage. The infatuation of Orgon, which increased in proportion to the measures which were taken to cure it, gave occasion to that singular and admirable scene of the fourth act, which the necessity of un-masking a vice so abominable as that of hypocrisy, rendered indis-pensible.   The panegyric of Louis XIV put in the mouth of the Exempt at the end of the piece, could not justify the fault of the unravelling in the eyes of the critics.

ACTORS

Madam Pernelle, *mother to Orgon.*
Orgon, *husband to Elmira.*
Elmira, *wife to Orgon.*
Damis, *son to Orgon.*
Mariana, *daughter to Orgon.*
Valère, *in love with Mariana.*
Cleanthes, *brother-in-law to Orgon.*
Tartuffe, *a hypocrite.*
Dorina, *waiting-maid to Mariana.*
Mr. Loyal, *a sergeant.*
An Exempt.
Flipote, *Madam Perneile's maid.*

Scene: *Paris, in Orgon's house.*

ACT I

SCENE I

Madam Pernelle, Elmira, Mariana, Damis, Cleanthes, Dorina, Flipote.

Madam Pernelle. Come Flipote, let's be gone, that I may get rid of them.

Elmira. You walk so fast, that one has much ado to follow you.

Madam Pernelle. Stay, daughter, stay; come no farther; this is all needless ceremony.

Elmira. We only acquit ourselves of our duty to you: but pray, mother, what makes you in such haste to leave us?

Madam Pernelle. Because I can't endure to see such management, and nobody takes any care to please me. I leave your house, I tell you, very ill edified; my instructions are all contradicted. You show no respect for anything amongst you, every one talks aloud there, and the house is a perfect Dover Court.

Dorina. If——

Madam Pernelle. You are, sweetheart, a noisy and impertinent Abigail, and mighty free of your advice on all occasions.

Damis. But——

Madam Pernelle. In short, you are a fool, child; 'tis I tell you so, who am your grandmother; and I have told my son your father, a hundred times, that you would become a perfect rake, and would be nothing but a plague to him.

Mariana. I fancy——

Madam Pernelle. Good-lack, sister of his, you act the prude, and look as if butter would not melt in your mouth: but still waters, they say, are always deepest; and under your sly airs, you carry on a trade I don't at all approve of.

Elmira. But mother——

Madam Pernelle. By your leave, daughter, your conduct is absolutely wrong in everything: you ought to set them a good example; and their late mother managed 'em much better. You are a sorry economist, and what I can't endure, dress like

79

any princess. She who desires only to please her husband, daughter, needs not so much finery.

Cleanthes. But madam, after all—

Madam Pernelle. As for you, sir, her brother, I esteem you very much, I love and respect you; but yet, were I in my son's her husband's place, I should earnestly entreat you not to come within our doors. You are always laying down rules of life, that good people should never follow. I talk a little freely to you; but 'tis my humour; I never chew upon what I have at heart.

Damis. Your Mr. Tartuffe is a blessed soul, no doubt——

Madam Pernelle. He's a good man, and should be listened to; I can't bear, with patience, to hear him cavilled at by such a fool as you.

Damis. What! shall I suffer a censorious bigot to usurp an absolute authority in the family? And shall not we take the least diversion, if this precious spark thinks not fit to allow of it?

Dorina. If one were to hearken to him, and give in to his maxims, we could do nothing but what would be made a crime of; for the critical zealot controls everything.

Madam Pernelle. And whatever he controls is well controlled. He would fain show you the way to Heaven; and my son ought to make you all love him.

Damis. No, look you, madam, neither father, nòr anything else can oblige me to have any regard for him. I should belie my heart to tell you otherwise. To me his actions are perfectly odious; and I foresee, that, one time or other, matters will come to extremity between that wretch and me.

Dorina. 'Tis downright scandalous, to see an upstart take on him at that rate here. A vagabond, that had not a pair of shoes to his feet when he came hither, and all the clothes on his back would not fetch sixpence, that he should so far forget himself, as to contradict everything, and to play the master.

Madam Pernelle. Mercy on me! Matters would go much better, were everything managed by his pious directions.

Dorina. He passes for a saint in your imagination; but, believe me, all he does is nothing but hypocrisy.

Madam Pernelle. What a tongue!

Dorina. I would not trust him without good security, any more than I would his man Laurence.

Madam Pernelle. What the servant may be at bottom, I can't tell; but I'll answer for the master, that he is a good man;

you wish him ill, and reject him, only because he tells you the
naked truth. 'Tis sin that his heart can't brook, and the
interest of Heaven is his only motive.

Dorina. Ay; but why, for some time past, can't he endure
that anybody should come near us? How can a civil visit
offend Heaven, so much that we must have a din about it,
enough to stun one? Among friends, shall I give you my
opinion of the matter? [*Pointing to Elmira.*] I take him, in
troth, to be jealous of my lady.

Madam Pernelle. Hold your peace, and consider what you
say. He is not the only person who condemns these visits.
The bustle that attends the people you keep company with,
these coaches continually planted at the gate, and the noisy
company of such a parcel of footmen disturb the whole neighbourhood; I am willing to believe, there's no harm done; but
then it gives people occasion to talk, and that is not well.

Cleanthes. Alas, madam, will you hinder people from prating?
It would be a very hard thing in life, if for any foolish stories
that might be raised about people, they should be forced to
renounce their best friends; and suppose we should resolve to
do so, do you think it would keep all the world from talking?
There's no guarding against calumny. Let us therefore not
mind silly tittle-tattle, and let's endeavour to live innocently
ourselves, and leave the gossiping part of mankind to say what
they please.

Dorina. May not neighbour Daphne and her little spouse
be the persons who speak ill of us? People, whose own conduct
is the most ridiculous, are always readiest to detract from that
of others. They never fail readily to catch at the slightest
appearance of an affair, to set the news about with joy, and to
give things the very turn they would have them take. By
colouring other people's actions, like their own, they think to
justify their conduct to the world, and fondly hope, by way of
some resemblance, to give their own intrigues the air of innocence,
or to shift part of the blame elsewhere, which they find falls too
hard upon themselves.

Madam Pernelle. All these arguments are nothing to the
purpose. Orante is known to lead an exemplary life, her care
is all for Heaven; and I have heard say that she has but an
indifferent opinion of the company that frequents your house.

Dorina. An admirable pattern indeed! She's a mighty good
lady, and lives strictly, 'tis true, but 'tis age that has brought
this ardent zeal upon her; and we know that she's a prude in

her own defence. As long as 'twas in her power to make conquests, she did not balk any of her advantages; but when she found the lustre of her eyes abate, she would needs renounce the world that was on the point of leaving her; and under the specious mask of great prudence, conceals the decay of her worn-out charms. That is the antiquated coquettes' last shift. It is hard upon them to see themselves deserted by all their gallants. Thus forsaken, their gloomy disquiet can find no relief but in prudery; and then the severity of these good ladies censures all and forgives none. They cry out aloud upon every one's way of living, not out of a principle of charity, but envy, as not being able to suffer that another should taste those pleasures which people on the decline have no relish for.

Madam Pernelle. [*To Elmira.*] These are the idle stories that are told to please you, daughter. There's no getting in a word at your house, for madam here engrosses all the talk to herself. But I shall also be heard in my turn. I tell you my son never acted a wiser part, than when he took this devout man into his family; that Heaven in time of need sent him hither to reclaim your wandering minds; that 'tis your main interest to hearken to his counsels, and that he reproves nothing that is not blameable. These visits, balls, and assemblies are all the inventions of the wicked spirit; there's not one word of godliness to be heard at any of them, but idle stuff, nonsense, and tales of a tub, and the neighbours often come in for a share, whip you have 'em in tierce and quarte. In short, the heads of reasonable people are turned by the confusion of such meetings. A thousand different fancies are started about less than nothing; and as a good doctor said the other day very well, 'Tis a perfect Tower of Babel, for every one here babbles out of all measure. Now to give you an account what brought it in was this. [*Pointing to Cleanthes.*] What! is that spark giggling already? Go look for your fool to make a jest of, and unless—— [*To Elmira.*] Good-bye t'ye, daughter, I shall say no more. Depend on it, I have not half the esteem for your house I had, and it shall be very fine weather when I set my foot in your doors again. [*Giving Flipote a box on the ear.*] Come you, you're dreaming and gaping at the crows; i'fakins! I'll warm your ears for you. Let's march, trollop, let's march.

SCENE II

Cleanthes, Dorina.

Cleanthes. I won't go, for fear she should fall foul on me again. That this good old lady——

Dorina. 'Tis pity, truly, she does not hear you call her so; she'd give you to understand how she liked you, and that she was not old enough to be called so yet.

Cleanthes. What a heat has she been in with us about nothing! And how fond does she seem of her Tartuffe!

Dorina. Oh! truly, all this is nothing compared to the infatuation of her son, and were you to see him you'd say he was much worse. His behaviour in our public troubles had procured him the character of a man of sense, and of bravery for his prince; but he's grown quite besotted since he became fond of Tartuffe. He calls him brother, and loves him in his heart a hundred times better than either mother, son, daughter, or wife. He's the only confidant of all his secrets, and the wise director of all his actions; he caresses, he embraces him, and I think one could not have more affection for a mistress. He will have him seated at the upper end of the table, and is delighted to see him guttle as much as half a dozen. He must be helped to all the tit-bits, and whenever he but belches, he bids G—d bless him. In short, he dotes upon him, he's his all, his hero; he admires all he does, quotes him on all occasions, looks on every trifling action of his as a wonder, and every word an oracle. At the same time the fellow, knowing his blind side, and willing to make the most on't, has a hundred tricks to impose upon his judgment, and get his money from him in the way of bigotry. He now pretends truly to take the whole family to task; even the awkward fool his foot-boy takes upon him to lecture us with his fanatic face, and to demolish our patches, paint, and ribbons. The rascal, the other day, tore us a fine handkerchief that lay in the *Pilgrim's Progress*, and cried, That it was a horrid profanation, to mix hellish ornaments with sanctified things.

SCENE III

Elmira, Mariana, Damis, Cleanthes, Dorina.

Elmira. [*To Cleanthes.*] You are very happy in not having come to the harangue she gave us at the gate. But I saw my husband, and as he did not see me. I'll go up to wait his coming.

Cleanthes. I'll wait for him here by way of a little amusement, only bid him good-morrow.

Scene IV

Cleanthes, Damis, Dorina.

Damis. Hint something to him about my sister's wedding; I suspect that Tartuffe's against it, and that he puts my father upon these tedious evasions; you are not ignorant how nearly I am concerned in it. If my friend Valère and my sister are sincerely fond of one another, his sister, you know, is no less dear to me, and if it must——
Dorina. Here he is.

Scene V

Orgon, Cleanthes, Dorina.

Orgon. Hah! brother, good-morrow.
Cleanthes. I was just going, and am glad to see you come back. The country at present is not very pleasant.
Orgon. Dorina. [*To Cleanthes.*] Brother, pray stay; you'll give me leave just to inquire the news of the family; I can't be easy else. [*To Dorina.*] Have matters gone well the two days I have been away? What has happened here? How do they all do?
Dorina. My lady the day before yesterday had a fever all day, and was sadly out of order with a strange headache.
Orgon. And Tartuffe?
Dorina. Tartuffe? Extremely well, fat, fair, and fresh-coloured.
Orgon. Poor man!
Dorina. At night she had no stomach, and could not touch a bit of supper, the pain in her head continued so violent.
Orgon. And Tartuffe?
Dorina. He supped by himself before her, and very heartily ate a brace of partridge, and half a leg of mutton hashed.
Orgon. Poor man!
Dorina. She never closed her eyes, but burnt so that she could not get a wink of sleep; and we were forced to sit up with her all night.
Orgon. And Tartuffe?
Dorina. Being agreeably sleepy, he went from table to his

chamber, and so into a warm bed, and slept comfortably till next morning.

Orgon. The poor man!

Dorina. At length my lady, prevailed upon by our persuasions, resolved to be let blood; then she soon grew easier.

Orgon. And Tartuffe?

Dorina. He plucked up his spirit, as he should; and fortifying his mind against all evils, to make amends for the blood my lady lost, drank at breakfast four swingeing draughts of wine.

Orgon. The poor man!

Dorina. At present they both are pretty well, and I shall go before and let my lady know how glad you are of her recovery.

SCENE VI

Orgon, Cleanthes.

Cleanthes. She jokes upon you, brother, to your face; and without any design of making you angry, I must tell you freely, that 'tis not without reason. Was ever such a whim heard of? Is it possible, that a man can be so bewitching at this time of day, as to make you forget everything for him? That after having, in your own house, relieved his indigence, you should be ready to——

Orgon. Hold there, brother, you don't know the man you speak of.

Cleanthes. Well, I don't know him, since you will have it so. But then, in order to know what a man he is,——

Orgon. Brother, you would be charmed did you know him, and there would be no end of your raptures. He's a man— that—ah—a man—a man, in short, a man. Who always practises as he directs, enjoys a profound peace, and regards the whole world no more than so much dung. Ay, I am quite another man by his conversation. He teaches me to set my heart upon nothing; he disengages my mind from friendships or relations; and I could see my brother, children, mother, wife, all expire, and not regard it more than this.

Cleanthes. Humane sentiments, brother, I must confess!

Orgon. Ah! had you but seen him as I first met with him, you would have loved him as well as I do. He came every day to church with a composed mien, and kneeled down just against me. He attracted the eyes of the whole congregation by the fervency with which he sent up his prayers to Heaven. He sighed and groaned very heavily, and every moment humbly kissed the earth. And when I was going out, he would advance before and offer me holy water at the door. Understanding by his boy (who copied him in everything), his low condition, and who he was, I made him presents; but he always modestly would offer to return me part. 'Tis too much, he'd say, too much by half. I am not worth your pity. And when I refused to take it again, he would go and give it among the poor before my face. At length Heaven moved me to take him home, since which everything here seems to prosper. I see he reproves without distinction; and that even with regard to my wife, he is extremely cautious of my honour. He acquaints me who ogles her, and is six times more jealous of her than I am. But you can hardly imagine how very good he is. He calls every trifle in himself a sin; he's scandalised at the smallest thing imaginable, so far, that the other day he told me he had caught a flea, as he was at his devotions, and had killed it, he doubted, in rather too much anger.

Cleanthes. S'death! you must be mad, brother, I fancy; or do you intend to banter me by such stuff? What is it you mean? All this fooling——

Orgon. Brother, what you say savours of libertinism; you are a little tainted with it; and, as I have told you more than once, you'll draw down some heavy judgment on your head one day or other.

Cleanthes. This is the usual strain of such as you. They would have everybody as blind as themselves. To be clear-sighted is libertinism, and such as don't dote upon empty grimaces, have neither faith nor respect to sacred things. Come, come, all this discourse of yours frights not me; I know what I say, and Heaven sees my heart. We are not to be slaves to your men of form. There are pretenders to devotion as well as to courage. And as we never find the truly brave to be such as make much noise wheresoever they are led by honour, so the good and truly pious, who are worthy of our imitation, are never those that deal much in grimace. Pray, would you make no distinction between hypocrisy and true devotion? Would you term them both alike, and pay the same regard to the mask as you do to the face? Would you put artifice on the level with sincerity, and confound appearance with reality? Is the phantom of the same esteem with you as the figure? and is bad money of the same value as good? Men generally are odd creatures. They never keep up to true nature. The bounds of reason are too narrow for them. In every character they overact their parts, and the noblest designs very often suffer in their hands, because they will be running things into extremes, and always carry things too far. This, brother, by the by.

Orgon. Yes, yes, you are without doubt, a very reverend doctor; all the knowledge in the world lies under your cap. You are the only wise and discerning man, the oracle, the Cato of the present age; all men, compared to you, are downright fools.

Cleanthes. No, brother, I am none of your reverend sages, nor is the whole learning of the universe vested in me; but I must tell you, I have wit enough to distinguish truth from falsehood. And as I see no character in life more great or valuable than to be truly devout, nor anything more noble, or more beautiful, than the fervour of a sincere piety; so I think nothing more abominable than the outside daubing of a pretended zeal; than those mountebanks, those devotees in show, whose sacrilegious and treacherous grimace deceives with impunity, and according as they please, make a jest of what is most venerable and sacred among men. Those slaves of interest, who make a trade of godliness, and who would purchase honours and reputation with a hypocritical turning up of the eyes, and affected transports. Those people, I say, who show an uncommon zeal for the next world in order to make their fortunes in this, who, with great affectation and earnestness, daily recommend solitude, while they live in courts. Men who know how to make their own vices consistent with their zeal; they are passionate, revengeful, faithless, full of artifice; and to effect a man's destruction, they insolently urge their private resentment as the cause of Heaven; being so much the more dangerous in their wrath, as they point against us those weapons which men reverence, and because their passions prompt them to assassinate us with a consecrated blade. There are too many of this vile character; but the sincerely devout are easily known; our age, brother, affords us some of these, who might serve for glorious patterns to us. Observe Aristo, Periander, Orontes, Alcidamas, Polidore, Clitander; that title is refused to them by nobody. These are not braggadocios in virtue. We see none of this insufferable haughtiness in their conduct; and their devotion is humane and gentle. They censure not all we do, they think there's too much pride in these corrections, and leaving the fierceness of words to others, reprove our actions by their own. They never build upon the appearance of a

fault, and are always ready to judge favourably of others.   They
have no cabals, no intrigues to carry on; their chief aim is to
live themselves as they should do.   They never worry a poor
sinner; their quarrel is only with the offence.   Nor do they ever
exert a keener zeal for the interest of Heaven, than Heaven
itself does.   These are the men for me; this is the true practice,
and this the example fit to be followed.   Your man is indeed
not of this stamp.   You cry up his zeal out of a good intention,
but, I believe you are imposed on by a very false gloss.

Orgon.   My dear brother, have you done?

Cleanthes.   Yes.

Orgon.   [*Going.*]   Then I'm your humble servant.

Cleanthes.   Pray one word more, brother; let us leave this
discourse.   You know you promised to take Valère for your
son-in-law.

Orgon.   Yes.

Cleanthes.   And have appointed a day for this agreeable
wedding.

Orgon.   True.

Cleanthes.   Why then do you put off the solemnity?

Orgon.   I can't tell.

Cleanthes.   Have you some other design in your head?

Orgon.   Perhaps so.

Cleanthes.   Will you break your word then?

Orgon.   I don't say that.

Cleanthes.   I think there's no obstacle can hinder you from
performing your promise.

Orgon.   That's as it happens.

Cleanthes.   Does the speaking of a single word require so
much circumspection then?   Valère sends me to you about it.

Orgon.   Heaven be praised!

Cleanthes.   What answer shall I return him?

Orgon.   What you will.

Cleanthes.   But 'tis necessary I should know your intentions;
pray what are they?

Orgon.   To do just what Heaven pleases.

Cleanthes.   But to the point pray.   Valère has your promise,
do you stand to it, ay or no?

Orgon.   Good be t'ye.

Cleanthes. [*Alone.*]   I am afraid he'll meet with some misfortune in his love.   I ought to inform him how matters go.

ACT II

Scene I

Orgon, Mariana.

Orgon. Mariana!

Mariana. Sir.

Orgon. Come hither; I have something to say to you in private.

Mariana. [*To Orgon, who is looking into a closet.*] What are you looking for, sir?

Orgon. I'm looking if anybody's there who might overhear us. This little place is fit for such a purpose. So, we're all safe. I have always, Mariana, found you of a sweet disposition, and you have always been very dear to me.

Mariana. I am very much obliged to you, sir, for your fatherly affection.

Orgon. 'Tis very well said, daughter, and to deserve it, your chief care should be to make me easy.

Mariana. That is the height of my ambition.

Orgon. Very well. Then what say you of Tartuffe, our guest?

Mariana. Who, I?

Orgon. Yes, you; pray take heed how you answer.

Mariana. Alas! sir, I'll say what you will of him.

Scene II

Orgon, Mariana, Dorina (coming in softly, and standing behind Orgon without being seen).

Orgon. That's discreetly said. Tell me then, my girl, that he's a very deserving person; that you like him, and that it would be agreeable if, with my consent, you might have him for a husband, ha?

Mariana. How, sir?

Orgon. What's the matter?

Mariana. What said you?

Orgon. What?

Mariana. Did I mistake you?

Orgon. As how?

Mariana. Whom would you have me say I liked, sir, and should be glad, with your approbation, to have for a husband?

Orgon. Tartuffe.

Mariana. I protest to you, sir, there's nothing in it. Why would you make me tell you such a story?

Orgon. But I would have it to be no story; and 'tis enough that I have pitched upon him for you.

Mariana. What, would you, sir——

Orgon. Ay, child, I purpose, by your marriage, to join Tartuffe to my family. I have resolved upon't, and as I have a right to——[*Spying Dorina.*] What business have you there? Your curiosity is very great, sweetheart, to bring you to listen in this manner.

Dorina. In troth, sir, whether this report proceeds from conjecture, or chance, I don't know; but they have been just telling me the news of this match, and I have been making a very great jest of it.

Orgon. Why, is the thing so incredible?

Dorina. So incredible, that were you to tell me so yourself, I should not believe you.

Orgon. I know how to make you believe it, though.

Dorina. Ay, ay, sir, you tell us a comical story.

Orgon. I tell you just what will prove true in a short time.

Dorina. Stuff!

Orgon. Daughter, I promise you I'm not in jest.

Dorina. Go, go; don't believe your father, madam, he does but joke.

Orgon. I tell you——

Dorina. No, 'tis in vain, nobody will believe you.

Orgon. My anger at length——

Dorina. Well, sir, we will believe you; and so much the worse on your side. What, sir, is it possible that with that air of wisdom, and that spacious beard on your face, you should be weak enough but to wish——

Orgon. Harkee, you have taken certain liberties of late, that I dislike. I tell you that, child.

Dorina. Good sir, let us argue this affair calmly. You really must banter people by this scheme. Your daughter is not cut out for a bigot; he has other things to think on. And then, what will such an alliance bring you in? For what reason would you go, with all your wealth, to choose a beggar for a son-in-law——

Orgon. Hold your tongue! If he has nothing, know that

we ought to esteem him for it. His poverty is an honest poverty, which raises him above all grandeur, because he has suffered himself, in short, to be deprived of his fortune by his negligence for things temporal, and his strong attachment to things eternal. But my assistance may put him in a way of getting out of trouble, and of recovering his own. As poor as he is, he's a gentleman, and the estate he was born to is not inconsiderable.

Dorina. Yes, he says so; and this vanity, sir, does not very well suit with piety. He that embraces the simplicity of a holy life, should not set forth his name and family so much. The humble procedure of devotion does but ill agree with the glare of ambition. To what purpose all this pride?——But this talk offends you. Then let us lay aside his quality, and speak to his person. Can you have the heart to fling away such a girl as this upon such a man as he? Should you not consult propriety, and look a little forward to the consequences of such a union as this? Depend upon't, a young woman's virtue is in some danger when she isn't married to her mind; that her living virtuously afterward depends, in a great measure, upon the good qualities of her husband; and that those whom people everywhere point at with the finger to the forehead, often make their wives what we find they are. It is no easy task to be faithful to some sorts of husbands; and he that gives his daughter a man she hates, is accountable to Heaven for the slips she makes. Consider then to what danger your design exposes you.

Orgon. I tell you, she is to learn from me what to do.

Dorina. You could not do better with her than to follow my advice.

Orgon. Don't let us amuse ourselves, daughter, with this silly stuff. I am your father, and know what you must do. I had indeed promised you to Valère, but, besides that 'tis reported he is given to play, I suspect him of being a little profligate. I don't observe that he frequents the church.

Dorina. Would you have him run to church at your precise hours, as people do who go there only to be taken notice of?

Orgon. I am not consulting you about it. The other, in short, is a favourite of Heaven, and that is beyond any other possessions. This union will crown your wishes with every sort of good; it will be one continued scene of pleasure and delight. You'll live in faithful love together, really like two children, like two turtle-doves. No unhappy debate will e'er rise between you; and you'll make anything of him you can well desire.

Dorina. She? She'll ne'er make anything but a fool of him, I assure you.

Orgon. Hey! What language!

Dorina. I say, he has the look of a fool; and his ascendant will overbear all the virtue your daughter has.

Orgon. Have done with your interruptions. Learn to hold your peace, and don't you put in your oar where you have nothing to do.

Dorina. Nay, sir, I only speak for your good.

Orgon. You are too officious. Pray hold your tongue, if you please.

Dorina. If one had not a love for you——

Orgon. I desire none of your love.

Dorina. But I will love you, sir, in spite of your teeth.

Orgon. Ha!

Dorina. I have your reputation much at heart, and can't bear to have you made the subject of every gossip's tale.

Orgon. Then you won't have done?

Dorina. It would be a sin to let you make such an alliance as this.

Orgon. Will you hold your tongue, you serpent, whose impudence——

Dorina. Oh! what, a devotee, and fly into such a rage?

Orgon. Yes; my choler is moved at this impertinence; and I'm resolved you shall hold your tongue.

Dorina. Be it so. But though I don't speak a word, I don't think the less.

Orgon. Think if you will; but take care not to say a syllable to me about it, or——Enough—— [*To his daughter.*] I have maturely weighed all things as a wise man should.

Dorina. [*Aside.*] It makes me mad that I must not speak now!

Orgon. Tartuffe, without foppery, is a person so formed——

Dorina. [*Aside.*] Yes, 'tis a pretty phiz.

Orgon. That should you have no great relish for his other qualifications——

Dorina. [*Aside.*] She'll have a very fine bargain of him! [*Orgon turns about towards Dorina, and eyes her with his arms across.*] Were I in her place though, no man alive should marry me against my will, with impunity. I'd let him see, soon after the ceremony was over, that a wife has a revenge always at hand.

Orgon. [*To Dorina.*] Then what I say, stands for nothing with you?

Dorina. What do you complain of? I don't speak to you.

Orgon. What is it you do then?

Dorina. I talk to myself.

Orgon. [*Aside.*] Very well! I must give her a slap on the face, to correct her prodigious insolence. [*He puts himself into a posture to strike Dorina, and at every word he speaks to his daughter he casts his eyes upon Dorina, who stands bolt-upright, without speaking.*] Daughter, you must needs approve of my design——and believe that the husband——which I have picked out for you——[*To Dorina.*] Why dost thou not talk to thyself now?

Dorina. Because I have nothing to say to myself.

Orgon. One little word more.

Dorina. I've no mind to it.

Orgon. To be sure I watched you.

Dorina. A downright fool, i'faith.

Orgon. In short, daughter, you must obey, and show an entire deference for my choice.

Dorina. [*As she runs off.*] I should scorn to take such a husband myself.

Orgon. [*Strikes at her, but misses.*] You have a pestilent hussy with you there, daughter, that I can't live with any longer, without sin. I'm not in a condition to proceed at present; her insolence has put my spirits into such a ferment, that I must go take the air to recover myself a little.

SCENE III

Mariana, Dorina.

Dorina. Pray tell me, have you lost your tongue? Must I play your part for you on this occasion? What, suffer a silly overture to be made you, without saying the least word against it!

Mariana. What should one do with a positive father?

Dorina. Anything, to ward off such a menace.

Mariana. But what?

Dorina. Why, tell him, that hearts admit of no proxies; that you marry for yourself, and not for him; that you being the person, for whom the whole affair is transacted, your inclinations for the man, should be consulted, not his; and that if Tartuffe seems so lovely in his eyes, he may marry him himself without let or hindrance.

Mariana. A father, I own, has such a command over one, that I never had courage to make him a reply.

Dorina. But let us reason the case. Valère has made advances for you: pray, do you love him, or do you not?

Mariana. Nay, you do injustice to my love, to question my affections! Ought you, Dorina, to ask me that? Have I not opened my heart to you a hundred times on that subject? and are you still a stranger to the warmth of my passion?

Dorina. How do I know whether your heart and words keep pace together? or whether you really have any particular regard for this lover, or not?

Mariana. You do me wrong, Dorina, to doubt it; and the sincerity of my sentiments, in that matter, has been but too plain.

Dorina. You really love him then?

Mariana. Ay, extremely.

Dorina. And according to all appearance, he loves you as well.

Mariana. I believe so.

Dorina. And you two have a mutual desire to marry?

Mariana. Assuredly.

Dorina. What is then your expectation from this other match?

Mariana. To kill myself, if they force me to it.

Dorina. Very good! That's a relief I did not think of; you need only to die to get rid of this perplexity. 'Tis a wonderful remedy, for certain. It makes one mad to hear folks talk at this rate.

Mariana. Bless me, Dorina! what a humour are you got into! You have no compassion upon people's afflictions.

Dorina. I have no compassion for people who talk idly, and give way in time of action as you do.

Mariana. But what would you have, if one is timorous?

Dorina. But love requires a firmness of mind.

Mariana. But have I wavered in my affections towards Valère? And is it not his business to gain me of my father?

Dorina. But what? if your father be a downright humorist, who is entirely bewitched with his Tartuffe, and would set aside a match he had agreed on, pray is that your lover's fault?

Mariana. But should I, by a flat and confident refusal, let everybody know, that I am violently in love? Would you have me, for his sake, transgress the modesty of my sex, and the bounds of my duty? Would you have my passion become a perfect town-talk?

Dorina. No, no, I don't want anything. I see you'd fain have Mr. Tartuffe; and now I think of it, I should be in the wrong to dissuade you from so considerable an alliance. To what purpose should I oppose your inclinations? The match is in itself too advantageous. Mr. Tartuffe, oh! is this a trifling offer? If we take it right, he's no simpleton. It will be no small honour to be his mate. All the world has a prodigious value for him already; he is well born, handsome in his person, he has a red ear, and a very florid complexion; you'll, in short, be but too happy with such a husband.

Mariana. Heavens!

Dorina. You can't conceive what a joy 'twill be to you, to be the consort of so fine a man!

Mariana. Poh! prithee give over this discourse, and rather assist me against this match. 'Tis now all over; I yield, and am ready to do whatever you'd have me.

Dorina. No, no, a daughter should do as she's bid, though her father would have her marry a monkey. Besides what reason have you to complain? Yours is a benefit ticket. You'll be coached down to his own borough-town, which you'll find abounds in cousins and uncles. It will be very diverting to you to entertain them all. Then Madam Tartuffe will be directly introduced to the beau-monde. You'll go visit, by way of welcome, the bailiff's lady, and the assessor's wife; they'll do you the honour of the folding chair. At a good time you may hope for a ball, and a great consort, to wit, two pair of bagpipes; and perchance you may see merry-Andrew, and the puppet-show; if however your husband——

Mariana. Oh! you kill me! rather contrive how to help me by your advice.

Dorina. Your humble servant for that.

Mariana. Nay, Dorina, for Heaven's sake——

Dorina. No, it must be a match, to punish you.

Mariana. Dear girl, do!

Dorina. No.

Mariana. If my professions——

Dorina. No, Tartuffe's your man, and you shall have a taste of him.

Mariana. You know how much I always confided in you; be so good——

Dorina. No, in troth; you shall be Tartuffed.

Mariana. Well, since my misfortunes can't move you, henceforth leave me entirely to my despair. That shall lend my heart relief, and I know an infallible remedy for all my sufferings.

[*Offers to go.*

Dorina. Here, here, come back; I'm appeased. I must take compassion on you, for all this.

Mariana. I tell you, d'y' see, Dorina, if they do expose me to this torment, it will certainly cost me my life.

Dorina. Don't vex yourself, it may easily be prevented——But see; here's your humble servant Valère.

SCENE IV

Valère, Mariana, Dorina.

Valère. I was just now told an odd piece of news, madam, that I knew nothing of, and which to be sure is very pretty.

Mariana. What's that?

Valère. That you are to be married to Tartuffe.

Mariana. 'Tis certain my father has such a design in his head.

Valère. Your father, madam——

Mariana. Has altered his mind, and has been just now making the proposal to me.

Valère. What, seriously?

Mariana. Ay, seriously. He has been declaring himself strenuously for the match.

Valère. And pray, madam, what may be your determination in the affair?

Mariana. I don't know.

Valère. The answer is honest! You don't know?

Mariana. No.

Valère. No?

Mariana. What would you advise me to?

Valère. I advise you to accept of him for a husband.

Mariana. Is that your advice?

Valère. Yes.

Mariana. In good earnest?

Valère. No doubt of it. The choice is good, and well worth attending to.

Mariana. Well, sir, I shall take your counsel.

Valère. You will have no difficulty to follow it, I believe.

Mariana. Hardly more than your counsel gave you.

Valère. I gave it, madam, to please you.

Mariana. And I shall follow it, to do you a pleasure.

Dorina. [*Retiring to the farther part of the stage.*] So. Let's see what this will come to.

Valère. Is this then your affection? And was it all deceit, when you——

Mariana. Pray let's talk no more of that. You told me frankly that I ought to accept of the offer made me. And I tell you, I shall do so, only because you advise me to it as the best.

Valère. Don't excuse yourself upon my intentions. Your resolution was made before; and you now lay hold of a frivolous pretence, for the breaking of your word.

Mariana. 'Tis true; it's well said.

Valère. Doubtless; and you never had any true love for me.

Mariana. Alas! You may think so if you please.

Valère. Yes, yes, may think so; but my offended heart may chance to be beforehand with you in that affair; and I can tell where to offer both my addresses and my hand.

Mariana. I don't doubt it, sir. The warmth that merit raises——

Valère. Lack-a-day! Let us drop merit. I have little enough of that, and you think so; but I hope, another will treat me in a kinder manner; and I know a person whose heart, open to my retreat, will not be ashamed to make up my loss.

Mariana. The loss is not great, and you will be comforted, upon this change, easily enough.

Valère. You may believe I shall do all that lies in my power. A heart that forgets us, engages our glory; we must employ our utmost cares to forget it too; and if we don't succeed, we must at least pretend we do; for to show a regard for those that forsake us, is a meanness one cannot answer to one's self.

Mariana. The sentiment is certainly noble and sublime.

Valère. Very well, and what everybody must approve of. What? would you have me languish for ever for you? See you fly into another's arms before my face, and not transfer my slighted affections somewhere else?

Mariana. So far from that, 'tis what I would have; and I wish 'twere done already.

Valère. You wish it done?

Mariana. Yes.

Valère. That's insulting me sufficiently, madam; I am just going to give you that satisfaction.   [*He offers to go.*

Mariana. 'Tis very well.

Valère. [*Returning.*] Be pleased to remember at least, that 'tis yourself who drive me to this extremity.

Mariana. Yes.

Valère. [*Returning again.*] And that the design I have conceived is only from your example.

Mariana. My example be it.

Valère. [*Going.*] Enough; you shall soon be punctually obeyed.

Mariana. So much the better.

Valère. [*Returning again.*] 'Tis the last time I shall ever trouble you.

Mariana. With all my heart.

Valère. [*Goes toward the door and returns.*] Hey?

Mariana. What's the matter?

Valère. Didn't you call me?

Mariana. Who, I? You dream sure.

Valère. Well then, I'll be gone; farewell, madam!

Mariana. Fare ye well, sir.

Dorina. [*To Mariana.*] I think, for my part, by this piece of extravagance, you've both lost your senses; I have let you alone thus long squabbling, to see what end you'd make of it. Heark ye, Mr. Valère!   [*She lays hold of Valère's arm.*

Valère. [*Pretending to resist.*] Hey! What would you have, Dorina?

Dorina. Come hither.

Valère. No, no, my indignation overpowers me; don't hinder me from doing as she would have me.

Dorina. Stay.

Valère. No, d'ye see, I'm resolved upon it.

Dorina. Ah!

Mariana. [*Aside.*] He's uneasy at the sight of me. My presence drives him away; I had much better therefore leave the place.

Dorina. [*Quitting Valère, and running after Mariana.*] What, t'other? whither do you run?

Mariana. Let me alone.

Dorina. You must come back.

Mariana. No, no, Dorina; in vain you'd hold me.

Valère. [*Aside.*] I find that my presence is but a plague to her. I had certainly better free her from it.

Dorina. [*Quitting Mariana, and running after Valère.*] What, again? Deuce take you for me. Leave this fooling, and come hither both of you.

[*She takes Valère and Mariana by the hand, and brings them back.*

Valère. But what's your design?

Mariana. What would you do?

Dorina. Set you two to rights again, and bring you out of this scrape. [*To Valère.*] Aren't you mad, to wrangle at this rate?

Valère. Didn't you hear how she spoke to me?

Dorina. [*To Mariana.*] Weren't you a simpleton, to be in such a passion?

Mariana. Didn't you see the thing, and how he treated me?

Dorina. Folly on both sides; [*To Valère.*] she has nothing more at heart, than that she may be one day yours; I am witness to it. [*To Mariana.*] He loves none but yourself, and has no other ambition than to become your husband, I answer for it upon my life.

Mariana. [*To Valère.*] Why then did you give me such advice?

Valère. [*To Mariana.*] And why was I consulted upon such a subject?

Dorina. You're a couple of fools. Come, come, your hands, both of you; [*To Valère.*] come you.

Valère. [*Giving his hand to Dorina.*] What will my hand do?

Dorina. [*To Mariana.*] So; come, now yours.

Mariana. [*Giving her hand.*] To what purpose is all this?

Dorina. Come along, come quick: you love one another better than you think of.

Valère. [*Turning towards Mariana.*] But don't do things with an ill grace, and give a body a civil look.

[*Mariana turns toward Valère, and smiles a little.*

Dorina. In troth, lovers are silly creatures!

Valère. [*To Mariana.*] Now, have I not room to complain of you; and, without lying, were not you a wicked creature, to gratify yourself in saying a thing so very shocking to me?

Mariana. But are not you the ungratefullest man in the world——

Dorina. Come let's adjourn this debate till another time; and think how to ward off this plaguy wedding.

Mariana. Say then, what engines shall we set at work?

Dorina. We'll set them every way to work. [*To Mariana.*] Your father's in jest; [*To Valère.*] it must be nothing but talk. [*To Mariana.*] But for your part, your best way will be to carry the appearance of a gentle compliance with his extravagance, that so, in case of an alarm, you may have it more easily in your power to delay the marriage proposed. In gaining time we shall remedy everything. Sometimes you may fob 'em off with some illness, which is to come all of a sudden, and will require delay. Sometimes you may fob 'em off with ill omens. You unluckily met a corpse, broke a looking-glass, or dreamed dirty water; and at last, the best on't is, they can't possibly join you to any other but him, unless you please to say, Yes. But, the better to carry on the design, I think it proper you should not be seen conferring together. [*To Valère.*] Go you immediately and employ your friends, that he may be forced to keep his word with you. [*To Mariana.*] Let us go excite his brother's endeavours, and engage the mother-in-law in our party. Adieu.

Valère. [*To Mariana.*] Whatever efforts any of us may be preparing, my greatest hope, to say the truth, is in you.

Mariana. [*To Valère.*] I can't promise for the inclinations of a father, but I shall be none but Valère's.

Valère. How you transport me! And though I durst——

Dorina. Ah! These lovers are never weary of prattling. Away, I tell you.

Valère. [*Goes a step or two, and returns.*] Once more——

Dorina. What a clack is yours? Draw you off this way, and you t'other.

[*Pushing them each out by the shoulders.*

ACT III

Scene I

Damis, Dorina.

Damis. May thunder, this moment, strike me dead; let me be everywhere treated like the greatest scoundrel alive, if any respect or power whatever shall stop me, and if I don't strike some masterly stroke.

Dorina. Moderate your passion for .Heaven's sake; your father did but barely mention it. People don't do all they propose, and the distance is great from the project to the execution.

Damis. I must put a stop to this fool's projects, and tell him a word or two in his ear.

Dorina. Gently, gently pray; let your mother-in-law alone with him, as well as with your father. She has some credit with Tartuffe. He is mighty complaisant to all she says, and perhaps he may have a sneaking kindness for her. I would to Heaven it were true! That would be charming. In short, your interest obliges her to send for him; she has a mind to sound his intentions, with regard to the wedding that disturbs you; and represent to him the fatal feuds he will raise in the family, if he entertains any hopes of this affair. His man says that he's at prayers, and I could not see him. But this servant told me, he would not be long before he came down. Then pray be gone, and let me stay for him.

Damis. I may be present at this whole conference.

Dorina. No, they must be by themselves.

Damis. I shall say nothing to him.

Dorina. You're mistaken; we know the usual impatience of your temper, and 'tis the ready way to spoil all. Get away.

Damis. No, I will see him, without putting myself in a passion.

Dorina. How troublesome you are! He's coming; retire.

[*Damis conceals himself in a closet.*

Scene II

Tartuffe, Dorina.

Tartuffe. [*Upon seeing Dorina speaks aloud to his servant who is in the house.*] Laurence, lock up my hair-cloth and scourge, and beg of Heaven ever to enlighten you with grace. If anybody comes to see me, I am gone to the prisons to distribute my alms.

Dorina. [*Aside.*] What affectation and roguery!

Tartuffe. What do you want?

Dorina. To tell you——

Tartuffe. [*Drawing a handkerchief out of his pocket.*] Oh! lack-a-day! pray take me this handkerchief before you speak.

Dorina. What for?

Tartuffe. Cover that bosom, which I can't bear to see. Such objects hurt the soul, and usher in sinful thoughts.

Dorina. You mightily melt then at a temptation, and the flesh makes great impression upon your senses? Truly, I can't tell what heat may inflame you; but, for my part, I am not so apt to hanker. Now I could see you stark naked from head to foot, and that whole hide of yours not tempt me at all.

Tartuffe. Pray now speak with a little modesty, or I shall leave you this minute.

Dorina. No, no, 'tis I who am going to leave you to yourself; and I have only two words to say to you: My lady is coming down into this parlour, and desires the favour of a word with you.

Tartuffe. Alack! with all my heart.

Dorina. [*Aside.*] How sweet he grows upon it! I'faith, I still stand to what I said of him.

Tartuffe. Will she come presently?

Dorina. I think I hear her. Ay, 'tis she herself; I leave you together.

Scene III

Elmira, Tartuffe.

Tartuffe. May Heaven, of its goodness, ever bestow upon you health both of body and of mind! and bless your days equal to the wish of the lowest of its votaries!

Elmira. I am much obliged to you for this pious wish; but let us take a seat to be more at ease.

Tartuffe. [*Sitting down.*] Do you find your indisposition anything abated?

Elmira. [*Sitting.*] Very well, my fever soon left me.

Tartuffe. My prayers have not sufficient merit to have drawn down this favour from above; but I made no vows to Heaven that did not concern your recovery.

Elmira. Your zeal for me was too solicitous.

Tartuffe. Your dear health cannot be overrated; and, to re-establish it, I could have sacrificed my own.

Elmira. That is carrying Christian charity a great way; and I am highly indebted to you for all this goodness.

Tartuffe. I do much less for you than you deserve.

Elmira. I had a desire to speak with you in private on a certain affair, and am glad that nobody observes us here.

Tartuffe. I am also overjoyed at it; and, be sure, it can be no ordinary satisfaction, madam, to find myself alone with you. 'Tis an opportunity that I have hitherto petitioned Heaven for in vain.

Elmira. What I want to talk with you upon, is a small matter, in which your whole heart must be open, and hide nothing from me.

Tartuffe. And, for this singular favour, I certainly will unbosom myself to you, without the least reserve; and I protest to you, that the stir I made about the visits paid here to your charms, was not out of hatred to you, but rather out of a passionate zeal which induced me to it, and out of a pure motive——

Elmira. For my part I take it very well, and believe 'tis my good that gives you this concern.

Tartuffe. [*Taking Elmira's hand, and squeezing her fingers.*] Yes, madam, without doubt, and such is the fervour of my——

Elmira. Oh! you squeeze me too hard.

Tartuffe. 'Tis out of excess of zeal; I never intended to hurt you. I had much rather——

[*Puts his hand upon her knee.*

Elmira. What does your hand do there?

Tartuffe. I'm only feeling your clothes, madam; the stuff is mighty rich.

Elmira. Oh! Pray give over; I am very ticklish.

[*She draws away her chair, and Tartuffe follows with his.*

Tartuffe. Bless me! How wonderful is the workmanship of this lace! They work to a miracle nowadays. Things of all kinds were never better done.

Elmira. 'Tis true; but let us speak to our affair a little. They say that my husband has a mind to set aside his promise, and to give you his daughter. Is that true? Pray tell me?

Tartuffe. He did hint something towards it. But, madam, to tell you the truth, that is not the happiness I sigh after. I behold elsewhere the wonderful attractions of the felicity that engages every wish of mine.

Elmira. That is, you love no earthly things.

Tartuffe. My breast does not enclose a heart of flint.

Elmira. I am apt to think that your sighs tend all to Heaven, and that nothing here below can detain your desires.

Tartuffe. The love which engages us to eternal beauties, does not extinguish in us the love of temporal ones. Our senses may easily be charmed with the perfect works Heaven has formed. Its reflected charms shine forth, in such as you. But, in your person, it displays its choicest wonders. It has diffused such beauties o'er your face as surprise the sight, and transport the heart; nor could I behold you, perfect creature, without admiring in you the Author of nature, and feeling my heart touched with an ardent love, at sight of the fairest of portraits, wherein he has delineated himself. At first I was under apprehensions lest this secret flame might be a dexterous surprise of the foul fiend; and my heart even resolved to avoid your eyes, believing you an obstacle to my future happiness. But at length I perceived, most lovely beauty, that my passion could not be blameable, that I could reconcile it with modesty, and this made me abandon my heart to it. It is, I confess, a very great presumption in me, to make you the offer of this heart; but, in my vows, I rely wholly on your goodness, and not on anything in my own weak power. In you centre my hope, my happiness, my quiet; on you depend my torment or my bliss; and I am on the point of being, by your sole decision, happy if you will, or miserable if you please.

Elmira. The declaration is extremely gallant, but, to say the truth, it is a good deal surprising. Methinks you ought to have fortified your mind better, and to have reasoned a little upon a design of this nature. A devotee as you are, whom every one speaks of as——

Tartuffe. Ah! being a devotee does not make me the less a man; and when one comes to view your celestial charms, the heart surrenders, and reasons no more. I know, that such language from me, seems somewhat strange; but, madam, after all, I am not an angel, and should you condemn the declaration I make, you must lay the blame upon your attractive charms. From the moment I first set eyes upon your more than human splendour, you became the sovereign of my soul. The ineffable sweetness of your divine looks broke through the resistance which my heart obstinately made. It surmounted everything, fastings, prayers, tears, and turned all my vows on the side of your charms. My eyes and my sighs have told it you a thousand times, and the better to explain myself I here make use of words. Now if you contemplate with some benignity of soul, the tribulations of your unworthy slave; if your goodness will give me consolation, and deign to debase itself so low as my nothingness, I shall ever entertain for you, miracle of sweetness, a devotion which nothing can equal. Your honour, with me, runs no risk, it need fear no disgrace on my part. All those courtly gallants the ladies are so fond of, make a bustle in what they do, and are vain in what they say. We see they are ever vaunting of their success; they receive no favours that they don't divulge, and their indiscreet tongues, which people confide in, dishonour the altar on which their hearts offer sacrifice. But men of our sort burn with a discreet flame, with whom a secret is always sure to remain such. The care we take of our own reputation, is an undeniable security to the persons beloved. And 'tis with us, when they accept our hearts, that they enjoy love without scandal, and pleasure without fear.

Elmira. I hear what you say, and your rhetoric explains itself to me in terms sufficiently strong. Don't you apprehend that I may take a fancy now, to acquaint my husband with this gallantry of yours? and that an early account of an amour of this sort, might pretty much alter his present affections towards you?

Tartuffe. I know that you are too good, and that you will rather pardon my temerity; that you will excuse me, upon the score of human frailty, the sallies of a passion that offends you; and will consider, when you consult your glass, that a man is not blind, and is made of flesh and blood.

Elmira. Some might take it perhaps in another manner; but I shall show my discretion, and not tell my husband of it. But in return, I will have one thing of you, that is honestly and sincerely to forward the match between Valère and Mariana, and that you yourself renounce the unjust power whereby you hope to be enriched with what belongs to another. And——

SCENE IV

Elmira, Damis, Tartuffe.

Damis. [*Coming out of the closet where he was hidden.*] No, madam, no, this ought to be made public; I was in this place, and overheard it all; and the goodness of Heaven seems to have directed me thither to confound the pride of a traitor that wrongs me; to open me a way to take vengeance of his hypocrisy and insolence; to undeceive my father, and show him, in a clear light, the soul of a villain that talks to you of love.

Elmira. No, Damis, 'tis enough that he reforms, and endeavours to deserve the favour I do him. Since I have promised him, don't make me break my word. 'Tis not my humour to make a noise; a wife will make herself merry with such follies, and never trouble her husband's ears with them.

Damis. You have your reasons for using him in that manner, and I have mine too for acting otherwise. To spare him would be ridiculous; the insolent pride of his bigotry has triumphed too much over my just resentment, and created too many disorders among us already. The rascal has, but too long, governed my father, and opposed my passion, as well as Valère's. 'Tis fit the perfidious wretch should be laid open to him, and Heaven for this purpose offers me an easy way to do it. I am greatly indebted to it for the opportunity; it is too favourable a one to be neglected, and I should deserve to have it taken from me now I have it, should I not make use of it.

Elmira. Damis——

Damis. No, by your leave, I must take my own counsel. My heart overflows with joy, and all you can say would in vain dissuade me from the pleasure of avenging myself. Without going any farther, I will make an end of the affair, and here's just what will give me satisfaction.

SCENE V

Orgon, Elmira, Damis, Tartuffe.

Damis. We are going to entertain you, sir, with an adventure spick and span new, which will very much surprise you. You are well rewarded for all your caresses; and this gentleman makes a fine acknowledgment of your tenderness. His great zeal for you is just come to light; it aims at nothing less than the dishonour of your bed, and I took him here making an injurious declaration of a criminal love to your wife. She is good-natured, and her over-great discretion, by all means, would have kept the secret; but I can't encourage such impudence, and think that not to apprise you of it is to do you an injury.

Elmira. Yes, I am of opinion that one ought never to break in upon a husband's rest with such idle stuff, that our honour can by no means depend upon it; and that 'tis enough we know how to defend ourselves. These are my thoughts of the matter; and you would have said nothing, Damis, if I had had any credit with you.

SCENE VI

Orgon, Damis, Tartuffe.

Orgon. Heavens! What have I heard? Is this credible?

Tartuffe. Yes, brother, I am a wicked, guilty, wretched sinner, full of iniquity, the greatest villain that ever breathed. Every instant of my life is crowded with stains; 'tis one continued series of crimes and defilements; and I see that Heaven, for my punishment, designs to mortify me on this occasion. Whatever great offence they can lay to my charge, I shall have more humility than to deny it. Believe what they tell you, arm your resentment, and like a criminal, drive me out of your house. I cannot have so great a share of shame but I have still deserved a much larger.

Orgon. [*To his son.*] Ah, traitor! darest thou, by this falsehood, attempt to tarnish the purity of his virtue?

Damis. What! shall the feigned meekness of this hypocritical soul make you give the lie——

Orgon. Thou cursed plague! hold thy tongue.

Tartuffe. Ah! let him speak; you chide him wrongfully; you had much better believe what he tells you. Why so favourable to me upon such a fact? Do you know after all what I may be capable of? Can you, my brother, depend upon my outside? Do you think me the better for what you see of me? No, no, you suffer yourself to be deceived by appearances, and I am neither better nor worse, alas! than these people think me. The world indeed takes me for a very good man, but the truth is, I am a very worthless creature. [*Turning to Damis.*] Yes, my dear child, say on, call me treacherous, infamous, reprobate, thief, and murderer; load me with names still more detestable; I don't gainsay you; I have deserved them all, and am willing on my knees to suffer the ignominy, as a shame due to the enormities of my life.

Orgon. [*To Tartuffe.*] This is too much, brother. [*To his son.*] Does not thy heart relent, traitor?

Damis. What, shall his words so far deceive you as to——

Orgon. Hold your tongue, rascal! [*Raising Tartuffe.*] For Heaven's sake, brother, rise. [*To his son.*] Infamous wretch!

Damis. He can——

Orgon. Hold thy tongue.

Damis. Intolerable! What! am I taken for——

Orgon. Say one other word and I'll break thy bones.

Tartuffe. For Heaven's sake, brother, don't be angry; I had rather suffer any hardship, than that he should get the slightest hurt on my account.

Orgon. [*To his son.*] Ungrateful monster!

Tartuffe. Let him alone; if I must on my knees ask forgiveness for him——

Orgon. [*Throwing himself also at Tartuffe's feet, and embracing him.*] Alas! You are in jest, sure? [*To his son.*] See his goodness, sirrah!

Damis. Then——

Orgon. Have done.

Damis. What! I——

Orgon. Peace, I say. I know what put you upon this attack

well enough; ye all hate him, and I now see wife, children, servants, are all let loose against him. They impudently try every way to remove this devout person from me. But the more they strive to get him out, the greater care will I take to keep him in; and therefore will I hasten his marriage with my daughter, to confound the pride of the whole family.

Damis. Do you think to force her to accept of him?

Orgon. Yes, traitor, and this very evening, to plague you. Nay, I defy you all, and shall make you to know that I am master, and will be obeyed. Come, sirrah, do you recant; immediately throw yourself at his feet to beg his pardon.

Damis. Who, I? of this rascal, who by his impostures——

Orgon. What, scoundrel, do you rebel, and call him names? A cudgel there, a cudgel. [*To Tartuffe.*] Don't hold me. [*To his son.*] Get you out of my house this minute, and never dare to set foot into it again.

Damis. Yes, I shall go, but——

Orgon. Quickly then leave the place; sirrah, I disinherit thee, and give thee my curse besides.

SCENE VII

Orgon, Tartuffe.

Orgon. To offend a holy person in such a manner!

Tartuffe. [*Aside.*] O Heaven! pardon him the anguish he gives me! [*To Orgon.*] Could you know what a grief it is to me that they should try to blacken me with my dear brother——

Orgon. Alack-a-day!

Tartuffe. The very thought of this ingratitude wounds me to the very quick!——Lord, what horror!——My heart's so full that I can't speak; I think I shan't outlive it.

Orgon. [*Running all in tears to the door out of which he drove his son.*] Villain! I'm sorry my hand spared, and did not make an end of thee on the spot. [*To Tartuffe.*] Compose yourself, brother, and don't be troubled.

Tartuffe. Let us by all means put an end to the course of these unhappy debates; I see what uneasiness I occasion here, and think there's a necessity, brother, for my leaving your house.

Orgon. How? You're not in earnest sure?

Tartuffe. They hate me, and seek, I see, to bring my integrity into question with you.

Orgon. What signifies that? Do you see me listen to them?

Tartuffe. They won't stop here, you may be sure; and those very stories which you now reject, may one day meet with more credit.

Orgon. No, brother, never.

Tartuffe. Ah! brother, a wife may easily deceive a husband.

Orgon. No, no.

Tartuffe. Suffer me, by removing hence, immediately to remove from them all occasion of attacking me in this manner.

Orgon. No, you must stay, or it will cost me my life.

Tartuffe. Well, then I must mortify myself. If you would, however——

Orgon. Ah!

Tartuffe. Be it so. Let's talk no more about it. But I know how I must behave on this occasion. Honour is delicate, and friendship obliges me to prevent reports, and not to give any room for suspicion; I'll shun your wife, and you shall never see me——

Orgon. No, in spite of everybody, you shall frequently be with her. To vex the world is my greatest joy, and I'll have you seen with her at all hours. This is not all yet; the better to brave them. I'll have no other heir but you; and I'm going forthwith to sign you a deed of gift for my whole estate. A true and hearty friend, that I fix on for a son-in-law, is far dearer to me than either son, wife, or kindred. You won't refuse what I propose?

Tartuffe. Heaven's will be done in all things.

Orgon. Poor man! Come, let's get the writings drawn up, and then let envy burst itself with spite.

ACT IV

Scene I

Cleanthes, Tartuffe.

Cleanthes. Yes, 'tis in everybody's mouth, and you may believe me. The noise this rumour makes is not much to your credit; and I have met with you, sir, very opportunely, to tell you plainly, in two words, my thoughts of the matter. I shan't inquire into the ground of what's reported, I pass that by, and take the thing at worst. We'll suppose that Damis has not used you well, and that they have accused you wrongfully. Is it not the part of a good Christian to pardon the offence, and extinguish in his heart all desire of vengeance? Ought you to suffer a son to be turned out of his father's house, on account of your differences? I tell you once again, and tell you frankly, there is neither small nor great but are scandalised at it. And if you take my advice, you'll make all up, and not push matters to extremity. Sacrifice your resentment to your duty, and restore the son to his father's favour.

Tartuffe. Alas! for my own part, I would do it with all my heart; I, sir, bear him not the least ill-will; I forgive him every-thing; I lay nothing to his charge, and would serve him with all my soul. But the interests of Heaven cannot admit of it: and if he comes in here again, I must go out. After such an un-paralleled action, it would be scandalous for me to have anything to do with him. Heaven knows what all the world would immediately think on't. They would impute it to pure policy in me, and people would everywhere say, that knowing myself guilty, I pretended a charitable zeal for my accuser; that I dreaded him at heart, and would practise upon him, that I might, underhand, engage him to silence.

Cleanthes. You put us off here with sham excuses, and all your reasons, sir, are too far fetched. Why do you take upon you the interests of Heaven? has it any occasion for our assist-ance in punishing the guilty? Leave, leave the care of its own vengeance to itself, and only think of that pardon of offences, which it prescribes; have no regard to the judgment of men, when you follow the sovereign orders of Heaven! What! shall the paltry interest of what people may believe, hinder the glory of a good action! No, no, let us always do what Heaven has prescribed, and perplex our heads with no other care.

Tartuffe. I have told you already that I forgive him from my heart, and that is doing, sir, what Heaven ordains; but after the scandal and affront of to-day, Heaven does not require me to live with him.

Cleanthes. And does it require you, sir, to lend an ear to what mere caprice dictates to the father? And to accept of an estate where justice obliges you to make no pretensions?

Tartuffe. Those that know me will never have the thought that this is the effect of an interested spirit. All the riches of this world have few charms for me; I am not dazzled by their false glare, and if I should resolve to accept this present, which the father has a mind to make me, it is, to tell you the truth, only because I'm afraid this means will fall into wicked hands; lest it should come amongst such, as will make an ill use on't in the world, and not lay it out, as I intend to do, for the glory of Heaven, and the good of my neighbour.

Cleanthes. Oh, entertain none of these very nice scruples, which may occasion the complaints of a right heir. Let him, without giving yourself any trouble, keep his estate at his own peril, and consider that 'twere better he misused it, than that people should accuse you for depriving him of it. I only wonder, that you could receive such a proposal without confusion. For, in short, has true zeal any maxim, which shows how to strip a lawful heir of his right? And if it must be that Heaven has put into your heart an invincible obstacle to living with Damis, would it not be better, like a man of prudence, that you should fairly retire from hence, than thus to suffer the eldest son, contrary to all reason, to be turned out of doors for you? Believe me, sir, this would give your discretion——

Tartuffe. It is half an hour past three, sir. Certain devotions call me above stairs, and you'll excuse my leaving you so soon.

Cleanthes. [*Alone.*] Ah!

Scene II

Elmira, Mariana, Cleanthes, Dorina.

Dorina. [*To Cleanthes.*] For goodness' sake, lend her what assistance you can, as we do. She's in the greatest perplexity, sir, imaginable; the articles her father has concluded for to-night, make her every moment ready to despair. He's just a-coming, pray let us set on him in a body and try, either by force or cunning, to frustrate the unlucky design, that has put us all into this consternation.

Scene III

Orgon, Elmira, Mariana, Cleanthes, Dorina.

Orgon. Hah! I'm glad to see you all together. [*To Mariana.*] I bring something in this contract, that will make you smile; you already know what this means.

Mariana. [*Kneeling to Orgon.*] Oh! sir, in the name of Heaven that is a witness of my grief, by everything that can move your heart, forgo a little the right nature has given you, and dispense with my obedience in this particular. Don't compel me, by this hard law, to complain to Heaven of the duty I owe you. Do not, my father, render the life, which you have given me, unfortunate. If, contrary to the tender hopes, I might have formed to myself, you won't suffer me to be the man's I presumed to love; at least, out of your goodness, which upon my knees I implore, save me from the torment of being the man's I abhor; and drive me not to despair by exerting your full power over me.

Orgon. [*Aside*.] Come, stand firm, my heart; no human weakness.

Mariana. Your tenderness for him gives me no uneasiness. Show it in the strongest manner, give him your estate; and if that's not enough, add all mine to it; I consent with all my heart, and give it up; but at least go not so far as to my person, suffer a convent, with its austerities, to wear out the mournful days allotted me by Heaven.

Orgon. Ay, these are exactly your she devotees, when a father crosses their wanton inclinations. Get up, get up; the more it goes against you, the more you'll merit by it. Mortify your senses by this marriage, and don't din me in the head any more about it.

Dorina. But what——

Orgon. Hold you your tongue; speak to your own concerns. I absolutely forbid you to open your lips.

Cleanthes. If you would indulge me, in answer, to give one word of advice.

Orgon. Brother, your advice is the best in the world; 'tis very rational, and what I have a great value for. But you must not take it ill if I don't use it now.

Elmira. [*To Orgon*.] Seeing what I see, I don't know what to say; I can but wonder at your blindness. You must be mightily bewitched and prepossessed in his favour, to give us the lie upon the fact of to-day.

Orgon. I am your humble servant, and believe appearances. I know your complaisance for my rascal of a son, and you were afraid to disavow the trick he would have played the poor man. You were, in a word, too little ruffled to gain credit; you would have appeared to have been moved after a different manner.

Elmira. Is it requisite that our honour should bluster so vehemently at the simple declaration of an amorous transport? Can there be no reply made to what offends us, without fury in our eyes and invectives in our mouth? For my part, I only laugh at such overtures; and the rout made about them, by no means pleases me. I love that we should show our discretion with good nature, and cannot like your savage prudes, whose honour is armed with teeth and claws, and is for tearing a man's eyes out for a word speaking. Heaven preserve me from such discretion! I would have virtue that is not diabolical, and believe that a denial given with a discreet coldness, is no less powerful to give the lover a rebuff.

Orgon. In short I know the whole affair, and shall not alter my scheme.

Elmira. I admire, still more, at your unaccountable weakness. But what answer could your incredulity make, should one let you see that they told you the truth?

Orgon. See?

Elmira. Ay.

Orgon. Stuff!

Elmira. But how, if I should contrive a way to let you see it in a very clear light?

Orgon. A likely story indeed!

Elmira. What a strange man! At least give me an answer, I don't speak of your giving credit to us; but suppose a place could be found, where you might see and overhear all, what would you then say of your good man?

Orgon. In this case, I should say that—I should say nothing: for the thing can't be.

Elmira. You have been too long deluded, and too much have taxed me with imposture. 'Tis necessary that by way of diversion, and without going any farther, I should make you a witness of all they told you.

Orgon. Do so; I take you at your word. We shall see your address, and how you'll make good your promise.

Elmira. [*To Dorina.*] Bid him come to me.

Dorina. [*To Elmira.*] He has a crafty soul of his own, and perhaps it would be a difficult matter to surprise him.

Elmira. [*To Dorina.*] No, people are easily duped by what they love, and self-love helps 'em to deceive themselves. [*To Cleanthes and Mariana.*] Call him down to me, and do you retire.

Scene IV

Elmira, Orgon.

Elmira. Now do you come and get under this table.

Orgon. Why so?

Elmira. 'Tis a necessary point that you should be well concealed.

Orgon. But why under this table?

Elmira. Lack-a-day! do as I'd have you, I have my design in my head, and you shall be judge of it. Place yourself there, I tell you, and when you are there, take care that no one either sees or hears you.

Orgon. I must needs say, I am very complaisant: but I must see you go through your enterprise.

Elmira. You will have nothing, I believe, to reply to me. [*To Orgon under the table.*] However, as I am going to touch upon a strange affair, don't be shocked by any means. Whatever I may say, must be allowed me, as it is to convince you, according to my promise. I am going by coaxing speeches, since I am reduced to it, to make this hypocritical soul drop the mask, to flatter the impudent desires of his love, and give a full scope to his boldness. Since 'tis for your sake alone, and to confound him, that I feign a compliance with his desires, I may give over when you appear, and things need go no farther than you would have them. It lies on you to stop his mad pursuit, when you think that matters are carried far enough, to spare your wife, and not to expose me any farther than is necessary to disabuse you. This is your interest, it lies at your discretion, and——He's coming; keep close, and take care not to appear.

Scene V

Tartuffe, Elmira, Orgon under the table.

Tartuffe. I was told you desired to speak with me here.

Elmira. Yes, I have secrets to discover to you; but pull to that door before I tell 'em you, and look about, for fear of a surprise. [*Tartuffe goes and shuts the door and returns.*] We must not surely make such a business of it, as the other was just now. I never was in such a surprise in my whole life: Damis put me into a terrible fright for you; and you saw very well that I did my utmost to baffle his designs, and moderate his passion. I was under so much concern, 'tis true, that I had not the thought of contradicting him; but thanks to Heaven, everything was the better for that, and things are put upon a surer footing. The esteem you are in laid that storm, and my husband can have no suspicion of you. The better to set the rumour of ill tongues at defiance, he desires we should be always together, and from thence it is, that without fear of blame I can be locked up with you here alone, and this is what justifies me in laying open to

you a heart, a little perhaps, too forward in admitting of your
passion.

Tartuffe. This language, madam, is difficult enough to
comprehend, and you talked in another kind of style but just
now.

Elmira. Alas! if such a refusal disobliges you, how little
do you know the heart of a woman! and how little do you know
what it means, when we make so feeble a defence! Our modesty
will always combat, in these moments, those tender sentiments
you may inspire us with. Whatever reason we may find for
the passion that subdues us, we shall always be a little ashamed
to own it. We defend ourselves at first, but by the air with
which we go about it, we give you sufficiently to know, that
our heart surrenders; that our words oppose our wishes for the
sake of honour, and that such refusals promise everything.
Without doubt this is making a very free confession to you,
and having regard little enough to the modesty that belongs to
us; but in short, since the word has slipped me, should I have
been bent so much upon restraining Damis? Should I, pray,
with so much mildness, have hearkened to the offer at large
which you made of your heart? Should I have taken the thing
as you saw I did, if the offer of your heart had had nothing in it
to please me? And when I myself would have forced you to
refuse the match which had just been proposed, what is it
this instance should have given you to understand, but the
interest one was inclined to take in you, and the disquiet it
would have given me, that the knot resolved on, should at least
divide a heart which I wanted to have wholly my own?

Tartuffe. 'Tis no doubt, madam, an extreme pleasure to
hear these words from the lips one loves; their honey plentifully
diffuses through every sense a sweetness I never before tasted.
My supreme study is the happiness of pleasing you, and my
heart counts your affection its beatitude; but you must excuse
this heart, madam, if it presumes to doubt a little of its felicity.
I can fancy these words to be only a sort of artifice to make me
break off the match that's upon the conclusion; and if I may
with freedom explain myself to you, I shall not rely upon this
so tender language, till some of the favours which I sigh after,
assure me of the sincerity of what may be said, and fix in my
mind a firm belief of the transporting goodness you intend me.

Elmira. [*Coughing to give her husband notice.*] What!
proceed so fast? Would you exhaust the tenderness of one's
heart at once? One does violence to one's self in making you

the most melting declaration; but at the same time this is not enough for you, and one cannot advance so far as to satisfy you, unless one pushes the affair to the last favours.

Tartuffe. The less one deserves a blessing, the less one presumes to hope for it; our love can hardly have a full reliance upon discourses; one easily suspects a condition full fraught with happiness, and one would enjoy it before one believes it. For my particular, who know I so little deserve your favours, I doubt the success of my rashness, and I shall believe nothing, madam, till by realities you have convinced my passion.

Elmira. Good lack! how your love plays the very tyrant! What a strange confusion it throws me into? With what a furious sway does it govern the heart! and with what violence it pushes for what it desires! What, is there no getting clear of your pursuit? Do you allow one no time to take breath? Is it decent to persist with so great rigour? To insist upon the things you demand without quarter? To abuse in this manner, by your pressing efforts, the foible you see people have for you?

Tartuffe. But if you regard my addresses with a favourable eye, why do you refuse me convincing proofs of it?

Elmira. But how can one comply with your desires, without offending that Heaven which you are always talking of?

Tartuffe. If nothing but Heaven obstructs my wishes, 'tis a trifle with me to remove such an obstacle, and that need be no restraint upon your love.

Elmira. But they so terrify us with the judgments of Heaven?

Tartuffe. I can dissipate those ridiculous terrors for you, madam; I have the knack of easing scruples. Heaven, 'tis true, forbids certain gratifications. But then there are ways of compounding those matters. It is a science to stretch the strings of conscience according to the different exigences of the case, and to rectify the immorality of the action by the purity of our intention. These are secrets, madam, I can instruct you in; you have nothing to do, but passively to be conducted. Satisfy my desire, and fear nothing, I'll answer for you, and will take the sin upon myself. [*Elmira coughs loud.*] You cough very much, madam.

Elmira. Yes, I am on the rack.

Tartuffe. [*Presenting her with a paper.*] Will you please to have a bit of this liquorice?

Elmira. 'Tis an obstinate cold, without doubt, and I am satisfied that all the liquorice in the world will do no good in this case.

Tartuffe. It is, to be sure, very troublesome.

Elmira. Ay, more than one can express.

Tartuffe. In short your scruple, madam, is easily overcome. You are sure of its being an inviolable secret here, and the harm never consists in anything but the noise one makes; the scandal of the world is what makes the offence; and sinning in private is no sinning at all.

Elmira. [*After coughing again, and striking upon the table.*] In short, I see that I must resolve to yield, that I must consent to grant you everything; and that with less than this I ought not to expect that you should be satisfied, or give over. It is indeed very hard to go that length, and I get over it much against my will. But since you are obstinately bent upon reducing me to it, and since you won't believe anything that can be said, but still insist on more convincing testimony, one must e'en resolve upon it, and satisfy people. And if this gratification carries any offence in it, so much the worse for him who forces me to this violence; the fault certainly ought not to be laid at my door.

Tartuffe. Yes, madam, I take it upon myself, and the thing in itself——

Elmira. Open the door a little, and pray look if my husband be not in that gallery.

Tartuffe. What need you take so much care about him? Betwixt us two, he's a man to be led by the nose. He will take a pride in all our conversations, and I have wrought him up to the point of seeing everything, without believing anything.

Elmira. That signifies nothing, pray go out a little, and look carefully all about.

SCENE VI

Orgon, Elmira.

Orgon. [*Coming from under the table.*] An abominable fellow, I vow! I can't recover myself; this perfectly stuns me.

Elmira. How! do you come out so soon? You make fools of people; get under the table again, stay to the very last, to see things sure, and don't trust to bare conjectures.

Orgon. No, nothing more wicked ever came from Hell.

Elmira. Dear heart, you must not believe too lightly; suffer yourself to be fully convinced, before you yield, and don't be too hasty for fear of a mistake.

[*Elmira places Orgon behind her.*

Scene VII

Tartuffe, Elmira, Orgon.

Tartuffe. [*Not seeing Orgon.*] Everything conspires, madam, to my satisfaction. I have surveyed this whole apartment; nobody's there, and my ravished soul——

[*Tartuffe going with open arms to embrace Elmira, she retires, and Tartuffe sees Orgon.*

Orgon. [*Stopping Tartuffe.*] Gently, gently; you are too eager in your amours; you should not be so furious. Ah, ha, good man! you intended me a crest, I suppose! Good-lack, how you abandon yourself to temptations! What, you'd marry my daughter, and had a huge stomach to my wife? I was a long while in doubt whether all was in good earnest, and always thought you would change your tone; but this is pushing the proof far enough; I am now satisfied, and want, for my part, no further conviction.

Elmira. [*To Tartuffe.*] The part I have played was contrary to my inclination; but they reduced me to the necessity of treating you in this manner.

Tartuffe. [*To Orgon.*] What? Do you believe——

Orgon. Come, pray no noise; turn out, and without ceremony.

Tartuffe. My design——

Orgon. These speeches are no longer in season; you must troop off forthwith.

Tartuffe. 'Tis you must troop off, you who speak so magisterially. The house belongs to me, I'll make you know it, and shall plainly show you, that you have recourse in vain to these base tricks, to pick a quarrel with me; that you don't think where you are when you injure me; that I have wherewithal to confound and punish imposture, to avenge offended Heaven, and make them repent it who talk here of turning me out o' doors.

Scene VIII

Elmira, Orgon.

Elmira. What language is this? And what can it mean?

Orgon. In truth I'm all confusion, and have no room to laugh.

Elmira. How so?

Orgon. I see my fault by what he says, and the deed of gift perplexes me.

Elmira. The deed of gift?

Orgon. Ay, 'tis done; but I have something else that disturbs me too.

Elmira. And what's that?

Orgon. You shall know the whole; but let's go immediately and see if a certain casket is above stairs.

ACT V

Scene I

Orgon, Cleanthes.

Cleanthes. Whither would you run?

Orgon. Alas! how can I tell?

Cleanthes. I think we ought, the first thing we do, to consult together what may be done at this juncture.

Orgon. This casket entirely confounds me. It gives me even more vexation than all the rest.

Cleanthes. This casket then is some mystery of importance?

Orgon. It is a deposit that Argas, my lamented friend, himself committed as a great secret to my keeping. When he fled, he pitched on me for this purpose; and these are the papers, as he told me, whereon his life and fortune depend.

Cleanthes. Why then did you trust them in other hands?

Orgon. Merely out of a scruple of conscience. I went straight to impart the secret to my traitor, and his casuistry over-persuaded me rather to give him the casket to keep; so that to deny it, in case of any inquiry, I might have the relief of a subterfuge ready at hand, whereby my conscience would have been very secure in taking an oath contrary to the truth.

Cleanthes. You are in a bad situation, at least, if I may believe appearances; both the deed of gift, and the trust reposed, are, to speak my sentiments to you, steps which you have taken very inconsiderately. One might carry you great lengths by such pledges; and this fellow having these advantages over you, it is still a great imprudence in you to urge him; and you ought to think of some gentler method.

Orgon. What! under the fair appearance of such affectionate zeal, to conceal such a double heart, and a soul so wicked? And that I, who took him in poor and indigent——'Tis over, I renounce all pious folks. I shall henceforth have an utter abhorrence of them, and shall become, for their sakes, worse than a devil.

Cleanthes. Mighty well; here are some of your extravagances! You never preserve a moderate temper in anything. Right reason and yours are very different, and you are always throwing yourself out of one extreme into another. You see your error, and are sensible that you have been imposed on by a hypocritical zeal, but in order to reform, what reason is there that you should be guilty of a worse mistake; and that you should make no difference between the heart of a perfidious worthless wretch, and those of all honest people? What! because a rascal has impudently imposed upon you under the pompous show of an austere grimace, will you needs have it that everybody's like him, and that there are no devout people to be found in the world? Leave these foolish consequences to libertines; distinguish between virtue and the appearance of it; never hazard your esteem too suddenly; and, in order to this, keep the mean you should do; guard, if possible, against doing honour to imposture; but, at the same time, don't injure true zeal; and, if you must fall into one extreme, rather offend again on the other side.

Scene II

Orgon, Cleanthes, Damis.

Damis. What, sir, is it true that the rascal threatens you? That he has quite forgotten every favour he has received? And that his base abominable pride arms your own goodness against yourself?

Orgon. Yes, son, and it gives me inconceivable vexation.

Damis. Let me alone, I'll slice both his ears off. There's no dallying with such insolence as his. I'll undertake to rid you of your fears at once; and to put an end to the affair, I must do his business for him.

Cleanthes. That's spoken exactly like a young fellow. Pray moderate these violent transports; we live in an age, and under a government, in which violence is but a bad way to promote our affairs.

Scene III

Madam Pernelle, Orgon, Elmira, Cleanthes, Mariana, Damis, Dorina.

Madam Pernelle. What's all this? I hear terrible mysteries here.

Orgon. They are novelties that I am an eye-witness to; you see how finely I am fitted for my care. I kindly pick up a fellow in misery, entertain and treat him like my own brother, heap daily favours on him; I give him my daughter and my whole fortune; when at the same time the perfidious, infamous wretch forms the black design of seducing my wife. And not content with these base attempts, he dares to menace me with my own favours, and would make use of those advantages to my ruin, which my too indiscreet good-nature put into his hands; to turn me out of my estate, which I made over to him, and to reduce me to that condition from which I rescued him.

Dorina. The poor man!

Madam Pernelle. I can never believe, son, he could commit so black an action.

Orgon. How?

Madam Pernelle. Good people are always envied.

Orgon. What would you insinuate, mother, by this discourse?

Madam Pernelle. Why, that there are strange doings at your house; and the ill-will they bear him is but too evident.

Orgon. What has this ill-will to do with what has been told you?

Madam Pernelle. I have told you a hundred times when you were a little one,

> That virtue here is persecuted ever;
> That envious men may die, but envy never.

Orgon. But what is all this to the present purpose?

Madam Pernelle. They have trumped up to you a hundred idle stories against him.

Orgon. I have told you already, that I saw it all my own self.

Madam Pernelle. The malice of scandal-mongers is very great.

Orgon. You'll make me swear, mother. I tell you that I saw with my own eyes a crime so audacious——

Madam Pernelle. Tongues never want for venom to spit; nothing here below can be proof against them.

Orgon. This is holding a very senseless **argument**! I saw it, I say, saw it; with my own eyes I saw it. What you call, saw it. Must I din it a hundred times into your ears, and bawl as loud as four folks?

Madam Pernelle. Dear heart! Appearances very often deceive us. You must not always judge by what you see.

Orgon. I shall run mad.

Madam Pernelle. Nature is liable to false suspicions, and good is oftentimes misconstrued evil.

Orgon. Ought I to construe charitably his desire of kissing my wife?

Madam Pernelle. You ought never to accuse anybody but upon good grounds; and you should have stayed till you had seen the thing certain.

Orgon. What the devil! How should I be more certain? Then, mother, I should have stayed till he had——You'll make me say some foolish thing or other.

Madam Pernelle. In short, his soul burns with too pure a flame, and I can't let it enter my thoughts that he could attempt the things that are laid to his charge.

Orgon. Go, if you were not my mother I don't know what I might say to you, my passion is so great!

Dorina. [*To Orgon.*] The just return, sir, of things here below. Time was, you would believe nobody, and now you can't be believed yourself.

Cleanthes. We are wasting that time in mere trifles, which should be spent in taking measures; we shouldn't sleep when a knave threatens.

Damis. What, can his impudence come to this pitch?

Elmira. I can scarce think this instance possible, for my part; his ingratitude would in this be too visible.

Cleanthes. [*To Orgon.*] Don't you depend upon that, he will be cunning enough to give the colour of reason for what he does against you; and for a less matter than this, the weight of a cabal has involved people in dismal labyrinths. I tell you once again, that, armed with what he has, you should never have urged him so far.

Orgon. That's true; but what could I do in the affair? I was not master of my resentments at the haughtiness of the traitor.

Cleanthes. I wish with all my heart that there could be any shadow of a peace patched up between you.

Elmira. Had I but known how well he had been armed, I should never have made such an alarm about the matter, and my——

Orgon. [*To Dorina, seeing Mr. Loyal coming.*] What would that man have? Go quickly and ask. I'm in a fine condition to have people come to see me.

SCENE IV

Orgon, Madam Pernelle, Elmira, Mariana, Cleanthes, Damis, Dorina, Mr. Loyal.

Mr. Loyal. [*To Dorina at the farther part of the stage.*] Good-morrow, child; pray let me speak to your master.

Dorina. He's in company, and I doubt he can see nobody now.

Mr. Loyal. Nay, I am not for being troublesome here. I believe my coming will have nothing in it that will displease him; I come upon an affair that he'll be very glad of.

Dorina. Your name, pray?

Mr. Loyal. Only tell him that I come on the part of Mr. Tartuffe, for his good.

Dorina. [*To Orgon.*] 'Tis a man who comes in a civil way, upon business from Mr. Tartuffe, which he says you won't dislike.

Cleanthes. [*To Orgon.*] You must see who this man is, and what he wants.

Orgon. [*To Cleanthes.*] Perhaps he comes to make us friends. How shall I behave myself to him?

Cleanthes. Be sure don't be angry, and if he speaks of an agreement you must listen to him.

Mr. Loyal. [*To Orgon.*] Save you, sir! Heaven blast the man who would wrong you, and may it be as favourable to you as I wish.

Orgon. [*Aside to Cleanthes.*] This mild beginning favours my conjecture, and already forebodes some accommodation.

Mr. Loyal. I always had a prodigious value for all your family, and was servant to the gentleman your father.

Orgon. Sir, I am much ashamed, and ask pardon that I don't know you, or your name.

Mr. Loyal. My name is Loyal, sir, by birth a Norman, and I am tipstaff to the court in spite of envy. I have had the good fortune for forty years together to fill that office, thanks to Heaven, with great honour; I come, sir, with your leave, to signify to you the execution of a certain decree.

Orgon. What, are you here——

Mr. Loyal. Sir, without passion, 'tis nothing but a summons, an order to remove hence, you and yours, to take out your goods, and to make way for others, without remission or delay, so that 'tis necessary——

Orgon. I go from hence?

Mr. Loyal. Yes, sir, if you please. The house at present, as you know but too well, belongs to good Mr. Tartuffe, without dispute. He is henceforward lord and master of your estate, by virtue of a contract I have in charge. 'Tis in due form, and not to be contested.

Damis. [*To Mr. Loyal.*] Most certainly 'tis prodigious impudence, and what I can't but admire!

Mr. Loyal. [*To Damis.*] Sir, my business is not with you, [*Pointing to Orgon.*] but with this gentleman, who is mild and reasonable, and knows the duty of an honest man too well to oppose authority.

Orgon. But——

Mr. Loyal. [*To Orgon.*] Yes, sir, I know you would not rebel for a million, and that, like a good honest gentleman, you will suffer me here to execute the orders I have received.

Damis. You may chance, Mr. Tipstaff, to get your black jacket well brushed here.

Mr. Loyal. [*To Orgon.*] Either, sir, cause your son to be silent or withdraw. I should be very loath to put pen to paper, and see your names in my information.

Dorina. [*Aside.*] This Mr. Loyal has a disloyal sort of look with him!

Mr. Loyal. I have a great deal of tenderness for all honest people, and should not, sir, have charged myself with these writs but to serve and oblige you; and to prevent another's being pitched on, who not having the love for you which I have, might have proceeded in a less gentle manner.

Orgon. And what can be worse than to order people to go out of their house?

Mr. Loyal. Why, you are allowed time. And, till to-morrow, I shall suspend, sir, the execution of the warrant. I shall only come and pass the night here with half a score of my folks, without noise or scandal. For form's sake, if you please, the keys of the door must, before you go to bed, be brought me. I'll take care your rest shan't be disturbed, and suffer nothing that is improper to be done. But to-morrow morning you must be ready to clear the house of even the least utensil. My people shall assist you; and I have picked out a set of lusty fellows, that they may do you the more service in your removal. Nobody can use you better, in my opinion; and as I treat you with great indulgence, I conjure you, sir, to make a good use of it, and to give me no disturbance in the execution of my office.

Orgon. [*Aside.*] I'd give just now, a hundred of the best louis d'ors I have left, for the power and pleasure of laying one sound blow on your ass-ship's muzzle.

Cleanthes. [*Aside to Orgon.*] Give over; don't let's make things worse.

Damis. This impudence is too great; I can hardly refrain; my fingers itch to be at him.

Dorina. Faith, Mr. Brawny-backed Loyal, some thwacks of a cudgel would by no means sit ill upon you.

Mr. Loyal. Those infamous words are punishable, sweetheart; there's law against women too.

Cleanthes. [*To Mr. Loyal.*] Let us come to a conclusion, sir, with this; 'tis enough; pray give up your paper of indulgence, and leave us.

Mr. Loyal. Good-bye to ye. Heaven bless you all together!

Orgon. And confound both thee and him that sent thee!

SCENE V

Orgon, Madam Pernelle, Elmira, Cleanthes, Mariana, Damis, Dorina.

Orgon. Well mother, you see whether I am in the right or no; and you may judge of the rest by the warrant. Do you at length perceive his treacheries?

Madam Pernelle. I am stunned, and am tumbling from the clouds.

Dorina. [*To Orgon.*] You complain without a cause, and blame him wrongfully; this does but confirm his pious intentions. His virtue is made perfect in the love of his neighbour; he knows, very often, that riches spoil the man; and he would only, out of pure charity, take from you everything that may obstruct your salvation.

Orgon. Hold your tongue. Must I always be repeating that to you?

Cleanthes. [*To Orgon.*] Come let's consult what's proper for you to do.

Elmira. Go and expose the audaciousness of the ungrateful wretch. This proceeding of his invalidates the contract; and his perfidiousness must needs appear too black to let him have the success we are apt to surmise.

SCENE VI

Valère, Orgon, Madam Pernelle, Elmira, Cleanthes, Mariana, Damis, Dorina.

Valère. 'Tis with regret, sir, I come to afflict you; but I am constrained to it by the imminence of the danger. A very intimate friend of mine, who knows the interest I ought to take in everything that may concern you, has for my sake violated, by a delicate step, the secrecy due to the affairs of state, and has just sent me advice, the consequence of which reduces you to the expedient of a sudden flight. The rogue who has long imposed on you, has thought fit, an hour ago, to accuse you to your prince, and to put into his hands, among other darts he shoots at you, the important casket of a state-criminal, of which, says he, in contempt of the duty of a subject, you have kept the guilty secret. I am not informed of the detail of the crime laid to your charge, but an order is issued out against your person, and to execute it the better, he himself is appointed to accompany the person that is to arrest you.

Cleanthes. Now are his pretensions armed, and this is the way that the traitor seeks to make himself master of your estate.

Orgon. The man, I must own, is a vile animal!

Valère. The least delay may be fatal to you; I have my coach at the door to carry you off, with a thousand louis d'ors that here I bring you. Let's lose no time, the shaft is thrown, and these blows are only parried by flight. I offer myself to conduct you to a place of safety, and to accompany you in your escape, even to the last.

Orgon. Alas, what do I not owe to your obliging care! I must take another time to thank you, and I beseech Heaven to be so propitious to me, that I may one day acknowledge this generous service. Farewell, take care the rest of you——

Cleanthes. Go quickly; we shall take care, brother, to do what is proper.

SCENE VII

Tartuffe, An Exempt, Madam Pernelle, Orgon, Elmira, Cleanthes, Mariana, Valère, Damis, Dorina.

Tartuffe. [*Stopping Orgon.*] Softly, sir, softly, don't run so fast, you shan't go far to find you a lodging; we take you prisoner in the king's name.

Orgon. Traitor, thou hast reserved this shaft for the last. 'Tis the stroke by which thou art to dispatch me, and this crowns all the rest of thy perfidies.

Tartuffe. Your abuses have nothing in them that can incense me; I'm instructed to suffer everything for the sake of Heaven.

Cleanthes. The moderation is great, I must confess.

Damis. How impudently the varlet sports with Heaven?

Tartuffe. All your raving can't move me; I think of nothing but doing my duty.

Mariana. You have much glory to expect from hence; this employ is a mighty honourable one for you.

Tartuffe. The employ can't be other than glorious, when it proceeds from the power that sent me hither.

Orgon. But do you remember, ungrateful wretch, that my charitable hand raised you from a miserable condition?

Tartuffe. Yes, I know what succours I might receive from thence, but the interest of my prince is my highest duty. The just obligation whereof stifles in my heart all other acknowledgments; and I could sacrifice to so powerful a tie, friend, wife, kindred, and myself to boot.

Elmira. The hypocrite!

Dorina. How artfully he can make a cloak of what is sacred!

Cleanthes. But if the zeal that puts you on, and with which you trick yourself out, is so perfect as you say it is, how came it not to show itself till he found means of surprising you soliciting his wife? How came you not to think of informing against him, till his honour obliged him to drive you out of his house? I don't say, that the making over his whole estate to you lately should draw you from your duty; but intending to treat him, as now you do, like a criminal, why did you consent to take anything from him?

Tartuffe. [*To the Exempt.*] I beg you, sir, to free me from this clamour, and be pleased to do as you are ordered.

Exempt. Yes, 'tis certainly delaying the execution too long; you invite me to fulfil it apropos; and to execute my order, follow me immediately to the prison, which we are to allot you for your habitation.

Tartuffe. Who? I, sir?

Exempt. Yes, you.

Tartuffe. Why to prison, pray?

Exempt. You are not the person I shall give an account to. [*To Orgon.*] Do you, sir, compose yourself after so warm a surprise. We live under a prince who is an enemy to fraud, a prince whose eyes penetrate into the heart, and whom all the art of impostors can't deceive. His great soul is furnished with a fine discernment, and always takes things in a right light; there's nothing gets too much footing by surprise, and his solid reason falls into no excess. He bestows lasting glory on men of worth, but he dispenses his favours without blindness, and his love for the sincere, does not foreclose his heart against the horror that's due to those that are otherwise. Even this person was not able to surprise him, and we find he keeps clear of the most subtle snares. He soon pierced through all the baseness contained within his heart. Coming to accuse you, he betrayed himself, and by a just stroke of divine judgment, he discovered himself to be a notorious rogue, of whom His Majesty had received information under another name; the whole detail of whose horrid crimes is long enough to fill volumes of histories. This monarch, in a word, detesting his ingratitude and un-dutifulness to you, to his other confusions hath added the following, and hath sent me under his direction, only to see how far his assurance would carry him, and to oblige him to give you full satisfaction. He wills moreover that I should strip the traitor of all your papers to which he pretends a right, and give them you. By dint of sovereign power he dissolves the obligation of the contract, which gives him your estate, and he pardons moreover this secret offence in which the retreat of your friend involved you; and this recompense he bestows for the zeal he saw you formerly showed in maintaining his rights. To let you see that his heart knows, even when 'tis least expected, how to recompense a good action; that merit with him is never lost, and that he much better remembers good than evil.

Dorina.   May Heaven be praised!

Madam Pernelle.   Now I begin to revive.

Elmira.   Favourable success!

Mariana.   Who could have foretold this?

Orgon. [*To Tartuffe as the Exempt leads him off.*] Well, traitor, there you are——

Scene VIII

Madam Pernelle, Orgon, Elmira, Mariana, Cleanthes, Valère, Damis, Dorina.

Cleanthes.   Nay, brother, hold, and don't descend to indig-nities; leave the wretch to his evil destiny, and don't add to the remorse that oppresses him. Much rather wish that his heart may now happily become a convert to virtue; that he may reform his life, through detestation of his crimes, and may soften the justice of a glorious prince; while for his goodness you go and on your knees make the due returns for his lenity to you.

Orgon. Yes, 'tis well said. Let us, with joy, go throw ourselves at his royal feet, to glory in the goodness which he generously displays to us; then, having acquitted ourselves of this first duty, 'twill be necessary we should apply ourselves, with just care, to another:

> With Hymen's tend'rest joys to crown Valère
> The generous lover, and the friend sincere.

SQUIRE LUBBERLY

(A COMEDY)

Squire Lubberly, *a Comedy of Three Acts in Prose, acted at Cham-bord in the month of October, 1669, and at Paris at the Theatre of the Palace-Royal, the 15th of November the same year.*

The comedy of *Squire Lubberly* consists of a kind of comic humour, more adapted to divert than to instruct. The extravagant folly of a country gentleman gives occasion to a sharper, who is in the interest of Erastus, to invent divers stratagems both to divert Orontes from giving his daughter to Mr. Pourceaugnac, as well as Mr. Pourceaugnac from concluding the match which had brought him to Paris; the traps which Sbrigani drew the advocate of Limoges into will appear to have a greater similitude to truth, if we recollect that this dexterous Neapolitan, in order the better to manage the measures he had taken, went to accost him as he came out of the stage coach, to find out the character and genius of the man he was to take in hand.

ACTORS

SQUIRE LUBBERLY.

ORONTES.

JULIA, *daughter to Orontes.*

NERINA, *a woman of intrigue, pretending to be a woman of Picardy.*

LUCETTA, *a pretended Gascon.*

ERASTUS, *lover to Julia.*

SBRIGANI, *a Neapolitan, a man of intrigue.*

FIRST PHYSICIAN.

SECOND PHYSICIAN.

APOTHECARY.

COUNTRY-MAN.

COUNTRY-WOMAN.

FIRST MUSICIAN.

SECOND MUSICIAN.

FIRST COUNSELLOR.

SECOND COUNSELLOR.

FIRST SWISS.

SECOND SWISS.

OFFICER.

TWO SOLDIERS.

SEVERAL MUSICIANS, PLAYERS UPON INSTRUMENTS AND DANCERS.

SCENE: *Paris.*

ACT I

Scene I

Julia, Erastus, Nerina.

Julia. For Heaven's sake! Erastus, let's take care of being surprised—I tremble lest we should be seen together: 'twould ruin all, after the command I've had to the contrary.

Erastus. I look every way, and see nothing.

Julia. [*To Nerina.*] Do you too, Nerina, keep a watchful eye, and be very careful that nobody comes.

Nerina. [*Retiring to the farther end of the stage.*] Rely on me, and speak boldly what you have to say to one another.

Julia. Have you thought of anything that may be of service in our affair, Erastus? And do you believe it possible to prevent this impertinent match which my father has got in his head?

Erastus. At least let's earnestly endeavour it; and we've already prepared a good number of batteries to overturn this ridiculous design.

Nerina. [*Running to Julia.*] I'faith, here's your father!

Julia. Ah! let's part immediately.

Nerina. No, no, no, don't stir, I was mistaken.

Julia. Bless me! Nerina, what a fool you are to put us in these frights!

Erastus. Yes, charming Julia, we've contrived abundance of machines for that purpose, and shan't fail to set them all at work, since you have given me leave. Don't inquire what stratagems we shall employ, you shall have the diversion of 'em; and as, at a comedy, it's good to let you have the pleasure of being surprised, without informing you of all that's going to be shown, so 'tis sufficient now to tell you, that we've several projects in hand ready to produce upon occasion, and that the ingenious Nerina and the dexterous Sbrigani undertake the business.

Nerina. To be sure, your father's in the wrong to think of pestering you with his counsellor of Limoges, Squire Lubberly, whom he never saw in his whole life, and who's now coming by the stage coach to carry you off before our eyes. Should three

or four thousand crowns more, upon the word of your uncle,
make him reject a lover that you like? And could such a creature
as you are be formed for a Limosin? If he has an inclination to
marry, why doesn't he take one of his own country-women, and
let Christians be at peace? The very name of Squire Lubberly
puts me in a terrible passion. I'm provoked at Squire Lubberly.
Was it only for that name Lubberly, it should cost me dear or
I'd break off the match. You shall not be Mrs. Lubberly.
Lubberly! Can a body endure it? No, Lubberly is what I
cannot bear, and therefore we'll make such sport with him, and
play him so many tricks one after another, that we'll send this
Squire Lubberly back again to Limoges.

Erastus. Here's our cunning Neapolitan, who will tell us
news.

SCENE II

Julia, Erastus, Sbrigani, Nerina.

Sbrigani. Sir, your man is come, I saw him three leagues off
where the coach lay. I've studied him a good half-hour in the
kitchen, whither he went down to breakfast, and I have him
already by heart. As for his figure, I'll say nothing to you of it,
you'll see what an air nature has bestowed upon him, and
whether his dress is not exactly answerable. But for his understanding, I beforehand assure you it's the dullest that ever was,
and we shall find him entirely fit to work upon, as we've a mind.
He's a man, in short, that will fall into all the snares that people
will lay for him.

Erastus. Is this true that you tell us?

Sbrigani. Ay, if I've any skill in mankind.

Nerina. This is a famous man, madam. Your affair could
not be put into better hands; he's the hero of our age for the
exploits he performs; a man that for the service of his friends
has twenty times in his life generously braved the galleys. One
who at the hazard of his arms and shoulders knows excellently
well how to put an end to the most difficult enterprises, and who,
such as you see him, was banished from his country for I
know not how many honourable actions which he generously
engaged in.

Sbrigani. I'm confounded at the praises with which you
honour me, and might much more justly extol the wonders of
your life; and particularly the glory you acquired, when with so

much honesty you played with the young foreign nobleman that was brought to your house, and bubbled him of twelve thousand crowns; when you handsomely trumped up that false contract which was the ruin of a whole family; when with such greatness of soul you could deny the pledge you were entrusted with; and when you bravely gave your evidence to hang a couple of persons that were innocent.

Nerina. These are trifles not worth mentioning, and your compliments make me blush.

Sbrigani. I'll spare your modesty, and we'll have no more of it; but to begin our business, let's instantly go find our country squire, while on your part you get all the other actors of the comedy in a readiness against we want 'em.

Erastus. Do you, madam, be mindful of your part; and the better to conceal our aim, pretend, as you've been instructed, that you are perfectly well pleased with the resolutions of your father.

Julia. If it depended only on that, matters would go wondrous well.

Erastus. But, dear Julia, suppose all our contrivances should be unsuccessful.

Julia. I'll declare my real inclinations to my father.

Erastus. And if he should persist in his design, contrary to your inclinations?

Julia. I'd threaten him to put myself into a nunnery.

Erastus. But if, notwithstanding all that, he should endeavour to force you to this match?

Julia. What would you have me say to ye?

Erastus. What would I have you say to me?

Julia. Yes.

Erastus. What one that really loves would say.

Julia. What's that?

Erastus. That nothing shall force you, but that in spite of all your father's endeavours, you promise to be mine.

Julia. Heavens! Erastus, content yourself with what I'm now doing, and attempt not to find out what the future resolutions of my heart may be, nor perplex me in my duty by proposing the last sad expedient, which perhaps we may have no need of; but however, permit me, if it must be so, to be led into it by the course of things.

Erastus. Well then——

Sbrigani. Faith, here's our man, let's look about us.

Nerina. O what a figure he is!

Scene III

Squire Lubberly, Sbrigani.

Squire Lubberly. [*Turning to the side he came on, and talking to the people who are following him.*] Well, what? What's the matter? What's here to do? Would the foolish city and the foolish folk in it were at the devil! Can't a man go along without having a parcel of numskulls gaping and grinning at him? Eh, ye cockneys, mind your own business, and let people pass without twittering in their faces. Deuce take me an' I don't thrust my fist in the first man's face I see laugh.

Sbrigani. [*Speaking to the people.*] What's the matter, gentlemen? What does this mean? Who have you got amongst ye? Is it fitting to make game in this manner of gentlemen strangers that come hither?

Squire Lubberly. This here's a man of sense.

Sbrigani. What a proceeding is this of yours? What is it you find to laugh at?

Squire Lubberly. Right.

Sbrigani. Is there anything ridiculous in the gentleman?

Squire Lubberly. Ay.

Sbrigani. Isn't he like other people?

Squire Lubberly. Am I crooked, or humpbacked?

Sbrigani. Learn to distinguish people.

Squire Lubberly. Well said.

Sbrigani. The gentleman is of a mien to be respected.

Squire Lubberly. 'Tis true.

Sbrigani. A person of condition.

Squire Lubberly. Ay, a gentleman of Limoges.

Sbrigani. A man of wit.

Squire Lubberly. Who has studied the law.

Sbrigani. He does you too much honour by coming into your city.

Squire Lubberly. No doubt of it.

Sbrigani. The gentleman is not a person to occasion laughter.

Squire Lubberly. Certainly.

Sbrigani. And I shall call anybody to account that laughs at him.

Squire Lubberly. [*To Sbrigani.*] Sir, I'm infinitely obliged to ye.

Sbrigani. I'm sorry, sir, to see such a person as you are received in this manner, and I beg your pardon on behalf of the city.

Squire Lubberly. Your servant, sir.

Sbrigani. I saw you this morning, sir, where the coach inned, when you were at breakfast; and the becoming grace with which you ate your victuals immediately created in me a friendship for you. And as I'm sensible you were never here before, but are a perfect stranger, I'm very glad I've found you, to offer you my service at your arrival, and to assist you in your conduct amongst people who sometimes haven't all the respect they ought for persons of honour.

Squire Lubberly. You do me too great a favour.

Sbrigani. I have already told you, that I felt an inclination for you from the moment I first saw you.

Squire Lubberly. I'm obliged to ye.

Sbrigani. Your countenance pleased me.

Squire Lubberly. It's too great an honour to me.

Sbrigani. I saw something honest.

Squire Lubberly. I'm your humble servant.

Sbrigani. Something lovely.

Squire Lubberly. Oh, oh!

Sbrigani. Graceful.

Squire Lubberly. Oh, oh!

Sbrigani. Sweet.

Squire Lubberly. Oh, oh!

Sbrigani. Majestic.

Squire Lubberly. Oh, oh!

Sbrigani. Frank.

Squire Lubberly. Oh, oh!

Sbrigani. And cordial.

Squire Lubberly. Oh, oh!

Sbrigani. I assure you that I'm entirely yours.

Squire Lubberly. I'm mightily obliged to ye.

Sbrigani. I speak from the bottom o' my heart.

Squire Lubberly. I believe it.

Sbrigani. Had I the honour to be known to you, you'd find me to be a man that's perfectly sincere.

Squire Lubberly. I don't doubt it.

Sbrigani. An enemy to deceit.

Squire Lubberly. I'm persuaded of it.

Sbrigani. And one not capable of disguising his thoughts. You look at my clothes which are not made like other people's; but I'm originally of Naples, at your service, and am desirous to preserve a little the way of dress, and the sincerity of my country.

Squire Lubberly. That's mighty well done. I was desirous for my part to put myself into the court fashion for the credit of the country.

Sbrigani. Faith, it becomes you better than all our courtiers.

Squire Lubberly. So my tailor told me. The clothes are rich and decent, and will be talked of here.

Sbrigani. To be sure. Won't you go to the Louvre?

Squire Lubberly. I must go pay my court.

Sbrigani. The king will be overjoyed to see you.

Squire Lubberly. I believe so.

Sbrigani. Have you taken a lodging?

Squire Lubberly. No, I was going to look for one.

Sbrigani. I shall be very glad to go with you about it, and I know the whole place.

Scene IV

Erastus, Squire Lubberly, Sbrigani.

Erastus. Hah! Who's this! What do I see? What a happy meeting! Squire Lubberly! I'm overjoyed to see you! How? It seems as if you hardly remembered me.

Squire Lubberly. Sir, I'm your servant.

Erastus. Is it possible that five or six years can have made you forget me? and that you don't recollect the best friend to all the family of the Lubberlys!

Squire Lubberly. I beg your pardon. [*Low to Sbrigani.*] I don't know who he is, faith.

Erastus. There's not one of the Lubberlys at Limoges that I don't know, from the greatest to the least; I kept company with nobody but them during the time I was there, and I had the honour of seeing you almost every day.

Squire Lubberly. The honour was to me, sir.

Erastus. Don't you remember my face?

Squire Lubberly. Ay, ay. [*To Sbrigani.*] I don't know him.

Erastus. Don't you remember that I've had the happiness of drinking I can't tell how many times with you?

Squire Lubberly. Excuse me. [*To Sbrigani.*] I know nothing of it.

Erastus. How d'ye call that rogue at Limoges that used to treat so handsomely?

Squire Lubberly. What, little John?

Erastus. The same. We often went together to enjoy

ourselves at his house How is it you call the name of the place where they walk at Limoges?

Squire Lubberly. The churchyard.

Erastus. Right. 'Tis there I've enjoyed many sweet hours of your agreeable conversation. You don't recollect all this?

Squire Lubberly. Pardon me, I recollect it. [*To Sbrigani.*] Devil take me if I remember it.

Sbrigani. [*Low, to Squire Lubberly.*] A hundred such things as that get out of one's head.

Erastus. Prithee embrace me then, and let's renew our former friendship.

Sbrigani. [*To Squire Lubberly.*] This is a man that loves you mightily.

Erastus. Tell me some news of all your family. How does that gentleman your—he there—that's so honest a man.

Squire Lubberly. My brother the consul?

Erastus. Yes.

Squire Lubberly. He's as well as can be.

Erastus. Troth! I'm overjoyed at it. And that good-humoured man—there—Mr.—your——

Squire Lubberly. My cousin the counsellor?

Erastus. You are right.

Squire Lubberly. Always gay and merry.

Erastus. Faith! I'm mighty glad of it. And the gentleman, your uncle? the——

Squire Lubberly. I have no uncle.

Erastus. You had one at that time though.

Squire Lubberly. No. Nothing but an aunt.

Erastus. That's what I would have said. Madam your aunt, how does she do?

Squire Lubberly. She has been dead six months.

Erastus. Alas poor woman! She was so good a creature.

Squire Lubberly. We've also my nephew, the parson, who was like to die of the smallpox.

Erastus. What a pity 'twould have been?

Squire Lubberly. D'ye know him too?

Erastus. Do I know him truly! A lusty handsome young fellow.

Squire Lubberly. None of the lustiest.

Erastus. No, but of a good shape.

Squire Lubberly. O! ay.

Erastus. He is your nephew.

Squire Lubberly. True.

Erastus.   Your brother or your sister's son.

Squire Lubberly.   True.

Erastus.   Parson of the Church of —— What d'ye call the name?

Squire Lubberly.   Of St. Stephen.

Ersastus.   That's he, I don't know any other.

Squire Lubberly.   [*To Sbrigani.*]   He names all my relations.

Sbrigani.   He knows you better than you imagine.

Squire Lubberly.   By what I perceive you've lived a long while in our town.

Erastus.   Full two years.

Squire Lubberly.   You were there then, when our governor was godfather to my cousin the supervisor's child.

Erastus.   Ay, truly, I was one of the first invited.

Squire Lubberly.   It was genteel.

Erastus.   Ay, mighty genteel.

Squire Lubberly.   'Twas a very handsome entertainment.

Erastus.   Certainly.

Squire Lubberly.   You saw then the quarrel too, that I had with the Perigordin gentleman?

Erastus.   Ay.

Squire Lubberly.   Egad, he met with his match.

Erastus.   Ha, ha!

Squire Lubberly.   He gave me a box on the ear, but I told him his own very handsomely.

Erastus.   Sure enough—but I don't intend you shall take any other lodging than mine.

Squire Lubberly.   I don't care to——

Erastus.   You jest. I shall by no means suffer my very good friend to be anywhere else but in my house.

Squire Lubberly.   'Twill be to you——

Erastus.   Nay, it signifies nothing, you shall lodge at my house.

Sbrigani.   [*To Squire Lubberly.*]   Since he persists in it, I advise you to accept the offer.

Erastus.   Where are your things?

Squire Lubberly.   I left 'em with my servant, where I was set down.

Erastus.   Let's send somebody to fetch 'em.

Squire Lubberly.   No, I forbade him to stir, unless I should come myself, for fear of some roguery.

Erastus.   'Twas prudently thought of.

Squire Lubberly.   This place requires a little caution.

Erastus. One finds sharpers everywhere.

Sbrigani. I'll wait upon the gentleman, and conduct him where you please.

Erastus. Well, I shall be glad to give some directions, and you need only come to that house there.

Sbrigani. We'll be with you instantly.

Erastus. [*To Squire Lubberly.*] I expect you with impatience.

Squire Lubberly. [*To Sbrigani.*] Here's an acquaintance I hadn't the least thought of.

Sbrigani. He has the appearance of an honest man.

Erastus. [*Alone.*] Faith, Squire Lubberly, we'll be at you every way; matters are ready, and I need only knock. Soho there.

Scene V

The Apothecary, Erastus.

Erastus. I believe, sir, you're the doctor that somebody came to talk with from me.

Apothecary. No, sir, 'tis not I that am the doctor; that honour doesn't belong to me. I'm only an apothecary, an unworthy apothecary, at your service.

Erastus. Is the doctor within then?

Apothecary. Yes. He's busy dispatching some sick folks, and I'll go tell him that you are here.

Erastus. No, don't stir, I'll wait till he has done. 'Tis to put into his hands a certain relation of ours, (whom he has been told of), that's seized with a sort of madness, which we should be very glad to have him cured of, before he's married.

Apothecary. I know the matter, I know the matter; and I was with him when they spoke to him about this affair. Faith and troth, you could not have applied yourself to a more able physician, he's a man that understands medicine as fundamentally as I understand my criss-cross-row: and who, though a body should die for it, would not abate one tittle of the rules of the ancients. Ay, sir, he always follows the great road, the great road, and doesn't go look for noon at four o'clock: and for all the money in the world, he would not cure anybody with other medicines than what the faculty prescribes.

Erastus. He does very right, a patient should not desire to be cured, unless the faculty consents to it.

Apothecary. 'Tis not because we are intimate friends that I speak it; but it's a pleasure to be his patient, and I should rather die by his medicines than be cured by those of any other: for whatever happens, a man is certain that things are always regular; and should you die under his direction, your heirs would have nothing to reproach you for.

Erastus. That's a mighty comfort to a dead man.

Apothecary. To be sure. One would be glad, at least, to die methodically. Besides, he's not one of those doctors that make a market of their patients: he's a man that's expeditious, expeditious, who loves to dispatch his patients: and when they are to die, 'tis done with him the quickest in the world.

Erastus. Indeed, there's nothing like going through an affair speedily.

Apothecary. That's true: to what purpose serves so much humming and hawing, and beating round the bush? One should know out of hand the short or the long of a distemper.

Erastus. You're in the right.

Apothecary. Why there have been three of my children already whose illness he did me the honour to take care of, that died in less than four days: but in another's hands they would have languished three months.

Erastus. It's good to have such friends as these.

Apothecary. No doubt of it. I have only two children left, which he takes care of as if they were his own: he treats and orders 'em as he pleases, without my interposing; and very frequently, when I return out o' the city, I'm quite amazed to find 'em bleeding or purging by his direction.

Erastus. That's the most obliging care in the world.

Apothecary. Here he is, here he is, here he comes.

Scene VI

Erastus, First Physician, Apothecary, Country-Man, Country-Woman.

Country-Man. [*To the Physician.*] Sir, he can't hold out any longer, and he says that he feels in his head the violentest pains in the world.

First Physician. The patient is a fool, and by so much the more so, because in his distemper, it is not the head according to Galen, but the spleen that must disorder him.

Country-Man. Whatever it be, sir, he has had constantly along with it a looseness, for these six months.

First Physician. Good; that's a sign his inside is clear. I'll come to visit him in two or three days: but if he should die before that time, don't fail to give me notice: because it's not a point of civility for a physician to visit a dead person.

Country-Woman. [*To the Physician.*] My father, sir, grows continually worse and worse.

First Physician. That's not my fault. I give him medicines, why is not he cured? How many times has he been blooded?

Country-Woman. Fifteen, sir, in twenty days.

First Physician. Blooded fifteen times?

Country-Woman. Yes.

First Physician. And isn't he cured?

Country-Woman. No, sir.

First Physician. 'Tis a sign the distemper is not in the blood. We'll purge him as many times to see if it isn't in the humours, and if we've no success, we'll send him to the bath.

Apothecary. That is the end, that is the end of physic.

Scene VII

Erastus, First Physician, Apothecary.

Erastus. [*To the Physician.*] 'Twas I, sir, that sent to speak with you some days ago, about a relation that's a little disordered in his mind, whom I would place at your house, that he may be cured with the more conveniency, and be seen but by few people.

First Physician. Yes, sir, I've got everything in readiness, and promise to take all imaginable care of him.

Erastus. Here he comes very seasonably.

First Physician. It happens extremely lucky, for I've got an old physician, one of my friends, here, with whom I shall be very glad to consult about his disorder.

Scene VIII

Squire Lubberly, Erastus, First Physician, The Apothecary.

Erastus. [*To Squire Lubberly.*] A little affair is fallen out, which obliges me to leave you; [*Pointing to the Physician.*] but there's a person in whose hands I leave you, that will take care upon my account to treat you in the best manner he is able.

First Physician. The duty of my profession obliges me so to do, and it's sufficient that you lay this charge upon me.

Squire Lubberly. [*Aside.*] This is certainly his steward, and he must be a man of quality.

First Physician. [*To Erastus.*] Yes, I assure you, that I'll treat the gentleman methodically, and with all the regularity of our art.

Squire Lubberly. Od's life, I must not have so much ceremony, I don't come here to incommode you.

First Physician. 'Tis only a pleasure to me to be so employed.

Erastus. [*To the Physician.*] There are ten pistoles beforehand however, as an earnest of what I've promised.

Squire Lubberly. Nay, if you please, I don't understand that you should be at any expense, or send to buy anything for me.

Erastus. Pray now, give me leave, it's not for what you imagine.

Squire Lubberly. I beg you'll treat me only as a friend.

Erastus. That's what I'll do. [*Softly to the doctor.*] I chiefly recommend to you not to let him get out of your hands, for by fits he's for making his escape.

First Physician. Don't you give yourself any uneasiness.

Erastus. [*To Squire Lubberly.*] I beg you to excuse the incivility that I commit.

Squire Lubberly. You banter; why, you do me too great a favour.

SCENE IX

Squire Lubberly, First Physician, Second Physician,
The Apothecary.

First Physician. 'Tis a great deal of honour, sir, for me to be pitched upon to do you service.

Squire Lubberly. Your servant.

First Physician. Here's a skilful man, my brother, with whom I'm going to consult about the manner of our treating you.

Squire Lubberly. Pray not so much ceremony. I tell you I'm a man that likes the common way.

First Physician. Here, bring chairs.

[*Servants bring in chairs.*

Squire Lubberly. [*Aside.*] These are mighty dismal-looking servants for a young man!

First Physician. Come, sir, take your place, sir.

[*The Two Physicians sitting, seat Squire Lubberly between them.*

Squire Lubberly. [*Giving his hands.*] Your most humble servant. [*Perceiving they feel his pulse.*] What does this mean?

First Physician. D'ye eat well, sir?

Squire Lubberly. Yes, and drink still better.

First Physician. So much the worse. That great appetition of frigid and humid is an indication of the heat and aridity that is within. D'ye sleep much?

Squire Lubberly. Yes, when I've supped heartily.

First Physician. Have you dreams?

Squire Lubberly. Now and then.

First Physician. Of what nature are they?

Squire Lubberly. Of the nature of dreams. What the devil of a conversation is this?

First Physician. Your stools, how are they?

Squire Lubberly. Troth! I don't understand the meaning of all these questions, and had rather drink a glass.

First Physician. A little patience. We are going to reason upon your affair before you, and will do it in English to be understood the better.

Squire Lubberly. What great reasoning need there be about eating a morsel?

First Physician. Since so it is, that no one can cure a distemper which he does not understand perfectly, and no one can understand it perfectly, without rightly settling the particular idea and the true species of it, by its diagnostic and prognostic signs; you'll give me leave, (as you are my senior) to enter upon the consideration of the distemper that's now in hand, before we meddle with the therapeutic part, and the remedies which are proper for us to prescribe for the perfect curation of it. I say then, sir, with your permission, that our patient here present, is unhappily attacked, affected, possessed, and disordered by that sort of madness which we term very properly hypochondriac melancholy; a kind of madness the most troublesome, and which requires no less than an Æsculapius like you, consummate in our art. You, I say, who are grown grey in the service, as the saying is, and through whose hands so much business of all sorts has passed. I term it hypochondriac melancholy to distinguish it from the other two: for the celebrated Galen establishes in a most learned manner, as is usual with him, three species of that distemper which we call melancholy; so termed not only by the Latins, but likewise by the Greeks; which is worthy of observation in our case. The first,

which arises from a direct disorder in the brain: the second,
which proceeds from the whole mass of blood made and rendered
atrabilious: and the third, termed hypochondriac, which is our
kind, proceeding from a disorder in some part of the lower belly,
and from the inferior region, but particularly from the spleen,
the heat and inflammation whereof sends up to the brain of our
patient abundance of fuliginous, gross, and heavy particles, the
black and malignant effluvia of which occasion a depravation of
the functions of the supreme faculty, and produce that distemper, which by our ratiocination he is manifestly attainted
and convicted of.   But for an uncontestable diagnostic of what
I say, you need only consider that mighty seriousness which
you see, that sadness accompanied by fearfulness and suspicion.
Pathognomic and individual symptoms of this distemper, so
well remarked by the divine old man Hippocrates.   That
physiognomy, those eyes red and staring, that swingeing beard,
that habitude of body, slender, lank, black, and hairy, tokens
denoting him exceedingly affected by this distemper, proceeding from a default in the hypochondria: which distemper,
by lapse of time, being naturalised, antiquated, habituated, and
made free of his body, might well degenerate either into distraction, or phthisic, or apoplexy, or even into downright frenzy
and fury.   All this being supposed, as a disease well known is
half cured, for *ignoti nulla est curatio morbi*, 'twill be no difficulty
for you to conclude upon the medicines we ought to prescribe
the gentleman.   First of all, to remedy this obdurate plethora,
this luxuriant cacochymy throughout his whole body, I'm of
opinion that he should be liberally phlebotomised: I mean, that
he be let blood frequently and in abundance, first, in the *vena
basilica*, then in the *vena cephalica*, and if the distemper be
obstinate, even a vein in the forehead should be opened; and
let the orifice be large, that the gross blood may issue out.   At
the same time I advise that he purge, scour, and evacuate by
purgatives, suitable and convenient; that's to say, by chola-
gogues, melanagogues, etc.   And as the real source of all this
mischief, either is a feculent and foul humour, or a vapour
black and gross, which obscures, empoisons, and muddifies
the animal spirits, it is proper afterwards for him to have a bath
of pure and clean water, with a large quantity of whey; to
purify by the water the feculency of that foul humour, and by
the whey to clarify the blackness of that vapour.   But before
all things, I think it good to recreate him by agreeable conversation, songs and musical instruments, whereto it's not improper

to add dancers, to the end that their motions, disposition and
agility may stir up and awaken the inactivity of his languid
spirits, which occasions the thickness of his blood, from whence
the distemper proceeds. These are the remedies I propose, to
which may be added abundance more that are better, by you,
sir, my master and senior, according to the experience, judgment,
light, and sufficiency that you have acquired in our art. *Dixi.*

   Second Physician. Sir, Heaven forbid it should enter into
my head to add anything to what you have been now saying.
You have discoursed so well of all the signs, the symptoms, and
the causes of the gentleman's distemper, the arguments you
have used about it are so learned and fine, that it's impossible
for him not to be out of his wits, and hypochondriacally melancholy. Or were he not, he must certainly become so for the
beauty of the things you've spoken, and the justness of your
way of reasoning. Yes, sir, you have very graphically depicted,
graphicè depinxisti, everything that appertains to this distemper. Nothing can be more learnedly, judiciously, ingeni-
ously conceived, thought, imagined, than what you have delivered
upon the subject of this disorder, be it as to the diagnostic, the
prognostic, or the therapeutic. And nothing now remains for
me to do but to congratulate the gentleman upon falling into
your hands, and acquaint him that he's but too happy in being
disordered in his senses, to experience the efficacy and the
gentleness of the medicines which you so judiciously have
proposed. I approve them all, *manibus et pedibus descendo
in tuam sententiam.* All that I would add to them is, to let all
his bleedings and purgings be of an odd number, *numero deus
impare gaudet;* to take the whey before the bathing; to make
him a forehead-cloth lined with salt; salt is a symbol of wisdom;
to whitewash the walls of his chamber, to dissipate the gloominess
of his spirits, *album est disgregativum visus.* And to give him
a little clyster instantly, for to serve as a prelude and intro-
duction to those judicious medicines, from which, if he's curable,
he must receive relief. Heaven grant, sir, that these medicines
which are yours may succeed with the patient according to
our intention.

   Squire Lubberly. I've been listening to you for an hour,
gentlemen. Is it a comedy we are acting here?

   First Physician. No, sir, we're not in jest.

   Squire Lubberly. What does all this mean? What would
you be at with your gibberish and your nonsense?

   First Physician. Soh! injurious language. That's a

diagnostic which we wanted for the confirmation of his distemper; this may turn to distraction.

Squire Lubberly. [*Aside.*] In what company have they left me here?   [*He spits two or three times.*

First Physician. Another diagnostic; frequent sputation.

Squire Lubberly. Let's have done with this, and begone from hence.

First Physician. Another again. Inquietude to change place.

Squire Lubberly. What's the meaning of all this ado? What would you have with me?

First Physician. We'd cure you, according to the orders that were given us.

Squire Lubberly. Cure me?

First Physician. Ay.

Squire Lubberly. S'death! I'm not sick.

First Physician. A bad sign, when a patient is insensible of his illness.

Squire Lubberly. I tell you that I'm very well.

First Physician. We know how you are better than you yourself. We're physicians that see plainly into your constitution.

Squire Lubberly. If you're physicians, I've nothing at all to do with ye. I make a jest of physic.

First Physician. How! how! this man is madder than we imagined.

Squire Lubberly. My father and mother never would take physic, and they both died without the assistance of doctors.

First Physician. I don't wonder then if they got a son that's mad. [*To Second Physician.*] Come, let's proceed now to the cure, and by the exhilarating sweetness of harmony, let us dulcify, lenify, and pacify the acrimony of his spirits, which I see are ready to be inflamed.

Scene X

Squire Lubberly. [*Alone.*] What the devil is this? Are the people of this place distracted? I never saw the like in my life, and don't at all understand the meaning of it.

SCENE XI

Squire Lubberly, and Two Physicians in grotesque habits.

They all three at first sit down, the Physicians rise up at different times to make their compliments to Squire Lubberly, who rises up as often to bow to them.

The Two Physicians.

> Buon dì, buon dì, buon dì,
> Non vi lasciate uccidere
> Dal dolor malinconico,
> Noi vi faremo ridere
> Col nostro canto harmonico,
> Sol' per guarirvi
> Siamo venuti quì.
> Buon dì, buon dì, buon dì.

First Physician.

> Altro non è la pazzia
> Che malinconia.
> Il malato
> Non è disperato,
> Se vol pigliar un poco d'allegria.
> Altro non è la pazzia
> Che malinconia.

Second Physician.

> Sù, cantate, ballate, ridete:
> E, se far meglio volete,
> Quando sentite il deliro vicino,
> Pigliate del vino,
> E qualche volta un poco di tabac.
> Allegramente, Monsu Pourceaugnac.

SCENE XII

Squire Lubberly, The Apothecary with a syringe.

Apothecary. Here, sir, is a little medicine, a little medicine, which you must take if you please, if you please.
Squire Lubberly. What d'ye mean? I've no occasion for it.
Apothecary. 'Twas ordered, sir, 'twas ordered.
Squire Lubberly. Hah! What d'ye mutter!

Apothecary. Take it, sir, take it; 'twill do you no harm, 'twill do you no harm.

Squire Lubberly. Heh!

Apothecary. It's a little clyster, a little clyster, gentle, gentle; it's gentle, gentle; there, take it, take it, sir, it's to scour, to scour, to scour.

Scene XIII

Squire Lubberly, Apothecary, and Two Physicians in grotesque habits, and Morris-Dancers with clyster-pipes.

The Two Physicians.

> Piglia-lo sù
> Signor Monsu,
> Piglia-lo, piglia-lo, piglia-lo sù,
> Che non ti farà male,
> Piglia-lo sù questo servitiale,
> Piglia-lo sù,
> Signor Monsu,
> Piglia-lo, piglia-lo, piglia-lo sù.

Squire Lubberly. Get ye gone to the devil with it.

> [*Squire Lubberly holding his hat to keep off the clyster-pipes, is followed by the Two Physicians and Morris-Dancers ; he runs off the stage, and returns again to sit down in the chair, near which he finds the Apothecary who waits for him ; the Two Physicians and Morris-Dancers return likewise.*

ACT II

Scene I

First Physician, Sbrigani.

First Physician. He has forced through everything I had placed to hinder him, and is fled away from the medicines I was beginning to prepare for him.

Sbrigani. 'Tis being a great enemy to himself to avoid medicines so salutiferous as yours.

First Physician. The mark of a distempered brain and a depraved reason, to be unwilling to be cured.

Sbrigani. You would have cured him in an instant.

First Physician. No doubt of it, though he had had a complication of a dozen distempers.

Sbrigani. But he has lost you the getting of fifty good pistoles.

First Physician. For my part, I don't understand losing 'em; for I'm resolved to cure him in spite of what he has done. He's bound and engaged to take my medicines, and I'll have him seized wherever I find him, as a deserter from physic and an infringer of my prescriptions.

Sbrigani. You're in the right, your medicines are a sure hit, and 'tis money he has robbed you of.

First Physician. Where can I learn any news of him?

Sbrigani. At the house of that good man Orontes, to be sure, whose daughter he's come to marry, and who knowing nothing of the infirmity of his son-in-law that is to be, will be in a hurry perhaps to conclude the marriage.

First Physician. I'll go talk with him immediately.

Sbrigani. You'll not do amiss.

First Physician. He's a mortgage to my prescriptions, and a patient shan't make a fool of a physician.

Sbrigani. That's very well said of you, and would you take my advice, you'd not permit him to be married till you have prescribed him your belly-full.

First Physician. Let me alone.

Sbrigani. [*Aside, and going.*] I'm going, for my part, to raise another battery, for the father-in-law is as much a noodle as the son-in-law.

SCENE II

Orontes, First Physician.

First Physician. You have a certain gentleman, sir, one Squire Lubberly, who is to espouse your daughter.

Orontes. Ay, I expect him from Limoges, he should have been come ere now.

First Physician. So he is, and has run away from my house after being placed there; but I forbid you, on the behalf of the faculty, to proceed in the match you've made till I have duly prepared him for it, and put him into a state of procreating children well conditioned both in body and mind.

Orontes. How's this?

First Physician. Your intended son-in-law was entered my patient; his distemper, which was given me to cure, is a chattel that belongs to me, which I reckon amongst my effects, and I declare to you that I don't intend he shall marry, until he has previously made satisfaction to the faculty, and undergone the medicines that I have ordered him.

Orontes. Has he some distemper?

First Physician. Yes.

Orontes. And what is his distemper, pray?

First Physician. Give yourself no concern about it.

Orontes. Is it some distemper——

First Physician. Physicians are obliged to secrecy. 'Tis sufficient that I enjoin both you and your daughter not to celebrate your nuptials with him without my consent, upon pain of incurring the faculty's displeasures, and undergoing all the diseases we please.

Orontes. If that's the case I shall take care to put a stop to the wedding.

First Physician. He was put into my hands, and is obliged to be my patient.

Orontes. Well and good.

First Physician. 'Tis in vain for him to run away, I'll have him condemned by a decree to be cured by me.

Orontes. I consent to it.

First Physician. Yes, he shall die, or else I'll cure him.

Orontes. With all my heart.

First Physician. And if I don't find him, I'll come upon you, and cure you in his stead.

Orontes. I am very well.

First Physician. That's no matter, I must have a patient, and will take whom I can.

Orontes. Take whom you will, but it shan't be me. [*Alone.*] A fine way of reasoning!

Scene III

Orontes, Sbrigani (dressed like a Flemish merchant).

Sbrigani. Sur, vid your permisseong, me be one tranger, de marshand Flemish, dat you'd be glad to demaund you one letel news.

Orontes. What is it, sir?

Sbrigani. Poot your haut upon your hed, you pleese, sir.

Orontes. Tell me what you desire, sir?

Sbrigani. Me speke nothing, sur, if you no poot oon de haut.

Orontes. Well then. What is it, sir?

Sbrigani. You not know in dis sitty one certain Montsir Orontes?

Orontes. Yes, I know him.

Sbrigani. You pleese, sur, vat maun he be?

Orontes. He's a man like other men.

Sbrigani. Me demaund you, sur, vether he be reesh, he goot de monnoie?

Orontes. Yes.

Sbrigani. But he be ver mush grate deal reesh, sur?

Orontes. Yes.

Sbrigani. Me be very glad of dat, sur.

Orontes. And why so?

Sbrigani. It be, sur, for one letel raisonn of consequance for us.

Orontes. But once more, upon what account?

Sbrigani. It be, sur, dat dis Montsir Orontes vil give his dauter be marrie to one certain Montsir Lubberly.

Orontes. Well.

Sbrigani. And dis Montsir Lubberly, sur, be one maun dat owe mush, ver mush, to ten or douzain marshand Flemish wish he come hidder.

Orontes. Does Squire Lubberly owe a great deal to ten or twelve merchants?

Sbrigani. Oye, sur, and eight mont ago ve have obtain one letel sentaunce oon him, and he give up to paye his creditor all dat dis Montsir Orontes give for his dauter's portiong upoon dis marriage.

Orontes. How, how, has he given up that to pay his creditors?

Sbrigani. Oye, sur, and vid one grand devotion ve all expect dis marriage.

Orontes. [*Aside.*] This information is not amiss. I wish you a good morning.

Sbrigani. Me taunk you, sur, for de grand faveur.

Orontes. Your most humble servant.

Sbrigani. Me, sur, be more den ver mush obligee for the gudde news vish you me give. [*He takes off his beard, and pulls off the Flemish habit which was over his own.*] This doesn't go wrong at all. Let's have done with our Flemish dress to think of other measures, and endeavour to sow such discord and suspicion between the father-in-law and son-in-law as shall break off the intended match. They are both equally qualified to swallow the bait that's thrown out to 'em; and amongst us sharpers of the first class, it's merely a diversion, when we find game so easy to be caught as this.

Scene IV

Squire Lubberly, Sbrigani.

Squire Lubberly. [*Thinking himself alone.*]

Piglia-lo sù, piglia-lo sù,
Signor Monsu——

What the devil is that? [*Seeing Sbrigani.*] Oh!

Sbrigani. What's the matter, sir? What ails you?

Squire Lubberly. Everything I see, methinks, is a clyster.

Sbrigani. Why so?

Squire Lubberly. Don't you know what has befallen me at that house which you conducted me to the door of?

Sbrigani. No, really; what was it?

Squire Lubberly. I thought to have been regaled there in a proper manner.

Sbrigani. Well.

Squire Lubberly. I leave you in his hands, sir. Doctors dressed in black. In a chair. Feel the pulse. Since so it is. He is mad. Two great jolterheads. Swingeing hats. *Buon dì, buon dì.* Six merry-andrews. Ta, ra, ta, ta. Ta, ra, ta, ta. *Allegramente, Monsu Lubberly.* Apothecary. Clyster. Take it, sir, take it, take it. It is gentle, gentle, gentle. 'Tis to scour, to scour, to scour. *Piglia-lo sù, Signor Monsu, piglia-lo, piglia-lo, piglia-lo sù.* I never was so surfeited with impertinence in all my life.

Sbrigani. What does all that mean?

Squire Lubberly. It means that the man there with his mighty fondness is a deceitful rascal, who put me in a house to make a fool o' me, and play me a trick.

Sbrigani. Is that possible?

Squire Lubberly. Certainly. There were a dozen devils at my heels, and I had all the difficulty in the world to escape out of their clutches.

Sbrigani. Do but see. How deceitful are people's looks! I imagined him to be your most affectionate friend. 'Tis a wonder to me how 'tis possible such impostors should be in the world.

Squire Lubberly. Don't I stink of a clyster? Prithee smell.

Sbrigani. Faugh! here's something a little like it.

Squire Lubberly. My smelling and imagination are quite full of it, and methinks I see continually a dozen clyster-pipes levelled at me.

Sbrigani. What a grievous piece of villainy was there! and how treacherous and wicked people are!

Squire Lubberly. Pray tell me where Mr. Orontes lives; I should be glad to go thither immediately.

Sbrigani. So, so, you're of an amorous constitution then; and have heard that Mr. Orontes has a daughter——

Squire Lubberly. Ay, I'm come to marry her.

Sbrigani. To —— to marry her?

Squire Lubberly. Ay.

Sbrigani. In wedlock?

Squire Lubberly. How else can it be?

Sbrigani. Oh! 'tis another thing, I beg your pardon.

Squire Lubberly. What d'ye mean by that?

Sbrigani. Nothing.

Squire Lubberly. But pray.

Sbrigani. Nothing, I tell ye. I spoke a little too hastily.

Squire Lubberly. I desire you to tell me what the secret is.

Sbrigani. No, 'tis not necessary.

Squire Lubberly. Pray now.

Sbrigani. No, I beg you to excuse me there.

Squire Lubberly. What, are not you my friend?

Sbrigani. Ay marry, nobody can be more so.

Squire Lubberly. You should hide nothing from me then.

Sbrigani. 'Tis a thing wherein one's neighbour's interest is concerned.

Squire Lubberly. That I may oblige you to open your heart to me, here's a small ring I desire you to keep for my sake.

Sbrigani. Let me consider a little, if I can in conscience do it. [*After going a little way off from Squire Lubberly.*] Here's a man that pursues his own interest, that endeavours to provide for his daughter as advantageously as possible; and one must do harm to nobody. These things are indeed no secret, but I shall go discover 'em to a man that does not know 'em, and 'tis forbidden to speak evil of one's neighbour; that's true. But, on the other side, here's a stranger they would impose upon, who comes in an honest manner to marry a woman he knows nothing of, and whom he has never seen. An open-hearted gentleman, for whom I feel an inclination, who does me the honour to reckon me his friend, puts a confidence in me, and presents me a ring to keep for his sake. [*To Squire Lubberly.*] Well, I find I may tell you matters without wounding my conscience; but let's endeavour to tell 'em you in the gentlest way that's possible, and spare people the most we can. To acquaint you that this woman leads an infamous life would be a little too harsh; let's therefore seek some milder terms to express our meaning. The word sparkish does not come up to it; that of a complete coquette seems to me proper for our purpose, and I may make use of it to tell you honestly what she is.

Squire Lubberly. Would they take me then for a tom-noodle?

Sbrigani. Perhaps at the bottom there's not so much harm in it as everybody believes. There are people too, after all, who set themselves above these kinds of things, and don't fancy that their honour depends——

Squire Lubberly. I'm your servant for that, I'll not put such an hat as this upon my head, for the family of the Lubberlys love to show their faces.

Sbrigani. There's the father.

Squire Lubberly. That old fellow there?

Sbrigani. Yes. I'll withdraw.

Scene V

Orontes, Squire Lubberly.

Squire Lubberly. Good-morrow, sir, good-morrow.

Orontes. Servant, sir, servant.

Squire Lubberly. You are Mr. Orontes, aren't you?

Orontes. Yes.

Squire Lubberly. And I'm Squire Lubberly.

Orontes. Well and good.

Squire Lubberly. Do you believe, Mr. Orontes, that the people of Limoges are fools?

Orontes. Do you believe, Squire Lubberly, that the people of Paris are asses?

Squire Lubberly. Do you imagine, Mr. Orontes, that such a man as I am pining to death for a wife?

Orontes. Do you imagine, Squire Lubberly, that such a girl as my daughter is pining to death for a husband?

Scene VI

Julia, Orontes, Squire Lubberly.

Julia. I was told, father, that Squire Lubberly is come. O, to be sure that's he, for my heart tells me so. How handsome he is! What a fine air! And how pleased I am to have such a husband! Give me leave to embrace him and give him a proof——

Orontes. Softly, daughter, softly.

Squire Lubberly. [*Aside.*] Udsbud! how sparkish she is! how presently she takes fire!

Orontes. I'd be glad to know, Squire Lubberly, for what reason you come——

Julia. [*Comes near to Squire Lubberly, looks upon him with a languishing air, and is for taking him by the hand.*] How happy I am to see you! and how I burn with impatience——

Orontes. Heh! daughter, get ye gone, I tell ye.

Squire Lubberly. [*Aside.*] Hoh, hoh! What a coming wench!

Orontes. I'd be glad, I say, to know for what reason (if you please) you have the assurance to——

[*Julia continues the same action.*

Squire Lubberly. [*Aside.*] Od's my life!

Orontes. [*To Julia.*] Again! What's the meaning o' that?

Julia. Wouldn't you have me be fond of the husband you have chosen for me?

Orontes. No. Get ye in again.

Julia. Let me look on him.

Orontes. Go in, I tell ye.

Julia. I would stay here, if you please.

Orontes. I won't suffer it. If you don't go in this instant, I——

Julia. Well, I'm going in.

Orontes. My daughter's a fool, and doesn't understand how matters go.

Squire Lubberly. [*Aside.*] How she's delighted with me!

Orontes. [*To Julia.*] Won't you be gone?

Julia. When is it then that you will marry me to the gentleman?

Orontes. Never, you are not for him.

Julia. I will have him, so I will, since you promised him to me.

Orontes. If I promised him to you, I unpromise him to you again.

Squire Lubberly. [*Aside.*] She would fain lay hold o' me.

Julia. Do what you can we'll be married together, in spite of all the world.

Orontes. I shall prevent you both, I assure you. Bless me! what frenzy possesses her.

SCENE VII

Orontes, Squire Lubberly.

Squire Lubberly. S'bud, father-in-law that was-to-be, don't give yourself so much trouble. Nobody intends to run away with your daughter, and your grimaces won't take at all.

Orontes. All yours will have no great effect.

Squire Lubberly. Did you take it in your head that Leonard Lubberly was a man to buy a pig in a poke? and that he had not a bit of judgment in him to inform himself how the world goes, and see, in marrying, whether his honour was well secured?

Orontes. I can't tell what that means; but did you take it in your head, that a man of sixty-three has so few brains, and so little consideration for his daughter, as to marry her to a man that has you know what, and who was put into a doctor's house to be taken care of?

Squire Lubberly. That's a trick was put upon me, and I ail nothing.

Orontes. The doctor told it me himself.

Squire Lubberly. The doctor lied. I'm a gentleman, and I'll meet him sword in hand.

Orontes. I know what I should believe, and you shan't impose upon me in this matter, any more than about the debts which you are bound to pay upon my daughter's marriage.

Squire Lubberly. What debts?

Orontes. Shamming it here is to no purpose; for I've seen the Flemish merchant, who with other creditors obtained a decree against you six months ago.

Squire Lubberly. What Flemish merchant? What creditors? What decree obtained against me?

Orontes. You very well know what I mean.

SCENE VIII

Lucetta, Orontes, Squire Lubberly.

Lucetta. [*Counterfeiting a woman of Languedoc.*] Aw! thoo eart thare, and at last I ha' faund thee after sic muckle tramping. Caunst thoo, thoo wretch, caunst thoo endure thae sight o' mae?

Squire Lubberly. What would the woman have?

Lucetta. Whot would I ha', roscul! dust thoo mack as thoof hoot didst na knaw mae? dust thoo na blush, impudance as

thoo art, dust thoo na blush ta see mae? [*To Orontes.*] I wa
tald, measter, thot he wud morry ye'r dater; bout I assuer
yow thot I om hes weef, and thot seaven yeers peast, measter,
cooming ta Pézénas, he hod thae deevilish skill ta gaen ma
heert by hes flautterings, and faund thae certane way o' farcing
mae ta morry 'en.

Orontes. Alack! alack!

Squire Lubberly. What the devil is this?

Lucetta. Thae faulse loon gang'd awa frae mae thrae yeer
aufter, upo' pretaunce o' som motter that he mun ga do in hes
ain contry; and frae that teem I ha' hear na tedings of 'on;
bout whan I hod thae least thought aubout it, I wa tald thot
he wa coom ta thilk tawn, ta morry ane other yoong lass, hes
kinsfolk ha' proveded for hem, na heeding hes furst morriage.
Wharfour lefing a', I speeded ta thic place, wi' a' heast, ta
forefend thilk unlofu' morriage, and shaume afore a' thae woorld
thae fouest o' monkind.

Squire Lubberly. What amazing impudence!

Lucetta. Impudance, be na thoo ashaumed ta wroong mae?
dun na thae secreet gripings o' thy ain conshiance confoound
thee?

Squire Lubberly. Am I your husband?

Lucetta. Roscul, daurest thoo seay thae coontrary? thoo
kennest ta me farrow thot thoo beest bout too trewly sae. Wud
ta Heeven it was otherwise, and thot thoo hodst laft mae i' thot
steat o' innoceance and i' thot traunquillity of meind wic a'
tha chaurms and tha dilusions ha' unhoppily bereaved me o'.
Thon I shu' na maek thic ruefu' figure I neow do, ta see a crueel
husbond flout a' me foondness four him, and wi'out ane pitty
leef mae ta thae mortel greefings thot hes unfaithfu' doings
maek mae feel.

Orontes. I cannot forbear weeping. [*To Squire Lubberly.*]
Go, you're a wicked man.

Squire Lubberly. I know nothing of all this.

Scene IX

Nerina, Lucetta, Orontes, Squire Lubberly.

Nerina. [*Counterfeiting a woman of Picardy.*] Ho, hur con
no hould oot longer: hur pe quite chockt. Hoh roogg! hur hove
led hur a fine daunce, put now hur shon no eskcap her. [*To
Orontes.*] Justish! justish! hur wull poot a hindurmont to this

marriage. It be hur hosbon, sur, and her wull hong this hong-doog.

Squire Lubberly. Another!

Orontes. [*Aside.*] What a devil of a fellow is this?

Lucetta. And wat wud yow ha' wi' ye'r hindurmont and ye'r honging? i' thic mon ye'r husbond?

Nerina. Oye meistress, and hur pe his wiffe.

Lucetta. Thot i' na trew; I am hes weef; and 'gin he mun be hong, it be I mun hong 'en.

Nerina. Hur con no teel wot hur gabble?

Lucetta. I tall ye that I om hes weef.

Nerina. His wiffe?

Lucetta. Yees.

Nerina. Hur teel hur agin, it pe hur whoo pe soo.

Lucetta. And I assuer ye thot I om sae.

Nerina. Hur hos peen marridd to her foor years.

Lucetta. And I ha' bin hes weef thic seaven yeer.

Nerina. Hur hos witnesses oof aul hur sayes.

Lucetta. A' my contry knaws it.

Nerina. Hur toown con testifee it.

Lucetta. A' Pézénas rong o' our bridal.

Nerina. Aul Soint Quentin flock'd to hur wadding.

Lucetta. Nathing is sae trew.

Nerina. Nothung con pe mo certain.

Lucetta. [*To Squire Lubberly.*] Daurest thoo seay thae coontrary, villain?

Nerina. [*To Squire Lubberly.*] Con hur deny it to hur, roogg?

Squire Lubberly. One is as true as t'other.

Lucetta. Faw-shaumless-theef! Wreech! du' na ye remomber poor Feanny and poor Jeanny thae fruits o' our morriage?

Nerina. Donno pe zo brazen. Wo't, con hur forgget hur poorr shild, her littel Moggy, which hur leaft hur forr a tocken of hur faith?

Squire Lubberly. A couple of impudent jades!

Lucetta. Coom Feanny, coom Jeanny, coom Patie, coom Peggy, coom show an unnatural feether hes cruelty ta hes bairns.

Nerina. Cume hur shild Moggy, cume maak your vather aushame of his impeudance.

Scene X

Orontes, Squire Lubberly, Lucetta, Nerina, Several Children.

Jeanny, Feanny, Moggy. O papa! papa! papa!

Squire Lubberly. Devil take the little whore's birds!

Lucetta. Be na ye i' thae utmost confusion, villain, to tourn awae a' yer bairns, and ta shuut yer ears ta feetherly affection? Ye shu'na escape mae, roscul; I'll fallo ye ilka whare, and ding yer crime i' yer teeth, 'till I ha' me revenge, till I have ye punished; rogue! I wull ha' ye punished.

Nerina. Donno hur plush for zaying zo, and forr hur peing unsensible off the embrasses off the poor shild? Hur shonno get out off her honds. And forr aul hur flouts, her wull maak it known that hur pe hur wiffe, and hur wull hove hur hong.

The Children. Papa! papa! papa!

Squire Lubberly. Help, help! Where shall I run? I can bear no more of it.

Orontes. Go, you'll do right to have him punished; he deserves to be hanged.

Scene XI

Sbrigani. [*Alone.*] Everything is under my eye, and hitherto all goes right. We shall so weary out our country chap, that he'll knock off, i'faith.

Scene XII

Squire Lubberly, Sbrigani.

Squire Lubberly. Oh! I'm murdered! What vexation! What a confounded city! Assassinated on all sides.

Sbrigani. What's the matter, sir? has anything befallen you?

Squire Lubberly. Yes. It rains clysters and women in this country.

Sbrigani. How so?

Squire Lubberly. A couple of jabbering jades are come to accuse me of being married to both of 'em, and threaten me with justice.

Sbrigani. That's a plaguy affair, for in this country justice is as rigorous as the devil against that sort of crime.

Squire Lubberly. Ay; but though there should be an information, citation, decree and judgment obtained by surprise, default and contumacy, I've a way by disputing the jurisdiction of the court, to gain time, and bring about the means of invalidating the prosecution.

Sbrigani. Why this is talking of it in all the terms. And 'tis plain that you're of the profession, sir.

Squire Lubberly. I? Not at all; I, I am a gentleman.

Sbrigani. Certainly, to talk thus, you must have studied the practice.

Squire Lubberly. No, it's nothing but common sense, which makes me conclude I shall always be admitted to justify myself by facts, and that I cannot be condemned upon a simple accusation, without a re-examination and a confrontation with the parties.

Sbrigani. This is nicer still.

Squire Lubberly. These words come from me without my knowledge.

Sbrigani. Methinks the common sense of a gentleman may go so far as to conceive what is right, and the order of justice, but not to know the very terms of quibbling.

Squire Lubberly. These are some words I have remembered by reading romances.

Sbrigani. O very well.

Squire Lubberly. To show you that I understand nothing at all of the quirks of law, I beseech you to carry me to some counsellor to advise with upon my affair.

Sbrigani. I will so, and will carry you to a couple of very able men; but I warn you beforehand not to be surprised at their manner of speaking. They have contracted at the bar a certain habit of declaiming, which appears like singing, and you'll take all they say to you for music.

Squire Lubberly. What signifies it how they speak, so they tell me what I want to know?

Scene XIII

Squire Lubberly, Sbrigani, Two Counsellors, Two Attorneys, Two Bailiffs.

First Counsellor. [*Drawling out his words.*]
        In case of po-ly-ga-my,
        Hanging's what the laws decree.

Second Counsellor. [*Speaking very fast.*]
        What you've done
        Is clear and plain.

And in that case
'Tis very full
What the law says.
Consult our authors,
Legislators, and glossators;
Justinian, Papinian,
Ulpian, Tribonian,
Fernand, Rebuffe, John Imolus,
Paul Castro, Julian, Bartholus,
Jason, Alciat, and Cuja
That able man, you'll find they say:
I' th' case o' polygamy,
Hanging the laws decree.

Second Counsellor. [*Sings.*]
All people that are civilised
And well advised,
French, English, Hollanders,
Danes, Swedes, and Polanders,
Flemings, Spaniards, Portuguese,
Italians, Germans, all of these,
Herein you'll find
Are of a mind.
I' th' case o' polygamy
Hanging the laws decree.

First Counsellor. [*Sings.*]
I' th' case o' polygamy
Hanging the laws decree.
[*Squire Lubberly beats them off.*

ACT III

Scene I

Erastus, Sbrigani.

Sbrigani. Well, matters go on as we would have 'em; and as his natural parts are very poor, and his understanding the shallowest in the world, I've put him into such a terrible fright at the severity of the law in this country, and the preparations already making for his death, that he intends to fly; and to escape more easily from the people which I have told him are placed at the city gates to stop him, he's resolved to disguise himself, and the disguise he has taken is a woman's habit.

Erastus. I'd fain see him in that equipage.

Sbrigani. Take you care to complete the comedy, and whilst I'm playing my scenes with him, go you, [*Whispering him.*] you apprehend?

Erastus. Yes.

Sbrigani. And when I've placed him as I would——

[*Whispering him.*

Erastus. Very well.

Sbrigani. And when the father shall be apprised by me——

[*Whispering him again.*

Erastus. That does the best in the world.

Sbrigani. Here's our lass; away quick, that he mayn't see us together.

Scene II

Squire Lubberly (in woman's clothes), Sbrigani.

Sbrigani. For my part, I don't believe that in this condition one could ever know you, for you've an air like that of a woman o' quality.

Squire Lubberly. What amazes me is, that in this country the forms of law should not be observed.

Sbrigani. Ay, I have already told you they begin here with hanging a man, and then try him afterwards.

Squire Lubberly. That's very unjust justice.

Sbrigani. 'Tis as rigorous as the devil, particularly against these sorts of crimes.

Squire Lubberly. But when a body's innocent?

Sbrigani. No matter, they don't trouble themselves about that; and then they have in this city an intolerable hatred for the people of your country, and nothing can rejoice 'em more than to see a man of Limoges hanged.

Squire Lubberly. Why, what have the Limosins done to 'em?

Sbrigani. They are brutes, enemies to the gentility and merit of other cities. For my part, I protest I'm in a terrible fright about you; and I shall have no comfort of my life should you come to be hanged.

Squire Lubberly. 'Tis not so much the fear o' death that makes me fly, as that it is vexatious to a gentleman to be hanged; such a thing as that would injure one's titles of honour.

Sbrigani. You're in the right; they would contest with you after that the title of esquire. But be it your study, when I lead you by the hand, to walk as a woman does, and to use the language, and all the airs of a person of quality.

Squire Lubberly. Let me alone, I have seen people of fine carriage; all the matter is, I have somewhat of a beard.

Sbrigani. Your beard's nothing; there are women have as much as you. Come, let's see a little how you behave yourself. [*Squire Lubberly mimics a woman of quality.*] Good.

Squire Lubberly. Why, my cauch there. Where is my cauch? Lard, what a miserable thing it is to have such servants as these! Must I wait all day in the street, and will nabody call my cauch for me?

Sbrigani. Mighty well.

Squire Lubberly. So ho, here, cauchman, page. Little rascal! How I'll have ye lashed by and by! Page, page. Why where is this page? Can't the page be found? Will nabody call this page for me? have I na page in the warld?

Sbrigani. This is to a miracle. But one thing I observe, that hood is a little too thin, I'll fetch one that's thicker to conceal your face the better in case of any accident.

Squire Lubberly. What shall I do in the meanwhile?

Sbrigani. Stay for me here, I'll be with you in a moment. You need only walk about.

[*Squire Lubberly walks backward and forward the stage several times mimicking a woman of quality.*]

SCENE III

Squire Lubberly, Two Swiss.

First Swiss. [*Not seeing Squire Lubberly.*] Come aloong, broder, make hasht; ush both musht awoy to Teyburn to shee de execushong o' Squeer Lubberly dat ish condemn to be hong by te neack.

Second Swiss. [*Not seeing Squire Lubberly.*] Ush musht hire one window to shee dis execushong.

First Swiss. Day shay, dere be put up alreedy one greet quite new gallows, to hong dis Lubberly.

Second Swiss. By me shoul, me shall fiend one grand pleasure to shee hong dis Limosin.

First Swiss. Yesh, to shee him kick hish legs in de air befoie au de vorld.

Second Swiss. He be one pleashant roogue indeed. Day shay, he be marrie tree wife.

First Swiss. Dat be diable, tree wife to one mon; one be full enuff.

Second Swiss. [*Seeing Squire Lubberly.*] Gud morrow, maddome.

First Swiss. Vat do ye here alone?

Squire Lubberly. I stay for my attendants, gentlemen.

Second Swiss. She be pretty upo' my shoul.

Squire Lubberly. Softly, gentlemen.

First Swiss. Vill you, maddome, go and divert yourshelf at Teyburn? Ush vill show you one letel honging dat be ver pretty.

Squire Lubberly. I thank you.

Second Swiss. It be one gentlemon o' Limoges, dat vill be hong on one grand gallows.

Squire Lubberly. I have no curiosity.

First Swiss. Dis be one comical letel fubs.

Squire Lubberly. Fair and soft.

First Swiss. By me shoul, me vill go to bed vid you.

Squire Lubberly. Fie! this is going too far; such filthy language must not be used to a woman of my condition.

Second Swiss. Let her alone, it be me dat vill go to bed vid her for moi pistole.

First Swiss. Me vill not let her alone.

Second Swiss. Me vill have her myshelf.

> [*They pull him about violently.*]

First Swiss. Me vill have her.

Second Swiss. Dou lie.

First Swiss. Dou lie dyshelf.

Squire Lubberly. Help! a rape!

Scene IV

Squire Lubberly, An Officer, Two Soldiers, Two Swiss.

Officer. What's this? What violence is here? And what would ye do to the lady? Come, about your business, if you wouldn't have me put ye into prison.

First Swiss. By me shalvashon, dou sha' not have her.

Second Swiss. By me shalvashon, dou sha' not have her neider.

SCENE V

Squire Lubberly, An Officer.

Squire Lubberly. I'm obliged to you, sir, for delivering me from these insolent fellows.

Officer. Hah? here's a face that much resembles what was described to me.

Squire Lubberly. 'Tis not me, I assure you.

Officer. How, how, what's that——

Squire Lubberly. I can't tell.

Officer. Why did you talk so then?

Squire Lubberly. For nothing.

Officer. There's some meaning in what you said, and I seize you prisoner.

Squire Lubberly. O, sir, pray now!

Officer. No, no; by your appearance and your discourse you must needs be Squire Lubberly, whom we are hunting for, that has disguised himself in this manner; and you shall instantly go to prison.

Squire Lubberly. Alas!

SCENE VI

Squire Lubberly, Sbrigani, Officer, Soldiers.

Sbrigani. [*To Squire Lubberly.*] O Heaven! What does this mean?

Squire Lubberly. They know me.

Officer. Ay, that's what I am rejoiced at.

Sbrigani. [*To the Officer.*] Oh sir, for my sake? You know we have been friends a long while. I conjure you not to carry him to prison.

Officer. No, it's impossible.

Sbrigani. You're a man that will hear reason. Is there no way of adjusting this matter with a few pistoles?

Officer. [*To his soldiers.*] Stand off a little.

SCENE VII

Squire Lubberly, Sbrigani, An Officer.

Sbrigani. [*To Squire Lubberly.*] You must give him money to let you go. Do it quickly.

Squire Lubberly. [*Giving money to Sbrigani.*] O cursed town!
Sbrigani. Hold your hand, sir.
Officer. How much is there?
Sbrigani. One, two, three, four, five, six, seven, eight,
nine, ten.
Officer. No. My orders are too express.
Sbrigani. [*To the Officer who is going.*] Lord, stay. [*To
Squire Lubberly.*] Make haste, give him as much more.
Squire Lubberly. But——
Sbrigani. Make haste, I tell ye, and don't lose time. You'll
find a mighty pleasure, when you are hanged.
Squire Lubberly. [*Gives more money to Sbrigani.*] Oh!
Sbrigani. [*To the Officer.*] Here, sir.
Officer. [*To Sbrigani.*] I must run away with him then, for
there can be no safety here for me. Let me conduct him, and
don't you stir from this place.
Sbrigani. Pray take great care of him.
Officer. I promise you not to leave him till I put him in a
place of safety.
Squire Lubberly. [*To Sbrigani.*] Good-bye to ye. That's the
only honest man I've found in this city.
Sbrigani. Lose no time. I love you so much that I wish
you was far from hence already. [*Alone.*] May Heaven
conduct you. A fine bubble, i'faith! But here is——

Scene VIII

Orontes, Sbrigani.

Sbrigani. [*As if not seeing Orontes.*] Ah! what an amazing
accident! what an afflicting piece of news for a father! Poor
Orontes! how I pity thee!
Orontes. What is it? what misfortune dost thou forebode
to me?
Sbrigani. Ah! sir, that perfidious Limosin, that villain
Squire Lubberly is run away with your daughter.
Orontes. Run away with my daughter?
Sbrigani. Yes. She's become so mad for him, that she has
left you to go after him; and they say he has got a charm to
make all the women in love with him.
Orontes. Let's seek for justice immediately. A hue and
cry after 'em.

SCENE IX

Orontes, Erastus, Julia, Sbrigani.

Erastus. [*To Julia.*] Come along, you shall come in spite o' your teeth, and I'll put you in your father's hands again. Here, sir, here's your daughter whom I have taken by force from the man she was running away with; not for the love of her, but only in regard to you; for after her doing such an action as this, I ought to despise her, and cure myself absolutely of the passion I had for her.

Orontes. Ah! infamous creature as thou art!

Erastus. [*To Julia.*] What! to treat me thus, after all the marks of love that I have given you! I don't at all blame you for being obedient to the will of the gentleman your father; he is wise and judicious in what he does, and I don't complain of him at all for rejecting me for another. If he was worse than his word to me, he had his reasons for it. He was made believe that this other man is richer than I am by four or five thousand crowns; and four or five thousand crowns is a considerable sum, and what's well worth the trouble of a man's breaking his word for. But to forget in a moment all the passion I have shown for you; to let yourself be at first sight inflamed with love for a new comer, and shamefully to follow him without the consent of your father, after the crimes that were charged upon him, is what the whole world condemns, and for which my heart can't invent reproaches severe enough.

Julia. Why yes, I fell in love with him, and would follow him, since my father had chosen him for my husband. Notwithstanding what you say, he's a very honest man; and all the crimes they accuse him of are monstrous falsities.

Orontes. Hold your tongue; you're a fool, and I know better than you.

Julia. These are certainly tricks that have been played him, and perhaps 'tis he [*Pointing to Erastus.*] has contrived this artifice to give you a disgust to him.

Erastus. I! could I be capable of such a thing!

Julia. Yes, you.

Orontes. Hold your tongue, I tell ye, you're a fool.

Erastus. No, no, don't you imagine I have any desire to break off the match, or that it was my passion for you which forced me to pursue you. I have already told you 'twas only the regard I have for the gentleman your father. I could not endure that an honest man, as he is, should be exposed to the shame of all the tittle-tattle such an action as yours would occasion.

Orontes.   I'm infinitely obliged to ye, Erastus.

Erastus.   Fare you well, sir; I have had all the ardour in the world to enter into your family; and have done all that is in my power to obtain such an honour. But I have been unfortunate, and you did not judge me worthy of that honour. But that shall not prevent my retaining for you those sentiments of esteem and veneration which your person requires from me; and though I could not be your son-in-law, I shall however eternally be your servant.

Orontes.   Stay, Erastus, your behaviour touches my soul, and I give you my daughter in marriage.

Julia.   I'll have no other husband but Squire Lubberly.

Orontes.   And I'm resolved you shall have Erastus this moment. Here, your hand.

Julia.   No, I will not do it.

Orontes.   I shall give it you about your ears.

Erastus.   No, sir, no, don't use any violence towards her, I beseech you.

Orontes.   'Tis her place to obey me, and I know how to show myself master.

Erastus.   Don't you see what a love she has for that man? And would you have me possess a body which another has got the heart of.

Orontes.   'Tis some philter that he has given her; you'll see she'll change her mind before it's long. Give me your hand. Come.

Julia.   I don't——

Orontes.   What! d'ye make a noise! Come on, your hand I tell ye; ha, ha, ha!

Erastus. [*To Julia.*]   Don't believe it's for the love of you that I give you my hand; 'tis your father only that I'm in love with, and it's him I marry.

Orontes.   I'm mightily obliged to you, and I'll add ten thousand crowns to my daughter's portion. Let a notary be brought to draw the contract.

Erastus.   Whilst we wait for him, we may enjoy diversions suitable to the occasion, and fetch in those maskers whom the report of Squire Lubberly's marriage has brought hither from all parts of the city.

SCENE X

A Company of Dancers and Singers in masquerade habits.

Gipsy Woman.

>   Be gone, be gone, far hence away,
>   Sorrow, disquiet, carking care:
>   But hither come, ye pleasures gay,
>   Hither, ye laughing loves repair.
>   Let's think of nothing else but joy,
>   For pleasure is our grand employ.

Chorus of Singers.

>   Let's think of nothing else but joy,
>   For pleasure is our grand employ.

Gipsy Woman.

>   All here to follow me,
>   Uncommon ardour fires,
>   Hopeful that destiny
>   May favour your desires.
>   Love for ever, and confess
>   That's the road to happiness.

Gipsy Man.

>   Let us love till we die,
>   Does reason cry;
>   For, alas! what is living if love is away?
>   If love we can't have,
>   Let us haste to the grave;
>   Come death close our eyes, and adieu to the day.

Gipsy Man.   Riches,
Gipsy Woman.   Glory,
Gipsy Man.   Rank,
Gipsy Woman.   And power;

>   Which among mortals make such a rout,

Gipsy Man.

>   All signify nothing if love is left out.

Gipsy Woman.

>   For life without love has not one happy hour.

Both together.

>   Let's love for ever, and confess,
>   That's the road to happiness.

Chorus.

> Let's sing and dance,
> And sport and prance,
> And frolic be and jolly.

A Singer.   [*Habited like a pantaloon.*]

> For whene'er we
> To laugh agree,
> The wisest have most folly.

All together.

> Let's think of nothing else but joy,
> For pleasure is our grand employ.

GEORGE DANDIN
or THE HUSBAND DEFEATED

(A COMEDY)

GEORGE DANDIN, *or* THE HUSBAND DEFEATED, *a Comedy of Three Acts in Prose, acted at Versailles the 15th of July, 1668, and at Paris at the Theatre of the Palace-Royal the 9th of November the same year.*

Although experience has at all times shown that a disproportion in rank and fortune, and the difference of humour and education, are inexhaustible sources of discord between two persons, to whom interest on the one side, and vanity on the other, have been the motives of marrying each other; yet this is still a very common error in society, and 'tis what Molière here attempts to reform. The gross simplicity of the servants who deceived George Dandin, and the extravagant character of the country gentleman and his wife, are particulars happily inserted in this work to make that truth evident; but it would be in vain to endeavour to excuse the character of Angelica, who, without resisting her inclination for Clitander, lets her aversion to her husband appear too plainly, by giving into everything which is suggested to her in order to deceive him, or at least to make him uneasy; her proceedings which could not be entirely innocent, if we accused them of nothing but giddiness and imprudence, turned always to her advantage, by means of the expedients she found out to deliver herself from embarrassment, insomuch that people will sooner be tempted perhaps to imitate the conduct of the wife, who is always successful though always culpable, than to take example from the misfortune of the husband to avoid unsuitable matches; on which account this piece met with those that censured it, but with few critics.

ACTORS

GEORGE DANDIN, *a rich yeoman, husband of Angelica.*
ANGELICA, *wife of George Dandin, and daughter of Mr. de Sotenville.*
MR. DE SOTENVILLE, *a country gentleman, father of Angelisa.*
MRS. DE SOTENVILLE.
CLITANDER, *in love with Angelica.*
CLAUDINA, *waiting-woman to Angelica.*
LUBIN, *a countryman, servant to Clitander.*
COLIN, *George Dandin's valet.*

SCENE: *Before George Dandin's house in the country.*

ACT I

Scene I

George Dandin. Oh! what a plaguy business it is to have a gentlewoman for one's wife! and how instructive a lesson is my marriage to all yeomen that would exalt themselves above their station, and marry, as I have done, into the family of a gentleman! Gentility in itself is good; 'tis to be sure, a considerable thing; but it's attended by so many ugly circumstances, that the best way is not to meddle with it. I'm become well skilled in these affairs at my own expense, and understand what gentlefolks would be at when they take us ordinary people into their family. Our persons are little considered in the match; it's our money only that they marry; and I should have done much better, rich as I am, to have wedded some good plain country-wench, than to take a wife who thinks herself above me, is offended at bearing my name, and imagines that with all my wealth I've not paid dear enough for the honour of being her husband. George Dandin! George Dandin! Thou hast committed the most egregious folly in the world! My own house now is hateful to me, and I never enter it without finding something or other to disturb me there.

Scene II

George Dandin, Lubin.

George Dandin. [*Aside, seeing Lubin come out of his house.*] What the devil does that odd fellow there come to my house for?

Lubin. [*Aside, seeing George Dandin.*] There's a man looks at me.

George Dandin. [*Aside.*] He does not know me.

Lubin. [*Aside.*] He mistrusts something.

George Dandin. [*Aside.*] Hey-day! he'll scarce bow to me.

Lubin. [*Aside.*] I'm afraid he should tell, that he saw me come out there.

George Dandin. Good morrow to ye.

Lubin. Your servant.

George Dandin. You aren't of this place I believe.

Lubin. No, I come hither only to see the feast to-morrow.

George Dandin. But pray tell me a little, didn't you come out of yonder house?

Lubin. Hush.

George Dandin. Why so?

Lubin. Peace.

George Dandin. What's the matter?

Lubin. Not a word, you mustn't say you saw me come out there.

George Dandin. Why?

Lubin. Lack-a-day; be quiet.

George Dandin. But why?

Lubin. Softly. I'm afraid we should be heard.

George Dandin. No, no.

Lubin. Because I've been to speak with the mistress of that house, from a certain gentleman that makes love to her; but that must not be known. D'ye understand?

George Dandin. Ay.

Lubin. That's the reason. I was charged to take care that nobody might see me, and therefore pray don't say you saw me.

George Dandin. I warrant ye.

Lubin. I'm mighty glad to do things secretly, as I was ordered.

George Dandin. That's well.

Lubin. The husband, as they say, is a jealous fellow that won't let people make love to his wife, and he would make the devil to do, should it come to his ears. You take me right?

George Dandin. Very right.

Lubin. He must know nothing of all this.

George Dandin. To be sure.

Lubin. They'd fain deceive him cleverly. You understand me?

George Dandin. As well as possible.

Lubin. If you should say that you saw me come out of his house, you'd spoil the whole business. You apprehend?

George Dandin. Certainly. But what's his name that sent you thither?

Lubin. He's the Lord of our Manor; the Viscount of something—— Pox, I never remember how the deuce they pronounce that name; Mr. Cli——Clitander.

George Dandin. Is it the young courtier that dwells——

Lubin. Ay: by those trees.

George Dandin. [*Aside.*] That's the reason this fine fellow is lately come to lodge over-against me. I guessed right certainly, his neighbourhood gave me some suspicion before.

Lubin. Udszookers, he's the civilest man you ever saw. He gave me three pieces, only to tell the lady that he's in love with her, and that he mightily desires the honour of speaking to her. D'ye think I've had much trouble for so good pay? What is it to a day's work, for which I should have got but tenpence?

George Dandin. Well, have you delivered your message?

Lubin. Ay; I found one Claudina within there, who immediately understood my meaning, and got me to the speech of her mistress.

George Dandin. [*Aside.*] O jade of a maid!

Lubin. Odsbobs, that Claudina there is mighty pretty, she has gained my love, and 'twill be her own fault if we are not married.

George Dandin. But what answer did the mistress of the house return to this gentleman the courtier?

Lubin. She bid me tell him—hold, I don't know if I can remember all of it:—that she's obliged to him exceedingly for the affection he bears her, but because of her husband, who is whimsical, he must be careful that nothing of it be known, and must contrive some way for 'em to discourse together.

George Dandin. [*Aside.*] Ah! baggage of a wife!

Lubin. Odsbudikins, 'twill be comical; for the husband will mistrust nothing of the intrigue, that's good; and he'll be bamboozled with his jealousy. Isn't it so?

George Dandin. That's true.

Lubin. Good-bye to ye.——But not a word: keep the secret, that the husband mayn't know of it.

George Dandin. Ay, ay.

Lubin. For my part I'll seem as if nothing happened; I'm a sly cur, and it shan't be said that I've been meddling.

Scene III

George Dandin. [*Alone.*] Well, George Dandin, thou seest in what manner thy wife treats thee. Behold now what it is to desire marrying a gentlewoman. She fits thee every way without thy being able to revenge thyself, and gentility binds down thy hands. An equality of condition allows the husband, at least, the liberty of resentment, and if she had been a farmer's daughter, thou wouldst now be free to right thyself with a good cudgel. But thou wouldst be meddling with gentility, and wast weary of being master in thine own house. Ah! it vexes me to the very heart, and I could box myself willingly. What! to hearken impudently to the courtship of a spark, and at the same time promise him a correspondence! S'death, I won't let such an opportunity as this slip. I must go and complain immediately to her father and mother, and make them witnesses what cause of vexation and resentment their daughter gives me. But here they both come mighty luckily.

Scene IV

Mr. de Sotenville, Mrs. de Sotenville, George Dandin.

Mr. de Sotenville. What's the matter, son-in-law? You seem to me much disturbed.

George Dandin. Truly I have reason for it, and——

Mrs. de Sotenville. Laud, son-in-law, how little manners you have, not to bow to people when you come near 'em!

George Dandin. Faith, mother-in-law, 'tis because I've other things in my head, and——

Mrs. de Sotenville. Again? Is it possible, son-in-law, that you so little know what becomes you, and that there's no way of teaching you how to behave amongst persons of quality.

George Dandin. What do ye mean?

Mrs. de Sotenville. Will you never leave off that familiar word mother-in-law? Can't you use yourself to call me madam?

George Dandin. Zookers, if you call me son-in-law, methinks I may call you mother-in-law.

Mrs. de Sotenville. Much may be said against it, and the case is not the same. Be pleased to learn, it's not for you to use that word to a person of my condition; as much as you are our son-in-law, there's a wide difference between us and you, and you ought to know yourself.

Mr. de Sotenville. Enough of this, my dear, have done.

Mrs. de Sotenville. Good-lack, Mr. Sotenville, you're more indulgent than you ought to be, and don't know how to make people give you what's your due.

Mr. de Sotenville. Egad, I beg your pardon: I'm not to be taught on these occasions: I've shown by twenty vigorous actions in my life, I'm not a man that will recede one jot from my pretensions. But it's sufficient that we have given him a slight intimation. Let's know, son-in-law, what you have in your mind.

George Dandin. Then since I must speak downright, I'll tell you, Mr. de Sotenville, that I've room to——

Mr. de Sotenville. Softly, son-in-law. It's not respectful, remember, to call folks by their names, and to our superiors we should say, Sir, only.

George Dandin. Well, Mr. Sir Only, and no more Mr. de Sotenville, I must tell you that my wife gives me——

Mr. de Sotenville. Hold there——Learn likewise that you ought not to say my wife, when you speak of our daughter.

George Dandin. I'm out o' patience. What! isn't my wife my wife?

Mr. de Sotenville. Yes, son-in-law, she is your wife; but you're not allowed to call her so; you could do no more had you married one of your equals.

George Dandin. [*Aside.*] Ah! George Dandin, into what a condition hast thou brought thyself! [*Aloud.*] But, pray now, lay aside your gentility for one moment, and give me leave to speak to you now as well as I can. [*Aside.*] The devil take the tyranny of all these genealogies. [*To Mr. de Sotenville.*] I tell you then I'm dissatisfied at my marriage.

Mr. de Sotenville. Your reason, son-in-law?

Mrs. de Sotenville. What! do ye talk in this manner of a thing from whence you have reaped such great advantages?

George Dandin. And what advantages, madam, since you're thereabouts, madam? The matter has not been amiss for you; for, with your permission, your affairs had been in a sad way without me, and my money has served to stop up many a gap. But, for my part, what good have I got by it, pray now, unless it be the lengthening out my name, and receiving from you the title of Mr. Dandinière, instead of George Dandin?

Mr. de Sotenville. Son-in-law, d'ye reckon as nothing the advantage of being allied to the family of the Sotenvilles?

Mrs. de Sotenville. And to that of the Pruderies, from whence I have the honour to be descended. A family where the womb ennobles, and which by that valuable privilege will make your sons gentlemen.

George Dandin. Ay, that's good, indeed; my sons shall be gentlemen; but I shall be myself a cuckold unless care be taken of it.

Mr. de Sotenville. What d'ye mean by that, son-in-law?

George Dandin. I mean by that, that your daughter does not live as a wife ought to live, and that she does things which are contrary to honour.

Mrs. de Sotenville. Hold there. Take care what you say. My daughter is of a race too full of virtue to be inclined to do anything that honour can be wounded by; and as for the family of the Pruderies, there has not been a woman amongst 'em, thank Heaven, for more than three hundred years, that has occasioned any talk of her.

Mr. de Sotenville. Od's heart, a coquette never was in the Sotenville family; and valour is not more hereditary to the males than chastity to the females.

Mrs. de Sotenville. We had one Jacqueline Prudoterie, who would not be mistress of a duke and peer, governor of our province.

Mr. de Sotenville. And there was one Mathurina de Sotenville refused twenty thousand crowns from one of the king's favourites, that desired only the favour of speaking to her.

George Dandin. Well, but your daughter is not so difficult as that comes to: she's grown tractable since she has been with me.

Mr. de Sotenville. Explain yourself, son-in-law. We're not people that will support her in evil actions; but her mother and I shall be the foremost to do you justice.

Mrs. de Sotenville. We don't understand jesting in matters of honour, and we have brought her up with all the strictness possible.

George Dandin. All I can say to ye is, that here's a certain courtier whom you have seen, who is fond of her under my nose, and has made protestations of love to her, which she has hearkened to with a great deal of humanity.

Mrs. de Sotenville. By this light, I'd strangle her with my own hands, should the degenerate from her mother's virtue.

Mr. de Sotenville. Od's heart, I'd run my sword through both her and her gallant, should she have forfeited her honour.

George Dandin. I have told you what has passed, that I might expostulate with you; and I demand satisfaction in this affair.

Mr. de Sotenville. Don't trouble yourself at all, I'll get it you from them both; I'm a man that pushes matters home with everybody. But are you very certain of what you tell us?

George Dandin. Most certain.

Mr. de Sotenville. Take good care, however: for these are

ticklish points among gentlemen; it's not a business to make a mistake about.

George Dandin. I've said nothing, I tell you, but what is true.

Mr. de Sotenville. My dear, do you go and talk about it to your daughter, whilst I with my son-in-law discourse the man.

Mrs. de Sotenville. Is it possible, child, she should forget herself in this manner, after the prudent example which you yourself know that I have shown her.

Mr. de Sotenville. We're going to clear up the matter. Follow me, son-in-law, and give yourself no uneasiness. You shall see what mettle I am made of, when those that belong to me are meddled with.

George Dandin. This is he that's coming towards us.

Scene V

Mr. de Sotenville, Clitander, George Dandin.

Mr. de Sotenville. Sir, do you know me?

Clitander. Not that I remember, sir.

Mr. de Sotenville. I'm called Mr. de Sotenville.

Clitander. I am very glad of it.

Mr. de Sotenville. My name is known at Court, and I had the honour in my youth to distinguish myself amongst the foremost of the Arrière-Ban of Nancy.

Clitander. So much the better.

Mr. de Sotenville. My father, John Giles de Sotenville, had the glory, sir, to assist in person at the great siege of Montauban.

Clitander. I'm delighted to hear it.

Mr. de Sotenville. And I had a grandfather, Bertrand de Sotenville, who was so considerable in his time, that he was permitted to sell all his effects and go beyond sea.

Clitander. I am willing to believe it.

Mr. de Sotenville. Sir, I've been informed that you're in love with and follow a young person, who is my daughter; for whom I am interested, as well as for the man [*Pointing to George Dandin.*] you see, who has the honour to be my son-in-law.

Clitander. Who, I?

Mr. de Sotenville. Yes; and I'm mighty glad to talk with you, to learn, by your favour, the meaning of this affair.

Clitander. What a strange slander this is! Sir, who told it you?

Mr. de Sotenville. Somebody that believes he very well knows it.

Clitander. That somebody tells a lie. I'm a man of honour. D'ye think me capable of an action so base as that, sir! What! I love a young and handsome person that has the honour to be the daughter of Mr. de Sotenville! I respect you too much for that, and am too much your obedient servant. Whoever told you so, is a fool.

Mr. de Sotenville. Come on, son-in-law.

George Dandin. What?

Clitander. He's a rogue and a villain.

Mr. de Sotenville. [*To George Dandin.*] Answer him.

George Dandin. Answer him yourself.

Clitander. Did I know who it could be, I'd run him through before your face.

Mr. de Sotenville. [*To George Dandin.*] Make out the thing.

George Dandin. It is fully made out. It's true.

Clitander. Is it your son-in-law, sir, that——

Mr. de Sotenville. Yes, 'twas he himself that complained to me of it.

Clitander. Troth! he may be thankful for the advantage of belonging to you; I should teach him else to talk in this manner of such a person as I.

Scene VI

Mr. de Sotenville, Mrs. de Sotenville, Angelica, Clitander, George Dandin, Claudina.

Mrs. de Sotenville. As for the matter of that, jealousy is a wonderful thing. I bring my daughter hither to clear up the affair before all the world.

Clitander. [*To Angelica.*] Is it you then, madam, who told your husband that I'm in love with you?

Angelica. I! how could I tell him? Is it so then? Upon my word, I'd fain see you truly in love with me. Be at that sport, I beseech you, you shall find whom you speak to; it's a thing I advise you to undertake. Have recourse, by way of trial, to all the arts that lovers use. Attempt a little, as a diversion, to send me messages, write love-letters to me privately, watch the times of my husband's absence, or the time of my going abroad, to talk to me of your passion; you need only come hither, you shall be received as you ought, I promise you.

Clitander. So, so, madam, soft and fair; you've no need to give me so many instructions, or to be so much affronted. Who told you I thought of loving you?

Angelica. For my part, how can I account for the stories that were told me?

Clitander. Let 'em say what they please, but you are sensible whether or no I talked of love to you when I met you.

Angelica. You might have done it; you'd have been very welcome.

Clitander. I assure you, you have nothing to fear from me; I'm not a man that will make ladies uneasy: and I've too much respect for you and the gentlemen your relations to have the thought of being in love with you.

Mrs. de Sotenville. [*To George Dandin.*] Well, you see.

Mr. de Sotenville. Son-in-law, are you satisfied? What do ye say to this?

George Dandin. I say 'tis all an idle story. I know very well what I know; and since I must speak out, she just now received a message from him.

Angelica. I! did I receive a message?

Clitander. Did I send a message?

Angelica. Claudina?

Clitander. [*To Claudina.*] Is this true?

Claudina. By my faith, it's a strange untruth.

George Dandin. Hold your tongue, you jade as you are. I know your tricks; 'twas you brought in the messenger just now.

Claudina. Who, I?

George Dandin. Ay, you. Don't look so demurely.

Claudina. Alack! how full of wickedness is the world nowadays, to suspect me thus, me who am innocence itself!

George Dandin. Hold your tongue, impudence; you pretend to be a saint, but I've known you a long while, and you're a deceitful slut.

Claudina. [*To Angelica.*] Is it, madam, because——

George Dandin. Hold your tongue, I tell you; you may pay for your pranks dearer than the rest. For you haven't a father that's a gentleman.

Angelica. 'Tis so gross a falsehood, and what touches me so sensibly, that I scarce can have strength to answer it. 'Tis horrible to be accused by a husband, when a body has done nothing to him which one should not do. Alas! if I'm to blame, it's for treating him too well.

Claudina. Sure enough.

Angelica. All my misfortune is regarding him too much;

would to Heaven I was capable of permitting, as he talks, the addresses of somebody! I should not then have so much reason to complain. Adieu! I'll be gone, for I can't bear to be injured any more in this manner.

SCENE VII

Mr. de Sotenville, Mrs. de Sotenville, Clitander,
George Dandin, Claudina.

Mrs. de Sotenville. [*To George Dandin.*] Go, you don't deserve such a virtuous wife as you have got.

Claudina. By my faith, he deserves to have her do as he says; and was I in her place, I should be in no suspense about it. [*To Clitander.*] Yes, sir, you ought to make love to my mistress to punish him. Put yourself forward, I tell you, it will be worth your while, and I'll assist you in it, since he has already taxed me with so doing.   [*Claudina goes out.*

Mr. de Sotenville. Son-in-law, you deserve to have all this said to you; and your behaviour sets everybody against you.

Mrs. de Sotenville. Come, mind to treat a well-born gentle-woman better, and take care henceforward to make no more such blunders.

George Dandin. [*Aside.*] I'm vexed at my heart to be found fault with when I am in the right.

SCENE VIII

Mr. de Sotenville, Clitander, George Dandin.

Clitander. [*To Mr. de Sotenville.*] You see, sir, how falsely I've been accused, you're a man acquainted with the punctilios of honour, and I require satisfaction of you for the affront that has been offered me.

Mr. de Sotenville. That's reasonable; it's the right way of proceeding. Come, son-in-law, give satisfaction to this gentle-man.

George Dandin. How, satisfaction?

Mr. de Sotenville. Yes; it must be done according to the rules of honour, for having accused him wrongfully.

George Dandin. It's a thing I don't own, for my part, that I've accused him wrongfully. I know very well what I think of it.

Mr. de Sotenville. No matter; whatever you may think, he has denied it; that is satisfactory, and there's no pretence to complain of any man that disowns a thing.

George Dandin. Then, according to that, if I should find him in bed with my wife, he would clear himself by disowning it.

Mr. de Sotenville. No disputing; make your excuses to him as I instruct you.

George Dandin. I! Shall I excuse myself to him after——

Mr. de Sotenville. Come, I tell you. There's no occasion for consideration; you need not fear overdoing the matter, when you are under my direction.

George Dandin. I can't——

Mr. de Sotenville. S'heart, son-in-law, don't make me angry; I shall take his part against you. Come, suffer yourself to be governed by me.

George Dandin. [Aside.] Ah! George Dandin!

Mr. de Sotenville. Pull off your hat first, he is a gentleman, and you are not so.

George Dandin. [Aside, his hat in his hand.] It makes me mad.

Mr. de Sotenville. Repeat after me, Sir——

George Dandin. Sir——

Mr. de Sotenville. I ask your pardon—— *[Seeing George Dandin make a difficulty of obeying him.]* Ha!

George Dandin. I ask your pardon——

Mr. de Sotenville. For the ill thoughts I had of you.

George Dandin. For the ill thoughts I had of you.

Mr. de Sotenville. It was because I had not the honour to know you——

George Dandin. It was because I had not the honour to know you——

Mr. de Sotenville. And I desire you to believe——

George Dandin. And I desire you to believe——

Mr. de Sotenville. That I am your servant.

George Dandin. Would you have me be the servant of a man that wants to cuckold me?

Mr. de Sotenville. [Threatens him again.] Ha!

Clitander. Sir, 'tis sufficient.

Mr. de Sotenville. No, I'll have him go through with it, and everything shall be done according to form. That I am your servant.

George Dandin. That I am your servant.

Clitander. [To George Dandin.] Sir, I'm yours with all my heart, and shall think no more of what has passed. [*To Mr. de Sotenville.*] As for you, sir, I wish you a good morning, and am sorry for the little uneasiness you've had.

Mr. de Sotenville. I kiss your hand, and will entertain you with coursing an hare whenever you please.

Clitander. You do me too great honour.   [*Goes out.*

Mr. de Sotenville. See, son-in-law, how matters must be managed. Farewell. Be assured you're got into a family that will support you, and not suffer you to be affronted.

Scene IX

George Dandin. [*Alone.*] Ah! that I——Thou wouldst do it, thou wouldst do it, George Dandin, thou wouldst do it. Thou art fitted mighty well; thou art rightly served; thou hast exactly what thou deservest. Come, the matter now is only to disabuse her father and mother, and perhaps I may find out some way or other of succeeding in't.

ACT II

Scene I

Claudina, Lubin.

Claudina. Ay, indeed I guessed it must come from you, and that you had told it somebody who had told it again to my master.

Lubin. I'troth I didn't touch upon it, but to a man by the by, that he might not say he had seen me come out there; the people in this country must certainly be great blabs.

Claudina. Really the viscount has made a fine choice, to take you for his ambassador; he has employed a person on this occasion that is very cunning.

Lubin. Pooh, I shall be more cunning another time; and I'll be more cautious.

Claudina. Ay, ay, 'twill be high time.

Lubin. Let's talk no more of that. Hear me.

Claudina. What would you have me hear?

Lubin. Turn your face a little towards me.

Claudina. Well, what is it?

Lubin. Claudina.

Claudina. What?

Lubin. Well-a-day! doesn't thee know what I've a mind to say?

Claudina. No.

Lubin. Zooks, I love thee.

Claudina. In good earnest?

Lubin. Ay, or else the devil fetch me; you may believe me now I swear it.

Claudina Much good may it do you.

Lubin. I feel my heart quite out of sorts when I look at you.

Claudina. I'm overjoyed at it.

Lubin. What do ye do to be so pretty?

Claudina. I do like other folks.

Lubin. D'y' see, there's no need of many words to the bargain. If you've a mind, you shall be my wife, I shall be your husband, and we two shall be husband and wife.

Claudina. Maybe you'll be jealous like our master.

Lubin. No.

Claudina. For my part, I hate your suspicious husbands, and would have one that's alarmed at nothing; one so full of confidence, and so secure of my chastity, that he could see me in the midst of thirty men without being disturbed.

Lubin. Well, I shall be just so.

Claudina. It's the silliest thing in the world to mistrust a wife and torment her. The truth of the matter is, no good comes of it; it makes us think of naughty things; and husbands with their vagaries often make themselves what they are.

Lubin. Well, I'll give you leave to do everything you please.

Claudina. That's the way not to be deceived. When a husband relies on our discretion, we take no liberties but what we ought, and it happens to him as it does to those that open their purse to us, and cry, Take: we use it modestly, and are contented with what's reasonable. But those that are close-fisted towards us, oblige us to fleece 'em, and we spare 'em not at all.

Lubin. Pooh! I shall be one of those that open their purse, and you need only marry me.

Claudina. Well, well, we shall see.

Lubin. Come hither then, Claudina.

Claudina. What would you have?

Lubin. Come, I tell you.

Claudina.   O! fair and softly; I don't like your palmers.

Lubin.   Ah! a little bit of love.

Claudina.   Let me alone I tell you, I don't understand joking.

Lubin.   Claudina.

Claudina. [*Pushing Lubin away.*]   Ha!

Lubin.   Ah! how cross you are to poor folks!   Fie upon it, how rude that is to deny people!   Aren't you ashamed to be handsome and not willing to be caressed?   Oh, lud!

Claudina.   I'll give you a slap on the face.

Lubin.   O the wild creature! the savage! out upon't, faugh how cruel the slut is!

Claudina.   You take too great liberty.

Lubin.   What would it cost you to let me do it?

Claudina.   You must have patience.

Lubin.   Only one little kiss, to be abated upon our marriage.

Claudina.   I'm your humble servant for that.

Lubin.   Prithee, Claudina, be it e'er so little.

Claudina.   O! by no means, I've been caught that way already. Good-bye.   Go tell the viscount, I'll take care to deliver his letter.

Lubin.   Good-bye, pretty rudesbee.

Claudina.   That's an amorous word.

Lubin.   Good-bye, rock, flint, free-stone, and everything in the world that's hardest.

Claudina. [*Alone.*]   I'll go deliver it to my mistress——But here she is with her husband, let's get away and wait till she's alone.

Scene II

George Dandin, Angelica.

George Dandin.   No, no, one's not amused so easily, and I'm but too certain that what was told me is true.   I've better eyes than people fancy, and your rodomontades have not yet taken away my senses.

Scene III

Clitander, Angelica, George Dandin.

Clitander. [*At the farther part of the stage.*]   Ah! there she is. But the husband's with her.

George Dandin. [*Not seeing Clitander.*]   Through all your

pretences, I've found the truth of what was told me, and the
little respect you have for the tie that joins us. [*Clitander
and Angelica bow and curtsy to one another*.] Lack-a-day, let
alone your curtsies; 'tis not that kind of respect I talk of, and
you've no occasion to make your jests.

Angelica. I make my jests? Quite another thing.

George Dandin. I know your meaning, and understand——
[*Clitander and Angelica bow and curtsy again*.] What again?
Ah! no more of your jeering. I'm not ignorant that you think
me much below you because of your gentility, but the respect I
mean has nothing to do with my person. I speak of what you
owe to such sacred ties as those of wedlock. [*Angelica makes a
sign to Clitander*.] No shrugging up your shoulders, I don't
talk nonsense.

Angelica. Who dreams of shrugging up shoulders?

George Dandin. Lack-a-day, I see plainly. I tell you once
again, that marriage is an obligation which ought to have all
kind of respect shown it, and that it's very ill done of you to
use it as you do. [*Angelica makes a sign with her head*.] Ay,
indeed, ill done of you; and you needn't noddle your head and
make game of me.

Angelica. I? I don't know what you mean.

George Dandin. I know very well, and I know your contempt
of me too. Though I am not nobly born, I'm of a family however that's without reproach; and the race of the Dandins——

Clitander. [*Behind Angelica without being seen by George
Dandin*.] One moment's discourse.

George Dandin. [*Not seeing Clitander*.] Hey?

Angelica. What? I don't say a word.

[*George Dandin goes round his wife, and Clitander retires,
making a low bow to George Dandin*.]

SCENE IV

George Dandin, Angelica.

George Dandin. There's he that dangles after you.

Angelica. Well, is it my fault? what would you have me
do in it?

George Dandin. I'd have you do like a wife that desires to
please nobody but her husband. Let 'em say what they will
of it, gallants never form a siege but when they're encouraged.

There's a certain languishing air that draws 'em as honey does the flies, and modest women have a behaviour that drives 'em away immediately.

Angelica. I drive 'em away? For what reason? I am not affronted at being thought handsome, for that's a pleasure to me.

George Dandin. Ay? But what part would you have an husband act during this gallantry?

Angelica. The part of an honest man, that's glad to see his wife regarded.

George Dandin. Your servant. That's not my opinion; the Dandins haven't been accustomed to that fashion.

Angelica. O, the Dandins may accustom themselves to it, if they please. But I declare, for my part, that I don't intend to renounce the world, and bury myself alive with a husband. What? because a man takes it in his head to marry us, must we immediately have done with everything, and break off all intercourse with the living? The tyranny of these gentlemen husbands is wonderful; 'tis mighty fine of 'em, to desire we should be dead to all diversions, and only live for them. To me it's all a jest, and I'll not die so young.

George Dandin. Is it thus you perform the vows you made to me in public?

Angelica. I? I didn't make them to you voluntarily, but you forced them from me. Did you, before the wedding, ask my consent, or if I liked you? You advised about it with my father and mother only; it's they, properly speaking, that married you, and therefore you'll do well to make your complaints always to them of the wrongs that may be done you. For my part, who did not tell you that I'd marry you, and whom you took without consulting my inclinations, I don't think I'm bound to submit like a slave to your will; but will enjoy, by your leave, those happy days which youth offers me, make use of such dear liberties as the age permits, see the beau-monde a little, and indulge the pleasure of hearing fine things said to me. Prepare then for your punishment, and be thankful to Heaven that I'm incapable of doing anything that's worse.

George Dandin. Ay? Is that your way! I'm your husband, and I tell you, I don't understand this.

Angelica. As for my part, I'm your wife, and I tell you, I do understand it.

George Dandin. [*Aside.*] I've a temptation to beat that face of thine to a jelly, and make it in a condition never more to charm those complimenting sparks. Ah! come along, George Dandin, I can't command myself, and it's better for me to leave the place.

Scene V

Angelica, Claudina.

Claudina. I was out of patience, madam, till he was gone, to give you this letter from you know who.

Angelica. Let's see.

Claudina. [*Aside.*] As far as I can observe, she's not much displeased at what he writes to her.

Angelica. O! Claudina, in what a gallant manner is this letter written! what an agreeable air have people about the Court in all their words and actions! and what a difference there is between them and our folks in the country!

Claudina. I believe, after seeing them, the Dandins don't charm you much.

Angelica. Stay here, I'll go write an answer.

Claudina. [*Alone.*] I've no occasion, I suppose, to desire it may be favourable. But here he is——

Scene VI

Clitander, Lubin, Claudina.

Claudina. Really, sir, you choose there a clever messenger.

Clitander. I durst not send any of my own servants. But, dear Claudina, I must make you amends for the good offices which I know you've done me. [*He feels in his pocket.*

Claudina. Oh! sir, there's no occasion. No, sir, you need not give yourself that trouble. I do you service because you merit it, and I feel at my heart an inclination for you.

Clitander. [*Giving money to Claudina.*] I'm obliged to you.

Lubin. [*To Claudina.*] Since we're to be married, give it me, that I may put it to mine.

Claudina. I'll keep it for you as well as the kiss.

Clitander. [*To Claudina.*] Tell me, did you give my letter to your fair mistress?

Claudina. Yes; and she is gone to answer it.

Clitander. But, Claudina, is there no way for me to speak to her?

Claudina. Yes, come along with me, and I'll bring you to the speech of her.

Clitander. But will she take it well, and is there no danger in it?

Claudina. No, no, her husband isn't at home; besides, 'tis not he chiefly she has to manage, it's her father and mother; and provided they're but prepossessed, there's nothing at all to fear.

Clitander. I give up myself to your conduct.

Lubin. [*Alone.*] Odsbudikins, what a clever wife I shall have! She has the wit of four people.

Scene VII

George Dandin, Lubin.

George Dandin. [*Aside.*] Here's my man as before. Would to Heaven he could be brought to bear witness to her father and mother, of what they won't believe.

Lubin. Oh! there you are, Mr. Tittle-tattle, to whom I gave such a charge, not to speak, and who promised me so much you wouldn't. You're a blab, I find, you go and tell again what one says to you in private.

George Dandin. I?

Lubin. Ay. You've carried every word to the husband, and you are the cause of his making a clutter about it. I'm glad to know what a tongue you've got, and this shall teach me never to tell you anything more.

George Dandin. But hear me, friend.

Lubin. If you had not tattled, I'd have told you what's a-doing now; but for your punishment, you shall know nothing at all.

George Dandin. How? what's a-doing?

Lubin. Nothing, nothing. See now what you get by tattling: you shall find out no more, and so I leave your mouth to water.

George Dandin. Stay a little.

Lubin. No.

George Dandin. I'll say but one word to ye.

Lubin. No, no, forsooth; you've a mind to pump something out o' me.

George Dandin. Nay, it's not for that.

Lubin. Eh! some folly or another. I see what you would be at.

George Dandin. It's something else. Do but hear me.

Lubin. No more of the matter. You'd have me tell you that the viscount has been giving money to Claudina, and that she has carried him to her mistress. But I'm not such an ass.

George Dandin. Pray now——

Lubin. No.

George Dandin. I'll give ye——

Lubin. A fiddlestick.

Scene VIII

George Dandin. [*Alone.*] I could not make use of this idiot as I thought to do. But the fresh intelligence that has escaped him shall serve the same purpose; and if the gallant is at my house, that will be a plain case to her father and mother, and fully convince 'em of their daughter's impudence. The mischief is, I don't know how to make my advantage of this notice. If I go home, I shall drive the blade away; and whatever I to my dishonour may see myself, won't be believed, even upon my oath; but they'll say I rave. On the other side, if I fetch my father-in-law and mother-in-law, without a certainty of finding the gallant there, 'twill be the same thing, and I shall fall again into the trouble I did before. Can't I go softly and inform myself whether he's still there? [*After looking through the keyhole.*] Ah! Heaven! it's no longer doubtful. I perceived him through the keyhole! Fate gives me now an opportunity of putting 'em to confusion, and to finish the affair, it brings hither, in the nick of time, the judges that I wanted.

Scene IX

Mr. de Sotenville, Mrs. de Sotenville, George Dandin.

George Dandin. In short, you would not believe me just now, and your daughter got the better of me; but I'm at present prepared to show you how she uses me; and thank Heaven, my dishonour is now so plain, that you can't doubt on 't.

Mr. de Sotenville. How, son-in-law? are you again upon that matter?

George Dandin. Ay, I am: and I never had so much cause for 't.

Mrs. de Sotenville. D'ye still come to stun one's head?

George Dandin.   Ay, madam; for mine is served much worse.

Mr. de Sotenville.   Are not you weary of being troublesome?

George Dandin.   No.   But I'm very weary of being taken for a dupe.

Mrs. de Sotenville.   Will you never get rid of your chimeras?

George Dandin.   No, madam; but I'd fain get rid of a wife that disgraces me.

Mrs. de Sotenville.   Od's light, son-in-law, learn how you ought to speak.

Mr. de Sotenville.   S'heart, find out words less affronting than those.

George Dandin.   The loser can't laugh.

Mrs. de Sotenville.   Remember that you've married a gentle-woman.

George Dandin.   I remember it well enough, and shall remember it but too often.

Mr. de Sotenville.   Then if you remember it, think to speak of her with more respect.

George Dandin.   But why does not she think rather of treating me more decently?   What?   Because she's a gentlewoman, must she have the liberty to do by me as she pleases, and I not dare to breathe?

Mr. de Sotenville.   What is it you'd be at?   What can you say?   Did not you see this morning how she cleared herself of knowing the person you came to me to speak about?

George Dandin.   Ay.   But for your part, what could you say, should I now show you that the spark is with her?

Mrs. de Sotenville.   With her?

George Dandin.   Ay, with her, and in my house.

Mr. de Sotenville.   In your house?

George Dandin.   Ay, in my own house?

Mrs. de Sotenville.   If it's so, we shall take your part against her.

Mr. de Sotenville.   Yes.   The honour of our family is the dearest to us of all things; and if what you say be true, we shall disown her for our daughter, and abandon her to your resentment.

George Dandin.   You need only follow me.

Mrs. de Sotenville.   Take care you're not mistaken.

Mr. de Sotenville.   Don't do as you did before.

George Dandin.   Lack-a-day, come and see.   [*Pointing to Clitander who goes out with Angelica.*]   There have I told a lie?

Scene X

*Angelica, Clitander, Claudina, Mr. de Sotenville and Mrs. de
Sotenville, with George Dandin (at the farther part of the stage).*

Angelica. [*To Clitander.*] Farewell—I'm afraid you should
be found here; and I must be upon my guard.

Clitander. Then, madam, promise that I shall speak with
you at night.

Angelica. I'll endeavour it.

George Dandin. [*To Mr. and Mrs. de Sotenville.*] Let's get
behind 'em softly, and try not to be seen.

Claudina. Ah! madam, we're undone!—Here's your father
and mother, and your husband with 'em.

Clitander. [*Aside.*] O! Heaven!

Angelica. [*Aside to Clitander and Claudina.*] Take you no
notice, but leave it both of you to me. [*Aloud to Clitander.*]
What! dare you treat me in this fashion, after the late affair?
and is it thus you disguise your sentiments? I was informed
you were in love with me, and that you formed designs of making
court to me. I showed my displeasure at it, and publicly
expressed my meaning to you plain enough. You denied the
thing stoutly, and assured me you had no thought of offending
me; and yet the selfsame day have you the assurance to come
to my house and visit me? to tell me you're in love with me,
and say an hundred silly things to persuade me to answer your
extravagances? As if I was a woman that would violate the
vow I've made my husband, or ever depart from that virtue
my parents taught me. Should my father know it, he'd teach
you to attempt such enterprises; but a modest woman does not
like to make a bustle. [*Making a sign to Claudina to bring a
stick.*] I don't care to tell him of it, but will show you, though
I am a woman, that I've courage enough to revenge myself for
the affronts that are offered me. What you've done is not the
action of a gentleman, and therefore I shall not use you like a
gentleman.

> [*Angelica takes the stick, and goes to strike Clitander, who
> shifts his posture in such a manner that the blow falls
> upon George Dandin.*]

Clitander. [*Crying out as if he had been beaten.*] Oh, oh, oh,
oh, oh! gently.

SCENE XI

*Mr. de Sotenville, Mrs. de Sotenville, Angelica, George Dandin,
Claudina.*

Claudina. Hard, madam, strike to the purpose.

Angelica. [*Pretending to speak to Clitander.*] If you've anything lies at heart, I'm ready to answer it.

Claudina. Learn who it is you meddle with.

Angelica. [*Seeming astonished.*] Ah! father, are you there?

Mr. de Sotenville. Yes, daughter; and I find that in discretion and courage, thou provest thyself a worthy branch of the Sotenville family. Come hither to me that I may embrace thee.

Mrs. de Sotenville. Embrace me too, daughter. Alas! I weep for joy, and discover my own blood in what thou hast been doing.

Mr. de Sotenville. Son-in-law, how transported ought you to be, and what abundance of satisfaction must this accident afford you! You had just cause to be alarmed, but your suspicions are cleared up the most fortunately that can be.

Mrs. de Sotenville. No doubt, son-in-law, you ought now to be the most contented man alive.

Claudina. To be sure. What a wife is here! you're too happy in having her: and you ought to kiss the ground she treads on.

George Dandin. [*Aside.*] O traitress!

Mr. de Sotenville. What's the matter, son-in-law? don't you thank your wife at all for the affection you see she shows for you?

Angelica. No, no, father, that's needless. He's under no obligation to me for what he saw: all I did was for my own sake only.

Mr. de Sotenville. Whither are you going, daughter?

Angelica. I'll withdraw, father, that I may not be forced to receive his compliments.

Claudina. [*To George Dandin.*] She has reason to be angry. She's a wife that deserves to be adored, and you don't treat her as you should do.

George Dandin. [*Aside.*] Wicked jade!

SCENE XII

Mr. de Sotenville, Mrs. de Sotenville, George Dandin.

Mr. de Sotenville. It's a slight resentment for the late affair, and 'twill go over with fondling her a little. Son-in-law, adieu.

You're now in a condition to be no more uneasy. Go, be reconciled to one another, and endeavour to pacify her by excusing your passion to her.

Mrs. de Sotenville. You should consider she's a woman brought up to virtue, who hasn't been accustomed to be suspected of any base action. Adieu. I'm glad to see your uneasiness at an end, and the transports of joy which her conduct must afford you.

Scene XIII

George Dandin. [Alone.] I say not a word; for I should get nothing by speaking. Never anything was known equal to my disgrace. Indeed, I wonder at my misfortune, and the subtle contrivance of my confounded hussy of a wife to make herself seem always in the right, and me in the wrong. Is it possible that I shall always be outdone by her, that appearances will always turn against me, and that I shall ne'er be able to convict my impudent hussy? O Heaven! favour my designs, and vouchsafe to let people see that I'm dishonoured.

ACT III

Scene I

Clitander, Lubin.

Clitander. The night's pretty far gone; I'm afraid it should be too late. I can't see which way to go. Lubin?

Lubin. Sir.

Clitander. Is this the way?

Lubin. I think it is.* Odsbobs it's a silly night to be so dark as this.

Clitander. 'Tis certainly in the wrong. But if on the one hand it prevents our seeing, on the other hand it hinders our being seen.

Lubin. You are in the right. It's not so much in the wrong. I'd be glad to know, sir, you who are a scholar, why it is not day at night.

Clitander. That's a great question, and what is difficult. Thou art curious, Lubin.

Lubin. Ay, if I had studied, I should have thought of things that were never thought of.

Clitander. So I believe. Thou hast the appearance of a subtle penetrating mind.

Lubin. That's true. Hold. I can explain Latin, though I never learnt it. For the other day seeing *Collegium* written over a great gate, I guessed that it meant College.

Clitander. That's wonderful! Thou canst read then, Lubin?

Lubin. Ay, I can read print; but I never could learn to read writing.

Clitander. We're now against the house. [*After striking his hands.*] That's the signal Claudina gives me.

Lubin. O' my faith, that's a girl worth gold, and I love her with all my heart.

Clitander. And I brought you with me to talk with her.

Lubin. Sir, I am——

Clitander. Hush, I hear a noise.

SCENE II

Angelica, Claudina, Clitander, Lubin.

Angelica. Claudina.

Claudina. Well.

Angelica. Leave the door ajar.

Claudina. I have done so.

[*They search about in the dark for one another.*

Clitander. [*To Lubin.*] 'Tis they. St.

Angelica. St.

Lubin. St.

Claudina. St.

Clitander. [*To Claudina, whom he takes for Angelica.*] Madam.

Angelica. [*To Lubin, whom she takes for Clitander.*] How now?

Lubin. [*To Angelica, whom he takes for Claudina.*] Claudina?

Claudina. [*To Clitander, whom she takes for Lubin.*] Who is it?

Clitander. [*To Claudina, believing he's speaking to Angelica.*] Ah! madam, what joy I have!

Lubin. [*To Angelica, believing he's speaking to Claudina.*] Claudina, my dear Claudina.

Claudina. [*To Clitander.*] Softly, sir.

Angelica. [*To Lubin.*] Hold, Lubin.

Clitander. Is it you, Claudina?

Claudina. Yes.

Lubin. Madam, is it you?

Angelica. Ay.

Claudina. [*To Clitander.*] You took one for t'other.

Lubin. [*To Angelica.*] I'troth! Joan's as good as my lady in the dark.

Angelica. Clitander, isn't it you?

Clitander. Yes, madam.

Angelica. My husband's snoring finely, and I've taken this opportunity for us to converse here.

Clitander. Let's look some place for us to sit down.

Claudina. That's well thought of.

> [*Angelica, Clitander, and Claudina sit down at the farther part of the stage.*]

Lubin. [*Feeling about for Claudina.*] Claudina, where is it you are?

SCENE III

Angelica, Clitander and Claudina (*sit at the farther end of the stage*), *George Dandin* (*partly undressed*), *Lubin.*

George Dandin. [*Aside.*] I heard my wife go down, and hurried on my clothes to follow her. Whither can she be gone? Did she go out of doors?

Lubin. [*Still feeling about for Claudina.*] Where art thou, Claudina? [*Taking George Dandin for Claudina.*] O there you are. O' my faith, thy master's finely tricked, and I think this as comical as the beating-bout I was told of. He's now snoring like a devil, your mistress says, and little thinks the viscount and she are together whilst he naps it. I'd fain know what he's dreaming of now. It's perfectly comical. How comes it in his head to be so jealous of his wife, and want to keep her to himself? He's an impertinent fellow, and the viscount does him too great honour. You don't speak, Claudina. Come, let's follow 'em; give me your pretty little fist that I may kiss it. Ah, how sweet it is! methinks I am eating sugar-plums. [*To George Dandin, whom he takes for Claudina, and who pushes him roughly.*] Udsbud, what is it you do? That little pretty fist is woundy hard.

George Dandin. Who's there?

Lubin. Nobody.

George Dandin. He runs away, but leaves me informed of my jade's fresh treachery. Well, I must send instantly for her

father and mother, that this affair may be the means of getting
me a separation from her.   Soho! Colin, Colin.

SCENE IV

*Angelica and Clitander, with Claudina and Lubin (sit at the
    farther part of the stage), George Dandin, Colin.*

Colin. [*At the window.*]   Sir.

George Dandin.   Come down hither quickly.

Colin. [*Leaping out of the window.*]   Here I am.   Nobody can
come faster.

George Dandin.   Are you there?

Colin.   Ay, sir.

   [*Whilst George Dandin goes to speak to him on one side, Colin
      goes to the other and falls asleep.*

George Dandin. [*Turning to the side where he thinks Colin is.*]
Softly.   Speak low.   Hark ye.   Run to my father and mother-
in-law, and tell 'em I earnestly desire 'em to come hither immediately.   D'ye hear? heh? Colin? Colin?

Colin. [*From the other side wakening.*]   Sir.

George Dandin.   Where the devil are ye?

Colin.   Here.

George Dandin.   Plague on the booby for rambling from me.
[*As they hunt for one another, George Dandin crosses over to one
side, and Colin to the other side.*]   I tell ye, fly this moment to
find my father and mother-in-law, and tell 'em I conjure 'em to
come hither instantly.   D'ye understand me?   Answer; Colin,
Colin?

Colin. [*On the other side wakening.*]   Sir.

George Dandin.   This rascal will make me mad.   Come to
me, I say. [*They run against one another, and both fall.*]   O! the
rogue! he has crippled me!   Where is it you are?   Come hither
that I may drub you heartily.   I think he shuns me.

Colin.   Sure enough.

George Dandin.   Will you come?

Colin.   No, faith won't I.

George Dandin.   Come, I tell ye.

Colin.   No, you'll beat me.

George Dandin.   No indeed, I won't meddle with ye.

Colin.   Upon your word?

George Dandin. [*To Colin, whom he holds by the arm.*]   Ay,
come hither.   Right.   Happy it is for thee that I want thee.

Make haste to my father and mother-in-law, and desire them
from me to come hither as fast as they possibly can, and tell
'em it's about a matter of the utmost consequence.   And should
they make any difficulty on account of the time of night, don't
fail to press them to it, and assure 'em it's highly necessary
they should come, in whatever condition they may be.   D'ye
understand me now?

   Colin.   Ay, sir.

   George Dandin. [*Thinking himself alone.*] Get you gone
quickly, and make haste back again; for my part, I'll get into
the house and wait till——But I hear somebody.   Isn't it my
wife?   I must listen, and take advantage of this darkness.

[Standing close to the door of his house.

Scene V

Angelica, Clitander, Claudina, Lubin, George Dandin.

   Angelica. [*To Clitander.*]   Farewell, it's time to be gone.

   Clitander.   What, so soon?

   Angelica.   We've conversed enough.

   Clitander.   O! madam, can I possibly have enough of your
conversation, or find in so short a time words sufficient for my
purpose!   'Twould take me up whole days to express to you all
I feel, and I've not yet told you one half of what I have to
say to ye.

   Angelica.   We'll hear more of it another time.

   Clitander.   Alas!   With what a stroke you pierce my soul
when you talk to me of going, and under how much uneasiness
will you now leave me!

   Angelica.   We shall find means to see each other again.

   Clitander.   Ay, madam, but I consider that when you leave
me, you go to be with a husband.   That thought kills me; and
the privileges husbands have, are cruel things to a fond lover.

   Angelica.   Are you so simple to be uneasy on that score, or
d'ye imagine one can be able to love some sort of husbands?
One marries 'em, because one can't avoid it, because it depends
on parents, who have no regard for anything but riches; but
one knows how to be even with 'em, and it's a mighty jest to
value 'em more than they deserve.

   George Dandin. [*Aside.*]   These are our strumpets of wives.

   Clitander.   Ah! how readily must it be confessed, that he
they've got for you, little deserves the honour he has received,

and that the match they've made between a person like you, and such a man as he, is a thing extraordinary!

George Dandin. [*Aside.*] Poor husbands! thus it is you're served.

Clitander. You certainly deserve a quite different fate; and Heaven ne'er designed you to be a peasant's wife.

George Dandin. Would Heaven she were yours! You'd talk a different language. Let's go in; I've enough of it.

[*He goes in and shuts the door on the inside.*

SCENE VI

Angelica, Clitander, · Claudina, Lubin.

Claudina. Madam, if you've anything to say against your husband, dispatch quickly, for it's late.

Clitander. Oh! Claudina, how cruel are you!

Angelica. [*To Clitander.*] She's in the right. Let us part.

Clitander. It must be then submitted to, since you will have it so; but I conjure you to pity me at least for the wretched moments that I'm to pass.

Angelica. Adieu.

Lubin. Where are you, Claudina, that I may bid you good night?

Claudina. Go, go, I'll accept it at a distance, and return it you so too.

SCENE VII

Angelica, Claudina.

Angelica. Let's go in without making a noise.

Claudina. The door's shut.

Angelica. I've the master-key.

Claudina. Then open it softly.

Angelica. It's fastened within-side, and I don't know what we shall do.

Claudina. Call the boy, that lies there.

Angelica. Colin, Colin, Colin.

SCENE VIII

George Dandin, Angelica, Claudina.

George Dandin. [*Above at the window.*] Colin, Colin. O, I've caught you then, madam wife: you go a-caterwauling whilst

I'm asleep. I'm mighty glad of it, and to find you abroad at such an hour as this.

Angelica. Well, what great harm is there in taking the cool night-air?

George Dandin. Ay, ay. It's a rare time to take the cool air in. But it's a heat rather, Madam Jade. I know the whole intrigue between you and your spark. We've heard your gallant conversation, and the fine things you've said to one another, in praise of me. But it's my comfort, that I'm going to be revenged, and your father and mother will be now convinced of the justice of my complaints, and of your disorderly behaviour. I've sent to fetch 'em, and they'll be here in a moment.

Angelica. [*Aside.*] O Heaven!

Claudina. Madam.

George Dandin. This certainly is a stroke you did not expect. It's now my turn to triumph, and I've wherewithal to pull down your pride, and spoil your contrivances. You have till now made a jest of my complaints, cast a mist before your parents' eyes, and palliated your misdoings. I might see, or say what I would, your cunning always got the better of my veracity, and you've continually found out some way or other to appear in the right: but, at present, Heaven be thanked, matters will be made evident, and your impudence will be quite confounded.

Angelica But I beseech you let the door be opened for me.

George Dandin. No, no. You must stay the coming of those I've sent for; I'll have 'em find you abroad at this fine hour. And whilst you're expecting 'em, you may set your brains to work, if you please, for some new shift to bring you out of this scrape. Invent some means to excuse your wild pranks; find out some pretty artifice to deceive folks and appear innocent, some specious pretence of a nocturnal pilgrimage, or a friend in labour that you went to assist.

Angelica. Nay, it's not my intent to conceal anything from you. I don't pretend to vindicate myself, or deny things to you, since you're acquainted with them.

George Dandin. That's because you find all means of doing so are debarred you, and that you can't contrive any excuse for this business, but what may easily be proved false.

Angelica. Indeed I acknowledge I've done amiss, and that you've reason to complain; but I entreat the favour of you not to expose me this time to the displeasure of my parents, but let the door be opened quickly.

George Dandin. I'm your humble servant for that.

Angelica. Ah! poor dear husband! I conjure you do.

George Dandin. Ah! poor dear husband! Now I am your dear husband, because you find you're caught. I'm highly pleased at that, for you ne'er before thought fit to use such fond expressions to me.

Angelica. Hold. I assure you that I'll never give you any further occasion to be uneasy; and of me——

George Dandin. All that signifies nothing. I'll not lose the advantage of this adventure; it concerns me to have your behaviour, for once, fully discovered.

Angelica. Pray now let me speak to ye. I beg of you to hear me one moment.

George Dandin. Well, what d'ye say?

Angelica. It's true, I've been faulty, I confess it to you once more, that your resentment's just, that I took the opportunity of getting out whilst you were asleep, and that my going was upon an assignation I had made with the person you speak of. But, after all, you should forgive things of this nature, on the score of my age: the sallies of a young person who has seen nothing, and is but just entered upon the world; liberties one gives in to without thinking any harm, and which certainly at bottom have nothing of——

George Dandin. Ay, so you say, and this is one of those things that you want one piously to believe.

Angelica. I don't pretend by this that I've not been culpable towards you; I only beg of you to forget one fault, for which I sincerely ask your pardon, and to save me at this juncture from that vexation which the grating reproaches of a father and mother may give me. If you generously grant me the favour I've requested, that obliging conduct, that goodness of yours towards me, will entirely win me; 'twill thoroughly touch my heart, and produce there for you what all the power of my parents and the bands of marriage could not introduce. In short, 'twill be the cause of my renouncing all sorts of gallantry, and having no regard but for you alone. Yes, I give you my word, that for the future you shall find me the best of wives, and I'll show so much friendship, so much affection for you, that you shall be contented with it.

George Dandin. Ah! crocodile that fawns on people in order to murder 'em.

Angelica. Grant me this favour.

George Dandin. No more o' the matter. I'm inexorable.

Angelica.   Show yourself generous.

George Dandin.   No.

Angelica.   Pray do.

George Dandin.   Not at all.

Angelica.   I heartily conjure you, do.

George Dandin.   No, no, no.   I'll have 'em undeceived about you, and your shame shall appear publicly.

Angelica.   Well then, if you do drive me to despair, I forewarn you that a woman in this condition is capable of everything, and that I shall here do something for which you'll repent yourself.

George Dandin.   And, pray, what will you do?

Angelica.   My heart will give itself up even to the most desperate resolutions, and with this dagger here I'll kill myself upon the spot.

George Dandin.   Ha! ha! well and good.

Angelica.   Not so well and good for you as you imagine. All the neighbours know our quarrels, and the perpetual ill-will you bear me.   When I'm found dead, there's not a soul will doubt but that it was you who murdered me, and my parents, you may assure yourself, are not people that will let my death go unpunished, but will inflict upon you for it the severest punishment that the prosecutions of justice, and the warmth of their own resentment can afford.   By this means I shall find a way of revenging myself upon you, and I'm not the first of those that have had recourse to such kind of vengeance, that have made no difficulty of killing themselves, to destroy those that had the cruelty to drive 'em to the last extremity.

George Dandin.   I'm your humble servant for that.   People nowadays don't take it in their heads to kill themselves; that fashion's over long ago.

Angelica.   You may assure yourself of it; and if you persist in your refusal, if you don't order the door to be opened for me, I vow, that I'll show you instantly how far the resolution of one driven to despair can go.

George Dandin.   Fiddle faddle, fiddle faddle, it's only to frighten me.

Angelica.   Well, since it must be so, here's what will content us both, and prove if I'm in jest.   [*Pretending to kill herself.*] Ah! it's done.   Heaven grant my death may be revenged according to my wish, and that he who is the cause of it may meet with a just punishment for his cruelty to me!

George Dandin.   Hey-day! could she be so spiteful to kill

herself to make me be hanged?   Let's take a bit of candle and
go see.

Scene IX

Angelica, Claudina.

Angelica. [*To Claudina.*] Hist. Peace. Let's place ourselves immediately at the door, you on one side, and I on t'other.

Scene X

*Angelica and Claudina (entering the house the moment George
    Dandin comes out, and shutting the door on the inside),
    George Dandin (with a candle in his hand).*

George Dandin. Could the malice of a woman go so far as
this?   [*After looking about everywhere.*]   Here's nobody. Well,
I really suspected it.   The hussy is gone away, finding she could
gain nothing upon me, either by entreaties or threats.   So much
the better; 'twill make matters still worse o' her side, and her
father and mother, who are coming, will be the more sensible
of her guilt by it. [*Returning to the gate of his house, trying to
enter.*] Ah la! the door's shut. Soho there! somebody open
the door to me quickly.

Scene XI

Angelica and Claudina (at the window), George Dandin.

Angelica. What, is it you! Where have you been, you
rascal? Is this an hour to come home at, when the day is just
ready to appear? And is this the way of life an honest husband
ought to follow?
Claudina. Isn't it mighty pretty to go sotting the whole
night, and leave a poor young wife thus all alone at home?
George Dandin. How! you have——
Angelica. Go, go, traitor! I'm weary of your behaviour:
and without any more delay, I'll complain of it to my father
and mother.
George Dandin. What! Is it thus you dare——

SCENE XII

*Mr. de Sotenville and Mrs. de Sotenville (in their nightgowns),
Colin (carrying a lantern), Angelica and Claudina (at the
window), George Dandin.*

Angelica. [*To Mr. and Mrs. de Sotenville.*] Come hither, I
beseech you, and do me justice for the greatest insolence that
ever was, on a husband whose brain, wine and jealousy have
disordered in such a manner, that he neither knows what he
says, or does, but has sent for you himself to be witnesses of
the strangest extravagance that e'er was heard of. Here he's
come home, as you see, after making me wait the whole night
for him, and if you'll hearken to him, he'll tell you that he has
the most grievous complaints in the world to make to you of me;
that whilst he was asleep I stole from him to go a-rambling; and
a hundred other stories of the like nature which he raves about.

George Dandin. [*Aside.*] Here's a wicked jade.

Claudina. Ay, he'd fain make us believe that he was in the
house, and we were abroad; and 'tis a whim that there's no way
of getting out of his head.

Mr. de Sotenville. How! What does this mean?

Mrs. de Sotenville. Here's an outrageous piece of impudence,
to send for us!

George Dandin. Never——

Angelica. No, father, I can't bear any longer such a kind
of husband, my patience is at an end, he has been giving me
abundance of injurious words.

Mr. de Sotenville. [*To George Dandin.*] S'heart! thou art a
vile fellow.

Claudina. It's a matter of conscience to see a poor young
woman treated so, it cries to Heaven for vengeance.

George Dandin. Can one——

Mr. de Sotenville. Go, you ought to die with shame.

George Dandin. Let me only speak two words to ye.

Angelica. You need only hearken to him, he'll tell you a
fine heap of stories.

George Dandin. [*Aside.*] I'm out of all patience.

Claudina. He has drunk so much, I don't think one could
stay near him; the scent of the wine he breathes out, comes even
up to us.

George Dandin. Sir, father-in-law, I conjure you——

Mr. de Sotenville. Stand off, your breath stinks of wine.

George Dandin. Madam, I beseech you——

Mrs. de Sotenville. Fogh! don't come near me, your breath's infectious.

George Dandin. [*To Mr. de Sotenville.*] Suffer me——

Mr. de Sotenville. Stand off, I tell you, there's no bearing you.

George Dandin. [*To Mrs. de Sotenville.*] Pray now give me leave to——

Mrs. de Sotenville. Out upon it, you turn my stomach. Speak at a distance if you will.

George Dandin. Well then, I speak at a distance. I protest to you I haven't stirred out of the house, but 'twas she that went abroad.

Angelica. Isn't this what I told you?

Claudina. You see how probable this is?

Mr. de Sotenville. [*To George Dandin.*] Go, you make fools of people. Come down, daughter, and come hither.

Scene XIII

Mr. de Sotenville, Mrs. de Sotenville, George Dandin, Colin.

George Dandin. I call Heaven to witness that I was in the house, and that——

Mr. de Sotenville. Hold your tongue, it's an extravagance that is not supportable.

George Dandin. May thunder this moment strike me, if——

Mr. de Sotenville. Don't disturb our brains any more, but think of asking your wife's pardon.

George Dandin. I ask pardon!

Mr. de Sotenville. Yes, pardon, and upon the spot.

George Dandin. What! I——

Mr. de Sotenville. S'heart! if you dispute with me, I'll teach you what it is to make your sport of us.

George Dandin. Ah! George Dandin.

Scene XIV

Mr. de Sotenville, Mrs. de Sotenville, Angelica, George Dandin, Claudina, Colin.

Mr. de Sotenville. Here, come hither, daughter, that your husband may ask your pardon.

Angelica. I pardon all he has said to me? No, no, father, it's impossible to bring myself to that; and I beg you to separate me from a husband with whom I can live no longer.

Claudina. How can you refuse it?

Mr. de Sotenville. Such separations, daughter, cannot be without much scandal: you should show yourself wiser than he, and be patient this once more.

Angelica. How can one be patient after such affronts? No, father, it's what I can't consent to.

Mr. de Sotenville. It must be done, daughter, and 'tis I that command it you.

Angelica. That word stops my mouth, for you've an absolute power over me.

Claudina. What a sweet temper!

Angelica. It's vexatious to be obliged to forget such injuries; but whatever violence I do myself, it's my duty to obey you.

Claudina. Poor lamb!

Mr. de Sotenville. [*To Angelica.*] Come hither.

Angelica. All you make me do will signify just nothing, and you'll find that by to-morrow 'twill all be to do again.

Mr. de Sotenville. We'll take care about it. [*To George Dandin.*] Come, down upon your knees.

George Dandin. Upon my knees?

Mr. de Sotenville. Yes, upon your knees, and without delay.

George Dandin. [*Kneels down with the candle in his hand.*] O Heaven! [*Aside.*] [*To Mr. Sotenville.*] What must I say?

Mr. de Sotenville. Madam, I beg you to pardon me——

George Dandin. Madam, I beg you to pardon me——

Mr. de Sotenville. The extravagance I've committed——

George Dandin. The extravagance I've committed [*Aside.*] in marrying you——

Mr. de Sotenville. And I promise you to live better for the time to come.

George Dandin. And I promise you to live better for the time to come.

Mr. de Sotenville. [*To George Dandin.*] Take care you do so, and assure yourself this is the last of your impertinences we'll bear with.

Mrs. de Sotenville. Od's life! if you do thus again, we'll teach you the respect you owe your wife, and those from whom she is descended.

Mr. de Sotenville. The day begins to peep. [*To George*

Dandin.] Adieu. Get you in, and learn to be discreet. [*To Mrs. de Sotenville.*]   And for our parts, my dear, let's go away to bed.

Scene XV

George Dandin. [*Alone.*]   Ah! I give the affair quite over now, and can see no help for it. When anybody has married a wicked wife as I have done, the best method he can take, is to leap into the river head-foremost.

THE
CIT TURNED GENTLEMAN

(A COMEDY)

THE CIT TURNED GENTLEMAN, *a Comedy of Five Acts in Prose, acted
at Chambord in the month of October,* 1670, *and at Paris at the
Theatre of the Palace-Royal the* 29th *of November the same year.*

The court was not at all favourable to *The Cit Turned Gentleman*,
but ranked this piece in the number of those whose only merit
is that they make people laugh. However Louis XIV judged
better of it, and gave encouragement to the author, who was alarmed
at the ill success of the first representation. All Paris was struck
with the truth of the portrait which he had given them, and the town
soon silenced the critics; they saw in Mr. Jordan a folly common to
all men in all conditions of life, that is to say, the vanity of endeavouring to appear above what they are. This ridicule would not have
been striking in a person of too high a rank, nor would it have
appeared with grace in one of a rank too low; but to have a proper
effect in the comic scene, it was necessary that in the choice of the
character there should be a distance between his real condition and
that to which he aspired, sufficient to make the bare contrast of the
manners proper to the two conditions strongly paint out in one
single point, and in one and the same subject, the excess of the
general folly that was intended to be corrected. *The Cit Turned
Gentleman* answers this completely; for we see at the same time the
man and the character, the mask and the face placed in such an
opposition of light and shade, that we always perceive what he is
as well as what he would appear to be. The good sense of Mrs.
Jordan, the interested complaisance of Dorantes, the witty gaiety
of Nicola, the happy turn of wit in Lucilia, the noble frankness of
Cleontes, the pregnant subtlety of Coviel, and the burlesque vanity
of the different masters of arts and sciences, cast still a new light
on the character of Mr. Jordan, and he receives from everything
that's about him a new kind of ridicule which rebounds on him, and
from him, on all the conditions of life. The Turkish ceremony,
which Cleontes ought not to have been accessary to or assisting in,
passed pretty well by means of the excellence of the music, and the
singularity of the scenery.

ACTORS

Mr. JORDAN, *the Cit.*
Mrs JORDAN.
LUCILIA, *daughter to Mr. Jordan.*
CLEONTES, *in love with Lucilia.*
DORIMÈNE, *a marchioness.*
DORANTES, *a count, Dorimène's lover.*
NICOLA, *a maid-servant to Mr. Jordan.*
COVIEL, *servant to Cleontes.*
MUSIC-MASTER
MUSIC-MASTER'S SCHOLAR.
DANCING-MASTER.
FENCING-MASTER.
PHILOSOPHY-MASTER.
MASTER-TAILOR.
JOURNEYMAN-TAILOR.
TWO LACKEYS.

ACT I

SCENE I

Music-Master, a Scholar to the Music-Master (composing at a table in the middle of the stage), a Woman Singer, and Two Men Singers, a Dancing-Master and Dancers.

Music-Master. [*To the musicians.*] Here, step into this hall, and sit there till he comes.

Dancing-Master. [*To the dancers.*] And you too, on this side.

Music-Master. [*To his scholar.*] Is it done?

Scholar. Yes.

Music-Master. Let's see. . . . 'Tis mighty well.

Dancing-Master. Is it anything new?

Music-Master. Yes, 'tis an air for a serenade, which I set him to compose here, while we wait till our gentleman's awake.

Dancing-Master. May one see what it is?

Music-Master. You will hear it, with the dialogue, when he comes. He won't be long.

Dancing-Master. We have no want of business, either of us, at present.

Music-Master. 'Tis true. We have found a man here, just such a one as we both of us want. This same Mr. Jordan is a sweet income, with his visions of nobility and gallantry, which · he has got into his noddle; and it would be well for your capers and my crotchets, were all the world like him.

Dancing-Master. Not altogether so well; I wish, for his sake, that he were better skilled than he is in the things we give him.

Music-Master. It is true he understands 'em ill, but he pays for 'em well. And that's what our art has more need of at present than of anything else.

Dancing-Master. For my part, I own it to you, I regale a little upon glory. I am sensible of applause, and think it a very grievous punishment in the liberal arts, to display one's self to fools, and to expose our compositions to the barbarous judgment of the stupid. Talk no more of it, there is a pleasure in working for persons, who are capable of relishing the delicacies of an art; who know how to give a kind reception to the beauties of a work, and, by titillating approbation, regale you for your labour. Yes, the most agreeable recompense one can receive for the things one does, is to see them understood; to see 'em caressed with an applause that does you honour. There's nothing, in my opinion, which pays us better than this, for all our fatigues. And the praises of connoisseurs give an exquisite delight.

Music-Master. I grant it, and I relish them as well as you. There is nothing certainly that tickles more than the applause you speak of; but one cannot live upon this incense. Sheer praises won't make a man easy. There must be something solid mixed withal, and the best method of praising is to praise with the open hand. This indeed is one whose understanding is very shallow, who speaks of everything awry, and cross of the grain, and never applauds but in contradiction to sense. But his money sets his judgment right. He has discernment in his purse. His praises are current coin; and this ignorant cit is more worth to us, as you see, than that grand witty lord who introduced us here.

Dancing-Master. There's something of truth in what you say; but I find you lean a little too much towards the pelf. And mere interest is something so base, that an honest man should never discover an attachment to it.

Music-Master. For all that, you decently receive the money our spark gives you.

Dancing-Master. Certainly; but I don't place all my happiness in that: and I wish that, with his fortune, he had also some good taste of things.

Music-Master. I wish the same; 'tis what we both labour at as much as we can. But however he gives us the opportunity of making ourselves known in the world; and he'll pay for others, what others praise for him.

Dancing-Master. Here he comes.

SCENE II

Mr. Jordan (in a nightgown and cap), Music-Master, Dancing-Master, Scholar to the Music-Master, Violins, Musicians, Dancers, two Lackeys.

Mr. Jordan. Well, gentlemen? What have you there? will you let me see your little drollery?
Dancing-Master. How? what little drollery?

Mr. Jordan. Why the—how do you call that thing? your prologue, or dialogue of songs and dancing.

Dancing-Master. Ha, ha!

Music-Master. You see we are ready.

Mr. Jordan. I have made you wait a little; but 'tis because I am to be dressed out to-day like your people of quality; and my hosier has sent me a pair of silk-stockings, which I thought I should never have got on.

Music-Master. We are here only to wait your leisure.

Mr. Jordan. I desire you'll both stay till they have brought me my clothes, that you may see me.

Dancing-Master. As you please.

Mr. Jordan. You shall see me most exactly equipped from head to foot.

Music-Master. We don't doubt it.

Mr. Jordan. I have had this Indian thing made up for me.

Dancing-Master. 'Tis very handsome.

Mr. Jordan. My tailor tells me that people of quality go thus in a morning.

Music-Master. It fits you to a miracle.

Mr. Jordan. Why, hoh! Fellow there! both my fellows!

First Lackey. Your pleasure, sir?

Mr. Jordan. Nothing: 'Tis only to try whether you hear me readily. [*To the two masters.*] What say you of my liveries?

Dancing-Master. They are magnificent.

Mr. Jordan. [*Half-opens his gown and discovers a strait pair of breeches of scarlet velvet, and a green velvet jacket which he has on.*] Here again is a kind of dishabille to perform my exercises in a morning.

Music-Master. 'Tis gallant.

Mr. Jordan. Lackey!

First Lackey. Sir?

Mr. Jordan. T'other lackey!

Second Lackey. Sir?

Mr. Jordan. [*Taking off his gown.*] Hold my gown. [*To the music and dancing-masters.*] Do you like me so?

Dancing-Master. Mighty well; nothing can be better.

Mr. Jordan. Now for your affair a little.

Music-Master. I should be glad first to let you hear an air [*Pointing to his scholar.*] he has just composed for the serenade, which you gave me orders about. He is one of my scholars, who has an admirable talent for these sort of things.

Mr. Jordan. Yes; but that should not have been put

to a scholar to do; you were not too good for that business
yourself.

Music-Master. You must not let the name of scholar impose
upon you, sir. These sort of scholars know as much as the
greatest masters, and the air is as good as can be made. Hear
it only.

Mr. Jordan. [*To his servants.*] Give me my gown that I may
hear the better.——Stay, I believe I shall be better without
the gown.——No, give it me again, it will do better.

Musician.

> I languish night and day, nor sleeps my pain,
> Since those fair eyes imposed the rigorous chain;
> But tell me, Iris, what dire fate attends
> Your enemies, if thus you treat your friends?

Mr. Jordan. This song seems to me a little upon the dismal;
it inclines one to sleep; I should be glad you could enliven it a
little here and there.

Music-Master. 'Tis necessary, sir, that the air should be
suited to the words.

Mr. Jordan. I was taught one perfectly pretty some time
ago. Stay—um—how is it?

Dancing-Master. In good troth, I don't know.

Mr. Jordan. There's lamb in it.

Dancing-Master. Lamb?

Mr. Jordan. Yes——Hoh! [*He sings.*]

> I thought my dear Namby
> As gentle as fair-o:
> I thought my dear Namby
> As mild as a lamb-y.
> Oh dear, oh dear, oh dear-o!
> For now the sad scold, is a thousand times told,
> More fierce than a tiger or bear-o.

Isn't it pretty?

Music-Master. The prettiest in the world.

Dancing-Master. And you sing it well.

Mr. Jordan. Yet I never learnt music.

Music-Master. You ought to learn it, sir, as you do dancing.
They are two arts which have a strict connection one with
the other.

Dancing-Master. And which open the human mind to see
the beauty of things.

Mr. Jordan. What, do people of quality learn music too?

Music-Master. Yes, sir.

Mr. Jordan. I'll learn it then. But I don't know how I shall find time. For, besides the fencing-master who teaches me, I hav also got me a philosophy-master, who is to begin this morning.

Music-Master. Philosophy is something; but music, sir, music——

Dancing-Master. Music and dancing——Music and dancing, that is all that's necessary.

Music-Master. There's nothing so profitable in a state, as music.

Dancing-Master. There's nothing so necessary for men, as dancing.

Music-Master. A state cannot subsist without music.

Dancing-Master. Without dancing, a man can do nothing.

Music-Master. All the disorders, all the wars one sees in the world, happen only from not learning music.

Dancing-Master. All the disasters of mankind, all the fatal misfortunes that histories are replete with, the blunders of politicians, the miscarriages of great commanders, all this comes from want of skill in dancing.

Mr. Jordan. How so?

Music-Master. Does not war proceed from want of concord amongst men?

Mr. Jordan. That's true.

Music-Master. And if all men learnt music, would not that be a means of keeping them better in tune, and of seeing universal peace in the world?

Mr. Jordan. You're in the right.

Dancing-Master. When a man has been guilty of a defect in his conduct, be it in the affairs of his family, or in the government of the state, or in the command of an army; don't we always say, such a one has made a false step in such an affair?

Mr. Jordan. Yes, we say so.

Dancing-Master. And can making a false step proceed from anything but not knowing how to dance.

Mr. Jordan. 'Tis true, and you are both in the right.

Dancing-Master. This is to let you see the excellence and advantage of dancing and music.

Mr. Jordan. I now comprehend it.

Music-Master. Will you see each of our compositions.

Mr. Jordan. Yes

Music-Master. I have told you already that this is a slight essay which I formerly made upon the different passions that may be expressed by music.

Mr. Jordan. Very well.

Music-Master. [*To the musicians.*] Here, come forward. [*To Mr. Jordan.*] You are to imagine with yourself that they are dressed like shepherds.

Mr. Jordan. Why always shepherds? One sees nothing but such stuff everywhere.

Music-Master. When we are to introduce persons, as speaking in music, 'tis necessary to probability that we give into the pastoral way. Singing has always been appropriated to shepherds; and it is by no means natural in dialogue, that princes or citizens should sing their passions.

Mr. Jordan. Be it so, be it so. Let's see.

> *Dialogue in music between a Woman and two Men.*

Woman

> The heart that must tyrannic love obey,
> A thousand fears and cares oppress.
> Sweet are those sighs and languishments they say;
> Say what they will for me,
> Nought is so sweet as liberty.

First Man.

> Nothing so sweet as love's soft fire,
> Which can two glowing hearts inspire,
> With the same life, the same desire.
> The loveless swain no happiness can prove.
> From life take soothing love,
> All pleasure you remove.

Second Man.

> Sweet were the wanton archer's sway,
> Would all with constancy obey:
> But, cruel fate!
> No nymph is true:
> The faithless sex more worthy of our hate,
> To love should bid eternally adieu.

First Man.

> Pleasing heat!

Woman.

> Freedom blest!

Second Man.

> Fair deceit!

First Man.
>   O how I love thee!

Woman.
>   How I approve thee!

Second Man.
>   I detest!

First Man.
>   Against love's ardour quit this mortal hate.

Woman.
>   Shepherd, myself I bind here,
>   To show a faithful mate.

Second Man.
>   Alas! but where to find her?

Woman.
>   Our glory to retrieve,
>   My heart I here bestow.

Second Man.
>   But, nymph, can I believe
>   That heart no change will know?

Woman.
>   Let experience decide,
>   Who loves best of the two.

Second Man.
>   And the perjured side
>   May vengeance pursue.

All three.
>   Then let us kindle soft desire,
>   Let us fan the amorous fire.
>   Ah! how sweet it is to love,
>   When hearts united constant prove!

Mr. Jordan. Is this all?

Music-Master. Yes.

Mr. Jordan. I find 'tis very concise, and there are some little sayings in it pretty enough.

Dancing-Master. You have here, for my composition, a little essay of the finest movements, and the most beautiful attitudes with which a dance can possibly be varied.

Mr. Jordan. Are they shepherds too?

Dancing-Master. They're what you please. [*To the dancers.*] Hola!

II—*H 831

ACT II

SCENE I

Mr. Jordan, Music-Master, Dancing-Master.

Mr. Jordan. This is none of your stupid things, and these same fellows flutter it away bravely.

Music-Master. When the dance is mixed with the music, it will have a greater effect still, and you will see something gallant in the little entertainment we have prepared for you.

Mr. Jordan. That's however for by and by; and the person for whom I have ordered all this, is to do me the honour of dining with me here.

Dancing-Master. Everything's ready.

Music-Master. But in short, sir, this is not enough, 'tis necessary such a person as you, who live great, and have an inclination to things that are handsome, should have a concert of music at your house every Wednesday, or every Thursday.

Mr. Jordan. Why so? have people of quality?

Music-Master. Yes, sir.

Mr. Jordan. I'll have one then. Will it be fine?

Music-Master. Certainly. You must have three voices, a treble, a counter-tenor, and bass, which must be accompanied with a bass-viol, a theorbo-lute, and a harpsicord for the thorough-bass, with two violins to play the symphonies.

Mr. Jordan. You must add also a trumpet-marine. The trumpet-marine is an instrument that pleases me, and is very harmonious.

Music-Master. Leave us to manage matters.

Mr. Jordan. However don't forget by and by to send the musicians to sing at table.

Music-Master. You shall have everything you should have.

Mr. Jordan. But above all, let the entertainment be fine.

Music-Master. You will be pleased with it, and amongst other things, with certain minutes, you will find in it.

Mr. Jordan. Ay, the minuets are my dance; and I have a mind you should see me dance 'em. Come, master.

Dancing-Master. Your hat, sir, if you please. [*Mr. Jordan takes off his foot-boy's hat, and puts it on over his own nightcap ; upon which his master takes him by the hand, and makes him dance to a minuet-air which he sings.*] Tol, lol, lol, lol, lol, lol, Tol, lol,

lol, twice; Tol, lol, lol; tol, lol. In time, if you please, Tol, lol,
the right leg. Tol, lol, lol. Don't shake your shoulders so
much. Tol, lol, lol, lol, lol. Why, your arms are out of joint.
Tol, lol, lol, lol, lol. Hold up your head. Turn out your toes.
Tol, lol, lol. Your body erect.

Mr. Jordan. Heh?

Music-Master. Admirably well performed.

Mr. Jordan. Now I think of it, teach me how I must bow
to salute a marchioness; I shall have occasion for it by and by.

Dancing-Master. How you must bow to salute a marchioness?

Mr. Jordan. Yes, a marchioness whose name is Dorimène.

Dancing-Master. Give me your hand.

Mr. Jordan. No. You need only to do it, I shall remember
it easily.

Dancing-Master. If you would salute her with a great deal
of respect, you must first of all make a bow and fall back, then
advancing towards her, bow thrice, and at the last bow down
to her very knees.

Mr. Jordan. Do it a little. [*After the dancing-master has
made three bows.*] Right.

SCENE II

Mr. Jordan, Music-Master, Dancing-Master, Lackey.

Lackey. Sir, your fencing-master is here.

Mr. Jordan. Bid him come in that he may give me a lesson.
[*To the music and dancing-masters.*] I'd have you stay and
see me perform.

SCENE III

*Mr. Jordan, a Fencing-Master, Music-Master, Dancing-Master,
Lackey (holding two foils).*

Fencing-Master. [*Taking the two foils out of the lackey's
hand, and giving one to Mr. Jordan.*] Come, sir, your salute
Your body straight. A little bearing upon the left thigh.
Your legs not so much a straddle. Your feet both on a line.
Your wrist opposite to your hip. The point of your sword
over-against your shoulder. Your arm not quite so much
extended. Your left hand on a level with your eye. Your
left shoulder more square. Hold up your head. Your look

bold. Advance. Your body steady. Beat carte, and push carte. One, two. Recover. Again with it, your foot firm. One, two. Leap back. When you make a pass, sir, 'tis necessary your sword should disengage first, and your body make as small a mark as possible. One, two. Come, beat tierce, and push the same. Advance. Your body firm. Advance. Quit after that manner. One, two. Recover. Repeat the same. One, two. Leap back. Parry, sir, parry. [*The fencing-master gives him two or three home-thrusts, crying, Parry.*]

Mr. Jordan. Ugh!

Music-Master. You do wonders.

Fencing-Master. I have told you already; the whole secret of arms consists but in two things, in giving and not receiving. And as I showed you t'other day by demonstrative reason, it is impossible you should receive, if you know how to turn your adversary's sword from the line of your body; which depends only upon a small motion of your wrist, either inward, or outward.

Mr. Jordan. At that rate therefore, a man without any courage, is sure to kill his man, and not to be killed.

Fencing-Master. Certainly. Don't you see the demonstration of it?

Mr. Jordan. Yes.

Fencing-Master. By this one may see of what consideration such persons as we should be esteemed in a state, and how highly the science of arms excels all the other useless sciences, such as dancing, music, and——

Dancing-Master. Soft and fair, Mr. *Sa, sa.* Don't speak of dancing but with respect.

Music-Master. Pray learn to treat the excellence of music in a handsomer manner.

Fencing-Master. You're merry fellows, to pretend to compare your sciences with mine.

Music-Master. Do but see the importance of the creature!

Dancing-Master. The droll animal there, with his leathern stomacher!

Fencing-Master. My little master skipper, I shall make you skip as you should do. And you my little master scraper, I shall make you sing to some tune.

Dancing-Master. Mr. Tick-tack, I shall teach you your trade.

Mr. Jordan. [*To the dancing-master.*] Are you bewitched to quarrel with him, who understands tierce and carte, who knows how to kill a man by demonstrative reason?

Dancing-Master. I laugh at his demonstrative reason, and his tierce and his carte.

Mr. Jordan. [*To the dancing-master.*] Softly, I say.

Fencing-Master. [*To the dancing-master.*] How? Master Impertinence!

Mr. Jordan. Nay, my dear fencing-master!

Dancing-Master. [*To the fencing-master.*] How? You great dray-horse!

Mr. Jordan. Nay, my dancing-master.

Fencing-Master. If I lay my——

Mr. Jordan. [*To the fencing-master.*] Gently.

Dancing-Master. If I lay my clutches on you——

Mr. Jordan. Easily.

Fencing-Master. I shall curry you with such an air——

Mr. Jordan. [*To the fencing-master.*] For goodness' sake.

Dancing-Master. I shall drub you after such a manner——

Mr. Jordan. [*To the dancing-master.*] I beseech you.

Music-Master. Let us teach him a little how to speak.

Mr. Jordan. [*To the music-master.*] Lack-a-day, be quiet.

SCENE IV

Philosophy-Master, Mr. Jordan, Music-Master, Dancing-Master, Fencing-Master, Lackey.

Mr. Jordan. Hola, Mr. Philosopher, you are come in the nick of time with your philosophy. Come, and make peace a little amongst these people here.

Philosophy-Master. What's to do? What's the matter, gentlemen?

Mr. Jordan. They have put themselves into such a passion about the preference of their professions, as to call names, and would come to blows.

Philosophy-Master. O fie, gentlemen, what need was there of all this fury? Have you not read the learned treatise upon anger, composed by Seneca. Is there anything more base and shameful than this passion, which makes a savage beast of a man? And should not reason be master of all our commotions?

Dancing-Master. How, sir? Why he has just now been abusing us both, in despising dancing which is my employment, and music which is his profession.

Philosophy-Master. A wise man is above all foul language

that can be given him; and the grand answer one should make to all affronts, is moderation and patience.

Fencing-Master. They had both the assurance to compare their professions to mine.

Philosophy-Master. Should this disturb you? Men should not dispute about vainglory and rank; that which perfectly distinguishes one from another, is wisdom and virtue.

Dancing-Master. I maintained to him that dancing was a science, to which one cannot do sufficient honour.

Music-Master. And I, that music is one of those that all ages have revered.

Fencing-Master. And I maintained against 'em both, that the science of defence is the finest and most necessary of all sciences.

Philosophy-Master. And what becomes of philosophy then? You are all three very impertinent fellows, methinks, to speak with this arrogance before me; and impudently to give the name of science to things that one ought not to honour even with the name of art, that can't be comprised but under the name of a pitiful trade of gladiator, ballad-singer, and morris-dancer.

Fencing-Master. Out, ye dog of a philosopher.

Music-Master Hence, ye scoundrel of a pedant.

Dancing-Master. Begone, ye arrant pedagogue.

Philosophy-Master. How? Varlets as you are——

[*The philosopher falls upon them, they all three lay him on.*

Mr. Jordan. Mr. Philosopher!

Philosophy-Master. Infamous dogs! Rogues! Insolent curs!

Mr. Jordan. Mr. Philosopher!

Fencing-Master. Plague on the animal!

Mr. Jordan. Gentlemen!

Philosophy-Master. Impudent villains!

Mr. Jordan. Mr. Philosopher!

Dancing-Master. Deuce take the pack-saddled ass!

Mr. Jordan. Gentlemen!

Philosophy-Master. Profligate vermin!

Mr. Jordan. Mr. Philosopher!

Music-Master. De'el take the impertinent puppy!

Mr. Jordan. Gentlemen!

Philosophy-Master. Knaves!   Ragamuffins!   Traitors! Impostors!

Mr. Jordan. Mr. Philosopher! Gentlemen! Mr. Philosopher! Gentlemen! Mr. Philosopher!   [*They beat each other out.*

SCENE V

Mr. Jordan, Lackey.

Nay, beat your hearts out if you will, I shall neither meddle nor make with you, I shan't spoil my gown to part you. I should be a great fool to thrust myself among them, and receive some blow that might do me a mischief.

SCENE VI

Philosophy-Master, Mr. Jordan, Lackeys.

Philosophy-Master. [*Setting his band right.*] Now to our lesson.

Mr. Jordan. Ah! Sir, I'm sorry for the blows they have given you.

Philosophy-Master. 'Tis nothing at all. A philosopher knows how to receive things in a proper manner; and I'll compose a satire against 'em, in the manner of Juvenal, that shall cut 'em most gloriously. Let that pass. What have you a mind to learn?

Mr. Jordan. Everything I can, for I have all the desire in the world to be a scholar, and it vexes me that my father and mother had not made me study all the sciences, when I was young.

Philosophy-Master. 'Tis a very reasonable sentiment. *Nam, sine doctrinâ vita est quasi mortis imago.* You understand that, and are acquainted with Latin, without doubt?

Mr. Jordan. Yes; but act as if I were not acquainted with it. Explain me the meaning of that.

Philosophy-Master. The meaning of it is, that without learning, life is as it were an image of death.

Mr Jordan. That same Latin's in the right.

Philosophy-Master. Have you not some principles, some rudiments of science?

Mr. Jordan. Oh! yes, I can read and write.

Philosophy-Master. Where would you please to have us begin? Would you have me teach you logic?

Mr. Jordan. What may that same logic be?

Philosophy-Master. It's that which teaches us the three operations of the mind.

Mr. Jordan. What are those three operations of the mind?

Philosophy-Master. The first, the second, and the third. The first is to conceive well, by means of universals. The second, to judge well, by means of categories. The third, to draw the conclusion right, by means of figures: Barbara, Celarent, Darii, Ferio, Baralipton, etc.

Mr. Jordan. These words are too crabbed. This logic does not suit me by any means. Let's learn something else that's prettier.

Philosophy-Master. Will you learn morality?

Mr. Jordan. Morality?

Philosophy-Master. Yes.

Mr. Jordan. What means morality?

Philosophy-Master. It treats of happiness; teaches men to moderate their passions, and——

Mr. Jordan. No, no more of that. I'm as choleric as the devil, and there's no morality holds me; I will have my belly full of passion, whenever I have a mind to it.

Philosophy-Master. Would you learn physics?

Mr. Jordan. What is it that physics treat of?

Philosophy-Master. Physics are what explain the principles of things natural, and the properties of bodies; which discourse of the nature of elements, of metals, of minerals, of stones, of plants, and animals, and teach us the cause of all the meteors; the rainbow, *ignes fatui*, comets, lightnings, thunder, thunderbolts, rain, snow, hail, winds, and whirlwinds.

Mr. Jordan. There's too much hurly-burly in this, too much confusion.

Philosophy-Master. What would you have me teach you then?

Mr. Jordan. Teach me orthography.

Philosophy-Master. With all my heart.

Mr. Jordan. Afterwards you may teach me the almanack, to know when there's a moon, and when not.

Philosophy-Master. Be it so. To pursue this thought of yours right, and treat this matter like a philosopher, we must begin, according to the order of things, with an exact knowledge of the nature of letters, and the different manner of pronouncing them. And on this head I am to tell you, that letters are divided into vowels, called vowels because they express the voice: and into consonants, so called because they sound with the vowels, and only mark the different articulations of the voice. There are five vowels or voices, A, E, I, O, U.

Mr. Jordan. I understand all that.

Philosophy-Master.   The vowel A is formed by opening the mouth very wide, A.

Mr. Jordan.   A, A.   Yes.

Philosophy-Master.   The vowel E is formed by drawing the under-jaw a little nearer to the upper, A, E.

Mr. Jordan.   A, E.   A, E.   In troth it is.   How pretty that is!

Philosophy-Master.   And the vowel I, by bringing the jaws still nearer one to the other, and stretching the two corners of the mouth towards the ears, A, E, I.

Mr. Jordan.   A, E, I, I, I, I.   'Tis true.   Long live learning!

Philosophy-Master.   The vowel O is formed by re-opening the jaws, and drawing the lips near at the two corners, the upper and the under, O.

Mr. Jordan.   O, O.   There's nothing more just, A, E, I, O, I, O.   'Tis admirable!   I, O, I, O.

Philosophy-Master.   The opening of the mouth makes exactly a little ring, which resembles an O.

Mr. Jordan.   O, O, O.   You're right, O.   How fine a thing it is but to know something!

Philosophy-Master.   The vowel U is formed by bringing the teeth near together without entirely joining them, and pouting out both your lips, bringing them also near together without absolutely joining 'em, U.

Mr. Jordan.   U, U.   There's nothing more true, U.

Philosophy-Master.   Your two lips pout out, as if you were making faces.   Whence it comes that if you would do that to anybody, and make a jest of him, you need say nothing to him but U.

Mr. Jordan.   U, U.   It's true.   Ah! why did not I study sooner, that I might have known all this!

Philosophy-Master.   To-morrow we shall take a view of the other letters, which are the consonants.

Mr. Jordan.   Is there anything as curious in them, as in these?

Philosophy-Master.   Doubtless.   The consonant D, for example, is pronounced by clapping the tip of your tongue above the upper teeth, DE.

Mr. Jordan.   DE, DE.   'Tis so.   Oh! charming things! charming things!

Philosophy-Master.   The F, in leaning the upper teeth upon the lower lip, EF.

Mr. Jordan.   EF, EF.   'Tis truth.   Ah! father and mother o' mine, how do I owe you a grudge!

Philosophy-Master. And the R, in carrying the tip of the tongue up to the roof of your mouth; so that being grazed upon by the air which bursts out with a force, it yields to it, and returns always to the same part, making a kind of trill R, ra.

Mr. Jordan. R, r, ra. R, r, r, r, r, ra. That's true. What a clever man are you! And how have I lost time! R, r, r, ra.

Philosophy-Master. I will explain to you all these curiosities to the bottom.

Mr. Jordan. Pray do. But now, I must commit a secret to you. I'm in love with a person of great quality, and I should be glad you would help me to write something to her in a short *billet-doux*, which I'll drop at her feet.

Philosophy-Master. Very well.

Mr. Jordan. That will be very gallant, won't it?

Philosophy-Master. Without doubt. Is it verse that you would write to her?

Mr. Jordan. No, no, none of your verse.

Philosophy-Master. You would only have prose?

Mr. Jordan. No, I would neither have verse nor prose.

Philosophy-Master. It must be one or t'other.

Mr. Jordan. Why so?

Philosophy-Master. Because, sir, there's nothing to express one's self by, but prose, or verse.

Mr. Jordan. Is there nothing then but prose, or verse?

Philosophy-Master. No, sir, whatever is not prose, is verse? and whatever is not verse, is prose.

Mr. Jordan. And when one talks, what may that be then?

Philosophy-Master. Prose.

Mr. Jordan. How? When I say, Nicola, bring me my slippers, and give me my nightcap, is that prose?

Philosophy-Master. Yes, sir.

Mr. Jordan. On my conscience, I have spoken prose above these forty years, without knowing anything of the matter; and I have all the obligations in the world to you, for informing me of this. I would therefore put into a letter to her: Beautiful marchioness, your fair eyes make me die with love; but I would have this placed in a gallant manner; and have a gentle turn.

Philosophy-Master. Why, add that the fire of her eyes has reduced your heart to ashes: that you suffer for her night and day all the torments——

Mr. Jordan. No, no, no, I won't have all that——I'll have nothing but what I told you. Beautiful marchioness, your fair eyes make me die with love.

Philosophy-Master. You must by all means lengthen the thing out a little.

Mr. Jordan. No, I tell you, I'll have none but those very words in the letter: but turned in a modish way, ranged handsomely as they should be. I desire you'd show me a little, that I may see the different manners, in which one may place them.

Philosophy-Master. One may place them first of all as you said: Beautiful marchioness, your fair eyes make me die for love. Or suppose: For love die me make, beautiful marchioness, your fair eyes. Or perhaps: Your eyes fair, for love me make, beautiful marchioness, die. Or suppose: Die your fair eyes, beautiful marchioness, for love me make. Or however: Me make your eyes fair die, beautiful marchioness, for love.

Mr. Jordan. But of all these ways, which is the best?

Philosophy-Master. That which you said: Beautiful marchioness, your fair eyes make me die for love.

Mr. Jordan. Yet at the same time, I never studied it, and I made the whole of it at the first touch. I thank you with all my heart, and desire you would come in good time to-morrow.

Philosophy-Master. I shall not fail.

Scene VII

Mr. Jordan, Lackey.

Mr. Jordan. [*To his lackey.*] What? Are my clothes not come yet?

Lackey. No, sir.

Mr. Jordan. This cursed tailor makes me wait unreasonably, considering it's a day I have so much business in. I shall go mad. A quartan ague wring this villain of a tailor. D——l take the tailor. A plague choke the tailor. If I had him but here now, this detestable tailor, this dog of a tailor, this traitor of a tailor: I——

Scene VIII

Mr. Jordan, Master-Tailor, Journeyman-Tailor (bringing a suit of clothes for Mr. Jordan), Lackey.

Mr. Jordan. Oh! You're there. I was going to be in a passion with you.

Master-Tailor. I could not possibly come sooner; and I set twenty fellows to work at your clothes.

Mr. Jordan. You have sent me a pair of silk-hose so strait, that I had all the difficulty in the world to get 'em on, and there are two stitches broke in 'em.

Master-Tailor. They'll grow rather too large.

Mr. Jordan. Yes, if I break every day a loop or two. You have made me a pair of shoes too, that pinch me execrably.

Master-Tailor. Not at all, sir.

Mr. Jordan. How, not at all?

Master-Tailor. No, they don't pinch you at all.

Mr. Jordan. I tell you they do hurt me.

Master-Tailor. You fancy so.

Mr. Jordan. I fancy so, because I feel it. There's a fine reason indeed.

Master-Tailor. Hold, stay, here's one of the handsomest suits at court, and the best-matched. 'Tis a masterly work to invent a grave suit of clothes, that should not be black; and I'll give the cleverest tailor in town six trials to equal it.

Mr. Jordan. What a deuce have we here? You have put the flowers downwards.

Master-Tailor. Why, you did not tell me you would have 'em upwards.

Mr. Jordan. Was there any need to tell you of that?

Master-Tailor. Yes certainly. All the people of quality wear 'em in that way.

Mr. Jordan. Do people of quality wear the flowers downwards?

Master-Tailor. Yes, sir.

Mr. Jordan. Oh, 'tis very well then.

Master-Tailor. If you please I'll put 'em upwards.

Mr. Jordan. No, no.

Master-Tailor. You need only say the word.

Mr. Jordan. No, I tell you, you have done right. Do you think my clothes will fit me?

Master-Tailor. A pretty question! I defy a painter with his pencil to draw you anything that shall fit more exact. I have a fellow at home, who, for mounting a rhingrave, is the greatest genius in the world; another, who for the cut of a doublet, is the hero of the age.

Mr. Jordan. Are the peruke and feather as they should be?

Master-Tailor. Everything's well.

Mr. Jordan. [*Looking earnestly at the tailor's clothes.*] Ah, hah! Mr. Tailor, here's my stuff of the last suit you made for me. I know it very well.

Master-Tailor. The stuff appeared to me so handsome, that I had a mind to cut a coat out of it for myself.

Mr. Jordan. Yes, but you should not have cabbaged it out of mine.

Master-Tailor. Will you put on your clothes?

Mr. Jordan. Yes, give 'em me.

Master-Tailor. Stay; the matter must not go so. I have brought men along with me, to dress you to music; these sort of suits are put on with ceremony. Soho! come in there, you.

Scene IX

Mr. Jordan, Master-Tailor, Journeyman-Tailor, Journeymen-Tailors (dancing), Lackey.

Master-Tailor. [*To his journeymen.*] Put on this suit of the gentleman's, in the manner you do to people of quality. [*Enter four journeymen-tailors, two of which pull off his straight breeches made for his exercises, and two others his waistcoat ; then they put him on his new suit to music ; and Mr. Jordan walks amongst them to show them his clothes to see whether they fit or no.*]

Journeyman-Tailor. My dear gentleman, please to give the tailor's men something to drink.

Mr. Jordan. How do you call me?

Journeyman-Tailor. My dear gentleman.

Mr. Jordan. My dear gentleman! See what it is to dress like people of quality. You may go clothed like a cit all your days, and they'll never call you, my dear gentleman. [*Gives them something.*] Stay, there's for my dear gentleman.

Journeyman-Tailor. My lord, we are infinitely obliged to you.

Mr. Jordan. My lord! Oh, hoh! My lord! Stay, friend; my lord deserves something, My lord is none o' your petty words. Hold, there my lord gives you that.

Journeyman-Tailor. My lord, we shall go drink your grace's health.

Mr. Jordan. Your grace! oh, oh, oh! stay, don't go. Your grace, to me! [*Aside.*] I'faith if he goes as far as highness, he'll empty my purse. [*Aloud.*] Hold, there's for my grace.

Journeyman-Tailor. My lord, we most humbly thank your grace for your liberality.

Mr. Jordan. He did very well, I was going **to give him all.**

ACT III

Scene I

Mr. Jordan and his two Lackeys.

Mr. Jordan. Follow me, that I may go and show my clothes a little through the town; and especially take care, both of you, to walk immediately at my heels, that people may plainly see you belong to me.

Lackeys. Yes, sir.

Mr. Jordan. Call me Nicola, that I may give her some directions. You need not go, here she comes.

Scene II

Mr. Jordan, Nicola, Two Lackeys.

Mr. Jordan. Nicola?

Nicola. Your pleasure, sir?

Mr. Jordan. Harkee.

Nicola. [*Laughing.*] Ha, ha, ha, ha, ha.

Mr. Jordan. Who do ye laugh at?

Nicola. Ha, ha, ha, ha, ha, ha.

Mr. Jordan. What does this slut mean?

Nicola. Ha, ha, ha. How you are bedizened! Ha, ha, ha.

Mr. Jordan. How's that?

Nicola. Oh! oh! my stars! ha, ha, ha, ha, ha.

Mr. Jordan. What a jade is here! What! do ye make a jest of me?

Nicola. No, no, sir, I should be very sorry to do so. Ha, ha, ha, ha, ha, ha.

Mr. Jordan. I shall give ye a slap o' the chops, if you laugh any more.

Nicola. Sir, I cannot help it. Ha, ha, ha, ha, ha, ha.

Mr. Jordan. Won't ye have done?

Nicola. Sir, I ask your pardon; but you are so comical, that I cannot hold from laughing. Ha, ha, ha.

Mr. Jordan. Do but see the insolence!

Nicola. You are so thoroughly droll there! Ha, ha.

Mr. Jordan. I shall——

Nicola. I beg you would excuse me. Ha, ha, ha, ha.

Mr. Jordan. Hold, if you laugh again the least in the world, I protest and swear, I'll give ye such a box o' the ear, as ye never had in your life.

Nicola. Well, sir, I have done; I won't laugh any more.

Mr. Jordan. Take care you don't. You must clean out against by and by——

Nicola. Ha, ha.

Mr. Jordan. You must clean out as it should be——

Nicola. Ha, ha.

Mr. Jordan. I say, you must go clean out the hall, and——

Nicola. Ha, ha.

Mr. Jordan. Again?

Nicola. [*Tumbles down with laughing.*] Hold, sir, beat me rather, and let me laugh my belly-full, that will do me more good. Ha, ha, ha, ha.

Mr. Jordan. I shall run mad!

Nicola. For goodness' sake, sir, I beseech you let me laugh. Ha, ha, ha.

Mr. Jordan. If I take you in hand——

Nicola. Si—ir, I shall bu—urst, if I do—not laugh. Ha, ha, ha.

Mr. Jordan. But did ever anybody see such a jade as that, who insolently laughs in my face, instead of receiving my orders!

Nicola. What would you have me do, sir?

Mr. Jordan. Why, take care to get ready my house, for the company that's to come by and by.

Nicola. [*Getting up.*] Ay, i'fakins, I've no more inclination to laugh; all your company makes such a litter here, that the very word's enough to put one in an ill humour.

Mr. Jordan. What! I ought to shut my doors against all the world for your sake?

Nicola. You ought at least to shut it against certain people.

Scene III

Mrs. Jordan, Mr. Jordan, Nicola, Two Lackeys.

Mrs. Jordan. Ah, hah! Here's some new story. What means this, husband, this same equipage? D'ye despise the world, that you harness yourself out in this manner? Have you a mind to make yourself a laughing-stock wherever ye go?

Mr. Jordan. None but fools, wife, will laugh at me.

Mrs. Jordan. In truth, people have not stayed thus long to laugh, 'tis a good while ago that your ways have furnished all the world with a laugh.

Mr. Jordan. Who is that all the world, pray?

Mrs. Jordan. That all the world, is a world perfectly in the right, and much wiser than yourself. For my part, I am shocked at the life you lead. I don't know what to call our house. One would swear 'twere carnival here all the year round; and from break o' day, for fear there should be any respite, there's nothing to be heard here, but an uproar of fiddles and songsters, which disturb the whole neighbourhood.

Nicola. Madam says right. I shall never see my things set to rights again for that gang of folks that you bring to the house. They ransack every quarter of the town with their feet for dirt to bring here; and poor Frances is e'en almost slaved off her legs with scrubbing of the floors, which your pretty masters come to daub as regularly as the day comes.

Mr. Jordan. Hey-day! our maid Nicola! you have a pretty nimble tongue of your own, for a country-wench.

Mrs. Jordan. Nicola's in the right, and she has more sense than you have. I should be glad to know what you think to do with a dancing-master, at your age?

Nicola. And with a lubberly fencing-master, that comes here with his stamping to shake the whole house, and tear up all the pavement of the hall.

Mr. Jordan. Peace, our maid, and our wife.

Mrs. Jordan. What! will you learn to dance against the time you'll have no legs?

Nicola. What! have you a mind to murder somebody?

Mr. Jordan. Hold your prate, I tell you you are ignorant creatures, both of you, and don't know the advantage of all this.

Mrs. Jordan. You ought much rather to think of marrying your daughter, who is of age to be provided for.

Mr. Jordan. I shall think of marrying my daughter, when a suitable match presents itself; but I shall think too of learning the *belles sciences*.

Nicola. I've heard say further, madam, that to pin the basket, he has got him a philosophy-master to-day.

Mr. Jordan. Very well. I've a mind to have wit, and to know how to reason upon things with your genteel people.

Mrs. Jordan. Won't you go to school one of these days, and be whipped at your age?

Mr. Jordan. Why not? Would I were whipped this very

instant before all the world, so I did but know what they learn at school!

Nicola.   Yes, forsooth, that would be a mighty advantage t'ye.

Mr. Jordan.   Without doubt.

Mrs. Jordan.   This is all very necessary to the management of your house.

Mr. Jordan.   Certainly. You talk, both of you, like asses, and I'm ashamed of your ignorance. [*To Mrs. Jordan.*] For example, do you know, you, what it is you now speak?

Mrs. Jordan.   Yes, I know that what I speak is very right, and that you ought to think of living in another manner.

Mr. Jordan.   I don't talk of that. I ask you what the words are that you now speak?

Mrs. Jordan.   They are words that have a good deal of sense in them, and your conduct is by no means such.

Mr. Jordan.   I don't talk of that, I tell you. I ask you, what is that I now speak to you, which I say this very moment?

Mrs. Jordan.   Mere stuff.

Mr. Jordan.   Pshaw, no, 'tis not that. That which we both of us say, the language we speak this instant?

Mrs. Jordan.   Well?

Mr. Jordan.   How is it called?

Mrs. Jordan.   'Tis called just what you please to call it.

Mr. Jordan.   'Tis prose, you ignorant creature.

Mrs. Jordan.   Prose?

Mr. Jordan.   Yes, prose. Whatever is prose, is not verse; and whatever is not verse, is prose. Now, see what it is to study. And you, [*To Nicola.*] do you know very well how you must do to say U?

Nicola.   How?

Mr. Jordan.   Yes. What is it you do when you say U?

Nicola.   What?

Mr. Jordan.   Say U a little, to try.

Nicola.   Well, U.

Mr. Jordan.   What is it you do?

Nicola.   I say U.

Mr. Jordan.   Yes, but when you say U, what is it you do?

Nicola.   I do as you bid me.

Mr. Jordan.   O! what a strange thing it is to have to do with brutes! You pout out your lips, and bring your under-jaw to your upper, U, d'ye see? I make a mouth, U.

Nicola.   Yes, that's fine.

Mrs. Jordan. 'Tis admirable!

Mr. Jordan. 'Tis quite another thing, had but you seen O, and DE, DE, and EF, EF.

Mrs. Jordan. What is all this ridiculous stuff?

Nicola. What are we the better for all this?

Mr. Jordan. It makes one mad, to see these ignorant women.

Mrs. Jordan. Go, go, you should send all these folks apacking with their silly stuff.

Nicola. And especially that great lubberly fencing-master, who fills all my house with dust.

Mr. Jordan. Hey-day! This fencing-master sticks strangely in thy stomach. I'll let thee see thy impertinence presently. [*He orders the foils to be brought, and gives one to Nicola.*] Stay, reason demonstrative, the line of the body. When they push in carte one need only do so; and when they push in tierce one need only do so. This is the way never to be killed; and is not that clever to be upon sure grounds, when one has an encounter with anybody? There, push at me a little, to try.

Nicola. Well, how? [*Nicola gives him several thrusts.*]

Mr. Jordan. Gently! Hold! Oh! Softly; deuce take the hussy.

Nicola. You bid me push.

Mr. Jordan. Yes, but you push me in tierce, before you push in carte; and you have not patience while I parry.

Mrs. Jordan. You are a fool, husband, with all these whims, and this is come to you since you have taken upon you to keep company with quality.

Mr. Jordan. When I keep company with quality, I show my judgment; and that's much better than herding with your cits.

Mrs. Jordan. Yes, truly, there's a great deal to be got by frequenting your nobility; and you have made fine work with that count you are so bewitched with.

Mr. Jordan. Peace, take care what you say. Do you well know, wife, that you don't know whom you speak of, when you speak of him? He's a man of more importance than you think of; a nobleman of consideration at court, who speaks to the king just for all the world as I speak to you. Is it not a thing that does me great honour, that you see a person of that quality come so often to my house, who calls me his dear friend, and treats me as if I were his equal? He has more kindness for me than one would ever imagine; and he caresses me in such a manner before all the world, that I myself am perfectly confounded at it.

Mrs. Jordan. Yes, he has a great kindness for you, and caresses you; but he borrows your money of you.

Mr. Jordan. Well, and is it not a great honour to me to lend money to a man of that condition? And can I do less for a lord who calls me his dear friend?

Mrs. Jordan. And what is it this lord does for you?

Mr. Jordan. Things that would astonish you, if you did but know 'em.

Mrs. Jordan. And what may they be?

Mr. Jordan. Peace, I can't explain myself. 'Tis sufficient that if I have lent him money, he'll pay it me honestly, and that before 'tis long.

Mrs. Jordan. Yes, stay you for that.

Mr. Jordan. Certainly. Did he not tell me so?

Mrs. Jordan. Yes, yes, and he won't fail to disappoint you.

Mr. Jordan. He swore to me on the faith of a gentleman.

Mrs. Jordan. A mere song.

Mr. Jordan. Hey! You are mighty obstinate, wife of mine; I tell you he will keep his word with me, I am sure of it.

Mrs. Jordan. And I am sure that he will not; and all the court he makes to you, is only to cajole you.

Mr. Jordan. Hold your tongue. Here he comes.

Mrs. Jordan. That's all we shall have of him. He comes perhaps to borrow something more of you; the very sight of him gives me my dinner.

Mr. Jordan. Hold your tongue, I say.

SCENE IV

Dorantes, Mr. Jordan, Mrs. Jordan, Nicola.

Dorantes. My dear friend, Mr. Jordan, how do you do?

Mr. Jordan. Very well, sir, to do you what little service I can.

Dorantes. And Madam Jordan there, how does she do?

Mrs. Jordan. Madam Jordan does as well as she can.

Dorantes. Hah! Mr. Jordan, you're dressed the most genteely in the world!

Mr. Jordan. As you see.

Dorantes. You have a very fine air with that dress, and we have ne'er a young fellow at court, that's better made than you.

Mr. Jordan. He, he.

Mrs. Jordan. [*Aside.*] He scratches him where it itches.

Dorantes. Turn about. 'Tis most gallant.

Mrs. Jordan. [*Aside.*] Yes, as much of the fool behind as before.

Dorantes. 'Faith, Mr. Jordan, I was strangely impatient to see you. You're the man in the world I most esteem, and I was talking of you again this morning at the king's levee.

Mr. Jordan. You do me a great deal of honour, sir. [*To Mrs. Jordan.*] At the king's levee!

Dorantes. Come, be covered.

Mr. Jordan. Sir, I know the respect I owe you.

Dorantes. Lack-a-day, be covered; no ceremony pray between us two.

Mr. Jordan. Sir——

Dorantes. Put on your hat, I tell you, Mr. Jordan, you are my friend.

Mr. Jordan. Sir, I am your humble servant.

Dorantes. I won't be covered, if you won't.

Mr. Jordan. [*Puts on his hat.*] I choose rather to be unmannerly than troublesome.

Dorantes. I am your debtor, you know.

Mrs. Jordan. [*Aside.*] Yes, we know it but too well.

Dorantes. You have generously lent me money upon several occasions; and have obliged me, most certainly, with the best grace in the world.

Mr. Jordan. You jest, sir.

Dorantes. But I know how to repay what is lent me, and to be grateful for the favours done me.

Mr. Jordan. I don't doubt it, sir.

Dorantes. I'm willing to get out of your books, and came hither to make up our accounts together.

Mr. Jordan. [*Aside to Mrs. Jordan.*] Well, you see your impertinence, wife.

Dorantes. I'm one who love to be out of debt as soon as I can.

Mr. Jordan. [*Aside to Mrs. Jordan.*] I told you so.

Dorantes. Let's see a little what 'tis I owe you.

Mr. Jordan. [*Aside to Mrs. Jordan.*] You there, with your ridiculous suspicions.

Dorantes. Do you remember right all the money you have lent me?

Mr. Jordan. I believe so. I made a little memorandum of it. Here it is. Let you have at one time two hundred louis d'or.

Dorantes. 'Tis true.

Mr. Jordan. Another time, six-score.

Dorantes. Yes.

Mr. Jordan. And another time a hundred and forty.

Dorantes. You are right.

Mr. Jordan. These three articles make four hundred and sixty louis d'or, which come to five thousand and sixty livres.

Dorantes. The account is very right. Five thousand and sixty livres.

Mr. Jordan. One thousand eight hundred and thirty-two livres to your plume-maker.

Dorantes. Just.

Mr. Jordan. Two thousand seven hundred and four-score livres to your tailor.

Dorantes. 'Tis true.

Mr. Jordan. Four thousand three hundred and seventy-nine livres, twelve sols and eight deniers to your tradesman.

Dorantes. Very well. Twelve sols, eight deniers. The account is just.

Mr. Jordan. And a thousand seven hundred and forty-eight livres seven sols four deniers to your saddler.

Dorantes. 'Tis all true. What does that come to?

Mr. Jordan. Sum total, fifteen thousand eight hundred livres.

Dorantes. The sum total, and just. Fifteen thousand and eight hundred livres. To which add two hundred pistoles, which you are going to lend me, that will make exactly eighteen thousand francs, which I shall pay you the first opportunity.

Mrs. Jordan. [*Aside to Mr. Jordan.*] Well, did I not guess how 'twould be!

Mr. Jordan. [*Aside to Mrs. Jordan.*] Peace.

Dorantes. Will it incommode you to lend me what I tell you?

Mr. Jordan. Oh! no.

Mrs. Jordan. [*Aside to Mr. Jordan.*] This man makes a mere milch cow of you.

Mr. Jordan. [*Aside to Mrs. Jordan.*] Hold your tongue.

Dorantes. If this will incommode you, I'll seek it elsewhere.

Mr. Jordan. No, sir.

Mrs. Jordan. [*Aside to Mr. Jordan.*] He'll ne'er be satisfied till he has ruined you.

Mr. Jordan. [*Aside to Mrs. Jordan.*] Hold your tongue, I tell you.

Dorantes. You need only tell me if this puts you to any straits.

Mr. Jordan. Not at all, sir.

Mrs. Jordan. [*Aside to Mr. Jordan.*] 'Tis a true wheedler.

Mr. Jordan. [*Aside to Mrs. Jordan.*] Hold your tongue then.

Mrs. Jordan. [*Aside to Mr. Jordan.*] He'll drain you to the last farthing.

Mr. Jordan. [*Aside to Mrs. Jordan.*] Will you hold your tongue?

Dorantes. I've a good many people would be glad to lend it me, but as you are my very good friend, I thought I should wrong you if I asked it of anybody else.

Mr. Jordan. 'Tis too much honour, sir, you do me. I'll go fetch what you want.

Mrs. Jordan. [*Aside to Mr. Jordan.*] What! going to lend him still more?

Mr. Jordan. [*Aside to Mrs. Jordan.*] What can I do? Would you have me refuse a man of that rank, who spoke of me this morning at the king's levee.

Mrs. Jordan. [*Aside to Mr. Jordan.*] Go, you're a downright dupe.

Scene V

Dorantes, Mrs. Jordan, Nicola.

Dorantes. You seem to me very melancholy. What ails you, Mrs. Jordan?

Mrs. Jordan. My head's bigger than my fist, even if it is not swelled.

Dorantes. Where is Miss your daughter that I don't see her?

Mrs. Jordan. Miss my daughter is pretty well where she is.

Dorantes. How does she go on?

Mrs. Jordan. She goes on her two legs.

Dorantes. Won't you come with her, one of these days, and see the ball, and the play that's acted at court.

Mrs. Jordan. Yes truly, we've a great inclination to laugh, a great inclination to laugh have we.

Dorantes. I fancy, Madam Jordan, you had a great many sparks in your younger years, being so handsome and good humoured as you were.

Mrs. Jordan. Tredame, sir! what, is Madam Jordan grown decrepit, and does her head totter already with a palsy?

Dorantes. Odso, Madam Jordan, I ask your pardon. I was not thinking that you are young. I'm very often absent. Pray excuse my impertinence.

SCENE VI

Mr. Jordan, Mrs. Jordan, Dorantes, Nicola.

Mr. Jordan. [*To Dorantes.*] Here's two hundred pieces for you, hard money.

Dorantes. I do assure you, Mr. Jordan, I am absolutely yours; and I long to do you service at court.

Mr. Jordan. I'm infinitely obliged to you.

Dorantes. If Madam Jordan inclines to see the royal diversion, I'll get her the best places in the ballroom.

Mrs. Jordan. Madam Jordan kisses your hand.

Dorantes. [*Aside to Mr. Jordan.*] Our pretty marchioness, as I informed you in my letter, will be here by and by to partake of your ball and collation; I brought her, at last, to consent to the entertainment you design to give her.

Mr. Jordan. Let us draw to a distance a little, for a certain reason.

Dorantes. 'Tis eight days since I saw you, and I gave you no tidings of the diamond you put into my hands to make her a present of, as from you; but the reason was, I had all the difficulty in the world to conquer her scruples, and 'twas no longer ago than to-day, that she resolved to accept of it.

Mr. Jordan. How did she like it?

Dorantes. Marvellously; and I am much deceived if the beauty of this diamond has not an admirable effect upon her.

Mr. Jordan. Grant it, kind Heaven!

Mrs. Jordan. [*To Nicola.*] When he's once with him, he can never get rid of him.

Dorantes. I made her sensible in a proper manner, of the richness of the present, and the strength of your passion

Mr. Jordan. These kindnesses perfectly overwhelm me; I am in the greatest confusion in the world to see a person of your quality demean himself on my account as you do.

Dorantes. You jest sure. Does one ever stop at such sort of scruples among friends? And would not you do the same thing for me, if occasion offered?

Mr. Jordan. Oh! certainly, and with all my soul.

Mrs. Jordan. [*Aside to Nicola.*] How the sight of him torments me!

Dorantes. For my part, I never mind anything when a friend is to be served; and when you imparted to me the ardent passion you had entertained for the agreeable marchioness, with whom

I was acquainted, you see that I made an immediate offer of my service.

Mr. Jordan. 'Tis true, these favours are what confound me.

Mrs. Jordan. [*To Nicola.*] What will he never be gone?

Nicola. They are mighty great together.

Dorantes. You've taken the right way to smite her. Women, above all things, love the expense we are at on their account; and your frequent serenades, your continual entertainments; that sumptuous firework she saw on the water, the diamond she received by way of present from you, and the regale you are now preparing; all this speaks much better in favour of your passion than all the things you yourself could possibly have said to her.

Mr. Jordan. There's no expense I would not be at, if I could by that means find the way to her heart. A woman of quality has powerful charms for me, and 'tis an honour I would purchase at any rate.

Mrs. Jordan. [*Aside to Nicola.*] What can they have to talk of so long together? Go softly, and listen a little.

Dorantes. By and by you will enjoy the pleasure of seeing her at your ease, your eyes will have full time to be satisfied.

Mr. Jordan. To be at full liberty, I have ordered matters so, that my wife shall dine with my sister, where she'll pass the whole afternoon.

Dorantes. You have done wisely, for your wife might have perplexed us a little. I have given the proper orders for you to the cook, and for everything necessary for the ball. 'Tis of my own invention; and provided the execution answers the plan, I am sure 'twill be——

Mr. Jordan. [*Perceives that Nicola listens, and gives her a box on the ear.*] Hey, you're very impertinent. [*To Dorantes.*] Let us go if you please.

SCENE VII

Mrs. Jordan, Nicola.

Nicola. I'faith, curiosity has cost me something; but I believe there's a snake in the grass; for they were talking of some affair, which they were not willing you should be present at.

Mrs. Jordan. This is not the first time, Nicola, that I have had suspicions of my husband. I am the most deceived person in the world, or there is some amour in agitation, and I am labouring to discover what it should be. But let's think of my daughter. You know the love Cleontes has for her. He is a man who hits my fancy, and I have a mind to favour his addresses, and help him to Lucilia, if I can.

Nicola. In truth, madam, I am the most ravished creature in the world, to find you in these sentiments; for if the master hits your taste, the man hits mine no less; and I could wish our marriage might be concluded under favour of theirs.

Mrs. Jordan. Go, and talk with him about it, as from me, and tell him to come to me presently, that we may join in demanding my daughter of my husband.

Nicola. I fly, madam, with joy, and I could not have received a more agreeable commission. [*Alone.*] I believe I shall very much rejoice their hearts.

Scene VIII

Cleontes, Coviel, Nicola.

Nicola. [*To Cleontes.*] Hah, most luckily met. I'm an ambassadress of joy, and I come——

Cleontes. Be gone, ye perfidious slut, and don't come to amuse me with thy traitorous speeches.

Nicola. Is it thus you receive——

Cleontes. Be gone, I tell thee, and go directly and inform thy false mistress, that she never more, while she lives, shall impose upon the too simple Cleontes.

Nicola. What whim is this? My dear Coviel, tell me a little what does this mean.

Coviel. Thy dear Coviel, wicked minx? Away quickly out of my sight, hussy, and leave me at quiet.

Nicola. What dost thou too——

Coviel. Out o' my sight, I tell thee, and talk not to me, for thy life.

Nicola. [*Aside.*] Hey-day! What gadfly has stung 'em both? Well, I must march and inform my mistress of this pretty piece of history.

Scene IX

Cleontes, Coviel.

Cleontes. What! treat a lover in this manner; and a lover the most constant, the most passionate of all lovers!

Coviel. 'Tis a horrible trick they have served us both.

Cleontes. I discover all the ardour for her, all the tenderness one can imagine. I love nothing in the world but her, have nothing in my thoughts besides her. She is all my care, all my desire, all my joy. I speak of nought but her, think of nought but her, dream of nought but her, I breathe only for her, my heart lives wholly in her; and this is the worthy recompense of such a love! I am two days without seeing her, which are to me two horrible ages; I meet her accidentally, my heart feels all transported at the sight; joy sparkles in my face; I fly to her with ecstasy, and the faithless creature turns away her eyes, and brushes hastily by me, as if she had never seen me in her life!

Coviel. I say the same as you do.

Cleontes. Is it possible to see anything, Coviel, equal to this perfidy of the ungrateful Lucilia?

Coviel. Or to that, sir, of the villainous jade Nicola?

Cleontes. After so many ardent sacrifices of sighs and vows that I have made to her charms!

Coviel. After so much assiduous sneaking, cares, and services that I have paid her in the kitchen!

Cleontes. So many tears that I have shed at her feet!

Coviel. So many buckets of water that I have drawn for her!

Cleontes. Such ardour as I have shown, in loving her more than myself!

Coviel. So much heat as I have endured, in turning the spit in her place!

Cleontes. She flies me with disdain!

Coviel. She turns her back upon me with impudence!

Cleontes. This is a perfidy worthy the greatest punishment.

Coviel. This is a treachery that deserves a thousand boxes o' the ear.

Cleontes. Prithee, never think to speak once more to me in her favour.

Coviel. I, sir? marry Heaven forbid.

Cleontes. Never come to excuse the action of this perfidious woman.

Coviel. Fear it not.

Cleontes. No, d'ye see, all discourses in her defence will signify nothing.

Coviel. Who dreams of such a thing?

Cleontes. I'm determined to continue my resentment against her, and break off all correspondence.

Coviel. I give my consent.

Cleontes. This same count that visits her, pleases perhaps her eye; and her fancy, I see plainly, is dazzled with quality. But I must, for my own honour, prevent the triumph of her inconstancy. I'll make as much haste as she can do towards the change, which I see she's running into, and won't leave her all the glory of quitting me.

Coviel. 'Tis very well said, and for my share, I enter into all your sentiments.

Cleontes. Second my resentments, and support my resolutions against all the remains of love, that may yet plead for her. I conjure thee, say all the ill things of her thou canst. Paint me her person so as to make her despicable; and, in order to disgust me, mark me out well all the faults thou canst find in her.

Coviel. She, sir? A pretty mawkin, a fine piece to be so much enamoured with. I see nothing in her, but what's very indifferent, and you might find a hundred persons more deserving of you. First of all she has little eyes.

Cleontes. That's true, she has little eyes; but they are full of fire, the most sparkling, the most piercing in the world, the most striking that one shall see.

Coviel. She has a wide mouth.

Cleontes. Yes; but one sees such graces in it, as one does not see in other mouths, and the sight of that mouth inspires desire: 'tis the most attractive, the most amorous in the world.

Coviel. As to her height, she's not tall.

Cleontes. No; but she's easy, and well-shaped.

Coviel. She affects a negligence in speaking and acting.

Cleontes. 'Tis true; but all this has a gracefulness in her, and her ways are engaging; they have I don't know what charms, that insinuate into our hearts.

Coviel. A :to her wit——

Cleontes. Ah! Coviel, she has the most refined, the most delicate turn of wit.

Coviel. Her conversation——

Cleontes. Her conversation is charming.

Coviel. She's always grave.

Cleontes. Would you have flaunting pleasantry, a perpetual profuse mirth? And d'ye see anything more impertinent than those women who are always upon the giggle?

Coviel. But in short, she is the most capricious creature in the world.

Cleontes. Yes, she is capricious I grant ye; but everything sits well upon fine women; we bear with everything from the fair.

Coviel.   Since that's the case, I see plainly you desire always to love her.

Cleontes.   I! I should love death sooner; and I am now going to hate her as much as ever I loved her.

Coviel.   But how, if you think her so perfect?

Cleontes.   Therein shall my vengeance be more glaring; therein shall I better display the force of my resolution in hating her, quitting her, most beautiful as she is; most charming, most amiable, as I think her.   Here she is.

Scene X

Lucilia, Cleontes, Coviel, Nicola.

Nicola. [*To Lucilia.*]   For my part, I was perfectly shocked at it.

Lucilia.   It can be nothing else, Nicola, but what I said.   But there he comes.

Cleontes. [*To Coviel.*]   I won't so much as speak to her.

Coviel.   I'll follow your example.

Lucilia.   What means this, Cleontes, what's the matter with you?

Nicola.   What ails thee, Coviel?

Lucilia.   What trouble has seized you?

Nicola.   What cross humour possesses thee?

Lucilia.   Are you dumb, Cleontes?

Nicola.   Has thou lost thy speech, Coviel?

Cleontes.   The abandoned creature!

Coviel.   Oh! the Judas!

Lucilia.   I see very well that the late meeting has disordered your mind.

Cleontes. [*To Coviel.*]   O, hoh!   She sees what she has done.

Nicola.   The reception of this morning has made thee take snuff.

Coviel. [*To Cleontes.*]   She has guessed where the shoe pinches.

Lucilia.   Is it not true, Cleontes, that this is the reason of your being out of humour?

Cleontes.   Yes, perfidious maid, that is it, since I must speak; and I can tell you, that you shall not triumph, as you imagine, by your unfaithfulness, that I shall be beforehand in breaking with you, and you won't have the credit of discarding me.   I shall, doubtless, have some difficulty in conquering the passion I have for you: 'twill cause me uneasiness; I shall suffer for a while; but I shall compass my point, and I would sooner stab myself to the heart than have the weakness of returning to you.

Coviel. [*To Nicola.*] As says the master, so says the man.

Lucilia. Here's a noise indeed about nothing. I'll tell you, Cleontes, the reason that made me avoid joining you this morning.

Cleontes. [*Endeavouring to go to avoid Lucilia.*] No, I'll hear nothing.

Nicola. [*To Coviel.*] I'll let thee into the cause that made us pass you so quick.

Coviel. [*Endeavouring to go to avoid Nicola.*] I will hear nothing.

Lucilia. [*Following Cleontes.*] Know that this morning——

Cleontes. [*Walks about without regarding Lucilia.*] No, I tell you.

Nicola. [*Following Coviel.*] Learn that——

Coviel. [*Walks about likewise without regarding Nicola.*] No, traitress.

Lucilia. Hear me.

Cleontes. Not a bit.

Nicola. Let me speak.

Coviel. I'm deaf.

Lucilia. Cleontes!

Cleontes. No.

Nicola. Coviel!

Coviel. No.

Lucilia. Stay.

Cleontes. Idle stuff.

Nicola. Hear me.

Coviel. No such thing.

Lucilia. One moment.

Cleontes. Not at all.

Nicola. A little patience.

Coviel. A fiddle-stick.

Lucilia. Two words.

Cleontes. No, 'tis over.

Nicola. One word.

Coviel. No more dealings.

Lucilia. [*Stopping.*] Well, since you won't hear me, keep your opinion, and do what you please.

Nicola. [*Stopping likewise.*] Since that's thy way, e'en take it all just as it pleases thee.

Cleontes. Let's know the subject then of this fine reception.

Lucilia. [*Going in her turn to avoid Cleontes.*] I've no longer an inclination to tell it.

Coviel. Let us a little into this history.

Nicola. [*Going likewise in her turn to avoid Coviel.*] I won't inform thee now, not I.

Cleontes. [*Following Lucilia.*] Tell me——

Lucilia. No, I'll tell you nothing.

Coviel. [*Following Nicola.*] Say——

Nicola. No, I say nothing.

Cleontes. For goodness' sake.

Lucilia. No, I tell you.

Coviel. Of all charity.

Nicola. Not a bit.

Cleontes. I beseech you.

Lucilia. Let me alone.

Coviel. I conjure thee.

Nicola. Away with thee.

Cleontes. Lucilia!

Lucilia. No.

Coviel. Nicola!

Nicola. Not at all.

Cleontes. For Heaven's sake.

Lucilia. I will not.

Coviel. Speak to me.

Nicola. Not a word.

Cleontes. Clear up my doubts.

Lucilia. No, I'll do nothing towards it.

Coviel. Cure my mind.

Nicola. No, 'tis not my pleasure.

Cleontes. Well, since you are so little concerned to ease me of my pain, and to justify yourself as to the unworthy treatment my passion has received from you, ungrateful creature, 'tis the last time you shall see me, and I am going far from you to die of grief and love.

Coviel. [*To Nicola.*] And I'll follow his steps.

Lucilia. [*To Cleontes, who is going.*] Cleontes!

Nicola. [*To Coviel, who follows his master.*] Coviel!

Cleontes. [*Stopping.*] Hey?

Coviel. [*Likewise stopping.*] Your pleasure?

Lucilia. Whither do you go?

Cleontes. Where I told you.

Coviel. We go to die.

Lucilia. Do you go to die, Cleontes?

Cleontes. Yes, cruel, since you will have it so.

Lucilia. I? I have you die?

Cleontes. Yes, you would.

Lucilia. Who told you so?

Cleontes. [*Going up to Lucilia.*] Would you not have it so, since you would not clear up my suspicions?

Lucilia. Is that my fault? Would you but have given me the hearing, should I not have told you that the adventure you make such complaints about, was occasioned this morning by the presence of an old aunt who will absolutely have it, that the mere approach of a man is a dishonour to a girl; who is perpetually lecturing us upon this head, and represents to us all mankind as so many devils, whom one ought to avoid.

Nicola. [*To Coviel.*] There's the whole secret of the affair.

Cleontes. Don't you deceive me, Lucilia?

Coviel. [*To Nicola.*] Dost thou not put a trick upon me?

Lucilia. [*To Cleontes.*] There's nothing more true.

Nicola. [*To Coviel.*] 'Tis the very thing, as it is.

Coviel. [*To Cleontes.*] Shall we surrender upon this?

Cleontes. Ah, Lucilia, what art have you to calm my passions with a single word! How easily do we suffer ourselves to be persuaded by those we love!

Coviel. How easily is one wheedled by these plaguy animals!

Scene XI

Mrs. Jordan, Cleontes, Lucilia, Coviel, Nicola.

Mrs. Jordan. I am very glad to see you, Cleontes, and you are here apropos. My husband's acoming, catch your opportunity quick, and demand Lucilia in marriage.

Cleontes. Ah, madam, how sweet is that word, how it flatters my wishes? Could I receive an order more charming? A favour more precious?

Scene XII

Mr. Jordan, Mrs. Jordan, Cleontes, Lucilia, Coviel, Nicola.

Cleontes. Sir, I was not willing to employ any other person to make a certain demand of you, which I have long intended. It concerns me sufficiently to undertake it in my own person; and, without farther circumlocution, I shall inform you that the honour of being your son-in-law is an illustrious favour which I beseech you to grant me.

Mr. Jordan. Before I give you an answer, sir, I desire you would tell me whether you are a gentleman.

Cleontes. Sir, the generality of people don't hesitate much on this question. People speak out bluff, and with ease. They make no scruple of taking this title upon 'em, and custom nowadays seems to authorise the theft. For my part, I confess to you, my sentiments in this matter are somewhat more delicate. I look upon all imposture as unworthy an honest man; and that there is cowardice in denying what Heaven has made us; in tricking ourselves out, to the eyes of the world, in a stolen title; in desiring to put ourselves off for what we are not. I am undoubtedly born of parents who have held honourable employments. I have had the honour of six years' service in the army; and I find myself of consequence enough to hold a tolerable rank in the world; but for all this I won't give myself a name, which others in my place would think they might pretend to, and I'll tell you frankly that I am no gentleman.

Mr. Jordan. Your hand, sir, my daughter is no wife for you.

Cleontes. How?

Mr. Jordan. You are no gentleman, you shan't have my daughter.

Mrs. Jordan. What would you be at then with your gentlemen? D'ye think we sort of people are of the line of St. Louis?

Mr. Jordan. Hold your tongue, wife, I see you're acoming.

Mrs. Jordan. Are we either of us otherwise descended than of plain citizens?

Mr. Jordan. There's a scandalous reflection for you!

Mrs. Jordan. And was not your father a tradesman as well as mine?

Mr. Jordan. Plague take the woman. She never has done with this. If your father was a tradesman, so much was the worse for him; but as for mine, they are numskulls that say he was. All that I have to say to you is, that I will have a gentleman for my son-in-law.

Mrs. Jordan. Your daughter should have a husband that's proper for her; and an honest man who is rich and well made, would be much better for her than a gentleman who is deformed and a beggar.

Nicola. That's very true. We have a young squire in our town who is the most awkward looby, the veriest driveller that I ever set eyes on.

Mr. Jordan. Hold your prate, Mrs. Impertinence. You are always thrusting yourself into conversation. I've means sufficient for my daughter, and want nothing but honour, and I will have her a marchioness.

Mrs. Jordan. A marchioness!

Mr. Jordan. Yes, a marchioness.

Mrs. Jordan. Marry, Heavens preserve me from it.

Mr. Jordan. 'Tis a determined thing.

Mrs. Jordan. 'Tis what I shall never consent to. Matches with people above one, are always subject to grievous inconveniences. I don't like that a son-in-law should have it in his power to reproach my daughter with her parents, or that she should have children who should be ashamed to call me grandmother. Should she come and visit me with the equipage of a grand lady, and through inadvertency, miss curtsying to some of the neighbourhood, they would not fail, presently, saying a hundred idle things. Do but see, would they say, this lady marchioness, what haughty airs she gives herself! She's the daughter of Mr. Jordan, who was over and above happy, when she was a little one, to play children's play with us. She was not always so lofty as she is now; and her two grandfathers sold cloth near St. Innocent's Gate. They amassed great means for their children, which they are paying for now, perhaps very dear, in the other world. People don't generally grow so rich by being honest. I won't have all these tittle-tattle stories; in one word, I'll have a man who shall be beholden to me for my daughter, and to whom I can say, Sit you down there, son-in-law, and dine with me.

Mr. Jordan. See there the sentiments of a little soul, to desire always to continue in a mean condition. Let me have no more replies; my daughter shall be a marchioness in spite of the world; and if you put me in a passion, I'll make her a duchess.

Scene XIII

Mrs. Jordan, Lucilia, Cleontes, Nicola, Coviel.

Mrs. Jordan. Cleontes, don't be discouraged for all this. [*To Lucilia.*] Follow me, daughter, and come tell your father resolutely, that if you have not him, you won't marry anybody at all.

SCENE XIV

Cleontes, Coviel.

Coviel. You have made a pretty piece of work of it with your fine sentiments.

Cleontes. What wouldst thou have me do? I have a scrupulousness in this case that no precedents can conquer.

Coviel. You're in the wrong to be serious with such a man as that. Don't you see that he's a fool? And would it cost you anything to accommodate yourself to his chimeras?

Cleontes. You're in the right; but I did not dream it was necessary to bring your proofs of nobility, to be son-in-law to Mr. Jordan.

Coviel. [*Laughing.*] Ha, ha, ha.

Cleontes. What d'ye laugh at?

Coviel. At a thought that's come into my head to play our spark off, and help you to obtain what you desire.

Cleontes. How?

Coviel. The thought is absolutely droll.

Cleontes. What is it?

Coviel. There was a certain masquerade performed a little while ago, which comes in here the best in the world; and which I intend to insert into a piece of roguery I design to make for our coxcomb. This whole affair looks a little like making a joke of him; but with him we may hazard everything, there's no need here to study finesse so much, he's a man who will play his part to a wonder; and will easily give in to all the sham tales we shall take in our heads to tell him. I have actors, I have habits all ready, only let me alone.

Cleontes. But inform me of it.

Coviel. I am going to let you into the whole of it. Let's retire; there he comes.

SCENE XV

Mr. Jordan. [*Alone.*] What a deuce can this mean? They have nothing but great lords to reproach me with; and I for my part see nothing so fine as keeping company with your great lords; there's nothing but honour and civility among 'em; and I would it had cost me two fingers of a hand to have been born a count, or a marquis.

SCENE XVI

Mr. Jordan, Lackey.

Lackey. Sir, here's the count, and a lady, whom he's handing in.
Mr. Jordan. Good lack-a-day, I have some orders to give.
Tell 'em that I'm acoming in a minute.

SCENE XVII

Dorimène, Dorantes, Lackey.

Lackey. My master says that he's acoming in a minute.
Dorantes. 'Tis very well.

SCENE XVIII

Dorimène, Dorantes.

Dorimène. I don't know, Dorantes; I take a strange step
here in suffering you to bring me to a house where I know nobody.
Dorantes. What place then, madam, would you have a lover
choose to entertain you in, since, to avoid clamour, you neither
allow of your own house nor mine?
Dorimène. But you don't mention that I am every day
insensibly engaged to receive too great proofs of your passion.
In vain do I refuse things, you weary me out of resistance,
and you have a civil kind of obstinacy, which makes me come
gently into whatsoever you please. Frequent visits commenced,
declarations came next, which drew after them serenades and
entertainments, which were followed by presents. I opposed
all these things, but you are not disheartened, and you become
master of my resolutions step by step. For my part, I can
answer for nothing hereafter, and I believe in the end you will
bring me to matrimony, from which I stood so far aloof.
Dorantes. Faith, madam, you ought to have been there
already. You are a widow, and depend upon nobody but yourself. I am my own master, and love you more than my life.
What does it stick at then, that you should not, from this day
forward, complete my happiness?
Dorimène. Lack-a-day, Dorantes, there must go a great many
qualities on both sides, to make people live happily together;
and two of the most reasonable persons in the world have often
much ado to compose a union to both their satisfactions.

Dorantes. You're in the wrong, madam, to represent to yourself so many difficulties in this affair; and the experience you have had concludes nothing for the rest of the world.

Dorimène. In short, I always abide by this. The expenses you put yourself to for me, disturb me for two reasons; one is, they engage me more than I could wish; and the other is, I'm sure, no offence to you, that you can't do this, but you must incommode yourself, and I would not have you do that.

Dorantes. Fie, madam, these are trifles, and 'tis not by that——

Dorimène. I know what I say; and, amongst other things, the diamond you forced me to take, is of value——

Dorantes. Nay, madam, pray don't enhance the value of a thing my love thinks unworthy of you: and permit——Here's the master of the house.

SCENE XIX

Mr. Jordan, Dorimène, Dorantes.

Mr. Jordan. [*After having made two bows, finding himself too near Dorimène.*] A little farther, madam.

Dorimène. How?

Mr. Jordan. One step, if you please.

Dorimène. What then?

Mr. Jordan. Fall back a little for the third.

Dorantes. Mr. Jordan, madam, knows the world.

Mr. Jordan. Madam, 'tis a very great honour that I am fortunate enough to be so happy, but to have the felicity, that you should have the goodness, to grant me the favour, to do me the honour, to honour me with the favour of your presence; and had I also the merit to merit a merit like yours, and that Heaven——envious of my good——had granted me——the advantage of being worthy——of——

Dorantes. Mr. Jordan, enough of this; my lady does not love great compliments, and she knows you are a man of wit. [*Aside to Dorimène.*] 'Tis a downright cit, ridiculous enough, as you see, in his whole behaviour.

Dorimène. [*Aside to Dorantes.*] It is not very difficult to perceive it.

Dorantes. Madam, this is a very good friend of mine.

Mr. Jordan. 'Tis too much honour you do me.

Dorantes. A very polite man.

Dorimène. I have a great esteem for him.

Mr. Jordan. I have done nothing yet, madam, to merit this favour.

Dorantes. [*Aside to Mr. Jordan.*] Take good care however not to speak to her of the diamond you gave her.

Mr. Jordan. [*Aside to Dorantes.*] Mayn't I ask her only how she likes it?

Dorantes. [*Aside to Mr. Jordan.*] How! Take special care you don't. 'Twould be villainous of you; and to act like a man of gallantry, you should make as if it were not you who made the present. [*Aloud.*] Mr. Jordan, madam, says that he's in raptures to see you at his house.

Dorimène. He does me a great deal of honour.

Mr. Jordan. [*Aside to Dorantes.*] How am I obliged to you, sir, for speaking to her in that manner on my account!

Dorantes. [*Aside to Mr. Jordan.*] I have had a most terrible difficulty to get her to come hither.

Mr. Jordan. [*Aside to Dorantes.*] I don't know how to thank you enough for it.

Dorantes. He says, madam, that he thinks you the most charming person in the world.

Dorimène. 'Tis a great favour he does me.

Mr. Jordan. Madam, it's you who do the favours, and——

Dorantes. Let's think of eating.

SCENE XX

Mr. Jordan, Dorimène, Dorantes, Lackey.

Lackey. [*To Mr. Jordan.*] Everything is ready, sir.

Dorantes. Come then, let us sit down to table; and fetch the musicians.

ACT IV

Scene I

Dorimène, Mr. Jordan, Dorantes, three Musicians, Lackeys.

Dorimène. How, Dorantes? why here's a most magnificent repast!

Mr. Jordan. You are pleased to banter, madam, I would it were more worthy of your acceptance. [*Dorimène, Mr. Jordan, Dorantes, and three musicians sit down at the table.*]

Dorantes. Mr. Jordan, madam, is in the right in what he says, and he obliges me in paying you, after so handsome a manner, the honours of his house. I agree with him that the repast is not worthy of you. As it was myself who ordered it, and I am not so clearly sighted in these affairs, as certain of our friends, you have here no very learned feast; and you will find incongruities of good cheer in it, some barbarisms of good taste. Had our friend Damis had a hand here, everything had been done by rule; elegance and erudition would have run through the whole, and he would not have failed exaggerating all the regular pieces of the repast he gave you, and force you to own his great capacity in the science of good eating; he would have told you of bread *de rive*, with the golden kissing-crust, raised too all round with a crust that crumples tenderly in your teeth; of wine with a velvet sap, heightened with a smartness not too overpowering; of a breast of mutton stuffed with parsley; of a loin of veal *de rivière*, thus long, white, delicate, and which is a true almond paste between the teeth; of your partridges heightened with a surprising *goût*; and then by way of farce or entertainment, of a soup with jelly broth, fortified with a young plump turkey-pout, cantoned with pigeons, and garnished with white onions married to succory. But, for my part, I confess to you my ignorance; and, as Mr. Jordan has very well said, I wish the repast were more worthy of your acceptance.

Dorimène. I make no other answer to this compliment than eating as I do.

Mr. Jordan. Ah! what pretty hands are there!

Dorimène. The hands are so so, Mr. Jordan; but you mean to speak of the diamond which is very pretty.

Mr. Jordan. I, madam? Marry Heaven forbid I should

speak of it; I should not act like a gentleman of gallantry, and the diamond is a very trifle.

Dorimène.   You are wondrous nice.

Mr. Jordan.   You have too much goodness——

Dorantes. [*Having made signs to Mr. Jordan.*] Come, give some wine to Mr. Jordan, and to those gentlemen who will do us the favour to sing us a catch.

Dorimène.   You give a wondrous relish to the good cheer by mixing music with it; I am admirably well regaled here.

Mr. Jordan.   Madam, it is not——

Dorantes. Mr. Jordan, let us listen to these gentlemen, they'll entertain us with something better than all we can possibly say.

First and Second Musician together with a glass in their hands.

> Put it round, my dear Phyllis, invert the bright glass;
>   Oh what charms to the crystal those fingers impart!
> You and Bacchus combined, all resistance surpass,
>   And with passion redoubled have ravished my heart.
>   'Twixt him, you and me, my charmer, my fair,
>   Eternal affection let's swear.

> At the touch of those lips how he sparkles more bright!
>   And his touch, in return, those lips does embellish:
> I could quaff 'em all day, and drink bumpers all night.
>   What longing each gives me, what gusto, what relish!
>   'Twixt him, you and me, my charmer, my fair,
>   Eternal affection let's swear.

Second and Third Musician together.

> Since time flies so nimbly away,
>   Come drink, my dear boys, drink about;
> Let's husband him well while we may,
>   For life may be gone before the mug's out.
> When Charon has got us aboard,
>   Our drinking and wooing are past;
> We ne'er to lose time can afford,
>   For drinking's a trade not always to last.

> Let your puzzling rogues in the schools,
>   Dispute of the bonum of man;
> Philosophers dry are but fools,
>   The secret is this, drink, drink off your can.

> When Charon has got us aboard,
>   Our drinking and wooing are past,
> We ne'er to lose time can afford,
>   For drinking's a trade not always to last.

All three together.

> Why bob there! some wine, boys! come fill the glass, fill,
> Round and round let it go, till we bid it stand still.

Dorimène. I don't think anything can be better sung; and 'tis extremely fine.

Mr. Jordan. I see something here though, madam, much finer.

Dorimène. Hey! Mr. Jordan is more gallant than I thought he was.

Dorantes. How, madam! who do you take Mr. Jordan for?

Mr. Jordan. I wish she would take me for what I could name.

Dorimène. Again?

Dorantes. [*To Dorimène.*] You don't know him.

Mr. Jordan. She shall know me whenever she pleases.

Dorimène. Oh! Too much.

Dorantes. He's one who has a repartee always at hand. But you don't see, madam, that Mr. Jordan eats all the pieces you have touched.

Dorimène. Mr. Jordan is a man that I am charmed with.

Mr. Jordan. If I could charm your heart, I should be——

Scene II

Mrs. Jordan, Mr. Jordan, Dorimène, Dorantes, Musicians, Lackeys.

Mrs. Jordan. Hey-day! why here's a jolly company of you, and I see very well you did not expect me. It was for this pretty affair then, Mr. Husband o' mine, that you were in such a violent hurry to pack me off to dine with my sister; I just now found a play-house below, and here I find a dinner fit for a wedding. Thus it is you spend your money, and thus it is you feast the ladies in my absence, and present 'em with music and a play, whilst I'm sent abroad in the meantime.

Dorantes. What do you mean, Madam Jordan? And what's your fancy to take it into your head, that your husband spends his money, and that 'tis he who entertains my lady? Know, pray, that 'tis I do it, that he only lends me his house, and that you ought to consider a little better what you say.

Mr. Jordan. Yes, Mrs. Impertinence, 'tis the count that presents the lady with all this, who is a person of quality. He does me the honour to borrow my house, and is pleased to let me be with him.

Mrs. Jordan. 'Tis all stuff this. I know what I know.

Dorantes. Mrs. Jordan, take your best spectacles, take 'em.

Mrs. Jordan. I've no need of spectacles, sir, I see clear enough; I've smelt things out a great while ago, I am no ass. 'Tis base in you, who are a great lord, to lend a helping hand, as you do, to the follies of my husband. And you, madam, who are a great lady, 'tis neither handsome, nor honest in you, to sow dissension in a family, and to suffer my husband to be in love with you.

Dorimène. What can be the meaning of all this? Go, Dorantes, 'tis wrong in you to expose me to the silly visions of this raving woman.

Dorantes. [*Following Dorimène who goes out.*] Madam, why madam, where are you running?

Mr. Jordan. Madam——My lord, make my excuses to her and endeavour to bring her back.

SCENE III

Mrs. Jordan and Mr. Jordan, Lackeys.

Mr. Jordan. Ah! impertinent creature as you are, these are your fine doings; you come and affront me in the face of all the world, and drive people of quality away from my house.

Mrs. Jordan. I value not their quality.

Mr. Jordan. I don't know what hinders me, you plaguy hussy, from splitting your skull with the fragments of the feast you came here to disturb.   [*Lackeys take away the table.*

Mrs. Jordan. [*Going.*] I despise all this. I defend my own rights, and I shall have all the wives on my side.

Mr. Jordan. You do well to get out of the way of my fury.

SCENE IV

Mr. Jordan. [*Alone.*] She came here at a most unlucky time. I was in the humour of saying fine things, and never did I find myself so witty. What have we got here?

SCENE V

Mr. Jordan, Coviel (disguised).

Coviel. Sir, I don't know whether I have the honour to be known to you.

Mr. Jordan. No, sir.

Coviel. I have seen you when you were not above thus tall.

Mr. Jordan. Me?

Coviel. Yes. You were one of the prettiest children in the world; and all the ladies used to take you in their arms to kiss you.

Mr. Jordan. To kiss me?

Coviel. Yes, I was an intimate friend of the late gentleman your father.

Mr. Jordan. Of the late gentleman my father!

Coviel. Yes. He was a very honest gentleman.

Mr. Jordan. What is't you say?

Coviel. I say that he was a very honest gentleman.

Mr. Jordan. My father?

Coviel. Yes.

Mr. Jordan. Did you know him very well?

Coviel. Certainly.

Mr. Jordan. And did you know him for a gentleman?

Coviel. Without doubt.

Mr. Jordan. I don't know then what the world means.

Coviel. How?

Mr. Jordan. There is a stupid sort of people, who would face me down that he was a tradesman.

Coviel. He a tradesman? 'Tis mere scandal, he never was one. All that he did was, that he was very obliging, very officious, and as he was a great connoisseur in stuffs, he used to pick them up everywhere, have 'em carried to his house, and gave 'em to his friends for money.

Mr. Jordan. I'm very glad of your acquaintance, that you may bear witness that my father was a gentleman.

Coviel. I'll maintain it in the face of all the world.

Mr. Jordan. You will oblige me. What business brings you here?

Coviel. Since my acquaintance with the late gentleman your father, honest gentleman, as I was telling you, I have travelled round the world.

Mr. Jordan. Round the world?

Coviel. Yes.

Mr. Jordan.   I fancy 'tis a huge way off, that same country.

Coviel.   Most certainly.   I have not been returned from these tedious travels of mine but four days.   And because I have an interest in everything that concerns you, I come to tell you the best news in the world.

Mr. Jordan.   What?

Coviel.   You know that the son of the Great Turk is here.

Mr. Jordan.   I?   No.

Coviel.   How?   He has a most magnificent train.   All the world goes to see him, and he has been received in this country as a person of importance.

Mr. Jordan.   In troth, I did not know that.

Coviel.   What is of advantage to you in this affair is, that he is in love with your daughter.

Mr. Jordan.   The son of the Great Turk?

Coviel.   Yes, and wants to be your son-in-law.

Mr. Jordan.   My son-in-law, the son of the Great Turk?

Coviel.   The son of the Great Turk your son-in-law.   As I have been to see him, and perfectly understand his language, he held a conversation with me; and after some other discourse, says he to me: Acciam croc soler, onch alla moustaph gidelum amanahem varahini oussere carbulath.   That is to say, Have you not seen a young handsome person, who is the daughter of Mr. Jordan, a gentleman of Paris?

Mr. Jordan.   The son of the Great Turk said that of me?

Coviel.   Yes, as I made answer to him, that I knew you particularly well, and that I had seen your daughter.   Ah, says he to me, Marababa sahem; that is to say, Ah! how am I enamoured with her!

Mr. Jordan.   Marababa sahem means: Ah! how am I enamoured with her?

Coviel.   Yes.

Mr. Jordan.   Marry, you did well to tell me so, for as for my part, I should never have believed that Marababa sahem had meant, Ah! how am I enamoured with her!   'Tis an admirable language, this same Turkish!

Coviel.   More admirable than one can believe.   Do you know very well what is the meaning of Cacaramouchen?

Mr. Jordan.   Cacaramouchen?   No.

Coviel.   'Tis as if you should say, My dear soul.

Mr. Jordan.   Cacaramouchen means, My dear soul?

Coviel.   Yes.

Mr. Jordan.   Why, 'tis very wonderful!   Cacaramouchen,

my dear soul. Would one ever have thought it? I am perfectly confounded at it.

Coviel. In short, to finish my embassy, he comes to demand your daughter in marriage; and to have a father-in-law who should be suitable to him, he designs to make you a Mamamouchi, which is a certain grand dignity of his country.

Mr. Jordan. Mamamouchi?

Coviel. Yes, Mamamouchi: that is to say, in our language, a Paladin. Paladin, is your ancient —— Paladin in short: there's nothing in the world more noble than this; and you will rank with the grandest lord upon earth.

Mr. Jordan. The son of the Great Turk does me a great deal of honour, and I desire you would carry me to him, to return him my thanks.

Coviel. How? Why he's just acoming hither.

Mr. Jordan. Is he acoming hither?

Coviel. Yes. And he brings all things along with him for the ceremony of your dignity.

Mr. Jordan. He's main hasty.

Coviel. His love will suffer no delay.

Mr. Jordan. All that perplexes me, in this case, is, that my daughter is an obstinate hussy, who has took into her head one Cleontes, and vows she'll marry no person besides him.

Coviel. She'll change her opinion, when she sees the son of the Grand Turk; and then there happens here a very marvellous adventure, that is, that the son of the Grand Turk resembles this Cleontes, with a trifling difference. I just now came from him, they showed him me; and the love she bears for one, may easily pass to the other, and—I hear him coming; there he is.

SCENE VI

Cleontes (like a Turk), three Pages carrying the vest of Cleontes, Mr. Jordan, Coviel.

Cleontes. Ambousahim oqui boraf, Iordina, salamalequi.

Coviel. [*To Mr. Jordan.*] That is to say, Mr. Jordan, may your heart be all the year like a rose-tree in flower. These are obliging ways of speaking in that country.

Mr. Jordan. I am His Turkish Highness's most humble servant.

Coviel. Carigar camboto oustin moraf.

Cleontes. Oustin yoc catamalequi basum base alla moran.

Coviel. He says that Heaven has given you the strength of lions, and the prudence of serpents.

Mr. Jordan. His Turkish Highness does me too much honour; and I wish him all manner of prosperity.

Coviel. Ossa binamin sadoc babally oracaf ouram.

Cleontes. Bel-men.

Coviel. He says that you should go quickly with him, to prepare yourself for the ceremony, in order afterwards to see your daughter, and to conclude the marriage.

Mr. Jordan. So many things in two words?

Coviel. Yes, the Turkish language is much in that way; it says a great deal in a few words. Go quickly where he desires you.

Scene VII

Coviel. [*Alone.*] Ha, ha, ha. I'faith, this is all absolutely droll. What a dupe! Had he had his part by heart, he could not have played it better. O, hoh!

Scene VIII

Dorantes, Coviel.

Coviel. I beseech you, sir, lend us a helping hand here, in a certain affair which is in agitation.

Dorantes. Ah! ah! Coviel, who could have known thee? How art thou trimmed out there!

Coviel. You see, ha, ha.

Dorantes. What do ye laugh at?

Coviel. At a thing, sir, that well deserves it.

Dorantes. What?

Coviel. I could give you a good many times, sir, to guess the stratagem we are making use of with Mr. Jordan, to bring him over to give his daughter to my master.

Dorantes. I don't at all guess the stratagem, but I guess it will not fail of its effect, since you undertake it.

Coviel. I know, sir, you are not unacquainted with the animal.

Dorantes. Tell me what it is.

Coviel. Be at the trouble of withdrawing a little farther off, to make room for what I see acoming. You will see one part of the story, whilst I give you a narration of the rest.

Scene IX

The Turkish Ceremony.

The Mufti, Dervishes, Turks (assisting to the Mufti), Singers and Dancers.

Six Turks enter gravely, two and two, to the sound of instruments. They bear three carpets, with which they dance in several figures, and then lift them up very high. The Turks singing, pass under the carpets, and range themselves on each side of the stage. The Mufti accompanied by Dervishes, close the march.

Then the Turks spread the carpets on the ground, and kneel down upon them; the Mufti and the Dervishes standing in the middle of them; while the Mufti invokes Mahomet in dumb contortions and grimaces, the Turks prostrate themselves to the ground, singing Allah, raising their hands to heaven, singing Allah, and so continuing alternately to the end of the invocation. When they all rise up, singing Allahekber; then two Dervishes bring Mr. Jordan.

Scene X

The Mufti, Dervishes, Turkish Singers and Dancers, Mr. Jordan (clothed like a Turk, his head shaved, without a turban or sabre).

The Mufti to Mr. Jordan.

>If thou understandest,
>   Answer;
>If thou dost not understand,
>   Hold thy peace, hold thy peace.

>I am Mufti,
>   Thou! who thou art
>I don't know:
>   Hold thy peace, hold thy peace.
>   [*Two Dervishes retire with Mr. Jordan.*

Scene XI

The Mufti, Dervishes, Turks (singing and dancing).

Mufti. Say, Turk, who is this,
        An Anabaptist, an anabaptist?
The Turks. No.
Mufti. A Zuinglian?
The Turks. No.

Mufti. A Coffite?
The Turks. No.
Mufti. A Hussite? A Morist? A Fronest?
The Turks. No, no, no.
Mufti. No, no, no. Is he a Pagan?
The Turks. No.
Mufti. A Lutheran?
The Turks. No.
Mufti. A Puritan?
The Turks. No.
Mufti. A Brahmin? A Moffian? A Zurian?
The Turks. No, no, no.
Mufti. No, no, no. A Mahometan, a Mahometan?
The Turks. There you have it, there you have it.
Mufti. How is he called? How is he called?
The Turks. Jordan, Jordan.
Mufti. [*Dancing.*] Jordan! Jordan!
The Turks. Jordan, Jordan.
Mufti. To Mahomet for Jordan:
      I pray night and day,
      That he would make a Paladin
      Of Jordan, of Jordan.
      Give him a turban, and give a sabre,
      With a galley and a brigantine,
      To defend Palestine.
      To Mahomet for Jordan,
      I pray night and day.

                        [*To the Turks.*

      Is Jordan a good Turk?
The Turks. That he is, that he is.
Mufti. [*Singing and dancing.*] Ha, la ba, ba la chou, ba la ba, ba la da.
The Turks. Ha la ba, ba la chou, ba la ba, ba la da.

SCENE XII

Mufti, Dervishes, Mr. Jordan, Turks (singing and dancing).

The Mufti returns with the State Turban, which is of an immeasurable largeness, garnished with lighted wax candles, four or five rows deep, accompanied by two Dervishes bearing the Alcoran with conic caps, garnished also with lighted candles.

The two other Dervishes lead up Mr. Jordan, and place him on his knees with his hands to the ground, so that his back on which

the Alcoran is placed, may serve for a desk to the Mufti, who makes
a second burlesque invocation, knitting his eyebrows, striking his
hands sometimes upon the Alcoran, and tossing over the leaves with
precipitation ; after which, lifting up his hands, and crying with
a loud voice, Hou.

During this second invocation, the assistant Turks bowing down
and raising themselves alternately, sing likewise, Hou, hou, hou.

Mr. Jordan. [*After they have taken the Alcoran off his back.*]
Ouf.

Mufti. [*To Mr. Jordan.*] Thou wilt not be a knave?

The Turks. No, no, no.

Mufti. Not be a thief?

The Turks. No, no, no.

Mufti. [*To the Turks.*] Give the turban.

The Turks. Thou wilt not be a knave?

No, no, no.

Not be a thief?

No, no, no.

Give the turban.

[*The Turks dancing put the turban on Mr. Jordan's head at*
the sound of the instruments.

Mufti. [*Giving the sabre to Mr. Jordan.*]

Be brave, be no scoundrel,

Take the sabre.

The Turks. [*Drawing their sabres.*]

Be brave, be no scoundrel,

Take the sabre.

[*The Turks dancing strike Mr. Jordan several times with their*
sabres, to music.

Mufti. Give, give

The bastonade.

The Turks. Give, give

The bastonade.

[*The Turks dancing give Mr. Jordan several strokes with a*
cudgel to music.

Mufti. Don't think it a shame,

This is the last affront.

The Turks. Don't think it a shame,

This is the last affront.

The Mufti begins a third invocation. The Dervishes support
him with great respect, after which the Turks singing and dancing
round the Mufti, retire with him, and lead off Mr. Jordan.

ACT V

Scene I

Mrs. Jordan, Mr. Jordan.

Mrs. Jordan. Bless us all! Mercy upon us! What have we got here? What a figure! What! dressed to go a mumming, and is this a time to go masked? Speak therefore, what does this mean? Who has trussed you up in this manner?

Mr. Jordan. Do but see the impertinent slut, to speak after this manner to a Mamamouchi.

Mrs. Jordan. How's that?

Mr. Jordan. Yes, you must show me respect now I am just made a Mamamouchi.

Mrs. Jordan. What d'ye mean with your Mamamouchi?

Mr. Jordan. Mamamouchi, I tell you. I am a Mamamouchi.

Mrs. Jordan. What beast is that?

Mr. Jordan. Mamamouchi, that is to say, in our language, a Paladin.

Mrs. Jordan. A Paladin? Are you of an age to be a morris-dancer?

Mr. Jordan. What an ignoramus! I say, Paladin. 'Tis a dignity, of which I have just now gone through the ceremony.

Mrs. Jordan. What ceremony then?

Mr. Jordan. Mahameta per Jordina.

Mrs. Jordan. What does that mean?

Mr. Jordan. Jordina, that is to say, Jordan.

Mrs. Jordan. Well, how Jordan?

Mr. Jordan. Voler far un Paladina de Jordina.

Mrs. Jordan. What?

Mr. Jordan. Dar turbanta con galera.

Mrs. Jordan. What's the meaning of that?

Mr. Jordan. Per deffender Palestina.

Mrs. Jordan. What is it you would say?

Mr. Jordan. Dara, dara, bastonnara.

Mrs. Jordan. What is this same jargon?

Mr. Jordan. Non tener honta, questa star l'ultima affronta.

Mrs. Jordan. What in the name of wonder, can all this be?

Mr. Jordan. [*Singing and dancing.*] Hou la ba, ba la chou, ba la ba, ba la da. [*Falls down to the ground.*

Mrs. Jordan.   Alas and well-a-day! My husband is turned fool.

Mr. Jordan. [*Getting up and walking off.*]   Peace, insolence, show respect to Mr. Mamamouchi.

Mrs. Jordan. [*Alone.*]   How could he lose his senses? I must run and prevent his going out. [*Seeing Dorimène and Dorantes.*] So, so, here come the rest of our gang. I see nothing but vexation on all sides.

Scene II

Dorantes, Dorimène.

Dorantes. Yes, madam, you'll see the merriest thing that can be seen; and I don't believe it's possible, in the whole world, to find another man so much a fool as this here. And besides, madam, we must endeavour to promote Cleontes's amour, and to countenance his masquerade. He's a very pretty gentleman and deserves that one should interest one's self in his favour.

Dorimène. I've a very great value for him, and he deserves good fortune.

Dorantes. Besides, we have here, madam, an entertainment that will suit us, and which we ought not to suffer to be lost; and I must by all means see whether my fancy will succeed.

Dorimène. I saw there magnificent preparations, and these are things, Dorantes, I can no longer suffer. Yes, I'm resolved to put a stop, at last, to your profusions; and to break off all the expenses you are at on my account, I have determined to marry you out of hand. This is the real secret of the affair, and all these things end, as you know, with marriage.

Dorantes. Ah! madam, is it possible you should form so kind a resolution in my favour?

Dorimène. I only do it to prevent you from ruining yourself; and without this, I see plainly, that before 'tis long you won't be worth a groat.

Dorantes. How am I obliged to you, madam, for the care you take to preserve my estate! 'Tis entirely at your service, as well as my heart, and you may use both of 'em just in the manner you please.

Dorimène. I shall make a proper use of them both. But here comes your man; an admirable figure.

SCENE III

Mr. Jordan, Dorimène, Dorantes.

Dorantes. Sir, my lady and I are come to pay our homage to your new dignity, and to rejoice with you at the marriage you are concluding betwixt your daughter and the son of the Grand Turk.

Mr. Jordan. [*Bowing first in the Turkish manner.*] Sir, I wish you the force of serpents, and the wisdom of lions.

Dorimène. I was exceeding glad to be one of the first, sir, who should come and congratulate you upon the high degree of glory to which you are raised.

Mr. Jordan. Madam, I wish your rose-tree may flower all the year round; I am infinitely obliged to you for interesting yourselves in the honour that's paid me; and I am greatly rejoiced to see you returned hither, that I may make my most humble excuses for the impertinence of my wife.

Dorimène. That's nothing at all, I can excuse a commotion of this kind in her; your heart ought to be precious to her, and 'tis not at all strange the possession of such a man as you are, should give her some alarms.

Mr. Jordan. The possession of my heart is a thing you have entirely gained.

Dorantes. You see, madam, that Mr. Jordan is none of those people whom prosperity blinds, and that he knows, in all his grandeur, how to own his friends.

Dorimène. 'Tis the mark of a truly generous soul.

Dorantes. Where is His Turkish Highness? We should be glad, as your friends, to pay our devoirs to him.

Mr. Jordan. There he comes, and I have sent to bring my daughter to join hands with him.

SCENE IV

Mr. Jordan, Dorimène, Dorantes, Cleontes (in a Turkish habit).

Dorantes. [*To Cleontes.*] Sir, we come to compliment Your Highness, as friends of the gentleman your father-in-law, and to assure you, with respect, of our most humble services.

Mr. Jordan. Where's the dragoman, to tell him who you are, and make him understand what you say; you shall see that he'll answer you, and he speaks Turkish marvellously. Hola!

there; where the deuce is he gone? [*To Cleontes.*] Stref,
strif, strof, straf. The gentleman is a grande segnore, grande
segnore, grande segnore; and madam is a granda dama, granda
dama. [*Seeing he cannot make himself be understood.*] Lack-
a-day! [*To Cleontes.*] Sir, he be a French Mamamouchi. and
madam a French Mamamouchess. I can't speak plainer.
Good, here's the dragoman.

SCENE V

*Mr. Jordan, Dorimène, Dorantes, Cleontes (in a Turkish habit),
Coviel (disguised).*

Mr. Jordan. Where do you run? We can say nothing
without you. [*Pointing to Cleontes.*] Inform him a little that
the gentleman and lady are persons of great quality, who come
to pay their compliments to him, as friends of mine, and to
assure him of their services. [*To Dorimène and Dorantes.*] You
shall see how he will answer.

Coviel. Alabala crociam, acci boram alabamen.

Cleontes. Catalequi tubal ourin soter amalouchan.

Mr. Jordan. [*To Dorimène and Dorantes.*] Do ye see?

Coviel. He says that the rain of prosperity waters, at all
seasons, the garden of your family.

Mr. Jordan. I told you that he speaks Turkish.

Dorantes. This is admirable.

SCENE VI

Cleontes, Mr. Jordan, Lucilia. Dorimène, Dorantes, Coviel.

Mr. Jordan. Come, daughter, come nearer, and give the
gentleman your hand, who does you the honour of demanding
you in marriage.

Lucilia. What's the matter, father, how are you dressed
here? what! are you playing a comedy?

Mr. Jordan. No, no, 'tis no comedy, 'tis a very serious
affair; and the most honourable for you that possibly can be
wished. [*Pointing to Cleontes.*] This is the husband I bestow
upon you.

Lucilia. Upon me, father?

Mr. Jordan. Yes upon you, come take him by the hand, and
thank Heaven for your good fortune.

Lucilia. I won't marry.

Mr. Jordan. I'll make you, am I not your father?

Lucilia. I won't do it.

Mr. Jordan. Here's a noise indeed! Come, I tell you. Your hand here.

Lucilia. No, father, I've told you before that there's no power can oblige me to take any other husband than Cleontes; and I am determined upon all extremities rather than——— [*Discovering Cleontes.*] 'Tis true that you are my father; I owe you absolute obedience; and you may dispose of me according to your pleasure.

Mr. Jordan. Hah, I am charmed to see you return so readily to your duty; and it is a pleasure to me to have my daughter obedient.

SCENE VII

Cleontes, Mrs. Jordan, Mr. Jordan, Lucilia, Dorimène, Dorantes, Coviel.

Mrs. Jordan. How, how, what does this mean? They tell me you design to marry your daughter to a mummer.

Mr. Jordan. Will you hold your tongue, impertinence? You're always coming to mix your extravagances with everything; there's no possibility of teaching you common sense.

Mrs. Jordan. 'Tis you whom there's no teaching to be wise, and you go from folly to folly. What's your design, what would you do with this flock of people?

Mr. Jordan. I design to marry my daughter to the son of the Grand Turk.

Mrs. Jordan. To the son of the Grand Turk?

Mr. Jordan. Yes. [*Pointing to Coviel.*] Make your compliments to him by the dragoman there.

Mrs. Jordan. I have nothing to do with the dragoman, and I shall tell him plainly to his face that he shall have none of my daughter.

Mr. Jordan. Will you hold your tongue once more?

Dorantes. What, Mrs. Jordan, do you oppose such an honour as this? Do you refuse His Turkish Highness for a son-in-law?

Mrs. Jordan. Lack-a-day, sir, meddle you with your own affairs.

Dorimène. 'Tis a great honour, 'tis by no means to be rejected.

Mrs. Jordan. Madam, I desire you too not to give yourself any trouble about what no ways concerns you.

Dorantes. 'Tis the friendship we have for you, that makes us interest ourselves in what is of advantage to you.

Mrs. Jordan. I shall easily excuse your friendship.

Dorantes. There's your daughter consents to her father's pleasure.

Mrs. Jordan. My daughter consent to marry a Turk?

Dorantes. Certainly.

Mrs. Jordan. Can she forget Cleontes?

Dorantes. What would one not do to be a great lady?

Mrs. Jordan. I would strangle her with my own hands, had she done such a thing as this.

Mr. Jordan. Here's tittle-tattle in abundance. I tell you this marriage shall be consummated.

Mrs. Jordan. And I tell you that it shall not be consummated.

Mr. Jordan. What a noise is here?

Lucilia. Mother!

Mrs. Jordan. Go, you are a pitiful hussy.

Mr. Jordan. [*To Mrs. Jordan.*] What! do you scold her for being obedient to me?

Mrs. Jordan. Yes, she belongs to me as well as you.

Coviel. [*To Mrs. Jordan.*] Madam.

Mrs. Jordan. What would you say to me, you?

Coviel. One word.

Mrs. Jordan. I've nothing to do with your word.

Coviel. [*To Mr. Jordan.*] Sir, would she hear me but one word in private, I'll promise you to make her consent to what you have a mind.

Mrs. Jordan. I won't consent to it.

Coviel. Only hear me.

Mrs. Jordan. No.

Mr. Jordan. [*To Mrs. Jordan.*] Give him the hearing.

Mrs. Jordan. No, I won't hear him.

Mr. Jordan. He'll tell you——

Mrs. Jordan. He shall tell me nothing.

Mr. Jordan. Do but see the great obstinacy of the woman! Will it do you any harm to hear him?

Coviel. Only hear me; you may do what you please afterwards.

Mrs. Jordan. Well, what?

Coviel. [*Aside to Mrs. Jordan.*] We have made signs to you, madam, this hour. Don't you see plainly that all is done purely to accommodate ourselves to the visions of your husband; that we are imposing upon him under this disguise, and that it is Cleontes himself who is the son of the Great Turk?

Mrs. Jordan. [*Aside to Coviel.*] Oh, oh?

Coviel. [*Aside to Mrs. Jordan.*] And that 'tis me, Coviel, who am the dragoman?

Mrs. Jordan. [*Aside to Coviel.*] Oh! in that case, I give up.

Coviel. [*Aside to Mrs. Jordan.*] Don't seem to know anything of the matter.

Mrs. Jordan. [*Aloud.*] Yes, 'tis all done, I consent to the marriage.

Mr. Jordan. Ay, all the world submits to reason. [*To Mrs. Jordan.*] You would not hear him. I knew he would explain to you what the son of the Great Turk is.

Mrs. Jordan. He has explained it to me sufficiently, and I'm satisfied with it. Let us send to see for a notary.

Dorantes. 'Tis well said. And, Mrs. Jordan, that you may set your mind perfectly at rest, and that you should this day quit all jealousy which you may have entertained of the gentleman your husband, my lady and I shall make use of the same notary to marry us.

Mrs. Jordan. I consent to that too.

Mr. Jordan. [*Aside to Dorantes.*] 'Tis to make her believe.

Dorantes. [*Aside to Mr. Jordan.*] We must by all means amuse her a little with this pretence.

Mr. Jordan. Good, good. [*Aloud.*] Let somebody go see for the notary.

Dorantes. In the meantime, till he comes and has drawn up the contracts, let us see our entertainment, and give His Turkish Highness the diversion of it.

Mr. Jordan. Well advised; come let us take our places.

Mrs. Jordan. And Nicola?

Mr. Jordan. I give her to the dragoman; and my wife, to whosoever pleases to take her.

Coviel. Sir, I thank you. [*Aside.*] If it's possible to find a greater fool than this, I'll go and publish it at Rome.

THE IMPERTINENTS

(A COMEDY)

THE IMPERTINENTS, *a Comedy of Three Acts in Verse, acted at Vaux in the month of August, 1661, and at Paris at the Theatre of the Palace-Royal the 4th of November the same year.*

The theatre again resounded with the just applause which was given to *The School for Husbands*, when *The Impertinents* was acted at Vaux in the house of Monsieur Fouquet, Superintendent of the Finances, before the king and court; Paul Pellisson, less famous for the delicacy of his wit, than for his inviolable attachment to the person of M. Fouquet, even in his misfortunes composed the prologue to it in praise of the king; the scene of the hunter, the hint of which was given to Molière by the king, was afterwards added when it was acted at St. Germains. This kind of comedy is almost void of all plot, the scenes have no necessary connection with one another, you may change the order of them, leave out some, and substitute others without injuring the work; but the essential point was to keep up the attention of the spectator by the variety of characters, the justness of the portraits, and the continued elegance of the style; 'twas the assemblage of these exquisite beauties, 'twas this image, or rather reality itself of the embarrassments and importunities of a court, which gave success to *The Impertinents*.

ACTORS

Damis, *guardian of Orphisa.*
Orphisa.
Erastus, *in love with Orphisa.*
Alcidorus,
Lysander,
Alcander,
Alcippus,
Orante,
Climène,   *Impertinents.*
Dorantes,
Caritides,
Ormin,
Philintes,
Montaign, *servant of Erastus.*
L'Espine, *servant of Damis.*
La Rivière, *and two other servants of Erastus.*

Scene: *Paris.*

ACT I

SCENE I

Erastus, Montaign.

Erastus. Under what planet, kind Heaven, must I be born, to be always plagued to death with impertinents! I think fortune throws 'em in my way wherever I go, and I see some new species of 'em every day. But there's nothing can equal to-day's impertinent, I thought I should never have got rid of him; and a hundred times did I curse that innocent fancy, which took me at dinner, of seeing a play; where, thinking to divert myself, I unhappily met with a most severe punishment for my sins; I must give thee an account of the whole affair; for I find my passion is still up when I think of it. I was got upon the stage in an humour of hearkening to the piece, which I had heard cried up by several persons. The actors began, and everybody was silent, when, with a blustering air, and full of extravagance, in brushes a man with huge pantaloons, crying out, Soho there! a chair, quickly; and surprised the audience with his great noise; being interrupted in one of the most beautiful passages of the piece. Heaven defend us! says I, will our Frenchmen who are so often corrected, never behave themselves with an air of men of sense? Must we, through excess of folly, expose ourselves in a public theatre, and so confirm, by the noise of fools, what is everywhere said of us among our neighbours? While I was shrugging up my shoulders at this, the actors were willing to go on with their parts. But the fellow, in seating himself, made a new disturbance, and crossing the stage again with large strides, though he might have sat at his ease on either side, he planted his chair in the middle of the front, and insulting the spectators with his brawny back, he hid the actors from three-fourths of the pit. There was a noise set up, that would have shamed another man; but he, steady and firm, did not at all mind it, and would have continued just as he had placed himself, had he not, to my misfortune, spied out me. Ha! marquis, says he to me, placing himself by me, How dost thou do? Let me embrace thee. I immediately blushed that people

285

should see I was acquainted with such a shittle-brained mortal: though I was very little so. But it will be seen in those people, who will be hugely great with you from nothing at all, whose kisses you must endure, as you tender your happiness, and who are so familiar with you, as even to thee and thou you. He asked me, immediately, a hundred frivolous questions, exalting his voice above the actors. Everybody cursed him, and to stop him, I should be very glad, says I, to hear the play. Thou hast not seen this, marquis, heh! Rat me, I think it droll enough, and I'm no ass in these things; I know by what rules a work is to be finished, and Corneille reads everything he does to me. Upon this, he gave me a summary of the whole piece, telling me scene by scene, what was to be done next, and even the verses he could say by heart, he repeated aloud to me before the actors. 'Twas in vain for me to resist, he pushed his point, and towards the end got up a good while before the time; for these fine fellows, to act genteelly, take special care above all things not to hear the conclusion. I thanked Heaven, and reasonably thought that with the play my misery would have ended: but, as if I had come off too cheap, my gentleman joined me afresh; rehearsed to me his exploits, his uncommon virtues, spoke of his horses, his good fortune, and the favour he had at court, offering me his service there with all his heart. I thanked him gently, with a nod, meditating at every turn a handsome retreat; but he observing me upon the move in order to leave him, Come, says he to me, let's go, everybody's gone: and being got out of that place, giving it me more home, Marquis, let us go to the ring and see my chariot, 'tis well contrived, and more than one duke and lord have bespoken one of the same fashion of my coachmaker. I thanked him, and the better to get off, told him that I had a certain entertainment to make. Hah! I'll make one at it, egad, being in the number of thy friends, and balk the man of quality, to whom I was engaged. Our poor pittance of cheer, says I, is by much too small to dare invite a person of your condition to it. No, answered he, I'm a man of no ceremony, and I only go there to have a little chat with thee; I swear to thee, I'm tired with great entertainments. But, says I, 'twill be wrong if they expect you. Thou art out, marquis, we have all a good understanding together; and I think entertainments much pleasanter with thee. I stormed within myself, was melancholy and confused at the unhappy success my excuse had had, and knew not whither to betake myself to get rid of a trouble that was death to me; when a

chariot, made after a most sumptuous manner, and loaded
with footmen before and behind, happened to stop with a huge
noise just before us; from whence out jumps a young fellow,
dressed out after an ample manner; my impertinent and he
rushing to embrace, surprised the passers-by with their furious
encounter; and whilst they were both thrown into the con-
vulsions of their civilities, I stole slyly away without saying a
word; not without having groaned long under the torture, and
cursed the impertinent whose obstinate fondness kept me from
the rendezvous which had been appointed me here.

Montaign. There are vexations mixed with the pleasures
of life; everything, sir, goes not exactly to our liking; Heaven
thinks fit we should all have our impertinents here below, and
without this, men would be too happy.

Erastus. But of all my impertinents, the most impertinent
still is Damis, guardian to her I adore; who dashes all the hopes
she is pleased to give me in my addresses; and notwithstanding
her kindness prevents her to see me. I'm afraid I have already
passed the hour appointed, and 'twas in this walk Orphisa was
to be.

Montaign. The hour of an appointment has generally some
latitude, and is not confined to the limits of an instant.

Erastus. 'Tis true; but I tremble, and the excess of my
passion makes a crime even of nothing towards her I love.

Montaign. If this perfect love, which you so well testify,
makes a crime of nothing, towards her you love; in return, the
just passion she entertains for you, makes nothing of all your
crimes.

Erastus. But dost thou, in good earnest, believe she loves me?

Montaign. What! do you still doubt of a confirmed love?

Erastus. Ah! 'tis with great difficulty that in such a matter
a heart much enamoured, rests entirely satisfied. It is afraid
of flattering itself, and amidst its various cares, what it most
wishes is what it least believes. But let us endeavour to find
the delightful creature.

Montaign. Sir, your band gapes before.

Erastus. No matter.

Montaign. Pray, let me set it right.

Erastus. Pho! you strangle me, blockhead, let it alone as
it is.

Montaign. Let me comb a little——

Erastus. Was ever such stupidity! Thou hast almost took
off one of my ears with a tooth of the comb.

Montaign.   Your pantaloons——
Erastus.   Let 'em alone, you are over careful.
Montaign.   They are all rumpled.
Erastus.   I'll have 'em so.
Montaign.   Permit me, for goodness' sake, to brush this hat, which is full of dust.
Erastus.   Brush it then, since I must go through all this.
Montaign.   Will you wear it cocked, as it is?
Erastus.   S'death! make haste.
Montaign.   'Twould be a shame——
Erastus. [*Having waited some time.*]   'Tis enough.
Montaign.   Have a little patience.
Erastus.   He kills me.
Montaign.   Where have you been thrusting yourself?
Erastus.   D'ye design to keep the hat for ever?
Montaign.   'Tis done.
Erastus.   Give it me then.
Montaign. [*Letting the hat fall.*]   Hey!
Erastus.   There, 'tis down!   I'm finely helped forward.   A plague to thee.
Montaign.   Let me but with a rub or two take off——
Erastus.   I'll not have it done.   A deuce take all trouble-some servants who fatigue their masters, and do nothing but displease by mere affectation of being necessary.

Scene II

Orphisa, Alcidorus, Erastus, Montaign.

Erastus.   But don't I see Orphisa?   Yes, 'tis she that comes. Whither is she going so fast, and who is he that hands her?
   [*He salutes her as she passes by, and she turns her head another way.*

Scene III

Erastus, Montaign.

Erastus.   What! see me here plainly before her and pass me pretending not to know me?   What can I think?   What say you?   Speak if you will.
Montaign.   Sir, I say nothing, for fear of being impertinent.
Erastus.   And it is in reality being so, to say nothing to me, in the extremity of this cruel torture?   Make some answer to

my dejected heart. What am I to imagine? Speak, what d'ye think of it? Tell me your opinion.

Montaign. Sir, I'll be silent, and don't desire to affect being necessary.

Erastus. Plague on the impertinent puppy! Go follow them; and see what becomes of 'em, and don't quit them.

Montaign. [*Coming back.*] Must I follow them at a distance?

Erastus. Yes.

Montaign. [*Coming back.*] Without their seeing me, or making the least show of being sent after them?

Erastus. No, you'll do better to give them notice that you follow them by my express order.

Montaign. [*Coming back.*] Shall I find you here?

Erastus. Heaven confound thee, for the most impertinent fellow, in my opinion, in the world.

Scene IV

Erastus. [*Alone.*] Oh! What trouble do I feel! How happy had it been for me, had they made me balk this fatal appointment! I thought to have found everything propitious to me; and my eyes have seen what stabs me to the heart.

Scene V

Lysander, Erastus.

Lysander. I knew thee, my dear marquis, at a great distance under these trees, and immediately made up to thee. I must sing to thee, as one of my friends, a certain air of a little courant that I have made, which pleases all the people at court, who have any skill; and to which more than twenty have already made verses. I have wealth, birth, and a good tolerable employment, and make a figure in France, considerable enough; but I would not, for all I'm worth, but have made that air, which I am going to show thee: La, la, hem, hem; prithee mind it. [*He sings his courant.*] Isn't it pretty?

Erastus. Oh!

Lysander. This close is pretty. [*He sings the close over again four or five times successively.*] What think you of it?

Erastus. Very pretty, certainly.

Lysander. The steps I have made to it are not less agreeable; and above all, the figure has a marvellous grace. [*He sings, talks, and dances all together.*] Stay, the man crosses thus: then the woman crosses again. Together, then they quit, and the woman comes there. Dost thou see this pretty touch of a feint here? This fleuret? These coupees running after the fair one? Back to back; face to face pressing up close to her? What dost thou think of it, marquis?

Erastus. All these steps are fine.

Lysander. For my part, I despise the dancing-masters.

Erastus. I see so.

Lysander. Then the steps?

Erastus. Have nothing but what is surprising.

Lysander. Wouldst thou have me teach 'em thee out of friendship?

Erastus. Faith, for the present, I have a certain perplexity—

Lysander. Well then, it shall be when you please; if I had these new words about me, we would read them together, and see which were prettiest.

Erastus. Another time.

Lysander. Adieu. My dearest Baptist has not seen my courant, and I am going to seek for him. We have a mighty sympathy in our taste for tunes, and I'll desire him to add the parts to it. [*Exit, singing as he goes.*

Scene VI

Erastus. [*Alone.*] Heavens! must quality, which people would make a cover for everything, oblige us daily to endure a hundred fools! and make us demean ourselves frequently, even to the complaisance of applauding their impertinencies!

Scene VII

Erastus, Montaign.

Montaign. Sir, Orphisa is alone, and coming this way.

Erastus. Oh! what hurry and disorder am I in! I have still a fondness for this inhuman beauty, and my reason bids me hate her.

Montaign. Your reason, sir, neither knows what it would have, nor what power a mistress has over a man's heart. Though one has ever so just cause to be in a passion, a fine woman can adjust everything with a word speaking.

Erastus. Alas! I confess it, and the sight of her has already impressed a respect upon all my resentment.

SCENE VIII

Orphisa, Erastus, Montaign.

Orphisa. Your countenance seems to me not very cheerful,
should it be my presence, Erastus, that offends you? What
means this? What's the matter with you? What uneasiness
makes you sigh so deep at the sight of me?

Erastus. Alas! Can you then ask me, cruel creature, what
it is that occasions this mortal sorrow of heart? Is it not the
effect of a malicious temper to pretend ignorance of what you
have done—— He whose conversation made you pass me full
in view——

Orphisa. [*Laughing.*] Is that what you are disturbed about?

Erastus. Do, inhuman creature, still insult my misery; go,
it ill becomes you to rally my sorrow; to abuse, ungrateful as
you are, and to injure my passion, on account of the foible which
you know is owing to yourself.

Orphisa. Certainly one must laugh at you, and confess too,
that you are very silly to give yourself such uneasiness. The
man you speak of, so far from pleasing me, is an impertinent
fellow whom I was contriving to shake off; one of those troublesome and officious fools, who can't suffer one to be alone anywhere, come immediately, with fawning compliments, to offer
you their hand, which one wishes 'em hanged for. I pretended
to be going away, to hide my design; and he would hand me even
to my coach. I got rid of him presently in that way, and came
in again by the other gate to see for you.

Erastus. Shall I give credit to this story of yours, Orphisa?
And is your heart sincere to me?

Orphisa. You are a pretty gentleman indeed, to talk in this
manner; when I justify myself against your frivolous complaints. I am very simple too, and my foolish kindness——

Erastus. Ah! be not angry, too severe beauty. Being
absolutely under your command, I will implicitly believe everything you are so good as to tell me. Deceive, if you please,
an unhappy lover; I shall respect you, even to the grave. Abuse
my love, and refuse me yours; expose to my sight the triumph
of my rival; yes, I'll bear with everything from those heavenly
charms; I'll die for it, but, in short, never will complain.

Orphisa. When such sentiments reign in your breast, I shall
on my part——

SCENE IX

Alcander, Orphisa, Erastus, Montaign.

Alcander. Marquis, a word with thee. [*To Orphisa.*]
Madam, be so good to pardon the indiscretion of presuming to
whisper before you.   [*Orphisa goes out.*

SCENE X

Alcander, Erastus, Montaign.

Alcander. 'Tis with reluctance, marquis, I make thee this
request; but there's a man has just now palpably affronted me,
and I heartily wish, not to be behind-hand with him, that thou
wouldst immediately carry him a challenge from me. Thou
knowest that, in the like case, I should gladly repay thee in
the same coin.
Erastus. [*Having stood silent some time.*] I will not now act
the bravo; yet I have been a soldier before I was a courtier;
I served fourteen years and think I may fairly withdraw myself
from such a scrape, with a good grace, and not fear that the
refusal of my sword will be imputed to me as any cowardice.
Duelling puts people in a wretched posture; and our king is no
mere painted monarch, he will be obeyed by the people of first
rank in his kingdom; and I think he acts in this like a worthy
prince. When his service calls me I have a heart to do it: but
I don't find I have one to displease him. I regard his order as
a supreme law; seek somebody else, and not me, to disobey
him. I talk with great frankness to thee, marquis, and am,
in any other affair, thy most obedient. Adieu.

SCENE XI

Erastus, Montaign.

Erastus. A legion take all impertinents for me. Where is
this dear object of my vows retired to?
Montaign. I don't know.
Erastus. Go search everywhere to find her out. I shall wait
in this walk.

ACT II

Scene I

Erastus. What, have my impertinents dispersed at last? I think it rains impertinents from all quarters. I fly from 'em, and meet 'em; and for an additional torment, I cannot find her I wish to find. The thunder and rain are quickly over, and have not chased away the beau-monde. Would Heaven, among the favours it bestows here so profusely, they had but chased away the people that tease me! The sun goes down apace, and I am astonished my man is not come back yet.

Scene II

Alcippus, Erastus.

Alcippus. A good day to ye.

Erastus. [*Aside.*] What, always my love diverted?

Alcippus. Give me consolation, marquis, for the strange hand I yesterday lost at piquet, with one St. Bovain, to whom I could have given fifteen, and the eldest hand. 'Tis a blow would make one mad, it plagues me ever since yesterday, and would make one wish all gamesters at the devil; a blow most certainly to make one hang one's self at the market-cross. I want but two, the other wants a pique. I deal, he takes six, and demands to deal over again. I seeing myself almost up, would not consent to it. I go out Ace of Clubs (do but admire my misfortune) the Ace, King, Knave, Ten, and Eight of Hearts; and throw out, as my policy was to go for Point, Queen and King of Diamonds; Ten and Queen of Spades. To my Five Hearts that I went out, I took in also the Queen, which made me exactly a Quint Major. But my gentleman with the Ace, not without my extreme surprise, spreads upon the table a Sixième of low Diamonds. I had thrown out the Queen of the same with the King, but he missing of his pique, I recovered my fright, and reasonably thought I should make at least two poor tricks. With the seven Diamonds he had four Spades; and playing the last of 'em, it puzzled me cruelly, as not knowing which of my two Aces to keep. I threw away the Ace of Hearts, as I think, with good reason, but he had discarded four Clubs. And there was I capoted with a Six of Hearts, without being able, through vexation, to utter one word. S'heart, do me justice for this horrible stroke; had one not seen it, could one possibly have believed it?

Erastus. The greatest strokes of fortune are observed to be in play.

Alcippus. S'death, you yourself shall be judge whether I am wrong; and whether 'tis without reason that this accident puts me out of all patience, for here are our two games, which I have directly about me; stay, this is the hand I went out, as I told you; and here——

Erastus. I comprehended it all by your description of it, and see the justice of the passion which ruffles you; but I must leave you, upon a certain affair. Adieu, comfort yourself however under your misfortune.

Alcippus. Who? I? I shall always have it next my heart: 'tis to my mind, worse than a thunderbolt, I'm determined to show it to all the world. [*He goes a little way, and ready to turn back, calls out.*] A Six o' Hearts! Two tricks!

Erastus. [*Alone.*] What place are we got into? Turn which way one will one sees nothing but fools.

Scene III

Erastus, Montaign.

Erastus. Hah! How hast thou suffered me to languish through impatience!

Montaign. Sir, I could make no more haste.

Erastus. But dost thou bring me any news at last?

Montaign. Doubtless, and from the object, on whom depends your destiny, I have, by her express order, something to tell you.

Erastus. What? My heart already longs to hear this. Speak.

Montaign. Do you wish to know what it is?

Erastus. Yes, say quick.

Montaign. Stay, sir, if you please; I've almost put myself out o' breath with running.

Erastus. Dost thou take pleasure in keeping me in pain?

Montaign. Since you desire immediately to know the order I received from this charming object, I'll tell you——Troth, without bragging to you of my diligence, I went a huge way to find the lady; and if——

Erastus. Plague o' thy digressions.

Montaign. Fie! you should moderate a little your passions; and Seneca——

Erastus. Seneca's a fool, in thy mouth, since he tells me not a word that concerns me.   Give me the order, quick.

Montaign. To satisfy your longing, your Orphisa——there's an insect got into your hair.

Erastus. Let it be there.

Montaign. This fair one bids me tell you on her part——

Erastus. What?

Montaign. Guess.

Erastus. Dost thou know I'm not in a laughing humour?

Montaign. Her order is, that you are to stay in this place, assuring yourself that in a little while you shall see her here, when she has got rid of some country ladies, who are a troublesome sort of animals to courtiers.

Erastus. Let us then keep in the place that she was pleased to choose: but since this appointment gives me here some leisure, leave me to think a little; [*Montaign goes out.*] I have a design of making her some verses, to a tune which I know she takes delight in.   [*Musing.*

SCENE IV

Orante, Climène, Erastus (at a corner of the stage without being seen).

Orante. All the world will be of my opinion.

Climène. Do you think to carry it by obstinacy?

Orante. I think my reasons better than yours.

Climène. I wish somebody would give us both the hearing.

Orante. [*Seeing Erastus.*] I see a man here who is no ignoramus; he may be judge in our difference. [*To Erastus.*] Marquis, a word with you, pray; allow us to appeal to you, to be judge in a quarrel betwixt us two, in a debate arising from our different sentiments, about what is a sign of the most perfect lover.

Erastus. 'Tis a difficult question to decide, and you had best see for a more skilful judge.

Orante. No, these stories you tell us are to no purpose: you are a noted wit, and we know you well; we know that everybody, with justice, gives you the character——

Erastus. Oh! I beseech you——

Orante. In one word, you shall be our arbitrator, and you must bestow a minute or two upon us.

Climène. [*To Orante.*] You retain here a person who is to condemn you: for in short, if what I venture to believe of him is true, the gentleman will honour my reasons with the victory.

Erastus. [*Aside.*] That I can't beat it into my rascal's head, to invent something to get me off!

Orante. [*To Climène.*] For my part, I have too good proof of his wit, to fear he should pronounce anything to my disadvantage. [*To Erastus.*] In short, this grand debate which is kindled betwixt us, is whether a lover should be jealous.

Climène. Or the better to explain our thoughts, Who should please most, one that is jealous, or one that is otherwise.

Orante. For my part, without dispute, I am for the last.

Climène. And I hold, in my sentiment, for the former.

Orante. I think we should give our vote on the side of him who shows most respect.

Climène. And I, that if our inclinations must appear it should be in favour of him who discovers most love.

Orante. Yes, but one discovers the warmth of a lover's passion much better in respect, than jealousy.

Climène. And 'tis my opinion, that whoever has an attachment to us, is by so much the more amorous, as he is the more jealous.

Orante. Fie, Climène, talk not to me of those people for lovers, whose love resembles hatred, and who instead of respect, and gentle addresses, never apply themselves to anything but being troublesome; whose minds, being ever prompted by a gloomy passion, busy themselves in converting our least actions into a crime; subject our innocence to their blindness, and want an explanation from us upon the least glance of an eye; who perceiving in us any appearance of sadness, presently complain it arises from their presence; and when the least joy brightens up in our eyes, will have their rivals to be at the bottom of it. In short, who taking privilege from the fury of their love, never speak to us but with a design to pick a quarrel; they presume to forbid everybody approaching us, and set themselves up for tyrants over their very conquerors. The lovers for me, are such as respect inspires, and their submission is a surer mark of our power.

Climène. Fie, talk not to me of those persons as true lovers, who feel no manner of transports; those lukewarm gallants, whose peaceable hearts reckon already upon all things as sure in their favour; have no fear of losing us, and through too great confidence, suffer their love, at every turn, to fall asleep; have a good intelligence with their rivals, and leave them a clear stage to push their point.   A love so sedate raises my choler, not to be jealous is loving with indifference; and I would have a lover, to convince me of his passion, float on eternal suspicions; one who, by his hasty transports, gives a glaring token of the esteem he has for her to whom he makes his pretensions.   One then applauds one's self for his disquiet; and if he sometimes treats us in too rude a manner, the pleasure of seeing him on his knees before us, to excuse himself for the violence of his passion, his tears, his vexation for having displeased us, are a charm sufficient to appease all our anger.

Orante.   If there must go so much raving to please you, I can tell who could content you; and I know some five or six people in Paris, who, as they make it appear, love to such a degree as to go to cuffs about it.

Climène.   If to please you there must be no jealousy, I know some certain people would hit you exactly.   Men of so patient a humour in their love, that they could see you in the arms of thirty, without being concerned at it.

Orante.   In short, you are to declare, by your sentence, which person's love appears preferable to you.

[*Orphisa appears at the farther end of the stage and sees Erastus between Orante and Climène.*

Erastus.   Since I can't get clear without giving sentence, I'll satisfy you both at once; and not to blame what is agreeable to either of you, the jealous loves most, and the other loves much the best.

Climène.   The sentence is very judicious; but——

Erastus.   No more, I am clear of it.   After what I have said, permit me to leave you.

Scene V

Orphisa, Erastus.

Erastus. [*Seeing Orphisa, and going up to her.*]   How long you stay, madam, and how plainly I see——

Orphisa.   No, no, by no means quit such pleasant conversation.   You are in the wrong to accuse me for being too long acoming; and you had something could make you easily dispense with my absence.

Erastus.   Will you fall into a passion with me without cause, and do you reproach me for the plague they have given me? Nay, I beseech you stay——

Orphisa.   Pray let me alone, and go join your company again.

Scene VI

Erastus [*Alone.*] Heavens! must impertinents of both sexes conspire this day to frustrate the dearest of my wishes! But let me follow her, in spite of her opposing it, and clear up my innocence to her.

Scene VII

Dorantes, Erastus.

Dorantes. Ha! marquis, what swarms of impertinents does one every day meet with, to interrupt the course of one's pleasures! Here am I in such a rage at a very fine chase, which a booby——'Tis a story that I must tell thee.

Erastus. I'm looking for a certain person here, and can't stay.

Dorantes. Egad, I'll tell it thee as we go along. We were an agreeable select company of us, who made a party yesterday to hunt a stag; and we went on purpose into the country to lie upon the spot, that is to say, my dear, in the thickest part of the forest. As this exercise is my supreme delight, I had a mind, that the thing might be well done, to go into the wood myself; and we all concluded to bend all our efforts upon a stag, which everybody told us was a full-made stag; but for my part, my judgment was, without standing to observe the marks, that he was only a stag of the second head. We had separated our relays, as was proper, and were breakfasting in haste, upon some new-laid eggs, when a plain countryman, with a long rapier, proudly mounting his breeding-mare, which he honoured with the title of his good mare, came to make us an awkward compliment, presenting us also, to complete the vexation, with a great looby of a son, as much a fool as his father. He called himself a great hunter, and begged of us that he might have the favour of the chase along with us. Heaven preserve every skilful person, when hunting, from a fellow that blows his horn unseasonably, from people who having half a score scabby beagles at their heels, cry, My pack, and are marvellous hunters. His request being granted, and his virtues esteemed, we were all pursuing our blinks. Within the distance of three bow-shots, all of a sudden was cried, Ilho! Ilho! The dogs were laid on the stag; I second it, and blow aloud; my stag unharbours, and passes a pretty long plain, and my dogs after him, but so well in breath that you might have covered them all with a cloak.

He made to the forest. We then slip the old pack upon him,
and I in great haste take my chestnut horse. Have you seen him?

Erastus.   I think not.

Dorantes.   How! 'tis a horse as good as he is handsome, and
which I bought a few days ago of Gaveau. I leave you to judge
whether he would deceive me in such a matter as this, he that
considers who I am; so that I am perfectly easy about him;
and in reality, he never sold a better horse, nor a better made
one. The head of a barb, with a fair star, the neck of a swan,
slender, and very straight; no more shoulders than a hare, short-
jointed, and that shows his vivacity by his carriage; feet, egad,
such feet! double-reined; to say the truth, I was the only
person could find the way to master him, and young Jack
Gaveau never mounted him without trembling, though he
endeavoured to set a good face on it. His buttocks are not to
be equalled for largeness, and legs, mercy o' me! In short he's
a miracle; if you'll believe me, I refused a hundred pieces for
him, and one of the king's horses to boot. I mount therefore,
and was in high pleasure to see the vintagers in rows at a great
distance on the plain; I spur on, and find myself in a by-thicket
at the heels of the dogs, only I and Drecar. Within that our
stag stood at bay for an hour; upon this I cheer the dogs, and
played the deuce and all among them. In short, never was
hunter in higher glee; I imprimed him myself, and all things
went swimmingly; ours joined company with a young hind; one
part of my dogs divided from the other, and then, marquis,
as you may easily imagine, they all hunted timorous, and
Fowler was at a loss; he turned all o' the sudden, which made
my heart jump for joy; he struck in afresh upon the track, and
I found my horn, and cry, Hark to Fowler, hark to Fowler;
I traced him again with pleasure upon a molehill, and sounded
again a long while. Some of the dogs came back to me, when,
as ill-luck would have it, the young hind, marquis, passes my
country bumpkin. My hairbrains, as was likely, falls ablowing
his horn, and bellowing aloud, Ilho, Ilho, Ilhoy. My dogs all
quitted me, and make directly to my booby; I puts on thither,
and discovered the track again in the high road; but no sooner,
my dear, had I cast my eyes on the ground, but I found out
the change, and was heartily mortified. In vain did I show
him all the differences between the edge of my stag's hoofs,
and his marks, he still maintains to me, like a blockhead of a
sportsman, that 'tis the pack-stag, and by this dispute he gave
time for the dogs to get a great way off. I stormed at it, and

cursing the mortal with all my heart, I spurs my horse full speed o'er hill and dale, who brushed through boughs as thick as my arm. I recovered the dogs to my first scent, who, to my great joy, run upon the quest of our stag, as if they had been in full view. They imprime him afresh; but was ever such a trick seen before? To tell thee the truth, marquis, it frets me to death; our stag being imprimed, runs by our spark, who thinking to do the exploit of a most laudable huntsman, with a holster-pistol, that he had brought along with him, shoots him directly through the head, and cries out to me a vast way off, I've fetched the beast down. Good Heaven! Did ever anybody hear of pistols in stag-hunting? For my part, when I arrived at the spot, I thought it was so out of the way an action, that I claps both spurs to my horse in a rage, and never stopped gallop till I got home, without saying so much as one word to this ignorant puppy.

Erastus. You could not do better, thy prudence is admirable; just so should we shake off all impertinents. Adieu.

Dorantes. When you please, we'll go to some place where we shall have no fear of your country hunters.

Erastus. Very well. [*Alone.*] I think at last I shall lose all patience. Let me make all haste possible to excuse myself.

ACT III

SCENE I

Erastus, Montaign.

Erastus. 'Tis true. my diligence hath succeeded on one hand: the dear object was at last appeased: but on the other, they quite weary me, and my cruel stars have persecuted me, in my amour, with double fury. Yes, her tutor, Damis, one of my most shocking impertinents, afresh opposes my most tender addresses; has forbidden me the sight of his lovely niece; and designs to provide her another husband to-morrow. Orphisa, however, in spite of his discharging her, deigns this evening to grant one favour to my love; and I have prevailed upon the fair one to permit me to wait upon her in private, at her own house. Love delights, above everything, in secret favours, it finds a pleasure in breaking through opposition; and when 'tis forbidden, the least conversation with the beloved beauty becomes a supreme favour. I must to my appointment: 'tis near upon the hour: and besides, I would choose to be there rather before than after the time.

Montaign. Shall I follow you?

Erastus. No, I should be afraid you would discover me to some suspicious person or other.

Montaign. But——

Erastus. I would not have you.

Montaign. I must obey your commands: but at a distance, at least——

Erastus. Twenty times over must I bid thee hold thy tongue? Wilt thou never leave off this way of making thyself troublesome, at every turn, for an impertinent valet?

Scene II

Caritides, Erastus.

Caritides. Sir, 'tis an unseasonable time to do myself the honour of waiting upon you, the morning is most proper for the performance of that duty: but it is not very easy to meet with you; for you are always either asleep, or abroad; at least your servants always tell me so; and I took this opportunity to find you; 'tis a great happiness too that fortune favours me with, for two moments later, and I had missed of you again.

Erastus. Sir, do you want anything with me?

Caritides. I acquit myself, sir, of the duty I owe you; and come—excuse the boldness that inspires me, if——

Erastus. Without so much ceremony, what have you to say to me?

Caritides. As the rank, the wit, the generosity, which everybody extols in you——

Erastus. Yes, I am very much extolled; proceed, sir.

Caritides. Sir, it is an extreme difficulty upon a man, when he is obliged to produce himself to any person: and one should always be introduced to great men, by people who set us forth a little; whose discourse being hearkened to, displays, with some weight, what our little merit can show: for my part, I should have been glad that somebody, who were well apprised of it, could have told you, sir, who I am.

Erastus. I see sufficiently, sir, what you are, and your manner of accosting me gives me to know that.

Caritides.   Yes, I am a man of learning, who am charmed
with your virtues; none of those learned men whose name ends
only in *us*: there is nothing so common as a name after the
Latin termination; they who are habited after the Greek
manner, have a much better mien; and that I might have one
which should terminate in *es*, I call myself Mr. Caritides.

Erastus.   Mr. Caritides be it.   What would you say?

Caritides.   I have a petition, sir, which I would read to you,
and which, in the situation your employment places you, I
presume to conjure you to present to the king.

Erastus.   Lack-a-day, sir, you can present it yourself.

Caritides.   It is true, sir, the king grants this extreme favour,
but through this very excess of his unparalleled goodness, so
many villainous petitions, sir, are presented, that they stifle
the good ones; and what my hope rests upon, is, that somebody
would give mine, when the king is alone.

Erastus.   Well, you can do it, and take your own time.

Caritides.   Ah! sir, the door-keepers are terrible fellows,
they treat men of learning with a fillip o' the nose, as if they
were mere scoundrels; and I can get no farther than the guard-
room.   The ill-treatment I must endure would make me retire
from court for ever, had I not conceived strong hope that you
will be my Mæcenas with His Majesty.   Yes, your credit is a
certain means——

Erastus.   Well, give it me, I will present it.

Caritides.   Here it is; but please to hear it read however.

Erastus.   No——

Caritides.   That you may be acquainted with it, sir, I conjure
you.

A PETITION TO THE KING

Sir,

*Your most humble, most obedient, most faithful, and most
learned subject and servant, Caritides, a Frenchman by nation,
a Grecian by profession, having considered the great and notable
abuses committed in the inscriptions upon signs of houses, shops,
taverns, ninepin-alleys, and other places of your good city of Paris ;
in that certain ignorant composers of the said inscriptions, do
subvert, by a barbarous, pernicious, and detestable orthography,
all manner of sense and reason, without regard to any etymology,
analogy, energy, or allegory whatsoever, to the great scandal of the
Republic of Letters, and of the French nation, which is discredited
and dishonoured by the said abuses and gross faults, in respect*

to strangers, *and notoriously, in respect to the Germans, curious readers and inspectors of the said inscriptions——*

Erastus. This petition is very long, and may **very** likely weary——

Caritides. Oh! sir, not a word can be retrenched from it.

[*He goes on.*]

Humbly supplicates your Majesty, for the good of your kingdom, and glory of your government, to institute an office of comptroller, intendant, corrector, reviser, and restorer-general of the said inscriptions ; and to honour your supplicant with this, as well in consideration of his rare and eminent erudition, as of the great and signal services he has done to the state, and to your Majesty in composing an anagram upon your said Majesty in French, Latin, Greek, Hebrew, Syriac, Chaldee, Arabic——

Erastus. [*Interrupting him.*] Very well: give it me quick, and retire; the king shall see it; the thing is as good as done.

Caritides. Oh! sir, if you but show my petition, 'tis all in all. If the king but sees it, I am sure of my point: for as his justice is, in everything, so great, he cannot refuse my demand. And now, to exalt your name to the skies, give me your name and surname in writing, and I'll make a poem that shall have the form of an acrostic, at both ends of the verse, and in each hemistich.

Erastus. Yes, Mr. Caritides, you shall have it to-morrow. [*Alone.*] In good truth, such learned fellows are most admirable asses. Another time I should have laughed heartily at his folly.

Scene III

Ormin, Erastus.

Ormin. Though an affair of great consequence brings me hither, I was willing that man should leave you before I spoke with you.

Erastus. Very well, but dispatch for I must be gone.

Ormin. I don't in the least doubt, but the fellow who has just left you, has very much tired you, sir, with his visit. 'Tis a troublesome old mortal, who is a little crack-brained; and to get rid of whom I have always some contrivance ready at hand. In the Mall, at Luxembourg, and in the Tuilleries, he fatigues all the world with his idle notions: and such persons as you should avoid the conversation of these pedantic scholars who are good for nothing. For my part, I have no fear of being troublesome to you, since I come, sir, to make your fortune.

Erastus. [*Aside.*] This is some whiffling alchymist, one of those fellows who are not worth a groat; and are ever promising you so much wealth. [*Loud.*] You have hit upon that blessed stone, sir, which of itself can enrich all the kings of the earth?

Ormin. A pretty fancy! Oh! you are out, sir; Heaven preserve me from being one of those sort of fools! I don't feed upon frivolous visions, I bring you here solid words of a proposal which I would communicate by you to the king, and which I always carry about me safe under seal. None of those foolish projects, those vain chimeras which the superintendents have dinned in their ears; none of those beggarly proposals, whose pretensions go no farther than to talk of twenty or thirty millions of livres; but one which shall annually, at a moderate computation, bring in to the king four hundred millions hard money; with ease, without risk or suspicion, and without the least hardship upon the subject. In short, 'tis a hint of inconceivable gain, and which, at the first word you will find to be feasible. Yes, provided I can but be encouraged by you——

Erastus. Well, we shall talk of it; I am a little in haste.

Ormin. If you would promise me to keep it secret, I would discover to you this important project.

Erastus. No, no, I won't be let into your secret.

Ormin. Sir, I believe you too discreet to betray it, and will, with great frankness, inform you of it in two words——we must mind lest somebody should overhear us.——[*Whispers Erastus.*] This marvellous project, of which I am the inventor, is that——

Erastus. A little farther off, sir, for a certain reason.

Ormin. You know, without my needing to tell you, the vast profit the king receives annually from his seaports. Now the project, which nobody has hit upon as yet, and 'tis an easy matter, is that you should turn all the coasts of France into famous seaports. This would amount to immense sums; and if——

Erastus. The project is good, and will please the king exceedingly. Adieu. We shall see you.

Ormin. At least stand by me for having discovered the first hint of it.

Erastus. Yes, yes.

Ormin. If you would lend me a brace of pieces, which you might repay yourself, sir, out of the profits of the invention——

Erastus. [*Gives two pieces of gold to Ormin.*] Yes, with all my heart. [*Alone.*] Would Heaven I could get rid of all the impertinents at this rate! To see the unseasonableness of their visits! I hope at last I shall get clear. Won't somebody else come and divert me?

Scene IV

Philintes, Erastus.

Philintes. Marquis, I have heard strange news just now.

Erastus. What?

Philintes. That a man has quarrelled with thee a little while ago.

Erastus. With me?

Philintes. What signifies dissembling the matter? I have it from good hands, that you have had a challenge sent you; and as your friend, I come, at all events, to offer my service to you against all the world.

Erastus. I'm obliged to you; but believe me, you——

Philintes. You won't confess it; but you come abroad without servants. Stay you in town, or go into the country, you shall go nowhere but I will accompany you.

Erastus. [*Aside.*] Plague! I shall run mad.

Philintes. To what end do you hide it from me?

Erastus. I swear, marquis, they have imposed upon you.

Philintes. In vain do you deny it.

Erastus. May I be thunderstruck, if I have had any quarrel——

Philintes. Do you think I believe you?

Erastus. Bless me! I tell you without disguise, that——

Philintes. Don't imagine me either a dupe or credulous upon this point.

Erastus. Will you oblige me?

Philintes. No.

Erastus. Pray leave me.

Philintes. By no means, marquis.

Erastus. A little gallantry calls me this evening to a certain place——

Philintes. I shan't leave you. I shall follow you, be it to what place it will.

Erastus. S'death! since you will have me have a quarrel, I consent to it, to satisfy your zeal; it shall be with you who plague me to distraction, and from whom I cannot, by fair means, disengage myself.

Philintes. This is accepting a piece of service not at all like a friend: but since I do you so ill an office, adieu. Determine all your affairs without me.

Erastus. You'll be my friend when you leave me. [*Alone.*] But what misfortunes persecute me! They'll have made me slip the hour appointed.

SCENE V

Damis, L'Espine, Erastus, La Rivière and his comrades.

Damis. [*To L'Espine.*] What! does the traitor hope to gain her in spite of me? My just vengeance shall prevent him.

Erastus. [*Aside.*] I have a glimpse of somebody there, before Orphisa's door. What! must I always have some obstacle or other in the way of a passion she is pleased to authorise?

Damis. [*To L'Espine.*] Yes, I have learnt that my niece, in spite of all my care, is to have a private interview this evening with Erastus, in her chamber, no witnesses present.

La Rivière. [*To his comrades.*] What do I hear those people there talking of our master? let us draw nearer softly, without discovering ourselves.

Damis. [*To L'Espine.*] But before he has room to accomplish his design, I must stab that traitorous heart of his in a thousand places. Go and fetch those folks I spoke of just now, to place 'em in ambush where I would have 'em; that at the mention of the name of Erastus, you may be ready to revenge my honour, which his passion has the insolence to injure; break off the assignation which calls him hither, and smother his criminal passion in his blood.

La Rivière. [*With his comrades attacking Damis.*] Traitor, before they can sacrifice him to thy fury, thou must have something to say to us.

Erastus. Though he would have destroyed me, the point of honour urges me to succour my mistress's uncle. [*To Damis.*] I'm your man. [*Draws his sword against Rivière and his companions, whom he drives off.*]

Damis. Heavens! by what succour is my life preserved from certain death? To whom am I obliged for so singular a piece of service?

Erastus. [*Returning.*] I have only done an act of justice in saving you.

Damis. O Heaven ! can I believe my ears? Is it Erastus's hand——

Erastus. Yes, sir, yes, 'tis I; too happy in that my hand has saved you; too unhappy, in that I have deserved your displeasure.

Damis. What? Is he whose death I had resolved upon, the person who has fought in my favour? Oh! 'Tis too much; my heart is forced to surrender; and whatever, this night, might be the intention of your love, this surprising piece of generosity ought to stifle all animosity. I blush at my crime, and blame my caprice. My hatred has too long injured you; and that I may, by a most shining instance, condemn it, I join you this very night to the object of your wishes.

Scene VI

Orphisa, Damis, Erastus.

Orphisa. [*Coming out of her house with a candle.*] Sir, what accident has occasioned that dreadful disturbance——

Damis. Nothing, my niece, but what is very agreeable, since, after my so long blaming your passion, 'tis what gives you Erastus for a husband. His arm has saved me from a death I most narrowly escaped; and I desire the gift of your hand may requite him for me.

Orphisa. Sir, if it is to discharge the debt you owe, I agree to it; above all on the account of the life he has saved.

Erastus. My heart is so surprised at such a wonder, that in this ecstasy I doubt whether I am awake.

Damis. Let us celebrate the happy state you are going to enjoy and let our violins come and regale us.

[*A knocking at Damis's door.*

Erastus. Who knocks so loud there?

Scene VII

Damis, Orphisa, Erastus, L'Espine.

L'Espine. Sir, here are masks with their kits and tabors.

[*Enter Masks who take up the whole stage.*

Erastus. What, impertinents for ever! Soho, there! Swiss, drive out these tatterdemalions.

THE LEARNED LADIES

(A COMEDY)

THE LEARNED LADIES, *a Comedy of Five Acts in Verse, acted at Paris at the Theatre of the Palace-Royal, March 11, 1672.*

Molière composed *The Learned Ladies* more at leisure than many other of his pieces, in which he ridicules the folly of false wit, and a pedantic education. A subject in appearance very unlikely to furnish anything which could be entertaining on the stage; a prejudice which at first hindered the success of the piece, but which did not continue long, for they soon perceived with what art the author had spun out into five acts a subject which was dry in itself, without mixing anything foreign with it; and they applauded him for presenting in a comic dress what did not appear susceptible of it.

Some confused and superficial notions of sciences, ill-chosen terms of art, and an ill-placed affectation of grammatical purity, composed in different colours the grounds of the characters of Philaminta, Armanda, and Belisa. Henrietta alone preserved herself from the contagion, and from thence became a greater favourite of her father, who was made uneasy by the distemper without having the power to cure it. The infatuation of Philaminta, and the high notion she had conceived of the talents and wit of Trissotin, make the plot of the piece. A sonnet and madrigal, which this pretended wit very emphatically recites in the second scene of the third act, confirm her in the resolution she had already taken to marry Henrietta as soon as possible to him whom she esteemed above any man in the world. It were to be wished that Philaminta had been undeceived by a more likely and better-combined incident than that of the two letters which Aristus brings in the fifth act; but the reciprocal generosity of Clitander and Henrietta makes amends in some measure for this fault. It is pretended that the quarrel between Trissotin and Vadius was copied after one that happened at the palace of Luxembourg at the king's sister's, between two authors of that time.

ACTORS

CHRISALUS, *a citizen*.
PHILAMINTA, *wife to Chrisalus*.
ARMANDA, ⎫
HENRIETTA, ⎬ *daughters to Chrisalus and Philaminta*.
ARISTUS, *brother to Chrisalus*.
BELISA, *sister to Chrisalus*.
CLITANDER, *in love with Henrietta*.
TRISSOTIN, *a wit*.
VADIUS, *a pedant*.
MARTINA, *a cook-maid*.
L'EPINE, *a footman*.
JULIAN, *a servant to Vadius*.
NOTARY.

SCENE: *Paris in Chrisalus's house*.

ACT I

Armanda, Henrietta.

Armanda. What! is the lovely name of maid a title, sister, that you would quit the charming delight of? Dare you entertain the thoughts of marrying? Can this vulgar design enter your head?

Henrietta. Yes, sister.

Armanda. Ah! can one support that Yes? or can one hear it without a sickness at heart?

Henrietta. What has matrimony then in it that obliges you, sister——

Armanda. Ah! Heavens, fie.

Henrietta. What's the matter?

Armanda. Ah! fie, I tell you. Don't you conceive what a surfeit such a word offers to one's imagination whenever one hears it? What a strange image it shocks one with? To what a nasty prospect it leads the mind? Don't you shiver at it? And can you bring yourself to endure the consequences of that word, sister?

Henrietta. The consequences of that word, when I consider them, set before me a husband, children, and a family. And I see nothing in this, if I may talk rationally upon it, which shocks one's imagination or makes one shiver.

Armanda. O Heavens! can you be pleased with such attachments?

Henrietta. Why, what can one do better at my age than to bind a man to one's self under the title of husband, who loves one, and is beloved by one, and from this tender union to secure the delights of an innocent life? Has such a tie, when well-matched, no charms?

Armanda. Lard! what a grovelling mind is yours! What a mean part do you act in the world to immure yourself with family affairs, and not to discover more sensible pleasures than an idol of a husband, and monkeys of children! Leave the low amusements of these kind of affairs to gross creatures and vulgar people; elevate your desires to more lofty objects;

endeavour to get a taste for more noble pleasures; and, treating sense and matter with contempt, give yourself, like us, entirely up to understanding. You have our mother for an example before your eyes, who is everywhere honoured with the title of learned; endeavour like me to show yourself her daughter; aspire to the brightness which is in the family, and bring yourself to be sensible of the charming pleasures which the love of study pours into the heart. Instead of being in servile bondage to the will of a man, marry yourself, sister, to philosophy, which raises you above the rest of human kind, and gives the sovereign empire to reason, subjecting the animal part to its laws, the gross appetite of which debases us to beasts. These are the lovely flames, the soft attachments which ought to employ the moments of life; and the cares which I see so many women affected with, appear in my eyes most horrible meannesses.

Henrietta. Heaven, whose order we perceive to be almighty, forms us in our birth for different offices, and every mind is not composed of materials to fit it for making a philosopher. If yours is created fit for those heights which the speculations of the learned mount to, mine is made, sister, to crawl upon earth, and its weakness confines it to trifling cares. Let us not disorder the just regulations of Heaven, but follow the instigations of our several instincts. Do you, by the flight of a great and fine genius, inhabit the lofty regions of philosophy, whilst my imagination, seeing itself here below, tastes the terrestrial charms of matrimony; thus in our designs, so contrary to each other, we shall both imitate our mother; you, with regard to the mind and noble desires; I with regard to sense and the grosser pleasures; you in the productions of genius and light, I in those of matter, sister.

Armanda. When we pretend to regulate ourselves by any one person, 'tis in their finest parts which we ought to resemble them; and 'tis not at all taking her for a model, sister, only to cough and spit like her.

Henrietta. But you would not have been what you boast yourself to be, if my mother had only had those fine parts; and well you know, sister, that her noble genius did not always apply itself to philosophy. Pray now leave me, out of a little goodness, to those meannesses to which you owe the light; and don't suppress a little scholar which would come into the world, by desiring that I should imitate you.

Armanda. I see your mind can't be cured of the foolish infatuation of getting a husband. But let us know, pray, who you think to have? You don't aim at Clitander, sure?

Henrietta. For what reason should I not? Does he want merit? Is it a low choice?

Armanda. No, but 'tis a design which would be very dishonest to endeavour to take away another's conquest; and 'tis not a thing unknown to the world that Clitander has deeply sighed for me.

Henrietta. Yes, but all those sighs are vain things with you, for you don't fall into human meannesses; your mind has renounced matrimony for ever, and philosophy has all your affection. Having thus no design in your heart upon Clitander, what does it concern you if another may pretend to him?

Armanda. This empire which reason holds over the senses, does not make us renounce the sweets of praise; and one may refuse a man of merit for a husband, whom one would willingly have in the train of our adorers.

Henrietta. I did not hinder him from continuing his adorations to your perfections, but only received one who came to offer me the homage of his passion on your refusal.

Armanda. But do you think, pray, that there's an entire surety in the offer of a disgusted lover's vows? Do you believe his passion for your charms to be mighty strong, and that all ardour for me is quite dead in his heart?

Henrietta. He tells me so, sister, and for my part I believe him.

Armanda. Don't have so strong a faith, sister; but be assured when he says that he leaves me and loves you, that he does not really mean it, but deceives himself.

Henrietta. I don't know; but in short, if you please, it is very easy for us to inform ourselves of the thing. I see him coming hither, and he'll be able to give us a full light into the matter.

Scene II

Clitander, Armanda, Henrietta.

Henrietta. To deliver me from a doubt, my sister has involved me in, betwixt her and me, Clitander, lay open your heart, discover the bottom of it, and be so good as to let us know which of us has a right to pretend to your addresses.

Armanda. No, no, I will not impose the hardship of an explanation on your passion; I don't love to be troublesome to people, and I know how perplexing the constraint of such a confession to the face must be.

Clitander. No, madam, my heart, which seldom dissembles,

feels no constraint to make a free acknowledgment; such a step does not throw me into any perplexity, and I'll loudly own, with a frank and clear heart, that the tender cords with which I am bound, [*Pointing to Henrietta.*] my love and my addresses are all on this side. Let not this confession give you any emotion, you desired that things should be so; your attractions had caught me, and my tender sighs sufficiently proved to you the ardour of my desires; my heart consecrated an immortal flame to you, but your eyes did not think their conquest great enough; I suffered under their yoke a hundred different slights, they reigned like proud tyrants over my heart, till, tired with so much torment, I sought more humane conquerors, and chains less cruel. [*Pointing to Henrietta.*] I have found 'em, madam, in these eyes, and their bonds shall be always precious to me. With a compassionate regard they dried up my tears, and did not disdain the refuse of your charms; they touched me so deeply by such uncommon favours, that there's nothing can ever deliver me from my chains; and now I presume to conjure you, madam, never to make any attempt on my passion, nor ever endeavour to recall a heart resolved to die in this soft ardour.

Armanda. Lack-a-day! who told you, sir, that they had any such desire, or in short cared so much for you? I think you are a pleasant mortal for imagining it, and very impertinent for declaring it to me.

Henrietta. Oh, softly, sister. Where is now the moral part which so well regulates the animal, and bridles the sallies of wrath?

Armanda. But how do you, who talk to me of it, practise it yourself, in answering a passion which is discovered to you, without the leave of those who gave you being? Know that duty subjects you to their laws, that you are not permitted to love but according to their choice, that they have a supreme authority over your heart, and that 'tis criminal to dispose of it yourself.

Henrietta. I thank you for the kindness you show me in teaching me so well what belongs to my duty; my heart will regulate its conduct by your instructions; and to let you see, sister, that I profit by it, Clitander, take care to support your love by the concurrence of those from whom I received birth; procure a lawful power over my desires, and secure me a way to love you without a crime.

Clitander. I'll go and labour after it with the utmost diligence, for I only waited for this kind permission from you.

Armanda. You triumph, sister, and seem to imagine that this gives me disturbance.

Henrietta. I, sister, not at all. I know that the laws of reason are always prevalent over your senses, and that, by strength of the lessons of wisdom you learn, you are above such a weakness. So far from suspecting you of being in any concern, I believe that you'll condescend to employ your interest for me here to second his demand, and by your approbation to press the happy moment of our marriage. I beg it of you, and to labour after it——

Armanda. Your little wit pretends to raillery, and you appear mighty proud of a heart one throws to you.

Henrietta. As much thrown as this heart is, you don't much dislike it; and if you could pick it up from me you'd readily take the pains to stoop for it.

Armanda. I scorn to descend to make any answer to that, and these are foolish discourses which one ought not to hear.

Henrietta. 'Tis very well done of you, and you discover inconceivable moderation.

Scene III

Clitander, Henrietta.

Henrietta. Your sincere confession has not a little surprised her.

Clitander. She sufficiently deserves such a freedom; and all the haughtiness of her proud folly is worthy at least of my plain-dealing. But since I'm permitted, I go to your father, madam——

Henrietta. The surest way is to gain my mother; my father is of a humour to consent to anything; but places little weight on what he resolves; he has received from Heaven a certain gentleness of soul which makes him submit at once to what his wife wills; 'tis she that governs, and in an absolute manner dictates for a law whatever she has resolved on. I heartily wish, I must own, that you were of a temper a little more complaisant to her and to my aunt, of a spirit which might procure you their esteem, by flattering their fancies.

Clitander. My heart is so sincere that it could never, even in your sister, flatter their characters. These female doctors are not to my taste. I agree that a woman should have an insight into everything; but I would not have her indulge a monstrous passion, to make herself learned for the sake of being learned; and I love to have her often know, when questions are put to her, how to appear ignorant of things which she knows. In short, I would have her hide her study, and have knowledge without desiring the world should know it, without citing authors, without speaking bombast words, and being constantly learned on the least occasions. I have a great deal of respect for your mother, but I can't entirely approve of her chimera, and make myself an echo of what she says, to the incense she offers her heroes of genius. Her Mr. Trissotin vexes and grieves me, and I'm enraged to see her esteem such a man, to place in the rank of great and fine geniuses a blockhead whose writings are everywhere damned; a pedant, whose liberal pen furnishes the market-hall with officious papers.

Henrietta. His writings and conversation are both very tiresome, in my opinion, and I find I am much of your taste and opinion; but as he has great power over my mother, you ought to force yourself to a little complaisance. A lover makes his court where his heart is engaged; he would willingly gain the favour of the whole world with regard to that; and that no creature may oppose his flame, he obliges himself to please even the very house-dog.

Clitander. Yes, you are in the right; but Mr. Trissotin inspires the very bottom of my soul with a prevailing spleen. I can't consent to dishonour myself by praising his works, in order to gain his approbation. 'Tis by those he first appeared to my sight, and I knew him before I had seen him. I perceive in the trash of those writings he gives us, what his pedant person everywhere displays; the constant haughtiness of his presumption, the intrepidity of a good opinion of himself; that indolency of an extreme confidence which makes him always so satisfied with himself, which makes him incessantly laugh at his own merit, which makes him in such good humour with everything he writes, and that he would not change his renown for all the honours of the greatest general.

Henrietta. You must have had good eyes to see all this.

Clitander. Nay, the thing goes farther, even to his very figure; I see by the verses which come from his head what an air the poet must be of; and I so well guessed at every mark of him, that meeting a man one day in the palace I laid a wager that 'twas Trissotin in person, and I found indeed that the wager was good.

Henrietta. What a fable is this!

Clitander. No, I tell the thing as it is. But I see your aunt.
Pray give me leave to declare our secret to her, and gain her
good offices with your mother.

Scene IV

Belisa, Clitander.

Clitander. Suffer a lover, madam, to take the opportunity
of this happy moment to speak to you, and to discover to you
the sincere passion——

Belisa. Ah, softly, take care not to open your heart too far
to me; if I have placed you in the rank of my lovers, be contented that your eyes be your only interpreters, and don't
explain to me, by any other language, desires which pass with
me for an affront; love me, sigh, burn for my charms, but let
me be permitted not to know it. I can shut my eyes to your
secret flames as long as you keep yourself to dumb interpreters;
but if the mouth comes to be meddling in the matter, I must
banish you for ever from my sight.

Clitander. Take no alarm at the intentions of my heart;
Henrietta, madam, is the object which charms me, and I come
ardently to conjure your goodness to second the love I have
for her beauty.

Belisa. Hah! this turn is certainly very witty, I confess.
This subtle evasion deserves to be praised; and in all the romances
I ever cast my eyes on, I never met with anything more ingenious.

Clitander. This is no stroke of wit, madam, but a pure
confession of what I have in my breast. Heaven has bound my
heart to Henrietta's beauty by the ties of an immutable ardour;
Henrietta retains me in her amiable empire, and to marry
Henrietta is the happiness I aspire to. You can do a great deal
towards it, and all I desire is that you would condescend to
favour my addresses.

Belisa. I see where the demand would gently aim, and know
what I should understand under that name. The figure is
artful, and, not to depart from it in what my heart offers me to
reply to you, I must tell you that Henrietta is a rebel to matrimony, and that you must burn for her without pretending
to anything.

Clitander. Alas! madam, to what good is this perplexing
things, and why will you imagine what is not?

Belisa. Lack-a-day! no formalities; forbear to deny what

your looks have often given me to understand; 'tis enough that we are content with the turn which your passion artfully pitched on, and that under the figure which respect obliges it to, we are willingly resolved to suffer its homage, provided that its transports be enlightened by honour, and offer only pure vows at my altar.

Clitander. But——

Belisa. Adieu. This ought to satisfy you for this time, and I have told you more than I would have told you.

Clitander. But your error——

Belisa. Enough. I blush now, and my modesty has endured a surprising attack.

Clitander. I'll be hanged if I love you, and wise——

Belisa. No, no, I'll hear nothing more.

SCENE V

Clitander. [*Alone.*] Deuce take the fool with her visions! Did one ever see anything equal to these prepossessions? I'll go and commit this business to another, and take the assistance of some wiser person.

ACT II

SCENE I

Aristus. [*Leaving Clitander, but continuing to speak to him.*] Yes, I'll bring you the answer presently; I'll insist, press, do all that should be done. What a deal has a lover to say for one word! and how impatient he is for what he desires! Never——

SCENE II

Chrisalus, Aristus.

Aristus. Oh! save you, brother.

Chrisalus. And you too, brother.

Aristus. Do you know what brings me hither?

Chrisalus. No; but I'm ready to know it, if you please.

Aristus. You have known Clitander a long time since.

Chrisalus. Undoubtedly; and he comes often to our house.

Aristus. And what esteem is he in with you, brother?

Chrisalus. As a man of honour, wit, courage, and conduct; and I know very few people who have his merit.

Aristus. A certain desire of his, brought me hither, and I rejoice that you have an esteem for him.

Chrisalus. I was acquainted with his late father in my journey to Rome.

Aristus. Very well.

Chrisalus. He was, brother, a very honest gentleman.

Aristus. So they say.

Chrisalus. We were then but twenty-eight years of age, and troth we were a couple of brisk sparks.

Aristus. I believe so.

Chrisalus. We followed the Roman ladies, and all the world talked of our pranks there; we made some people jealous.

Aristus. That was well enough; but let's come to what brought me hither.

SCENE III

Belisa (entering softly, and listening), Chrisalus, Aristus.

Aristus. Clitander makes me his interpreter to you, and his heart is smitten with Henrietta's charms.

Chrisalus. What, my daughter?

Aristus. Yes. Clitander is enamoured with her, and I never saw a lover more passionate.

Belisa. [*To Aristus.*] No, no, I understand you. You don't know the story; the thing is not what you may imagine.

Aristus. How, sister?

Belisa. Clitander deceives you; 'tis with another object that his heart is smitten.

Aristus. You jest. What! is it not Henrietta that he's in love with?

Belisa. No, I'm sure it is not.

Aristus. He told it me himself.

Belisa. Oh, ay.

Aristus. You see me here, sister, commissioned by him to ask her of her father this very day.

Belisa. Very well.

Aristus. And his love made him very earnest with me to hasten the time for such an alliance.

Belisa. Better still. Nobody could have made use of a more gallant deception. Henrietta, between us, is an amusement, an ingenious veil, a pretext, brother, to cover another flame which I know the mystery of, and I am desirous to undeceive you both.

Aristus. But since you know so much, sister, tell us, pray, who's this other object he loves?

Belisa. You would know it then?

Aristus. Yes. Whom?

Belisa. 'Tis I.

Aristus. You!

Belisa. I myself.

Aristus. Hah, sister!

Belisa. What does that Hah! mean? And what is there surprising in my discourse? We are formed of an air, I fancy, to be able to say that we have one heart in subjection to our empire; and Dorantes, Damis, Cleontes, and Lycidas, may plainly show that we have some charms.

Aristus. Do those men love you?

Belisa. Yes, with all their might.

Aristus. They have told you so?

Belisa. No one ever took that liberty; they have hitherto so very much revered me, that they have never said a word to me of their love; but the dumb interpreters have all done their office in offering me their heart, and devoting their service to me.

Aristus. Why, we seldom or never see Damis come here.

Belisa. That's to show me a more submissive respect.

Aristus. Dorantes is always affronting you with satirical language.

Belisa. That's the transport of a jealous rage.

Aristus. Cleontes and Lycidas have both of 'em taken wives.

Belisa. That was done through a despair which I reduced their passion to.

Aristus. Faith, my dear sister, this is mere chimera.

Chrisalus. [*To Belisa.*] You ought to lay aside these chimeras.

Belisa. Ah, chimeras! are these chimeras, say you? I, chimeras! chimeras truly is very good! I rejoice much at chimeras, brothers, and I did not know that I had chimeras.

SCENE IV

Chrisalus, Aristus.

Chrisalus. Our sister is mad, I think.

Aristus. This grows upon her every day; but once more let us return to our discourse. Clitander asks Henrietta of you to wife. Consider what answer should be made to his passion.

Chrisalus. Need you ask? I consent to it with all my heart, and esteem his alliance a singular honour.

Aristus. You know that he has not abundance of wealth, that——

Chrisalus. That's a concern of no great importance; he is rich in virtue, and that's worth treasures; and besides, his father and I were but one in two bodies.

Aristus. Let's speak to your wife, and let us see and make her favourable——

Chrisalus. 'Tis enough, I accept him for a son-in-law.

Aristus. Yes, but to support your consent, brother, 'tis not amiss to have her agree to it. Come——

Chrisalus. You jest. It is not necessary, I'll answer for my wife, and take the business upon myself.

Aristus. But——

Chrisalus. Let me alone, I say, and don't be apprehensive; I'll go immediately and set things in order.

Aristus. Be it so. I'll go sound Henrietta upon this, and will return to know——

Chrisalus. 'Tis a done thing, and I'll go to my wife to talk to her of it without delay.

SCENE V

Chrisalus, Martina.

Martina. I'm mighty lucky, indeed! Alas! 'tis a true saying, He that would drown a dog accuses him of madness; another's service is no inheritance.

Chrisalus. What's the matter? What ails you, Martina?

Martina. What ails me?

Chrisalus. Yes.

Martina. My ailment is, that I'm discharged to-day, sir.

Chrisalus. Discharged?

Martina. Yes. Madam has turned me away.

Chrisalus. I don't understand that. How is it?

Martina. They threaten me with a sound beating, if I don't march off.

Chrisalus. No, you shall stay; I am satisfied with you; my wife is often a little hot-headed; and I won't——

Scene VI

Philaminta, Belisa, Chrisalus, Martina.

Philaminta. [*Seeing Martina.*] What! Do I see you, hussy? Quick, begone, jade; go, leave this place, and never come into my sight again.

Chrisalus. Softly.

Philaminta. No, 'tis done.

Chrisalus. Hey!

Philaminta. I'll have her be gone.

Chrisalus. But what has she done, that you resolve in this manner——

Philaminta. What! do you uphold her?

Chrisalus. By no means.

Philaminta. Do you take her part against me?

Chrisalus. Lack-a-day! no. I only ask what her crime is.

Philaminta. Am I one that would turn her away without just cause?

Chrisalus. I don't say that; but I ought, with respect to the servants, to——

Philaminta. No, she shall be gone out of our house, I say.

Chrisalus. Well, yes. Does anybody say anything to the contrary to you?

Philaminta. I'll have no obstacle to my desires.

Chrisalus. Agreed.

Philaminta. And you ought, if you'd be like a reasonable husband, to take my part against her, and join in my anger.

Chrisalus. [*Turning towards Martina.*] So I do. Yes, my wife turns you away with reason, gipsy, and your crime is unworthy of pardon.

Martina. What is it I have done then?

Chrisalus. [*Aside.*] Faith! I don't know.

Philaminta. She's in a humour still to make it of no consequence.

Chrisalus. Has she occasioned your hatred by breaking some looking-glass, or china?

Philaminta. Would I turn her away, do you imagine, and put myself in a passion for so small a matter?

Chrisalus. [*To Martina.*] What does this mean? [*To Philaminta.*] The thing is considerable then?

Philaminta. Undoubtedly. Am I an unreasonable woman?

Chrisalus. Has she, through negligence, suffered some ewer, or piece of plate, to be stolen?

Philaminta. That would be nothing.

Chrisalus. [*To Martina.*] Oho! Plague! Gipsy! [*To Philaminta.*] What! have you surprised her in some dishonesty?

Philaminta. Worse than all that.

Chrisalus. Worse than all that?

Philaminta. Worse.

Chrisalus. [*To Martina.*] What the deuce! jade. [*To Philaminta.*] Hey? has she committed——

Philaminta. She has, with an unparalleled insolence, after thirty lectures about it, insulted my ear with the impropriety of a vulgar savage word, which Vaugelas condemns in express terms.

Chrisalus. Is that——

Philaminta. What! in spite of our remonstrances, continually to shock the foundation of all the sciences; grammar, which even rules over kings, and makes 'em with an high hand obey its laws?

Chrisalus. I thought she had been guilty of a much greater offence.

Philaminta. What! don't you think this crime unpardonable?

Chrisalus. Yes indeed.

Philaminta. I should wish you'd excuse her.

Chrisalus. I shall take care of that.

Belisa. 'Tis a pity, 'tis true, that all construction should be destroyed by her, when she has a hundred times been instructed in the laws of language.

Martina. All you preach is fine and good, I believe; but I can't talk your jargon, not I.

Philaminta. O impudence! To call a language founded upon reason and polite custom, jargon.

Martina. When one makes one's self understood, one always speaks well, and all your fine terms are not of no use.

Philaminta. So, her own style still, Are not of no use.

Belisa. O indocible animal! Shall we never be able to teach you to talk congruously, with all the pains we incessantly take? *Not* put with *No* makes a recidivation, and is, as we have told you, too much of a negative.

Martina. Zooks! I are not a scollard like you, I speak just as they speak in our country.

Philaminta. Ah! Can this be endured!

Belisa. What a horrible solecism!

Philaminta. 'Tis enough to kill a sensible ear.

Belisa. Thy genius is very gross, I must own. *I* is but singular, *are* is plural. Wilt thou all thy life offend grammar thus?

Martina. Who talks of offending either grandmother or grandfather?

Philaminta. O Heavens!

Belisa. You take grammar in a wrong sense, and I have told you already whence that word comes.

Martina. Let it come from Scotland, Ireland, or Wales, 'tis nothing to me.

Belisa. What a clownish soul 'tis! Grammar teaches us the laws of the nominative case, and the verb, as well as of the adjective and substantive.

Martina. I must tell you, madam, that I don't know these people.

Philaminta. What a torment this is!

Belisa. These are the names of words, and you ought to take notice in what it is that they must be made to agree together.

Martina. What matter is it whether they agree together, or quarrel?

Philaminta. [*To Belisa.*] Ah, Heavens! let us put an end to such a discourse. [*To Chrisalus.*] You will not make her be gone from me then, will you?

Chrisalus. Yes, yes. [*Aside.*] I must consent to her humour. go, don't provoke her; retire, Martina.

Philaminta. How! Are you afraid of offending the jade? You speak to her in a mighty obliging tone.

Chrisalus. I? not at all. [*In a rough tone.*] Go, begone. [*In a milder tone.*] Go thy ways, poor girl.

Scene VII

Philaminta, Chrisalus, Belisa.

Chrisalus. You are satisfied, and she's gone; but I don't approve of her going in this manner; she's a girl fit for her business, and you turn her out of my house for a trifling cause.

Philaminta. Would you have me always keep her in my service, to put my ear incessantly to torment? To break all the laws of custom and reason by a barbarous heap of vices in speech, of lame expressions, intermixed between times with proverbs taken from Billingsgate?

Belisa. It is true, it makes one sweat to bear her discourse. She pulls Vaugelas to pieces every day, and the least blunders of her gross genius are either pleonasm or cacophony.

Chrisalus. What matter is it if she does fail in the laws of Vaugelas, provided she does not fail in the kitchen? For my part, I had much rather that she joined the nouns and verbs falsely, and repeated a servile bad word a hundred times in picking her herbs, than have her burn my meat or oversalt my broth. I live by good soup, and not by fine language. Vaugelas does not teach how to make good soup; and Malherbe and Balzac, so learned in fine words, would have been blockheads perhaps in the kitchen.

Philaminta. How terribly this gross discourse shocks me! And how unworthy it is of one who calls himself a man, to be continually bent on material cares instead of raising himself up towards spiritual ones! Is the body, that rag, of importance enough, of a value to merit a single thought? And ought we not to leave that far behind?

Chrisalus. Ay, but my body is myself, and I'll take care of it. A rag, if you please, but my rag is dear to me.

Belisa. The body with the mind, brother, makes a figure; but if you'll believe all the learned world in the case, the mind ought to have the precedency over the body; and our greatest care, our first concern, should be to nourish it with the juice of science.

Chrisalus. I'faith! if you think about nourishing your mind, 'tis with very airy diet, as everyone says; and you have no care, no solicitude for——

Philaminta. Ah! Solicitude is coarse to my ear, it smells strangely of antiquity.

Belisa. 'Tis true the word is of high date.

Chrisalus. Will you let me speak? In short I must be plain, pull off the mask, and discharge my spleen; people treat you as if you were mad, and I'm heartily troubled——

Philaminta. How?

Chrisalus. [*To Belisa.*] 'Tis to you that I speak, sister. The least solecism in speech provokes you; but you make strange ones yourself in conduct. Your eternal folios don't please me; and, except a great Plutarch which I put my bands in, you ought to burn all this useless lumber, and leave learning to your great doctors about town; to do right, you should remove out of the garret that long telescope enough to frighten people, and a hundred knick-knacks the sight of which are offensive. Not to look after what is done in the moon, but to mind a little what's done at home, where we see everything go topsy-turvy. It is not right for a great many reasons, that a wife should study and know so many things. To form the minds of her children to good manners, to see her family go on well, to have an eye over her servants, and to regulate with economy what is expended, ought to be her study and philosophy. Our forefathers were very wise people in this point, who said that a wife always knew enough when the capacity of her genius raised her to understand a doublet and a pair of breeches. Their wives did not read, but they lived well; their families were all their learned discourse, and their books, a thimble, thread, and needles, with which they worked amidst their knot of maids. But the women of this age are very far from behaving themselves in that manner, they must write and turn authors. No science is too profound for 'em; and in my house, more than in any other place in the world, the most lofty secrets are conceived, and they understand everything but what they ought to understand. They know the motions of the moon, the Polar Star, Venus, Saturn, and Mars, which I have no business with; and with all this vain knowledge, which they go so far to look for, they don't know how my pot goes on, which I have occasion for. My servants too aspire after learning, to please you, and they all do nothing less than what they have to do; reasoning is the business of all my house, and reasoning banishes all reason out of it. One burns my roast meat while she's reading some history, the other raves in verse when I call for drink. In short, I perceive your example followed by 'em, and I have servants and yet am not served. One poor wench alone was left me who was not infected with this villainous air, and here she's turned away with a great clutter, because she did not speak according to Vaugelas. I tell you, sister, for 'tis to you, as I said, that I address myself, all this proceeding offends me. I don't like all your scholars should come to my house, and especially this Mr. Trissotin. 'Twas he who lampooned you in verse; all his discourses are foolish trash; one's at a loss for what he says after he has spoken; and I believe, for my part, that he's crack-brained.

Philaminta. What meanness, good Heaven, both of soul and language!

Belisa. Can there be a more stupid assemblage of corpuscula? or a mind composed of more city-like atoms? Is it possible that I am of the same blood? I heartily hate myself for being of your stock, and leave the place in confusion.

Scene VIII

Philaminta, Chrisalus.

Philaminta. Have you still some other arrow to shoot?

Chrisalus. I? No. Let's talk no more of dispute, 'tis over. Let us discourse of another affair. As for your elder daughter, she discovers a distaste for the marriage-knot; in short she's a philosopher, I say nothing more of her; she's well managed; and you do very right. But her younger sister is of quite another humour, and I believe 'tis good to provide Henrietta with a proper husband, that——

Philaminta. 'Tis what I have thought on: and will discover my intention to you. This Mr. Trissotin whom we are accused about, and who has not the honour to be in your esteem, is the person I pitch on for a husband for her, and I know better than you how to judge of his merit. All dispute is superfluous in this case; and I have fully resolved on the thing. However, don't say a word of the choice of this husband, I'll speak to your daughter about it before you. I have reasons to make my conduct approved of, and I shall know very well if you have instructed her.

Scene IX

Aristus, Chrisalus.

Aristus. Well? Your wife's gone, brother, and I see that you have just had some discourse together.

Chrisalus. Yes.

Aristus. What's the success of it? Shall we have Henrietta? Has she consented? Is the business done?

Chrisalus. Not quite yet.

Aristus. Does she refuse?

Chrisalus. No.

Aristus. Does she stay to consider?

Chrisalus. Not at all.

Aristus. What then?

Chrisalus. She offers me another man for a son-in-law.

Aristus. Another man for a son-in-law!

Chrisalus. Another.

Aristus. What's his name?

Chrisalus. Mr. Trissotin.

Aristus. What, that Mr. Trissotin——

Chrisalus. Yes, that always talks Latin and verses.

Aristus. Have you accepted of him?

Chrisalus. I! no, Heaven forbid.

Aristus. What answer did you make?

Chrisalus. None; and I am very glad I did not speak, lest I should have run myself into a scrape.

Aristus. The reason is very fine, and you have made a grand step. Did you propose Clitander to her however?

Chrisalus. No; for finding she talked of another son-in-law, I thought 'twas better for me not to make any advances.

Aristus. Your prudence is vastly extraordinary truly. Are you not ashamed of your effeminacy? Is it possible a man can be so weak to let his wife have an absolute power, and not to dare to oppose what she has resolved on.

Chrisalus. Lack-a-day! You talk of it, brother, with a great deal of ease, and don't know how noise weighs me down. I love repose, peace and tranquillity very much, and my wife is of a terrible humour; she makes a great ado about the name of philosopher, but she is not less passionate for that; and her morality, which despises wealth, has no effect on the eagerness of her choler; for the least opposition to what comes in her head we have a horrible tempest for eight days. She makes me tremble whenever she begins her note; she's such a perfect dragon, that I know not where to hide myself; and yet, with all her devilish temper, I'm obliged to call her, My heart, and My life.

Aristus. Go, 'tis a jest. Between us, your wife is an absolute mistress over you, through your cowardice. Her power is founded upon nothing but your weakness. 'Tis from you she takes the title of mistress. You give up yourself to her haughty command, and suffer yourself to be led by the nose like an ass. What, can't you for once resolve to be a man, seeing you are called so? To make a wife condescend to your wishes, and take heart enough to say once, I will have it so. Can you, without shame, leave your daughter to be sacrificed to the foolish visions which the family are possessed with; and to invest a nincompoop with all your wealth for six words of Latin which he bellows out to 'em? A pedant, whom your wife compliments every turn with the name of fine wit, and great philosopher, of a man that was never equalled for gallant verses, when everybody knows he's nothing of all this? Come, come; once more, 'tis a joke; and your cowardice deserves to be laughed at.

Chrisalus. You are in the right of it, and I find that I am in the wrong. Come, I'll now show a stouter heart, brother.

Aristus. That's well said.

Chrisalus. 'Tis an infamous thing to be so subject to the power of a wife.

Aristus. Very well.

Chrisalus. She has gained too much by my mildness.

Aristus. True.

Chrisalus. Played too much upon my easiness.

Aristus. Certainly.

Chrisalus. And I'll make her know this day that my daughter is my daughter, and that I am her master, and will choose a husband for her which shall be according to my mind.

Aristus. Now you are reasonable, and as I would have you.

Chrisalus. You are for Clitander, and know where he lives; bring him to me, brother, this moment.

Aristus. I'll run and do it immediately.

Chrisalus. 'Tis bearing too long, and I'll be a man in the face of the world.

ACT III

SCENE I

Philaminta, Armanda, Belisa, Trissotin, L'Epine.

Philaminta. Ah, let us sit down here, to hear at ease these verses, which we have need to weigh word by word.

Armanda. I burn to see 'em.

Belisa. And we are dying for it.

Philaminta. [*To Trissotin.*] Whatever comes from you are charms to me.

Armanda. 'Tis an unparalleled pleasure to me.

Belisa. 'Tis a delicious repast it affords to my ear.

Philaminta. Don't let us languish under such pressing desires.

Armanda. Make haste.

Belisa. Be quick, and hasten our pleasure.

Philaminta. Offer your epigram to our impatience.

Trissotin. [*To Philaminta.*] Alas, madam, 'tis a quite new-born babe. Its fate certainly ought to touch you, for 'twas in your courtyard that I brought it forth.

Philaminta. Its father is sufficient to make it dear to me.

Trissotin. Your approbation may serve for a mother to it.

Belisa. How witty he is!

SCENE II

Henrietta, Philaminta, Armanda, Belisa, Trissotin, L'Epine.

Philaminta. [*To Henrietta who is going away.*] Hey-day, why do you run away again?

Henrietta. For fear of disturbing such a sweet conversation.

Philaminta. Come hither, and come with both your ears to share the pleasure of hearing wonders.

Henrietta. I know but little of the beauties of writing, and things of genius are not my province.

Philaminta. No matter, I have a secret besides to tell you afterwards, which 'tis necessary you should be informed of.

Trissotin. [*To Henrietta.*] The sciences have nothing in 'em to inflame you, you don't pique yourself upon anything but to charm.

Henrietta. One as little as t'other, and I have no desire——

Belisa. Ah, pray let us think of the new-born babe.

Philaminta. [*To L'Epine.*] Come, boy, quickly, something to sit on. [*L'Epine falls down.*] Do you see the impertinent thing! Ought people to fall after having learnt the equilibrium of things?

Belisa. Doesn't thou see the cause of thy fall, ignorance? and that it proceeded from thy deviating from the fixed point, which we call the centre of gravity?

L'Epine. I perceived it, madam, when I was on the ground.

Philaminta. [*To L'Epine, who goes out.*] The booby!

Trissotin. 'Twas happy for him he was not made of glass.

Armanda. Ah! Wit for ever!

Belisa. That's never dried up.

Philaminta. [*All sit down.*] Serve up to us quickly your amiable repast.

Trissotin. A plate of only eight verses is a small matter, I think, for such a great hunger as you discover to me, and I believe I should not do amiss in this case if I joined to the epigram, or rather madrigal, the ragout of a sonnet which has been esteemed by a certain princess to have something of delicacy in it. It is seasoned with Attic salt throughout, and you'll think it, I believe, of a pretty good taste.

Armanda. Oh, I don't doubt it.

Philaminta. Let us give attention immediately.

Belisa. [*Interrupting Trissotin as often as he begins to read.*] I feel my heart leap for joy beforehand. I love poetry to distraction, and especially when the verses are gallantly turned.

Philaminta. If we talk continually, he can say nothing.

Trissotin. So——

Belisa. [*To Henrietta.*]   Silence, niece.

Armanda. Ah! let him read then.

Trissotin. A sonnet to the Princess Urania upon her fever

> Asleep your prudence sure must be,
> Magnificently thus to treat,
> And sumptuously lodge in state
> Your most pernicious enemy.

Belisa. Ah, what a lovely beginning!

Armanda. What a gallant turn it has!

Philaminta. He alone possesses the talent of making easy verses.

Armanda. We must give up the day to Prudence asleep.

Belisa. Lodge her enemy, is full of charms to me.

Philaminta. I like Sumptuously and Magnificently. Those two adverbs joined do admirably.

Belisa. Let's hearken to the rest.

Trissotin.

> Asleep your prudence sure must be,
> Magnificently thus to treat,
> And sumptuously lodge in state,
> Your most pernicious enemy.

Armanda. Prudence asleep!

Belisa. Sumptuously lodge her enemy!

Philaminta. Sumptuously! magnificently!

Trissotin.

> Whate'er is said, the serpent send
> From your apartment rich and great;
> Where insolently the ingrate
> Your precious life attempts to end.

Belisa. Ah! softly, pray let me breathe.

Armanda. Pray give us time to admire.

Philaminta. One feels at hearing these verses something run at the very bottom of one's heart, I don't know what, that makes one faint.

Armanda.

> Whate'er is said, the serpent send
> From your apartment rich and great.

How finely said is, Apartment rich and great! And with what wit is the metaphor introduced!

Philaminta.

Whate'er is said the serpent send.

Ah! that Whate'er is said, is admirable for taste! 'tis in my opinion an invaluable passage.

Belisa. I am likewise in love with Whate'er is said.

Armanda. I'm of your opinion, Whate'er is said, is a happy expression.

Armanda. I wish I had written it.

Belisa. 'Tis worth a whole piece.

Philaminta. But do you really comprehend the finesse of it as I do?

Armanda and Belisa. Oh! oh!

Philaminta.

Whate'er is said the serpent send.

Though they should take the fever's part, don't regard it, laugh at their babbling.

Whate'er is said the serpent send. Whate'er is said, whate'er is said. This Whate'er is said, says a great deal more than one thinks. I don't know, for my part, if everyone be like me, but I understand a million of words under it.

Belisa. 'Tis true, it says more things than it seems to do.

Philaminta. [*To Trissotin.*] But when you wrote this charming Whate'er is said, did you yourself comprehend all its energy? Did you really conceive yourself all that it says to us; and did you then think you were writing so much wit?

Trissotin. Ha, ha!

Armanda. I have likewise The ingrate, in my head; that ingrate of a fever, unjust, uncivil, to treat people ill who entertained it.

Philaminta. In short, both the stanzas of four lines are admirable. Let's come quickly to the triplets, pray.

Armanda. Ah, once more Whate'er is said, pray now.

Trissotin.

Whate'er is said the serpent send,

Philaminta, Armanda, and Belisa.

Whate'er is said!

Trissotin.

From your apartment rich and great.

Philaminta, Armanda, and Belisa.

Apartment rich and great!

Trissotin.

Where insolently the ingrate

Philaminta, Armanda, and Belisa.
> That ingrate of a fever!

Trissotin.
> Your precious life attempts to end.

Philaminta.
> Your precious life!

Armanda and Belisa.   Ah.

Trissotin.
> Who not respecting your high rank,
> Your noble blood has basely drank,

Philaminta, Armanda, and Belisa.   Ah!

Trissotin.
> And hourly plays some cruel prank.

> The next time to the bath you go,
> There take it without more ado,
> And in the cruel mischief throw.

Philaminta.   I can hold no longer.

Belisa.   I faint!

Armanda.   I die with pleasure.

Philaminta.   One finds one's self seized with a thousand gentle thrillings.

Armanda.
> The next time to the bath you go,

Belisa.
> There take it without more ado,

Philaminta.
> And in the cruel mischief throw.
> Take and drown it in the bath.

Armanda.   Every step in your verse one meets with some charming beauty.

Belisa.   One goes through it all with rapture.

Philaminta.   One can't tread but upon fine things.

Armanda.   They are paths strewed with roses.

Trissotin.   The sonnet then you think——

Philaminta.   Admirable, new, and nobody ever made anything so fine.

Belisa. [*To Henrietta.*]   What, without emotion during what has been read?   You make a strange figure there, niece.

Henrietta.   Everyone here below, aunt, makes such a figure as they can; and one can't be a wit at will.

Trissotin.   Perhaps my verses are troublesome to the lady.

Henrietta.   No, I don't hearken to 'em.

Philaminta.   Ah! let us see the epigram.

Trissotin.   Upon a coach of an amarant colour, given to a lady of his acquaintance.

Philaminta.   His titles have always something uncommon in 'em.

Armanda.   The novelty of 'em prepares one for a hundred witty strokes.

Trissotin.

  Love has so dearly sold to me his band——

Belisa, Armanda, and Philaminta.   Ah!

Trossotin.

  Already it has cost me half my land.
  And when this beauteous coach you do behold,
  Wherein there lies imbossed so much gold,
  That all the country round it does amaze,
  And yields a pompous triumph to my lays——

Philaminta.   Ah, My lays.   There's erudition!

Belisa.   The cover is pretty, and worth a million.

Trissotin.

  And when this beauteous coach you do behold,
  Wherein there lies imbossed so much gold,
  That all the country round it does amaze,
  And yields a pompous triumph to my lays;
  No longer say that it is amarant,
  But much, much rather say that 'tis my rent.

Armanda.   Oh, oh, oh! she there does not attend to it at all.

Philaminta.   Nobody but he can write in this taste.

Belisa.

  No longer say that it is amarant,
  But much, much rather say that 'tis my rent.

This may be declined, My rent, of my rent, to my rent.

Philaminta.   I don't know whether my mind might be prepossessed in your favour from the moment I knew you, but I admire your verse and prose throughout.

Trissotin. [*To Philaminta.*]   If you would show us something of yours, we likewise might admire it in our turn.

Philaminta.   I have done nothing in verse, but I have room to hope that I may in a little time be able to show you as a friend eight chapters of the plan of our academy.   Plato foolishly forbore the subject when he writ the treatise of his *Republic*; but I'll carry the idea, which I have upon paper formed in prose, to the full effect. For in short I am strangely vexed at the wrong they do us with regard to wit; and I'll revenge every one of us of the unworthy class men rank us in, by bounding our talents to trifling things, and shutting the door of sublime lights against us.

Armanda. 'Tis offering a great offence to our sex, to make the force of our understanding extend no farther than to judge of a petticoat, and the air of a mantua, or the beauties of a point, or a new brocade.

Belisa. We must get above this shameful condition, and bravely set our genius at liberty.

Trissotin. My respect for the ladies is everywhere known, and if I pay homage to the brilliance of their eyes, I likewise honour the brightness of their wit.

Philaminta. Our sex likewise do you justice in those things; but we would show certain wits whose pride makes 'em use us with contempt, that women are likewise furnished with learning; that, like them, they can hold learned assemblies, regulated in that case by better rules; that they'll unite there what's separated elsewhere, join fine language with sublime sciences, discover nature in a thousand experiments; and upon any questions that may be proposed, bring in each sect and espouse none.

Trissotin. For order, I am found of Peripateticism.

Philaminta. For abstractions, I love Platonism.

Armanda. Epicurus pleases me, for his dogmas are strong.

Belisa. For my part, I agree mightily to the atomical philosophy; but I think the vacuum difficult to be endured, and relish much better the subtle matter.

Trissotin. Descartes, for the magnetism, gives much into my opinion.

Armanda. I love his vortexes.

Philaminta. And I his falling worlds.

Armanda. I long to see our assembly opened, and to signalise ourselves by some discovery.

Trissotin. We expect it much from your lively lights, there's little of obscurity in nature to you.

Philaminta. For my part, without flattering myself, I have made one already, and have plainly seen men in the moon.

Belisa. I have not yet seen men, I think; but I have seen steeples as plain as I see you.

Armanda. We'll likewise dive into the profundity of grammar, history, poetry, morality, and politics, as well as of physics.

Philaminta. Morality has charms that my heart is smitten

with, and 'twas formerly the admiration of great geniuses; but I give the superiority to the Stoics, and I think nothing so fine as their *Wise Man*.

Armanda. As for language, they shall soon see our regulations in that, and we intend to make great changes in't. By either a just or natural antipathy, we have each of us taken a mortal hatred to a number of words, either verbs or nouns, which we shall mutually abandon; we are preparing deadly sentences against 'em, and design to open our learned conferences by the proscription of all those diverse words from which we would purge both verse and prose.

Philaminta. But the finest project of our academy, which is a noble enterprise, and with which I'm transported, a design full of glory, and which will be extolled amongst all the great geniuses of posterity, is the retrenching those filthy syllables, which in the finest words produce scandal; those eternal jests of the fools of all times; those nauseous commonplace things of our wretched buffoons; those sources of a heap of infamous equivocations with which they insult the modesty of women.

Trissotin. These are certainly admirable projects.

Belisa. You shall see our statutes when they are all made.

Trissotin. They can't fail of being all beautiful and wise.

Armanda. We shall by our laws be the judges of performances. By our laws prose and verse will be both subject to us; none shall have wit but we and our friends; we'll search everywhere to find something to blame, and will think no one knows how to write well but ourselves.

Scene III

Trissotin, Philaminta, Belisa, Armanda, Henrietta, L'Epine.

L'Epine. [*To Trissotin.*] Sir, here's a man would speak with you; he's dressed in black, and speaks in a soft tone.

[*They rise up.*

Trissotin. 'Tis that learned friend who has pressed me so much to procure him the honour of your acquaintance.

Philaminta. You have all liberty, sir, to introduce him.

Scene IV

Philaminta, Belisa, Armanda, Henrietta.

Philaminta. [*To Armanda and Belisa.*] Let us do him the honour of our wit at least. Harkee. [*To Henrietta who is going out.*] I told you in very plain words that I wanted you.

Henrietta. But for what?

Philaminta. Come hither, you shall know presently.

SCENE V

Philaminta, Belisa, Armanda, Henrietta, Vadius, Trissotin.

Trissotin. [*Presenting Vadius.*] This is the man that dies with desire to see you. When I introduce him to you, I don't fear being blamed for having admitted a profane person to you, madam; he may hold his place amongst the *beaux esprits*.

Philaminta. The hand that presents him speaks his value sufficiently.

Trissotin. He has a perfect knowledge of the ancient authors, and understands Greek, madam, as well as any man in France.

Philaminta. [*To Belisa.*] Greek! O Heavens! Greek! He understands Greek, sister.

Belisa. [*To Armanda.*] Ah! niece, Greek!

Armanda. Greek! What sweetness!

Philaminta. What! does the gentleman understand Greek? Ah! pray let me embrace you, sir, for Greek's sake.

[*Vadius embraces both Belisa and Armanda.*

Henrietta. [*To Vadius, who would embrace her likewise.*] Excuse me, sir, I don't understand Greek.   [*They sit down.*

Philaminta. I have a wonderful respect for Greek books.

Vadius. I'm afraid of being troublesome through the great desire which engaged me to pay you my homage to-day, madam, and I have disturbed some learned discourse.

Philaminta. Sir, with your Greek you can spoil nothing.

Trissotin. He likewise does wonders in verse, as well as prose, and might, if he would, show you something.

Vadius. The fault of authors in their productions is to tyrannise over conversation with them; to be at the palace, in courts, streets, or at table, indefatigable readers of their tiresome verses. For my part, I see nothing more ridiculous in my opinion, than an author who goes everywhere mumping for praise; who seizing the ears of the very first comers, makes 'em often martyrs to his lucubrations. They never saw me such a conceited fool; and in this I'm of the opinion of a certain Greek, who, by an express dogma, forbids all his wise men the unbecoming forwardness of reading their works. Here's some little verses for young lovers upon which I would gladly have your sentiments.

Trissotin.   Your verses have beauties which all others want.

Vadius.   Venus and the Graces reign in all yours.

Trissotin.   You have the free turn, and the fine choice of words.

Vadius.   We see everywhere the ethos and pathos with you.

Trissotin.   We have seen eclogues from you in a style which surpasses Virgil and Theocritus for sweetness.

Vadius.   Your odes have a noble, gallant, and tender air, which leaves your own Horace far behind.

Trissotin.   Is there anything so amorous as your lays?

Vadius.   Can one find anything equal to the sonnets you write?

Trissotin.   Anything more charming than your little rondeaus?

Vadius.   Anything so full of wit as all your madrigals?

Trissotin.   At ballads especially, you are admirable.

Vadius.   And I think you adorable in your crambos.

Trissotin.   If France could but know your worth——

Vadius.   If the age did but render justice to men of wit——

Trissotin.   You'd ride through the streets in a gilt coach.

Vadius.   We should see the public erect statues to you. Hum. [*To Trissotin.*] Here's a ballad, and I desire that you'll frankly——

Trissotin. [*To Vadius.*]   Have you seen a certain little sonnet upon the Princess Urania's fever?

Vadius.   Yes, 'twas yesterday read to me in company.

Trissotin.   Do you know the author of it?

Vadius.   No; but I know very well that, not to flatter him, his sonnet's worth nothing.

Trissotin.   A great many people, however, think it admirable.

Vadius.   That doesn't hinder its being miserable; and if you had seen it you would be of my opinion.

Trissotin.   I know I should not be at all so in that; and that few are capable of such a sonnet.

Vadius.   Heaven preserve me from making such.

Trissotin.   I maintain that a better can't be made; and my grand reason is, because I am the author of it.

Vadius.   You?

Trissotin.   I.

Vadius.   I can't tell then how the thing was.

Trissotin.   It was, that I was so unhappy as not to be able to please you.

Vadius.   I must have had my mind wandering when I heard

it, or else the reader spoilt the sonnet. But let's leave this discourse, and see my ballad.

Trissotin. A ballad, in my opinion, is an insipid thing; 'tis no longer in fashion, it smells of antiquity.

Vadius. A ballad however charms a great many people.

Trissotin. That doesn't hinder but it may displease me.

Vadius. It may be ne'er the worse for that.

Trissotin. It has wonderful charms for pedants.

Vadius. And yet it does not please you, we see.

Trissotin. You foolishly give your qualities to others.

[*They all rise.*

Vadius. You very impertinently cast yours upon me.

Trissotin. Go, schoolboy, paper-blotter.

Vadius. Go, pitiful rhymer; shame to thy profession!

Trissotin. Go, verse-stealer, impudent plagiary.

Vadius. Go, pedant——

Philaminta. Oh, gentlemen, what do you intend to do?

Trissotin. [*To Vadius.*] Go, go, restore the shameful thefts which the Greeks and Latins challenge from you.

Vadius. Go, go, and do penance on Parnassus for having lamed Horace in your verses.

Trissotin. Remember your book, and the little noise it made.

Vadius. Remember your bookseller, reduced to a hospital.

Trissotin. My glory is established, in vain you endeavour to mangle it.

Vadius. Yes, yes, I send you to the author of the *Satires* again.

Trissotin. I send you thither again likewise.

Vadius. I have the satisfaction that people see he has treated me more honourably. He cursorily gives me a slight touch amongst many authors that are esteemed at court, but he never leaves you at peace in his verses, and we see you throughout the butt of his lashes.

Trissotin. I hold the more honourable rank there for that. He puts you in the crowd for a miserable wretch, thinks it sufficient to crush you with one blow, and never does you the honour to redouble it; but he attacks me apart as a noble adversary, against whom he thinks all his effort necessary; and his redoubling his blows against me in all places, shows that he never thinks himself victorious.

Vadius. My pen shall teach you what sort of a man I am.

Trissotin. And mine shall make you know your master.

Vadius. I defy you in verse, prose, Greek, and Latin.

Trissotin. Well, we shall see one another alone at Barbin's.

Scene VI

Trissotin, Philaminta, Armanda, Belisa, Henrietta.

Trissotin. Don't blame my passion; 'tis your judgment that I defend, madam, in the sonnet which he had the boldness to attack.

Philaminta. I'll endeavour to reconcile you. But let us talk of another affair. Come hither, Henrietta. I have been a long time disturbed in mind because I could never discover any genius in you; but I have found a method of imparting some to you.

Henrietta. You take an unnecessary care for me; learned discourses are not my business; I love to live at ease, and one must be at too much pains in everything one says to have wit; 'tis an ambition that I have not in my head. I am very well satisfied, mother, in being a blockhead; and had rather have only a common way of talking, than torment myself to speak fine words.

Philaminta. Yes, but I am offended by it, and 'tis not my intention to suffer such a stain in my blood. The beauty of the face is a frail ornament, a fading flower, a moment's lustre, and which only cleaves to the epidermis; but that of the mind is inherent and firm. I have therefore sought a long time a way to give you the beauty which time cannot mow down, to inspire you with the love of learning, to insinuate into you fine knowledge; and the resolution my wishes have at last fixed on, is to join you to a man that's full of wit. [*Pointing to Trissotin.*] And that man is this gentleman, whom I determine to have you look on as the husband destined you by my choice.

Henrietta. I, mother?

Philaminta. Yes, you. Play the fool a little, do.

Belisa. [*To Trissotin.*] I understand you. Your eyes beg my consent to engage elsewhere a heart which I am in possession of. Come, I will so. I give you up to this union. 'Tis a match which will be the making of you.

Trissotin. [*To Henrietta.*] I know not what to say to you in my transport, madam; and this match which I see myself honoured with, puts me——

Henrietta. Softly, sir, 'tis not yet done; don't be in so much hurry.

Philaminta. How you answer! Do you know that if—— 'Tis enough, you understand me. [*To Trissotin.*] She'll grow wise. Come, let's leave her.

SCENE VII

Henrietta, Armanda.

Armanda.   You may see how your mother's care for you shines forth; and she could not have chosen a more illustrious spouse——

Henrietta.   If the choice is so lovely, why don't you take him?

Armanda.   'Tis to you, not to me, that his hand is given.

Henrietta.   I yield him up all to you, as my elder sister.

Armanda.   If matrimony appeared as charming to me as it does to you, I would accept of your offer with rapture.

Henrietta.   If I had pedants in my head, as you have, I should think it a very good match.

Armanda.   However different our tastes may be, we ought to obey our parents, sister.   A mother has an absolute power over us, and in vain you think by your resistance——

SCENE VIII

Chrisalus, Aristus, Clitander, Henrietta, Armanda.

Chrisalus. [*To Henrietta, presenting Clitander.*]   Come, daughter, I'll have my intention approved of.   Pull off this glove.   Give the gentleman your hand, and consider him henceforth in your heart as the man whose wife I intend you shall be.

Armanda.   On this side, sister, your inclinations are strong enough.

Henrietta.   We ought to obey our parents, sister; a father has an absolute power over our desires.

Armanda.   A mother has her share in our obedience.

Chrisalus.   What do you mean by this?

Armanda.   I say that I very much apprehend my mother and you won't agree in this, and there's another husband——

Chrisalus.   Hold your peace, Mrs. Pedantress; go, philosopher, whom she's so full of, and don't concern yourself with my actions.   Tell her my mind, and advise her not to come and set my ears on fire; go quickly.

SCENE IX

Chrisalus, Aristus, Henrietta, Clitander.

Aristus.   Mighty well; you do wonders.

Clitander.   What transport!   What joy!   How gentle is my fortune!

Chrisalus. [*To Clitander.*] Come, take her hand, and go before us; lead her into her chamber. What soft caresses! [*To Aristus.*] Hold, my heart is moved with all these tendernesses; this cheers up my old age wonderfully, and I begin to remember my youthful amours.

ACT IV

Scene I

Philaminta, Armanda.

Armanda. Yes, she did not in the least hesitate but made a vanity of her obedience, her heart scarce gave itself time to receive the order of surrendering, and seemed less to follow the will of a father than to affect to outbrave the orders of a mother.

Philaminta. I'll let her see to whose commands the laws of reason subject all her desires; and who ought to govern, her father or her mother, spirit or body, form or matter.

Armanda. They owed you at least a compliment upon it; and this little gentleman uses you strangely, to resolve to be your son-in-law in spite of your teeth.

Philaminta. He is not so now in the way his heart might have had pretensions to it. I thought him handsome, and approved of your loves; but he always displeased me by his proceedings; he knew that, thank Heaven, I undertook to write; and yet never desired me to read anything to him.

Scene II

Clitander (entering softly, and listening unseen), Armanda, Philaminta.

Armanda. I would not suffer, if I were you, that he should ever be Henrietta's husband. They would do me much wrong to have the least thought that I speak like an interested person in this case, and that the base trick which people find he has served me has occasioned any secret indignation in my heart. The soul is fortified against any such blows by the solid succour of philosophy, and by that one may raise one's self above everything; but to treat you so, is putting you to a nonplus. You are obliged by honour to be contrary to his inclinations, and in short he's a man you ought not to be pleased with. I never found, by talking together, that he has any esteem for you at the bottom.

Philaminta. Poor blockhead!

Armanda. Notwithstanding the noise your fame makes, he always appeared cold in praising you.

Philaminta. Brute!

Armanda. And I have twenty times read some of your verses as new things, which he did not think fine.

Philaminta. Impertinence!

Armanda. We often quarrelled about it, and you would not think how many follies——

Clitander. [*To Armanda.*] Oh, softly, pray. A little charity, madam, or at least a little honesty. What injury have I done you? And what is my offence, that you should arm all your eloquence against me? That you should endeavour to destroy me, and take so much pains to render me odious to those I stand in need of? Speak. Say whence this terrible wrath proceeds? I am desirous that this lady should be an impartial judge in the case.

Armanda. If I had the wrath you would accuse me of, I could find enough to authorise it. You would be too deserving of it; for first flames fix themselves by such sacred rights on the heart, that one ought to lose fortune, and renounce the light rather than burn with the fires of another love; no horror is equal to the changing one's vows, and every faithless heart is a monster in morality.

Clitander. Do you call that infidelity, madam, which the fierceness of your soul enjoined me; I only obey the laws it imposes on me, and if I offend you, that alone is the cause of it. Your charms had at first got entire possession of my heart. It burnt for two years with a constant ardour; there's no assiduous care, duty, respect, service, which it did not make amorous sacrifices of to you. But all my fires, all my care could do nothing with you, I found you still contrary to my softest addresses. That which you refuse, I offer to the choice of another. See. Is it my fault, madam, or yours? Did my heart run to a change, or did you drive it? Is it I that leave you, or you that turn me away?

Armanda. Do you call it, being contrary to your addresses, sir, to deprive 'em of what they had of vulgar in 'em; and to endeavour reducing 'em to that purity in which the beauty of perfect love consists? You can't for me keep your thought clear and disentangled from the commerce of sense; and you don't taste in the greatest of its charms that union of hearts, where the bodies are not concerned. You can't love but with a gross passion, but with all the train of material ties; and to nourish the fires which are produced in you, there must be marriage, with all that follows it. Foh! What strange love! How far are great souls from burning with these terrestrial flames! The senses have no share in all their ardours; this amiable passion would marry nothing but the heart, and leaves the rest behind as nothing worth; 'tis a fire pure and clear, like the celestial fires; with this they breathe only virtuous sighs, and never incline to base desires. Nothing impure has to do with the end they propose. They love for the sake of loving, and for nothing else; their transports are only to the mind; and none can perceive that they have a body.

Clitander. For my part, madam, I perceive, with your leave, that I have unluckily a body as well as a soul, and find it sticks too close to it to leave it behind; I don't understand the art of these separations; Heaven has denied me that philosophy, and my body and soul go together. There's nothing finer, as you have observed, than these purified desires which regard the mind only, that union of hearts, and those tender thoughts, so thoroughly disentangled from the commerce of sense. But these amours are too refined for me; I am a little grosser, as you accuse me; I love entire, myself, and I'm desirous, I must confess, that the love which anybody has for me, should be to my whole person. This is not a matter worthy of such great punishments, and, without doing any wrong to your fine sentiments, I see that my method is very much followed in the world, and that marriage is sufficiently in fashion, passes for a tie virtuous and tender enough to warrant the desire I had of becoming your husband, without giving you cause to appear offended at the liberty of such a thought.

Armanda. Mighty well, sir, extremely well, since your brutish sentiments will be satisfied without hearkening to me; since there must be carnal ties and corporeal chains to reduce you to a faithful ardour, if my mother consents to't, I'll bring my mind to agree with you in what we are speaking of.

Clitander. 'Tis too late, madam, another has taken place; and by such a return I should basely abuse my asylum, and wrong the goodness to which I fled from your haughtiness.

Philaminta. But in short, do you reckon upon my consent, sir, when you promise yourself this other match? Be pleased to know then, in your visions, that I have another husband ready for Henrietta.

Clitander. Pray, madam, consider of your choice; expose me, I beg you, to less disgrace; and don't doom me to the shameful fate of finding myself a rival of Mr. Trissotin's. The love of wits, which makes you so contrary to me, could not oppose to me a less noble adversary. There are many whom the ill taste of the age has reputed wits; but Mr. Trissotin has not been able to deceive anybody, and everyone does justice to his writings. They take him everywhere, but here, for what he is, and I have been twenty times surprised to see you raise to the skies silly verses which you would have disowned had you made 'em yourself.

Philaminta. If you judge of him quite otherwise than we, 'tis because we see him with other eyes than you.

Scene III

Trissotin, Philaminta, Armanda, Clitander.

Trissotin. [*To Philaminta.*] I'm come to tell you a great piece of news, madam. We have escaped finely while we slept. A world has passed along just by us, is fallen across our vortex, and if it had met our earth in the way, it had been dashed to pieces like glass.

Philaminta. Let us lay aside this discourse for another season, this gentleman finds neither rhyme nor reason in it; he professes to cherish ignorance, and to hate wit and learning above anything.

Clitander. This truth wants some softening. I must explain myself, madam; I only hate that wit and learning which spoil people. These are things which in themselves are fine and good; but I would rather choose to be in the rank of the ignorant, than see myself learned like some people.

Trissotin. For my part, I don't hold, whatever effect may be supposed, that learning can spoil anything.

Clitander. And 'tis my opinion that learning often makes very great fools, both in word and deed.

Trissotin. That's a great paradox.

Clitander. The proof of it would be easy enough, I believe, without being very wise. If reason should fail, I am sure famous examples won't fail me however.

Trissotin. You may cite, that will conclude nothing.

Clitander. I'll not go very far to find one to my purpose.

Trissotin. For my part, I don't see these famous examples.

Clitander. I see 'em so plain, that they almost strike me blind.

Trissotin. I have thought hitherto that 'twas ignorance which made great fools, not learning.

Clitander. You have thought very wrong; and I assure you that a learned fool is more foolish than an ignorant fool.

Trissotin. Common opinion is against your maxims, since ignorant and foolish are synonymous terms.

Clitander. If you'll take it according to the use of words, the alliance is greater between pedant and fool.

Trissotin. Folly in the one appears perfectly pure.

Clitander. And study in the other adds to nature.

Trissotin. Learning in itself has eminent merit.

Clitander. Learning in a blockhead becomes impertinent.

Trissotin. Ignorance must have very great charms for you, since you take up arms so eagerly in her defence.

Clitander. If ignorance has very great charms for me, 'tis because certain learned people offer themselves to my view.

Trissotin. Those certain learned people might, if we knew 'em, be as good as certain other people that we see appear.

Clitander. Yes, if it was to be left to those certain learned people; but the certain other people would not agree to this.

Philaminta. [*To Clitander.*] I think, sir——

Clitander. Good now, madam, the gentleman is able enough without your coming to his assistance; I have but too rough an assailant already, and I can only defend myself by retreating.

Armanda. But the offensive eagerness of each repartee which you——

Clitander. Another second! I have done then.

Philaminta. One may bear these sort of combats in conversation, provided the person be not attacked.

Clitander. Oh! lack-a-day, all this has nothing in it to offend him; he understands raillery as well as any man in France; and he can feel himself piqued with many other strokes, and yet his glory does nothing but make a jest of 'em.

Trissotin. I don't wonder in the combat I have undertaken, to see the gentleman take the thesis he maintains; he's much in at Court, that's enough; the Court, 'tis well known, does not stand up for wit; it has an interest in supporting ignorance, and 'tis as being a courtier that he undertakes its defence.

Clitander. You wish very ill to the poor Court, and its unhappiness is very great, to see you wits declaim against it every day; that when anything chagrins you, you quarrel with it; and arraigning its bad taste, accuse it alone for your ill success. Give me leave, Mr. Trissotin, to tell you with all the respect your name inspires me with, that you and your brethren would do very well to speak of the Court in a more tender manner; that, take it at the bottom, it is not so ignorant as you gentlemen imagine; that it has common sense to judge of everything; that something of good taste may be formed there; and that without flattery, the natural wit there is worth all the obscure learning of pedantry.

Trissotin.   We see the effects of its good taste, sir.

Clitander.   Do you see, sir, that it has so bad a one?

Trissotin.   What I see, sir, is, that Rasius and Baldus for learning do honour to France; and that all their merit, which is very visible, doesn't attract either the eyes or gifts of the Court.

Clitander.   I see your uneasiness, and that 'tis through modesty you don't place yourself, sir, with them. Not to bring you therefore into the discourse, What do your able heroes do for the State? What service do their writings do it, that they accuse the Court of horrible injustice, and complain in all places that it fails to pour down the favour of its gifts upon their learned names. Their learning is mighty necessary to France, and the Court has much to do with the books they write. Three beggarly fellows get it into their pitiful heads, that if they are but printed, and bound in calf, they are important persons in the State; that the destiny of crowns depends on their pen; that at the least rumour of their productions they should see pensions flying about 'em; that the eyes of the universe are fixed upon them; that the glory of their name is spread everywhere; and that they are famous prodigies in learning for knowing what others have said before 'em, for having had ears and eyes for thirty years, for having employed nine or ten thousand nights' labour to perplex themselves with Greek and Latin, and load their minds with an unintelligible booty of all the old trash that lies scattered in books; men that always appear drunk with their learning; meritoriously rich in importunate babble; unskilful in everything, void of common sense, and full of ridicule and impertinence to decry true wit and learning everywhere.

Philaminta.   Your warmth is very great, and this transport shows the movement of nature in you. 'Tis the name of rival that excites in your breast——

SCENE IV

Trissotin, Philaminta, Clitander, Armanda, Julian.

Julian. The learned person that paid you a visit just now, madam, and whose humble servant I have the honour of being, exhorts you to read this letter.

Philaminta. However important this may be which I am desired to read, know, friend, that 'tis a piece of rudeness to come and interrupt discourse; and that a servant, who knows how to behave, should have recourse to the people of the house to be introduced.

Julian. I'll note down that in my book, madam.

Philaminta. Trissotin boasts, madam, that he's to marry your daughter. I give you notice that his philosophy only aims at your wealth, and that you would do well not to conclude the match till you have seen the poem which I am composing against him. While you wait for this picture, in which I intend to set him forth to you in all his colours, I send you Horace, Virgil, Terence, and Catullus, where you'll see all the passages he has pilfered, marked in the margin.

Here's a merit attacked by a great many enemies, on account of the marriage I had promised myself; and this railing invites me to do an action directly which may confound envy, which may let him see that this endeavour of his has brought the sooner to effect what it thought to have broke off. [*To Julian.*] Relate all this to your master directly, and tell him, that in order to let him know what great value I set on his noble advice, and how worthy I think it to be followed, [*Pointing to Trissotin.*] I'll marry my daughter to the gentleman this night.

SCENE V

Philaminta, Armanda, Clitander.

Philaminta. [*To Clitander.*] You, sir, as friend to all the family, may assist at the signing of their contract, and I, on my part, invite you to it. Armanda, take care to send to a notary, and to go and give your sister notice of the business.

Armanda. There's no occasion to give my sister any notice, that gentleman there will take care to run and carry her this news immediately, and to dispose her heart to be rebellious to you.

Philaminta.   We shall see who has most power over her, and if I am able to bring her back to her duty.

Scene VI

Armanda, Clitander.

Armanda.   I am very sorry, sir, to see that things are not altogether disposed according to your intentions.

Clitander.   I'll go and labour, madam, with diligence that this great sorrow mayn't remain long at your heart.

Armanda.   I'm afraid that your labour won't have too good an issue.

Clitander.   Perhaps you may see your fear mistaken.

Armanda.   I hope I shall.

Clitander.   I'm persuaded of it; and that I shall be seconded by your assistance.

Armanda.   Yes, I'm going to serve you with all my might.

Clitander.   And that service is sure of my acknowledgment.

Scene VII

Chrisalus, Aristus, Henrietta, Clitander.

Clitander.   Without your assistance, sir, I shall be unhappy. Your wife has rejected my inclinations, and her heart is prepossessed in favour of Trissotin for a son-in-law.

Chrisalus.   What maggot has she got in her head then? Why the deuce would she have this Mr. Trissotin?

Aristus.   'Tis by the honour he has of rhyming in Latin, that he gains the advantage over his rival.

Clitander.   She'll have the wedding this very evening.

Chrisalus.   This evening?

Clitander.   This evening.

Chrisalus.   And this evening I'm resolved, in order to thwart her, that you two shall be married.

Clitander.   She has sent to the notary to draw up the contract.

Chrisalus.   And I'll fetch him to draw up that which he should do.

Clitander. [*Pointing to Henrietta.*]   And the lady is to be informed by her sister of the match she must prepare her heart for.

Chrisalus.   And I command her with full power to prepare her hand for this other alliance. I'll let 'em see that there's no other master to command in my house but myself. [*To Henrietta.*] We'll return presently, be sure stay for us.   Come, follow me, brother; and you, son-in-law.

Henrietta. [*To Aristus.*]   Alas!   Keep him but always in this humour.

Aristus.   I'll make use of everything to serve your love.

Scene VIII

Henrietta, Clitander.

Clitander.   Whatever powerful succours are promised my passion, my most solid hope is in your heart, madam.

Henrietta.   As for my heart, you may assure yourself of that.

Clitander.   I can't but be happy when I have that support.

Henrietta.   You see to what ties they intend to constrain it.

Clitander.   As long as it is for me, I see nothing to fear.

Henrietta.   I'll go and try everything in favour of our tender desires; and if all my endeavours can't give me to you, there's one retreat my heart's resolved on, which will hinder me from being anyone's else.

Clitander.   Just Heaven, defend me from ever receiving from you that proof of your love.

ACT V

Scene I

Henrietta, Trissotin.

Henrietta.   'Tis about the marriage, sir, for which my mother is preparing, that I was desirous to talk to you in private; thinking that in the confusion the house is in, I might be able to make you hearken to reason.   I know that you think me capable of bringing you a very considerable fortune in marriage; but money, which we see so many people esteem, has charms unworthy of a true philosopher.   And the contempt of wealth and frivolous greatness ought not to shine in your words alone.

Trissotin.   Neither is it that which I am charmed with in you; your sparkling charms, your eyes piercing and amorous, your gracefulness and air, are the wealth, the riches, which have attracted my tenders and addresses to you; 'tis with those treasures alone that I am enamoured.

Henrietta. I am much indebted to your generous passion. This obliging affection confounds me, and I'm grieved, sir, that I am not able to answer it. I esteem you as much as one can esteem anyone, but I find an obstacle that hinders me from loving you. A heart, you know, cannot be possessed by two, and I perceive that Clitander is master of mine. I know that he has much less merit than you, that I have ill eyes to choose him for a husband, and that you have a hundred fine talents which ought to please me. I see plainly that I'm in the wrong, but can't help it; and all the effect reason has upon me is to wish myself far enough for being so blind.

Trissotin. The gift of your hand, which I'm encouraged to make pretensions to, will deliver me that heart which Clitander now possesses; and I have room to presume, that by a thousand soft cares I shall be able to find the art of making myself beloved.

Henrietta. No; my soul is fixed to its first vows, and cannot be touched, sir, by your tendernesses. I dare to explain myself freely here to you, and my confession has nothing in it that should shock you. This amorous ardour which springs up in hearts is not, you know, the effect of merit; caprice has a share in it, and when anyone pleases us, we are often at a loss to say why he does. If people loved, sir, through choice and wisdom, you would have had my whole heart, and my whole affection; but one sees that love directs itself otherwise. I beg you'd leave me to my blindness, and not make use of the violence that for your sake is put upon my obedience. A man of honour will owe nothing to the power which parents have over us; he refuses to let what he loves be sacrificed to him, and will not obtain a heart from anyone but itself. Don't spur on my mother to exercise, by her choice, the rigour of her power upon my inclinations. Remove your love from me, and bear to some other the homage of a heart so precious as yours.

Trissotin. What way can this heart be able to satisfy you? Impose on it any commands that may be executed. Can it be capable of not loving you, unless you cease, madam, to be amiable, and to display in your eyes celestial charms——

Henrietta. Nay, sir, let us leave this idle stuff. You have so many Irises, Phyllises, and Amaranthas, whom you everywhere paint so charming in your verses, and for whom you vow such an amorous ardour——

Trissotin. 'Tis my wit that speaks, and not my heart. I'm

only in love with them as a poet; but I love the adorable Henrietta in earnest.

Henrietta. Oh! pray, sir——

Trissotin. If this offends you, I am not likely to give over my offence towards you. This ardour, hitherto unknown to you, consecrates vows of eternal duration to you; nothing can put a stop to their amiable transports; and notwithstanding your beauty may condemn my endeavours, I cannot refuse the assistance of a mother who intends to crown so dear a flame; and provided I obtain so great a happiness, provided I have you, 'tis no matter how.

Henrietta. But do you know that people run a greater risk than they imagine in using violence to a heart? That 'tis not very secure, let me tell you plainly, to marry a woman against her will; and that finding herself under constraint, she may be hurried to resentments which a husband ought to fear.

Trissotin. Such a discourse has nothing in it to make me alter my purpose. The wise man is prepared for all events; cured by reason of vulgar weaknesses, he sets himself above these sort of things, and does not take the least shadow of trouble about anything which is not to depend on himself.

Henrietta. In truth, sir, I'm transported with you; and I did not think that philosophy was so fine a thing as it is, to teach people to bear such accidents with constancy. This firmness of soul, so singular in you, deserves to have an illustrious subject given it; is worthy to find one who may take with pleasure continual pains to place it in full light; and as I dare not, to say the truth, think myself very proper to give it the whole lustre of its glory, I leave it to some other person, and swear to you, between ourselves, that I renounce the happiness of seeing you my husband.

Trissotin. [*Going.*] We shall see by and by, how the affair will go; for they have got the notary within already.

SCENE II

Chrisalus, Clitander, Henrietta, Martina.

Chrisalus. Daughter, I'm glad to see you. Come, come and do your duty, and submit your desires to the will of a father. I'll, I'll teach your mother how to behave; and to brave her the more, here I bring back Martina, and will fix her in the house again in spite of her teeth.

Henrietta. Your resolutions deserve praise. Take care that this humour doesn't change, father. Be firm in resolving on what you wish, and don't suffer yourself to be seduced from your good intentions. Don't slacken; but act so as to hinder my mother from getting the better of you.

Chrisalus. What! Do you take me for a booby?

Henrietta. Heaven forbid!

Chrisalus. Am I a simpleton, pray?

Henrietta. I don't say so.

Chrisalus. Am I thought incapable of the firm sentiments of a reasonable man?

Henrietta. No, father.

Chrisalus. At the age I am of, have not I sense enough to be master of my house?

Henrietta. Certainly.

Chrisalus. Have I such a weakness of soul to suffer myself to be led by the nose by my wife?

Henrietta. Oh! no, father.

Chrisalus. How now! What do you mean then? I think you are very merry in talking to me thus.

Henrietta. If I have offended you, it was not my intention.

Chrisalus. My will ought to be followed entirely in this house.

Henrietta. Very well, father.

Chrisalus. None besides myself has a right to govern in the house.

Henrietta. True, you are in the right.

Chrisalus. 'Tis I that hold the place of chief of the family.

Henrietta. Agreed.

Chrisalus. 'Tis I who ought to dispose of my daughter.

Henrietta. Yes.

Chrisalus. Heaven gives me a full authority over you.

Henrietta. Who says the contrary?

Chrisalus. And I'll let you see that in taking a husband, 'tis your father you must obey, not your mother.

Henrietta. Alas! In that you flatter my softest desires; all that I wish is to obey you.

Chrisalus. We shall see if my wife prove rebellious to my desires——

Clitander. Here she brings the notary with her.

Chrisalus. Second me, all of you.

Martina. Let me alone; I'll take care to encourage you, if there be any occasion for it.

SCENE III

*Philaminta, Belisa, Armanda, Trissotin, The Notary, Chrisalus,
Clitander, Henrietta, Martina.*

Philaminta. [*To the Notary.*] Can't you change your savage
style, and draw up a contract in good language?

Notary. Our style is very good, and I should be a blockhead,
madam, if I attempted to change the least word in it.

Belisa. Ah! What barbarism in the middle of France!
But however, sir, for learning's sake, instead of pounds, shillings,
and pence, let the portion be expressed in mines and talents;
and date by the words ides and kalends.

Notary. I? Why if I was to agree with your demands, I
should have all my companions hiss at me.

Philaminta. In vain we complain of this barbarism. Come,
sir, take the table and write. [*Seeing Martina.*] How, how!
Dares that impudent hussy show her face again? Pray, why
do you bring her to my house again?

Chrisalus. We shall tell you why by and by, at leisure. We
have another thing to determine now.

Notary. Let us proceed to the contract. Where's the bride
that is to be?

Philaminta. She I marry is the younger daughter.

Notary. Good.

Chrisalus. [*Pointing to Henrietta.*] Ay, here she is, sir; her
name is Henrietta.

Notary. Very well. And where's the bridegroom?

Philaminta. [*Pointing to Trissotin.*] The husband I give her
is this gentleman.

Chrisalus. [*Pointing to Clitander.*] And he that I myself
intend she shall marry, is this gentleman.

Notary. Two husbands! that's too many according to custom.

Philaminta. [*To the Notary.*] What do you stop for? Set
down, set down Mr. Trissotin for my son-in-law.

Chrisalus. For my son-in-law, set down, set down Mr.
Clitander.

Notary. Be at concord then; and upon mature judgment
see and agree between yourselves upon a bridegroom.

Philaminta. Follow, sir, follow the choice I have fixed on.

Chrisalus. Do, sir, do what I have resolved on.

Notary. Tell me first which of the two I must obey.

Philaminta. [*To Chrisalus.*] What! do you dispute my will
then?

Chrisalus. I can't bear that my daughter should be sought after only for love of the wealth that's in my family.

Philaminta. Truly your riches are much thought of here; and 'tis a very worthy suspicion for a wise man.

Chrisalus. In short, I have made choice of Clitander for her husband.

Philaminta. And here's the person, [*Pointing to Trissotin.*] I have pitched on for her husband; and my choice shall be followed, that's a resolved point.

Chrisalus. Hey-day! You pitch on him there in a very absolute manner.

Martina. 'Tis not for the wife to prescribe; and I am for giving the upper part in everything to the men.

Chrisalus. That's well said.

Martina. My discharge was given me a hundred times, that's certain; but the hen ought not to crow before the cock.

Chrisalus. Certainly.

Martina. And we see that people jeer at a man when his wife wears the breeches.

Chrisalus. True.

Martina. If I had a husband, I must needs say I would have him be master of the house; I should not love him if he proved a booby; and if I contested with him out of whim, or spoke too loud, I should think it right if he lowered my tone with a few stripes.

Chrisalus. She speaks as she ought to do.

Martina. My master is in the right to design an agreeable husband for his daughter.

Chrisalus. Yes.

Martina. For what reason should he refuse her Clitander, young and handsome as he is? And why, pray, should he give her a scholar, who is always a-criticising? She must have a husband, not a schoolmaster; and not desiring to understand Greek or Latin, she has no need of Mr. Trissotin.

Chrisalus. Very well.

Philaminta. We must suffer her to prate at her ease.

Martina. Scholars are good for nothing but to preach in a pulpit; and I have said it a thousand times, that I would never have a man of learning for my husband. Learning is not at all what is wanted in a family; books agree ill with matrimony; and if ever I plight my troth, I'll have a husband that has no other book but me; who, no offence to my mistress, knows neither A nor B; and, in one word, is a doctor only for his wife.

Philaminta. [*To Chrisalus.*] Have you done? And have I long enough hearkened quietly to your worthy interpreter?

Chrisalus. She has spoken truth.

Philaminta. To cut short all this dispute, I will absolutely have my desire executed. [*Pointing to Trissotin.*] Henrietta and the gentleman shall be joined immediately; I have said it, and I'll have it so; make me no reply. If you have given your word to Clitander, offer him her elder sister for a match.

Chrisalus. Here's an accommodation of this affair. See; [*To Henrietta and Clitander.*] do you give your consent.

Henrietta. What, father!

Clitander. [*To Chrisalus.*] How, sir!

Belisa. She might easily have proposals made to her which would please her much better; but we establish a kind of love which must be as refined as the morning-star; the thinking substance may be admitted into it, but we banish from it the extended substance.

SCENE IV

Aristus, Chrisalus, Philaminta, Belisa, Henrietta, Armanda, Trissotin, The Notary, Clitander, Martina.

Aristus. I am sorry to disturb these joyful rites by the grief I am obliged to bring hither. These two letters make me the bearer of two pieces of news, on account of which I have felt very great concern for you; [*To Philaminta.*] one for you, came to me from my attorney; [*To Chrisalus.*] the other, for you, came to me from Lyons.

Philaminta. What misfortune can be sent us word of, that ought to trouble us?

Aristus. This letter contains one, as you may read.

Philaminta. Madam, I have desired your brother to deliver you this letter, which will inform you of what I durst not come to tell you. Your great negligence in your affairs has been the cause that the clerk of your reporting-judge did not give me notice; and you have absolutely lost your suit, which you might have gained.

Chrisalus. [*To Philaminta.*] Your suit lost!

Philaminta. [*To Chrisalus.*] You are too much concerned! My heart is not at all shaken with this blow. Show a less common soul, and brave, like me, the strokes of fortune.

Your want of care costs you forty thousand crowns; and 'tis to pay that sum with the charges, that you are condemned by the order of court.

Condemned? Ah! That word is shocking, and was made for criminals only.

Aristus. He's in the wrong indeed, and you justly exclaim against him. He ought to have said, that you are desired by order of court to pay only forty thousand crowns, and the necessary charges.
Philaminta. Let us see the other.

Chrisalus. The friendship which binds me to your brother, makes me interest myself in all that concerns you. I know that you have put your money into the hands of Argantes and Damon, and I must acquaint you that they both became bankrupts on the same day.

O Heavens! to lose all my money at once thus!

Philaminta. [*To Chrisalus.*] Ah! What a shameful transport! Fie. All this is nothing; to a truly wise man, no change of fortune is fatal; and though he lose everything, he still remains firm to himself. Let us finish our affair, and quit your concern. His wealth, [*Pointing to Trissotin.*] may suffice both for us and himself.
Trissotin. No, madam, forbear to press this affair. I see the whole world is averse to this match, and I have no intention to put a force upon people.
Philaminta. This reflection came suddenly to you! It follows very close, sir, upon our misfortune.
Trissotin. At last I am tired with so much resistance. I had rather renounce all this confusion, and don't desire a heart that won't surrender itself.
Philaminta. I see, I see in you, not for your honour, what I have hitherto refused to believe.
Trissotin. You may see in me what you please, and I little regard how you take it. But I am not a man who would suffer the infamy of an injurious refusal, which I must have undergone here; I would have people set a greater value on me, and whoever will not, I kiss their hand.

Scene V

Aristus, Chrisalus, Philaminta, Belisa, Armanda, Henrietta, Clitander, The Notary, Martina.

Philaminta. How plainly has he discovered his mercenary soul! And how little philosophical is this action of his!

Clitander. I don't pretend to be one; but yet, madam, I cleave to your destiny; and dare offer you with my person whatever wealth fortune is known to have given me.

Philaminta. You charm me, sir, by this generous act; and I'll therefore crown your amorous desires. Yes, I grant Henrietta to the eager ardour——

Henrietta. No, mother, I now change my mind; suffer me to resist your intention.

Clitander. What, do you oppose my felicity? And when I find everyone agree to my love——

Henrietta. I know the smallness of your fortune, Clitander, and I always desired you for a husband, when I found that my marrying you would settle your affairs at the same time that it satisfied my tender desires; but since the fates are so contrary to us, I love you so much in this extremity as not to load you with our adversity.

Clitander. Any destiny with you would be agreeable to me; and, without you, none would be supportable.

Henrietta. Love always talks thus in its transports, but let us avoid the disquiet of vexatious reflections. Nothing wears out so much the ardour of the knot that ties us, as the grievous want of necessary possessions; and people often accuse one another of the direful sorrow which proceeds from such engagements.

Aristus. [*To Henrietta.*] Is what we have just now learnt, the only motive which makes you refuse to marry Clitander?

Henrietta. Otherwise you should see me fly to it with all my heart; and I only refuse to take him, because I love him too well.

Aristus. Suffer yourself then to be bound by such an amiable union. The news I brought you was false; 'twas a stratagem, a surprising device which I resolved to try, in order to serve your love, to undeceive my sister, and let her see what her philosopher would prove upon trial.

Chrisalus. Heaven be praised!

Philaminta. I'm glad at heart for the vexation which the base deserter will feel. To see this match concluded in a splendid manner, will be the greatest punishment to his sordid avarice.

Chrisalus. [*To Clitander.*]   I knew very well that you would have her.

Armanda. [*To Philaminta.*]   Will you sacrifice me then in this manner to their inclinations?

Philaminta.   It will not be you that I sacrifice to 'em; you have the support of philosophy, and can see their ardour crowned with a contented eye.

Belisa.   Let him take care however to retain me in his heart. People often marry through a sudden despair, which they afterwards repent of as long as they live.

Chrisalus. [*To the Notary.*]   Come, sir, follow the order I gave you, and draw up the contract as I said.

THE CHEATS OF SCAPIN

(A COMEDY)

THE CHEATS OF SCAPIN, *a Comedy of Three Acts in Prose acted at Paris,
at the Theatre of the Palace-Royal, the 24th of May,* 1671.

If we excuse the ridiculous incident of the sack, which has been
so often criticised upon after Despreaux, we shall find in *The Cheats
of Scapin* some riches of antiquity which have not displeased the
moderns. Plautus would not have even rejected the very incident
of the sack, nor the scene of the galley, corrected from Cyrano, and
would have discovered himself in the vivacity which animates the
plot. Terence would not have been ashamed of the simplicity and
elegance with which the piece opens, where Octavio relates to his
servant, or rather repeats himself, a piece of news which afflicts
him; whilst the valet, like an echo, confirms it by monosyllables.
Terence would have discovered himself again in that scene where
Argante talks aloud to himself, while Scapin answers him without
being either seen or heard by Argante, in order to let the spectator
into the cheat he was contriving. In short, although the servants,
who, like the slaves in Plautus and Terence, are the soul of this
piece, do not afford a comic humour so elegant as that which Molière
has first given an example of to his age, yet we can't help applauding
this inferior kind likewise.

ACTORS

ARGANTE, *father to Octavio and Zerbinetta.*
GÉRONTE, *father to Leander and Hiacintha.*
OCTAVIO, *son to Argante, and in love with Hiacintha.*
LEANDER, *son to Géronte, and in love with Zerbinetta.*
ZERBINETTA, *supposed a gipsy, and discovered to be daughter to Argante.*
HIACINTHA, *daughter to Géronte.*
SCAPIN, *valet to Leander.*
SILVESTER, *valet to Octavio.*
NERINA, *nurse to Hiacintha.*
CARLOS, *friend to Scapin.*
TWO PORTERS.

SCENE: *Naples.*

ACT I

Scene I

Octavio, Silvester.

Octavio. Sad news to an enamoured heart! What cruel extremities am I reduced to! You have just heard, Silvester, at the port, that my father is upon his return?

Silvester. Yes.

Octavio. That he arrived this very morning?

Silvester. This very morning.

Octavio. And that he comes back with a resolution to marry me?

Silvester. Yes.

Octavio. To a daughter of Signor Géronte?

Silvester. Of Signor Géronte.

Octavio. And that this young lady is ordered hither from Tarentum for that purpose?

Silvester. Yes.

Octavio. And you have this news from my uncle?

Silvester. From your uncle.

Octavio. Whom my father acquainted with this, by letter?

Silvester. By letter.

Octavio. And this uncle, you say, knows all our affairs?

Silvester. All our affairs.

Octavio. Pshaw! Prithee speak, and don't act on this fashion, catching the words out of my mouth.

Silvester. What can I say more? You forget not one circumstance, and you tell things just as they are.

Octavio. Advise me, at least, and tell me what I must do in this cruel conjuncture.

Silvester. Troth, I find myself as much embarrassed here as you are, and I've a good deal of occasion that somebody should give advice to me.

Octavio. I am killed by this plaguy return.

Silvester. And I am no less so.

Octavio. When my father comes to be let into affairs, I shall have a sudden storm of impetuous reprimands pour upon me.

Silvester. Reprimands are nothing, would Heaven I were quit at that rate! But for my part I am like to pay much dearer for your follies, I see a cloud of cudgel-blows forming at a distance which will burst upon my shoulders.

Octavio. Heavens! which way shall I get clear of the perplexity I find myself in?

Silvester. You should have thought of that before you had brought yourself into't.

Octavio. Pooh! you tease me to death with your unseasonable lectures.

Silvester. And you me much more, by your giddy actions.

Octavio. What must I do? What am I to resolve on? What remedy can I have recourse to?

SCENE II

Octavio, Scapin, Silvester.

Scapin. How now, Signor Octavio? What's the matter with you? What ails you? What disorder is this? You're much disturbed, I see.

Octavio. Ah! my dear Scapin, I'm undone, I'm lost irrecoverably, I am the most unfortunate of men.

Scapin. How so?

Octavio. Hast thou heard nothing in regard to me?

Scapin. No.

Octavio. My father's just a-coming with Signor Géronte, and they are determined to marry me.

Scapin. Well, what is there so horrible in that?

Octavio. Alas, you know the cause of my uneasiness.

Scapin. No, but 'tis your fault if I don't know it very soon, and I'm a man of consolation, one who interests myself in young people's affairs.

Octavio. Oh! Scapin, if thou couldst find any invention, forge any plot, to deliver me from the misery I'm in, I should think myself indebted to thee for more than life.

Scapin. To tell you the truth, there are few things impossible to me, when I am pleased to engage in 'em. Heaven has doubtless bestowed on me a fine genius enough for all those clean turns of wit, and those ingenious gallantries, to which the ignorant vulgar give the name of imposture; and without vanity, I can say that there has scarce been a man seen who was a more dexterous artist at expedients and intrigues, who acquired more glory in that noble profession, than myself. But in troth, merit is too ill rewarded nowadays, and I have renounced all these things ever since the chagrin of a certain affair which happened to me.

Octavio. How! What affair, Scapin?

Scapin. An adventure in which I was embroiled with justice.

Octavio. With justice?

Scapin. Yes. We had a trifling quarrel together.

Octavio. You, and justice?

Scapin. Yes, she used me but scurvily, and I was piqued to such a degree at the ingratitude of the age, that I resolved to act no longer. But enough. Go on with the story of your adventure.

Octavio. You know, Scapin, 'tis two months ago that Signor Géronte and my father embarked together upon a voyage which regards a certain commerce, wherein both their interests were concerned.

Scapin. I know it.

Octavio. And that Leander and I were left by our fathers; I under the conduct of Silvester, and Leander under thy direction.

Scapin. Yes. I have acquitted myself very well of my charge.

Octavio. Some time after, Leander met with a young gipsy, with whom he fell in love.

Scapin. That I know too.

Octavio. As we are great friends, he presently let me into the secret of his amour, and carried me to see this girl, whom I thought handsome, 'tis true, but not to such a degree as he would have had me think her. He entertained me with nothing but her, from day to day, at every turn exaggerated her beauty and her gracefulness to me; he extolled her wit, and spoke to me with transport of the charms of her conversation, which he reported to me even to the least word, and took pains to make me think 'em the most sprightly in the world. He sometimes quarrelled with me for not being sufficiently sensible of things he had told me, and blamed me for ever for the indifference I showed to the flames of love.

Scapin. I don't as yet see whither this tends.

Octavio. One day, as I accompanied him to visit the people in whose custody the dear object of his passion is, we heard, in a little house of a by-street, some lamentations mixed with a good deal of sobbing. We asked what it was. A woman told us, sighing, that we might there see something most piteous in the persons of foreigners; and that, except we were insensible, we should be touched with it.

Scapin. Whither will this lead us?

Octavio. Curiosity made me press Leander to see what it was. We enter into a hall, where we see an ancient woman dying, assisted by a maid-servant, who was making lamentation, and a young girl dissolved in tears, the handsomest and most touching that ever was seen.

Scapin. Oh! hoh!

Octavio. Another would have appeared frightful in the condition she was in; for she had nothing on but a wretched scanty petticoat, with a night waistcoat of plain dimity; and her headdress a yellow cornet, turned back upon the top of her head, which let her hair fall in disorder upon her shoulders; and yet thus dressed, she shone with a thousand allurements, and there was nothing but what was agreeable and charming in her whole person.

Scapin. I perceive things come towards.

Octavio. Hadst thou seen her, Scapin, in the condition I tell thee, thou hadst thought her admirable.

Scapin. Oh! I don't doubt it; and without seeing her, I see very plainly she was absolutely charming.

Octavio. Her tears were none of those disagreeable tears which disfigure a face. She had a most winning gracefulness in weeping; and her sorrow was the most beautiful in the world.

Scapin. I see all this.

Octavio. She melted everybody into tears, by throwing herself in the most tender manner upon the body of the dying woman, whom she called her dear mother; there was not a person there but was pierced to the soul to see so good a disposition.

Scapin. Really, this is very moving, and I see plainly this good disposition of hers made you in love with her.

Octavio. Ah! Scapin, a barbarian would have loved her.

Scapin. Certainly. How could one avoid it?

Octavio. After some words, with which I endeavoured to soften the grief of the afflicted charmer, we went from thence; and asking Leander what he thought of this person, he answered, me coldly, that he thought she was tolerably pretty. I was vexed at the indifference with which he spoke of her, and would not discover the effect her beauty had upon my heart.

Silvester. [*To Octavio.*] If you don't abridge this narrative, we are in for it till to-morrow morning. Let me finish it in two or three words. [*To Scapin.*] His heart takes fire from this moment. He can't live, if he goes not to comfort the amiable afflicted. His frequent visits are rejected by the maid-servant, who is become governante, by the death of the mother. Behold my gentleman in despair. He presses, supplicates, conjures; not a bit. They tell him the girl, though destitute of means or support, is of a good family; and that, without marrying her, they cannot allow of his addresses. His love is augmented by difficulties. He racks his brain, debates, reasons, ponders, takes his resolution. And lo! he has been married to her these three days.

Scapin. I understand.

Silvester. Now add to this the unthought-of return of the father, who was not expected this two months; the discovery the uncle has made of the secret of our marriage; and the other marriage intended between him and the daughter which Signor Géronte had by a second wife whom they say he married at Tarentum.

Octavio. And more than all this, add also the indigence this lovely creature labours under, and the incapacity I am in to get wherewithal to relieve her.

Scapin. Is that all? You are both mightily perplexed about a mere trifle. Is that a matter to be so much alarmed at? Art not ashamed to be caught short in such a small business? What the deuce! Thou art as large and as bulky as father and mother together; and canst thou not find in thy noddle, nor forge in thy invention, some gallant wile, some honest little stratagem, to adjust your affairs? Fie! Plague o' the booby. I should have been heartily glad formerly, would they but have given me our old fellows to bubble; I should have played 'em off with a jerk. I was no higher than this, when I had signalised myself by a hundred tricks of fine address.

Silvester. I confess that Heaven has not given me thy talents; and that I have not the wit, like thee, to be embroiled with justice.

Octavio. See here my lovely Hiacintha.

SCENE III

Hiacintha, Octavio, Scapin, Silvester.

Hiacintha. Ah! Octavio, is it true what Silvester has just told Nerina, that your father is upon his return, and intends to marry you?

Octavio. Yes, fair Hiacintha, and these tidings have struck me cruelly. But what do I see? Do you weep? Why these tears? Tell me, do you suspect me of any unfaithfulness? And have you not assurance of my love?

Hiacintha. Yes, Octavio, I am sure you love me; but I am not so that you will love me always.

Octavio. What, can one love you, and not love you for life?

Hiacintha. I've heard say, Octavio, that your sex loves not so long as ours does; and that the ardours men discover, are flames which are as easily extinguished as they are kindled.

Octavio. Ah! my dear Hiacintha, my heart then is not made like that of other men; I plainly perceive, for my part, that I shall love you till death.

Hiacintha. I'm willing to believe you think what you say, and I make no doubt but your words are sincere. But I fear a power which may oppose, in your heart, the tender sentiments you may have for me. You depend on a father who would marry you to another; and I'm sure, should this misfortune happen, 'twill be the death of me.

Octavio. No, lovely Hiacintha, there's no father shall force me to break my faith with you; and I am determined to quit my country, and even life itself, if 'tis necessary, rather than quit you. I have already, without having seen her, conceived a horrible aversion for her they have appointed me; and, without cruelty, I could wish the sea would drive her far hence for ever. Therefore pray, my lovely Hiacintha, weep not, for your tears kill me, and I cannot see 'em but they stab me to the heart.

Hiacintha. Since you will have it so, I will then dry up my tears, and wait with a fixed eye for what it shall please Heaven to determine about me.

Octavio. Heaven will be favourable to us.

Hiacintha. It cannot be averse to me, if you are faithful.

Octavio. I certainly shall be so.

Hiacintha. Then I shall be happy.

Scapin. [*Aside.*] She's not so much of a fool, in troth; and I think she's tolerably well to pass.

Octavio. [*Pointing to Scapin.*] Here's a man could be a marvellous help to us in all our necessities, were he but so pleased.

Scapin. I have made great protestations to meddle no more with the world; but if you entreat me very powerfully, both of you, perhaps——

Octavio. Nay, if it sticks only at strong entreaties to obtain thy assistance, I conjure thee, with all my heart, to take upon thee the conduct of our bark.

Scapin. [*To Hiacintha.*] And have you nothing to say to me?

Hiacintha. I conjure you, according to his example, by all in the world that's most dear to you, that you would assist us in our love.

Scapin. I must suffer myself to be overcome, and have a little humanity. Go, I'll employ myself in your favour.

Octavio. Be assured that——

Scapin. [*To Octavio.*] Hush. [*To Hiacintha.*] Get you hence, and make yourself easy.

SCENE IV

Octavio, Scapin, Silvester.

Scapin. [*To Octavio.*] And you prepare yourself firmly to endure the meeting of your father.

Octavio. I confess to thee, that this meeting makes me tremble beforehand; and I have such a natural timorousness as I don't know how to overcome.

Scapin. You must however appear firm at first encounter, for fear he takes the advantage of your faint-heartedness, and lead you about like a child. There, endeavour by study to compose yourself. A little boldness, and think how to answer resolutely upon everything I can say to you.

Octavio. I shall do the best I can.

Scapin. Come on, let's try a little to inure you to it. Let us con over your part, and see whether you'll act it well. Come. Your mind resolute, your head aloft, your looks bold.

Octavio. In this manner?

Scapin. A little more still.

Octavio. So?

Scapin. Good. Imagine me to be your father, just arrived, and only answer me as if I were he himself. How, scoundrel, worthless, infamous rascal, son unworthy of such a father as I am! Dare you appear before my face after this fine deportment of yours, after this base trick you have played me during my absence? Is this the fruit of all my cares, varlet? Is this the fruit of my cares? The respect that's due to me? The respect you retain for me? Come then. Have you the insolence, knave, to engage yourself without the consent of your father, to contract a clandestine marriage? Answer me, rogue, answer

me. Let me see your fine reasons.——What a plague! you're
absolutely nonplussed.

Octavio. 'Tis because I imagine 'tis my father I hear.

Scapin. Why, yes. 'Tis for that reason you must not look
like an idiot.

Octavio. I shall take upon me to be more resolute now, and
shall answer more stoutly.

Scapin. Certainly?

Octavio. Certainly.

Scapin. Here's your father a-coming.

Octavio. Heavens! I'm undone.

SCENE V

Scapin, Silvester.

Scapin. Soho! Octavio, stay; Octavio. There he's fled.
What a poor sort of man it is! Let's not delay waiting upon the
old gentleman.

Silvester. What shall I say to him?

Scapin. Leave me to speak to him, and only follow me.

SCENE VI

Argante, Scapin and Silvester (at the farther part of the stage).

Argante. [*Thinking himself alone.*] Did ever anybody hear
of an action like this?

Scapin. [*To Silvester.*] He has learnt the affair already; and
he has taken it so strongly into his head, that he talks on't
aloud now he's alone.

Argante. [*Thinking himself alone.*] Here's an instance of
great rashness!

Scapin. [*To Silvester.*] Let's hearken to him a little.

Argante. [*Thinking himself alone.*] I would be glad to know
what they can say to me upon this fine marriage.

Scapin. [*Aside.*] We have thought of that.

Argante. [*Thinking himself alone.*] Will they endeavour to
deny the thing?

Scapin. [*Aside.*] No, we don't think of that.

Argante. [*Thinking himself alone.*] Or will they undertake
to excuse it?

Scapin. [*Aside.*] That may possibly be.

Argante. [*Thinking himself alone.*] Will they pretend to amuse me with impertinent stories?

Scapin. [*Aside.*] Perhaps so.

Argante. [*Thinking himself alone.*] All their speeches will be to no purpose.

Scapin. [*Aside.*] We shall see that.

Argante. [*Thinking himself alone.*] They shan't impose upon me.

Scapin. [*Aside.*] Let us not swear to anything.

Argante. [*Thinking himself alone.*] I shall take care to secure my rascal of a son in a safe place.

Scapin. [*Aside.*] We shall see to that.

Argante. [*Thinking himself alone.*] And for that rogue, Silvester, I'll cudgel him to a mummy.

Silvester. [*To Scapin.*] I should have been much astonished had he forgot me.

Argante. [*Seeing Silvester.*] Oh! Hoh! Are you there then, most sage governor of a family? Fine director of young folks!

Scapin. Sir, I rejoice to see you returned.

Argante. A good day to you, Scapin. [*To Silvester.*] You have followed my orders, truly, in a pretty manner; and my son has behaved himself very sagely during my absence.

Scapin. You are mighty well, as far as I can see.

Argante. Pretty well. [*To Silvester.*] Dost not say a word, rascal? Dost not say one word?

Scapin. Have you had a good voyage?

Argante. Pshaw! A very good one. Let me alone a little, that I may have leisure to quarrel with the rascal.

Scapin. Would you quarrel?

Argante. Yes, I will quarrel.

Scapin. With whom, sir?

Argante. [*Pointing to Silvester.*] With that varlet there.

Scapin. Why so?

Argante. Have you not heard what has passed in my absence?

Scapin. I've heard indeed some trifling matter.

Argante. How! some trifling matter? An action of this nature!

Scapin. You are in some measure in the right.

Argante. So daring a thing as this!

Scapin. That's true.

Argante. A son marry without the consent of his father!

Scapin. Yes, there is something to be said to that. But I'm of opinion you should make no noise about it.

Argante. I'm not of that opinion, for my part; I will have my belly-full of making a noise. What! don't you think I've all the reason in the world to be in a passion.

Scapin. Yes. So was I at first, when I heard the thing; and so far interested myself in your favour, as to quarrel with your son. Ask him but what fine reprimands I gave him, and how I lectured him upon the little respect he retained for a father, whose footsteps he ought to kiss. One could not talk better to him, though't had been your own self. But what of that? I submitted to reason, and considered, that at the bottom he might not be so much in the wrong as one would be apt to think.

Argante. What's this you tell me? Is there no great wrong in going to marry himself, point blank, to a stranger?

Scapin. What would you have? He was pushed to't by his destiny.

Argante. Ho! ho! The prettiest reason, that, in the world! One has no more to do but to commit the greatest crimes imaginable, to cheat, steal, murder, and say for excuse, One was pushed to't by one's destiny.

Scapin. Lack-a-day! sir, you take my words in too philosophical a sense. I mean that he was fatally engaged in this affair.

Argante. And why did he engage in it?

Scapin. Would you have him as wise as yourself? Young folks are young, and have not all the prudence they should have, to do nothing but what's reasonable. Witness our Leander, who, notwithstanding all my lessons, notwithstanding all my remonstrances, has gone and done worse still than your son has done. I would be glad to know whether you yourself were not once young, and have not played as many pranks in your time as other people. I've heard say that formerly you were an excellent companion among the ladies; that you played the wag with the gallantest of 'em all at that time; and that you never made your approaches but you gained your point.

Argante. That's true, I grant it; but I always confined myself to gallantry, and never went so far as to do what he has done.

Scapin. What would you have had him done? He sees a young girl who had a kindness for him, for he takes after you to have all the women in love with him, he thinks her charming, he pays her visits, makes love to her, sighs after a gallant manner, acts the passionate lover. She yields to his addresses;

he pushes his fortune. When, lo! he is caught with her by her relations, who by force of arms oblige him to marry her.

Silvester. [*Aside.*] What a dexterous knave it is!

Scapin. Would you have had him suffer himself to be murdered? 'Tis much better to be married than to be dead.

Argante. They did not tell me the thing was done in this manner.

Scapin. [*Pointing to Silvester.*] Ask him rather; he won't say to the contrary.

Argante. [*To Silvester.*] Was it by force that he was married?

Silvester. Yes, sir.

Scapin. Would I tell you a lie?

Argante. He should have gone therefore immediately, and have entered his protest with a notary against the violence.

Scapin. That is what he would not do.

Argante. That would have made it easier for me to dissolve the marriage.

Scapin. Dissolve the marriage?

Argante. Yes.

Scapin. You won't dissolve it.

Argante. Shan't I dissolve it?

Scapin. No.

Argante. What, shan't I have the rights of a father, and have satisfaction for the violence they have done my son?

Scapin. 'Tis certain he'll by no means consent to it.

Argante. He not consent to it?

Scapin. No.

Argante. My son?

Scapin. Your son. Would you have him confess that he was capable of fear, and that they made him do things by force? He'll take care how he owns that. That were to injure himself, and show himself unworthy of such a father as you.

Argante. I care not for that.

Scapin. He must, for his own honour and yours, tell the world that he married her voluntarily.

Argante. And for my honour and his own I'll have him say the contrary.

Scapin. No, I am sure he won't do it.

Argante. I shall make him.

Scapin. He won't do it, I tell you.

Argante. He shall do it, or I'll disinherit him.

Scapin. You?

Argante. Yes, I.

Scapin. Good.

Argante. How, good?

Scapin. You shan't disinherit him.

Argante. Shan't I disinherit him?

Scapin. No.

Argante. No?

Scapin. No.

Argante. Ahah! That's merry enough; I shan't disinherit my son?

Scapin. No, I tell you.

Argante. Who shall hinder me?

Scapin. You yourself.

Argante. I myself?

Scapin. Yes. You won't have the heart to do it.

Argante. I shall.

Scapin. You're only in jest.

Argante. I am not in jest.

Scapin. Fatherly tenderness will prevail.

Argante. 'Twill do nothing at all.

Scapin. Yes, yes.

Argante. I tell you this shall be done.

Scapin. Trifles!

Argante. You mustn't call it trifles.

Scapin. Lack-a-day! I know ye, you are naturally good-humoured.

Argante. Let's have done with this discourse, for it provokes my choler. [*To Silvester.*] Get thee gone, hang-dog; get thee gone, and find out my rascal, while I join Signor Géronte, and tell him my misfortune.

Scapin. Sir, if I can serve you in anything, you need only command me.

Argante. I thank you. [*Aside.*] Oh! why was he an only son? And why have I not now the daughter which Heaven deprived me of, that I might make her my heir?

SCENE VII

Scapin, Silvester.

Silvester. Thou art a great man, I confess, and the affair is in a fine way. But the money, on the other hand, presses us sore for our subsistence, and we have people too on all hands barking after us.

Scapin. Let me alone, the plot is hatched; I'm only casting about in my noddle for a man who will be trusty to us, to act a part that I have occasion for. Stay. Hold a little. Pull thy hat over thy eyes like a bully. Bear upon one foot. Thy hand upon thy side. Thy eyes furious. Strut a little like a theatrical king. Very well. Follow me. I have some secrets to disguise thy face and thy voice.

Silvester. I conjure thee, however, engage me not in any broils with justice.

Scapin. Go, go. We share our dangers like brothers; and three years in the galleys, be they more or less, should not curb a noble spirit.

ACT II

Scene I

Géronte, Argante.

Géronte. Yes, without doubt, by the time, we should have our folks here to-day; a sailor who comes from Tarentum, assured me he had seen my man, who was ready to embark but my daughter's arrival will find things but in an ill dis position for what we proposed to ourselves; and what you have told me concerning your son, strangely breaks the measures we had concerted.

Argante. Give yourself no pain about that; I will be answerable to you for the removal of that obstacle; and I am going directly about it.

Géronte. In good truth, Signor Argante, give me leave to tell you; the education of children is a thing that requires the strongest application.

Argante. Doubtless. But to what purpose is this?

Géronte. To this purpose that the bad behaviour of young people most frequently proceeds from the bad education their fathers give 'em.

Argante. This happens sometimes. But what do you mean by that?

Géronte. What do I mean by that?

Argante. Yes.

Géronte. That if you, like a brave father, had well tutored your son, he would not have played you the trick he has done.

Argante. Mighty well. So that therefore you have tutored your son well?

Géronte. Without dispute; and I should be very sorry had he done anything that approaches to this.

Argante. And this son of yours, whom you like a brave father have so well tutored, has done still worse than mine. Heh!

Géronte. How!

Argante. How?

Géronte. What means this?

Argante. This means, Signor Géronte, that we should not be too hasty in condemning the conduct of others; and that they who will be carping, should look well at home whether there is not something lame there.

Géronte. I don't understand this riddle.

Argante. You'll have it explained.

Géronte. What, have you heard anything about my son?

Argante. It may be so.

Géronte. And what, pray?

Argante. In my vexation, your Scapin told me the thing only in gross; and you may, by him, or somebody else, be let into the detail. For my part, I go in haste to consult a lawyer, and advise what course I am to steer. Adieu.

Scene II

Géronte. [*Alone.*] What can this same affair be? Worse still than his! For my part, I don't see what one can do worse; and I think, that to marry without a father's consent, is an action which exceeds all that can be imagined.

Scene III

Géronte, Leander.

Géronte. Hah! You there.

Leander. [*Running to embrace his father.*] Oh! father, what joy is it to me to see you returned.

Géronte. [*Refusing to embrace him.*] Softly. Let us talk over the affair a little.

Leander. Permit me to embrace you, and——

Géronte. [*Still thrusting him away.*] Softly, I tell you.

Leander. What, father, do you refuse me expressing my transport by my embraces?

Géronte.   Yes. We have a certain matter to unravel together.
Leander.   And what may that be?
Géronte.   Hold still, that I may look you in the face.
Leander.   How?
Géronte.   Your eyes full upon mine a little.
Leander.   Well.
Géronte.   What is it that has passed here?
Leander.   What has passed here?
Géronte.   Yes. What have you done during my absence?
Leander.   What is't you would have had me done, father?
Géronte.   'Tis not I who would have had you done; but who ask you, What it is you have done?
Leander.   I? I have done nothing that you have reason to complain of.
Géronte.   Nothing?
Leander.   No.
Géronte.   You are very resolute.
Leander.   'Tis because I am sure of my innocence.
Géronte.   Scapin, for all that, has told some news about you.
Leander.   Scapin?
Géronte.   Hoh! hoh! This word makes you blush.
Leander.   Did he tell you anything about me?
Géronte.   This place is not altogether proper to determine this affair, and we shall examine into it elsewhere. Go home. I shall be back there presently. Ah! traitor, if it must be so that you disgrace me, I renounce you for my son, and you may well resolve to fly from my presence for ever.

Scene IV

Leander. [*Alone.*]   To betray me in this manner! A rascal, who, for a hundred reasons, ought to be the first to conceal the things I trust to him, is the first to discover 'em to my father. I vow to Heaven this treachery shall not remain unpunished.

Scene V

Octavio, Leander, Scapin.

Octavio.   My dear Scapin, what don't I owe to thy pains! What an admirable fellow art thou! And how propitious is Heaven to me in sending thee to my succour!
Leander.   Hoh! hoh! Are you there? I'm glad I've found you, Mr. Rascal.

Scapin. Sir, your servant. You do me too much honour.

Leander. [*Drawing his sword.*] You rally in a paltry manner. Oh! I shall teach you——

Scapin. [*Falling on his knees.*] Sir.

Octavio. [*Stepping between them, to hinder Leander from striking him.*] Nay, Leander.

Leander. No, Octavio, pray don't hold me.

Scapin. [*To Leander.*] Oh! sir.

Octavio. [*Holding Leander.*] Pray.

Leander. [*Wanting to strike Scapin.*] Let me satisfy my resentment upon him.

Octavio. In the name of friendship, Leander, don't use him ill.

Scapin. Sir, what have I done to you?

Leander. [*Going to strike him.*] What hast thou done to me, rascal.

Octavio. [*Still holding Leander.*] Nay, gently.

Leander. No, Octavio, I will have him instantly confess to me himself the perfidy he has been guilty of. Yes, rascal, I know the trick you've played me, they have just told me of it, and you did not think, perhaps, they should have blabbed the secret; but I'll have the secret from thy own mouth, or I'll whip my sword through thy body.

Scapin. Oh! sir, could you possibly have the heart?

Leander. Speak then.

Scapin. Have I done anything t'ye, sir?

Leander. Yes, rascal; and thy conscience tells it thee but too plainly what it is.

Scapin. I assure you, I don't know what 'tis.

Leander. [*Advancing to strike him.*] Don't you know?

Octavio. [*Holding him.*] Leander!

Scapin. Well, sir, since you will have it so, I confess that I drank with my friends that small vessel of Spanish wine that somebody made you a present of a few days ago; and 'twas I who made a vent in the cask, and poured water round about, to make you believe the wine was run out.

Leander. Was it thee, villain, who drank my Spanish wine, and was the occasion of my scolding the maid to such a degree, thinking 'twas she who had played me the trick?

Scapin. Yes, sir; I beg your pardon for it.

Leander. I'm very glad to find this; but that's not the affair in question at present.

Scapin. Isn't that it, sir?

Leander. No, 'tis another affair which concerns me much more, and I must have thee tell it me.

Scapin. I don't remember to have done anything else, sir.

Leander. [*Going to strike him.*] Won't you speak?

Scapin. Oh!

Octavio. [*Holding him.*] Softly.

Scapin. Yes, sir, 'tis true about three weeks ago you sent me in the evening to carry a watch to a young gipsy you were in love with. I came back to my lodging, my clothes all covered with dirt, and my face bloody, and told you I had met with thieves, who had beat me unmercifully, and robbed me of the watch. 'Twas I, sir, who kept it.

Leander. Did you keep the watch?

Scapin. Yes, sir, that I might see what o'clock it is.

Leander. So, so, these are fine things I learn here, and I have a most faithful servant, in good truth. But this is not all I want still.

Scapin. Isn't that it?

Leander. No, scoundrel, 'tis another thing yet that I must have thee confess.

Scapin. [*Aside.*] Plague!

Leander. Out with it, quick. I'm in haste.

Scapin. Sir, that's all I have done.

Leander. [*Going to strike him.*] Is that all?

Octavio. [*Getting before Leander.*] Nay.

Scapin. Well, yes, sir. You remember the hobgoblin six months ago, that gave you such a confounded drubbing one night, and you thought you should have broke your neck in a cave you fell into as you were running away.

Leander. Well?

Scapin. 'Twas I, sir, who acted the hobgoblin.

Leander. Was it thee, traitor, who acted the hobgoblin?

Scapin. Yes, sir, only to frighten you, and cure you of the fancy of making us ramble o' nights, as you were used to do.

Leander. I shall remember all I've learnt, in a proper time and place. But I must come to the fact, and have you confess what 'twas you told my father.

Scapin. Your father?

Leander. Yes, knave, my father.

Scapin. I haven't so much as seen him since his return.

Leander. Haven't you seen him?

Scapin. No, sir.

Leander. Really?

Scapin.   Really.   'Tis what he himself will tell you.
Leander.   I have it from his own mouth however——
Scapin.   With your leave, he did not speak truth.

SCENE VI

Leander, Octavio, Carlos, Scapin.

Carlos.   I bring you cruel news, sir, in regard to your amour.
Leander.   What?
Carlos.   Your gipsies are upon the point of carrying off
Zerbinetta; and she herself, with tears in her eyes, charged me
to come and tell you in all haste, that if you don't think of
carrying 'em the money they demanded for her in two hours,
you'll lose her for ever.
Leander.   In two hours?
Carlos.   In two hours.

SCENE VII

Leander, Octavio, Scapin.

Leander.   Oh! my dear Scapin, I implore thy assistance.
Scapin. [*Getting up, and walking by him with a haughty air.*]
Oh! my dear Scapin! I am my dear Scapin now you've
occasion for me.
Leander.   Go, I pardon everything thou hast told me, and
worse still, if thou hast done it.
Scapin.   No, no, don't pardon me anything; run your sword
through my body. I should be glad you'd kill me.
Leander.   No, rather I conjure thee to give me life, by serving
me in my amour.
Scapin.   No, no, you'd do better to kill me.
Leander.   Thou art too precious to me; and prithee employ
for me that admirable genius, which brings everything to bear.
Scapin.   No, kill me, I tell you.
Leander.   Nay, for Heaven's sake think of it no more, and
contrive to give me the succour I ask of thee.
Octavio.   Scapin, you must do something for him.
Scapin.   But how, after an insult of this kind?
Leander.   I beseech thee forget the passion I was in, and
lend me thy dexterity.
Octavio.   I join my petition to his.
Scapin.   I have that insult at heart.

Octavio. You must quit your resentment.

Leander. Dost abandon me, Scapin, in the cruel extremity to which my love is reduced?

Scapin. To come upon me with such an affront as that, unawares!

Leander. I'm in the wrong, I own it.

Scapin. To treat me as a rogue, a knave, a hang-dog, a scoundrel!

Leander. It gives me all the regret in the world.

Scapin. To design running me through the body!

Leander. I ask thy pardon for it with all my heart; and if it only sticks at falling down at thy feet, thou seest me there, Scapin, to conjure thee once more not to abandon me.

Octavio. Nay, faith, Scapin, you must yield to this.

Scapin. Rise up. Don't be so hasty another time.

Leander. Dost promise me to go to work for me?

Scapin. We shall consider of it.

Leander. But you know the time presses us.

Scapin. Give yourself no trouble. How much must you have?

Leander. Five hundred crowns.

Scapin. And you?

Octavio. Two hundred pistoles.

Scapin. I shall get these out of your dads. [*To Octavio.*] As to what concerns yours, the plot is all formed already; [*To Leander.*] and for yours, though covetous to an excess, there will need less ceremony still; for as to wit, thank Heaven, he has no great stock; and I give him up for a sort of mortal that one may at any time make believe anything one pleases. This is no scandal to you, there's not a suspicion of a resemblance betwixt him and you; and you know well enough the opinion of the world, which will have it that he's only your father for form's sake.

Leander. Soft, Scapin.

Scapin. Right, right; there's a good deal of scruple made about it. Don't you care for that? But I see Octavio's father a-coming. Let's begin with him, since he offers himself. [*To Octavio.*] And you, give your Silvester notice to come quickly and play his part.

Scene VIII

Argante, Scapin.

Scapin. [*Aside.*] There he is ruminating.

Argante. [*Thinking himself alone.*] To have so little conduct and consideration! To run headlong into an engagement like this! Ah! ah! the extravagance of youth!

Scapin. Sir, your servant.

Argante. A good day to you, Scapin.

Scapin. You are thinking of your son's affair.

Argante. I own to thee it gives me a plaguy uneasiness.

Scapin. Life, sir, is mixed with disappointments. 'Tis good to be always prepared for them. And I have heard, a long while ago, the saying of an ancient, which I have always retained.

Argante. What?

Scapin. That be a master of a family ever so little absent from home, he should run over in his mind all the vexatious accidents that may meet him at his return; to imagine with himself, his house burnt, his money stole, his wife dead, his son crippled, his daughter debauched; and what he finds has not happened to him, to impute it to good fortune. For my part, I have always practised this lesson in my little philosophy; and I never returned home but I held myself in readiness for the anger of my masters, for reprimands, hard language, kicks o' the posteriors, bastinadoes and strappadoes; and whatever did not happen, I thanked my good destiny for it.

Argante. This is very well; but this silly marriage, which breaks in upon that we are about, is a thing I can't suffer, and I have been consulting lawyers about dissolving of it.

Scapin. In good truth, sir, if you believe me, you'll try some way or other to accommodate the affair. You know what lawsuits are in this country, and you are going to plunge yourself in strange perplexities.

Argante. You're in the right. But what other way?

Scapin. I think I have found one. The compassion your uneasiness lately gave me, obliged me to cast about with myself some means to free you from your trouble; for I can't see honest fathers grieved by their children, but it moves me; and I always perceived in myself a particular inclination for your person.

Argante. I'm obliged to thee.

Scapin. I have been therefore to find out the brother of this wench he has married. 'Tis one of those bravoes by profession, one of those people who are all for foining; who talk of nothing but cutting and slashing, and make no more conscience of killing a man, than of swallowing a glass of wine. I got him upon this marriage; I showed him how easy it would be to dissolve it, on account of the violence; your prerogative from the name of father, and the countenance your right, your money and your friends would give you in a court of justice. In short, I so worked him about on all sides, that he gave ear to the propositions I made of adjusting the affair with a certain sum; and he gave his consent to dissolve the marriage, provided you'd give him money.

Argante.   And what did he demand?

Scapin.   Oh! At first very high things.

Argante.   But what?

Scapin.   Extravagant things.

Argante.   But what pray?

Scapin.   He talked of no less than five or six hundred pistoles.

Argante.   Five or six hundred quartan agues seize him. Does he banter one?

Scapin.   That's what I said to him. I utterly rejected all such-like proposals; and I gave him pretty well to understand you were no dupe, that he should demand five or six hundred pistoles of you. At last, after a great deal of discourse, the result of our conference was reduced to this. Time draws nigh, says he to me, when I must set out for the army. I am about equipping myself; and the occasion I have for some money makes me consent, in spite of me, to what is proposed. I must have a regimental horse, and I can't have one, that's ever so tolerable, under sixty pistoles.

Argante.   Well, as to the sixty pistoles, I give 'em.

Scapin.   There must be accoutrements and pistols, and that will amount to twenty pistoles more.

Argante.   Twenty pistoles, and sixty, that makes four-score.

Scapin.   Just.

Argante.   'Tis a great deal; but be it so. I consent to that.

Scapin.   He must have a horse too, to mount his servant on, which will likely cost thirty pistoles.

Argante.   How the deuce! Let him walk. He shall have none.

Scapin.   Sir.

Argante.   No, he's an extravagant fellow.

Scapin.   Would you have his servant walk o' foot?

Argante.   Let him walk as he pleases, and the master too.

Scapin. Lack-a-day, sir, don't stand upon small matters; pray don't go to law, but give it all to save yourself from the hand of justice.

Argante. Well, be it so. I resolve to give the thirty pistoles more.

Scapin. Further, says he, I must have a mule to carry——

Argante. Oh! let him and his mule go both to the devil; 'tis too much, and we must go before the judge.

Scapin. Pray, sir——

Argante. No, I'll do nothing.

Scapin. Sir, a small mule.

Argante. I won't give him so much as an ass.

Scapin. Consider——

Argante. No, I choose rather to go to law.

Scapin. Pho! sir, what do you talk of here, and what is it you resolve upon? Cast your eyes upon the windings and turnings of justice. See how many appeals, and degrees of jurisdiction, how many perplexing courses of pleadings, how many rapacious animals, through whose talons you are to pass; sergeants, attorneys, counsel at law, registers, substitutes, reporters, judges, and their clerks. There's not one of all these folks but is capable of blowing up the best cause in the world for a trifle. A sergeant shall deliver a false summons, upon which you'll be cast without knowing of it. Your attorney shall have an understanding with your adversary, and shall sell you for good ready money. Your counsel, bought off by the same, will not be found when he should plead your cause; or will give reasons that only beat about and about the bush, and never come home to the point. The register will issue out sentences and arrests against you for contumacy. The reporter's clerk will purloin some of your writings; or the reporter himself will not say what he has seen. And when, by all the precaution in the world, you have warded off all this, you will be surprised that your judges shall be solicited against you, either by your devout people, or by the women they love. Ah! sir, save yourself, if you can, from this hell. 'Tis damnation in this world to be at law; and the thought alone of a lawsuit were enough to make me fly to the very Indies.

Argante. How much does the mule amount to?

Scapin. Sir, for the mule, for his horse, and that of his man, for accoutrements and pistols, and to discharge some trifling things he owes his landlady, he demands in all two hundred pistoles.

Argante. Two hundred pistoles!

Scapin. Yes.

Argante. [*Walking about in a passion.*] Come, come, we'll stand it at law.

Scapin. Reflect——

Argante. I'll go to law.

Scapin. Don't go throw yourself——

Argante. I will try my cause.

Scapin. But to go to law, you must have money. You must have money for the summons; money for the rolls; money for the letter of attorney; money for appearance, counsel, evidence, and the solicitor's journeys. There must go some to the consultations and pleadings of counsel; for the right of dislodging your writings; for an engrossed copy of the instruments. You'll want money for the reports of the substitutes; for judges' fees in determination; for the enrolment of the register, the form of a decree, sentences, arrests, controls, signings, and the dispatches of their clerks. Without mentioning all the presents you must make. Give this man the money, and you are quit of the affair.

Argante. How! Two hundred pistoles?

Scapin. Yes, you will gain by it. I have made a small calculation within myself, of all the law charges; and I have found that, in giving your chap two hundred pistoles, you will have at least a hundred and fifty over and above, without reckoning the anxiety, the weary steps and vexation that you will spare. Were there nothing in it but being exposed to the impertinent things those wicked wags, the lawyers, will say before all the world, I'd rather give three hundred pistoles than go to law.

Argante. I despise all this, and defy the lawyers to say anything of me.

Scapin. You may do what you please; but if I were as you, I would avoid a lawsuit.

Argante. I won't give two hundred pistoles.

Scapin. Here comes the man we're talking of.

Scene IX

Argante, Scapin, Silvester (dressed like a bully).

Silvester. Scapin, bring me acquainted a little with that Argante, who is father to Octavio.

Scapin. Why, sir?

Silvester. I have just heard he intends to sue me, and dissolve by law the marriage of my sister.

Scapin. I don't know whether that be his intention; but he won't consent to the two hundred pistoles you expect, and he says 'tis too much.

Silvester. S'death, blood and guts! if I find him I'll make minced meat of him, were I to be broke alive on the wheel for it.

[*Argante, for fear of being seen, stands trembling behind Scapin.*

Scapin. Sir, this father of Octavio has courage, and perhaps he won't fear you.

Silvester. He? He? Blood and thunder! I'd whip my sword through his body in an instant. [*Seeing Argante.*] Who is that man there?

Scapin. 'Tis not he, sir; 'tis not he.

Silvester. Is it not one of his friends?

Scapin. No, sir; on the contrary, 'tis his mortal enemy.

Silvester. His mortal enemy?

Scapin. Yes.

Silvester. Hah! mass, I'm glad on't. Are you an enemy, sir, [*To Argante.*] to that scoundrel Argante? Heh?

Scapin. Yes, yes, I answer for it.

Silvester. [*Seizing Argante's hand in a rough manner.*] Shake hands, boy; shake hands. I give you my word, and swear to you by my honour, by the sword I wear, by all the oaths I can take, that before the day's at an end I'll rid you of that arrant villain, that scoundrel, Argante. Depend upon me.

Scapin. Violence is not allowed of, sir, in this country.

Silvester. I value nothing; I have nothing to lose.

Scapin. He will certainly be upon his guard; and he has relations, friends and domestics, who will be a protection from your resentment.

Silvester. That's what I want, s'bud, that's what I want. [*Drawing his sword.*] S'death and furies! Why have I him not here, with all his succours! Why does he not appear surrounded with thirty myrmidons! Why don't they pour upon me sword in hand! [*Standing upon his guard.*] How, villains, have you the insolence to attack me? S'heart! come on, kill and slay, no quarter. [*Pushing on every side, as if he had several persons to attack.*] Lay on. Firm. Push home. A sure foot, a quick eye. Hah! rascals, hah! Ragamuffins, if that's your play, I'll give you your bellies full. Stand to't, varlets, stand to't. Come on. Have at you here. Have at you there. [*Pushes as at Argante and Scapin.*] How? d'ye flinch? Stand your ground, pox, stand your ground.

Scapin. Nay, nay, nay, sir, we are none of 'em.
Silvester. This shall teach you to dare to play upon me.

Scene X

Argante, Scapin.

Scapin. Well, you see how many people are killed for two hundred pistoles. Pray come away, I wish you a good escape.
Argante. [*Trembling.*] Scapin.
Scapin. Your pleasure?
Argante. I determine to give the two hundred pistoles.
Scapin. I'm glad of it, out of respect to you.
Argante. Let's go find him out, I have 'em about me.
Scapin. You need only to give 'em to me. It won't be proper for your own honour that you should appear there, after having passed here for another person than what you are; and besides I should be afraid, lest upon your discovering yourself, he should take it into his head to demand more.
Argante. Yes; but I should have been very glad to see how I bestow my money.
Scapin. What, do you mistrust me?
Argante. No, no; but——
Scapin. S'bud, sir, I am a rogue, or I am an honest man; 'tis one of the two. Should I deceive you, and have I any other interest in all this, but yours and my master's, to whom you wish to be allied? If you suspect me, I shall meddle no more with anything; and from this time forward you have only to look out a person who will make up your affairs.
Argante. Take it then.
Scapin. No, sir; don't trust your money with me. I shall be very glad you would employ somebody else.
Argante. Pshaw! Take it.
Scapin. No. I tell you, don't trust me. Who knows whether I mayn't trick you out of your money?
Argante. Take it, I say, and don't make me dispute any longer. But take care to have good securities along with you.
Scapin. Let me alone; he has no fool to deal with.
Argante. I shall go wait for thee at home.
Scapin. I shall not fail being there. [*Alone.*] One caught. I have only to seek for the other. There he is. It looks as if Heaven brought 'em both, one after t'other, into my net.

SCENE XI

Géronte, Scapin.

Scapin. [*Making as if he saw not Géronte.*] Oh, Heavens! Unlooked-for misfortune! Miserable father! Poor Géronte, what will you do?

Géronte. [*Aside.*] What says he there of me, with that sorrowful face?

Scapin. Can nobody tell me where Signor Géronte is?

Géronte. What's the matter, Scapin?

Scapin. Oh, that I could meet with him, to tell him this unhappy accident!

Géronte. [*Running after Scapin.*] What is it then?

Scapin. In vain do I run all about to find him.

Géronte. Here I am.

Scapin. He must be hid in some corner, nobody can guess where.

Géronte. [*Stopping Scapin.*] Hola! Art thou blind, that thou dost not see me?

Scapin. Oh! sir, there's no possibility of meeting with you.

Géronte. I've been an hour here just at thy nose. What is the matter therefore?

Scapin. Sir——

Géronte. What?

Scapin. Sir, your son——

Géronte. Well, my son——

Scapin. Has fallen into the strangest misfortune in the world.

Géronte. What is it?

Scapin. I found him a little while ago very melancholy, at I don't know what, that you'd been saying to him, wherein you've very unseasonably involved me; and striving to divert this pensive mood, we took a turn upon the quay. There, among many other things, we fixed our eyes upon a Turkish galley very well equipped. A young Turk, of a very good mien, invited us aboard, and presented us his hand. Aboard we went, he showed us a thousand civilities, gave us a cold collation, where we ate the most excellent fruit that ever was seen, and drank wine which we thought the best in the world.

Géronte. What is there so grievous in all this?

Scapin. Stay, sir, there we were. While we were eating, he ordered the galley to put to sea; and when he was got off at some distance from the harbour, he put me into the skiff, and sends me to tell you, that if you don't send him immediately by me five hundred crowns he'll carry your son to Algiers.

Géronte. How the plague, five hundred crowns!

Scapin. Yes, sir; and more than that, he gave me but two hours for it.

Géronte. Oh! that villain of a Turk, to murder me in this manner!

Scapin. 'Tis your business, sir, to advise quickly in what way to save a son from slavery whom you so tenderly love.

Géronte. What the deuce had he to do aboard that galley?

Scapin. He ne'er thought of what has happened.

Géronte. Go, Scapin, begone, quick, and tell this Turk I'll send and arrest him.

Scapin. Arrest him in open sea! Have you a mind to joke with people?

Géronte. What the deuce had he to do aboard that galley?

Scapin. An evil destiny guides folks sometimes.

Géronte. You must, Scapin, you must in this case perform the part of a faithful servant.

Scapin. What, sir?

Géronte. Go, bid this Turk send me my son, and put thyself in his place, till such time as I have raised the sum he demands.

Scapin. Lack-a-day, sir, d'ye consider what you say? Do you imagine with yourself that this Turk has so little sense, to receive such a poor wretch as I am, in the place of your son?

Géronte. What the deuce had he to do aboard that galley?

Scapin. He didn't dream of this misfortune. Consider, sir, he gave me but two hours.

Géronte. You say that he asks——

Scapin. Five hundred crowns.

Géronte. Five hundred crowns! Has he no conscience?

Scapin. Truly, yes; the conscience of a Turk.

Géronte. Does he know what five hundred crowns are?

Scapin. Yes, sir, he knows 'tis fifteen hundred livres.

Géronte. Does the villain think that fifteen hundred livres are to be picked up in the highway?

Scapin. They are a people who have no notion of reason.

Géronte. But what the deuce had he to do aboard that galley?

Scapin. 'Tis true; but what then? One could not foresee things. For goodness sake, sir, dispatch.

Géronte. Stay, here's the key of my chest of drawers.

Scapin. Good.

Géronte. You'll open it.

Scapin. Very well.

Géronte. You'll find a large key on the left hand, which is that of my garret.

Scapin. Yes.

Géronte. You'll go and take all the goods that are in that great hamper, and you'll sell 'em to the brokers to redeem my son.

Scapin. [*Giving him back the key.*] Why, sir, are you dreaming? I should not get a hundred livres for all that you speak of; and besides, you know how little time is allowed me.

Géronte. But what the deuce had he to do aboard that galley?

Scapin. How many words lost! Drop this galley; think we are straitened for time, and that you run the risk of losing your son. Alas! My poor master, perhaps I shall never set eyes on you again while I live, and the moment I am speaking they are carrying you a slave to Algiers. But Heaven shall be my witness, I have done all I could for you, and that if you are not ransomed, there is nothing to blame but the too little affection of a father.

Géronte. Stay, Scapin, I'll go fetch this sum.

Scapin. Dispatch then quickly, sir, I tremble for fear the clock should strike.

Géronte. Isn't it four hundred crowns you said?

Scapin. No, five hundred crowns.

Géronte. Five hundred crowns?

Scapin. Yes.

Géronte. What the deuce had he to do in that galley?

Scapin. You're right; but make haste.

Géronte. Had he no other place to walk in?

Scapin. 'Tis true; but do it quickly.

Géronte. Oh, this cursed galley!

Scapin. [*Aside.*] This galley sticks in his stomach.

Géronte. Stay, Scapin, I did not remember I had just now received that sum in gold, and little did I think it would be so soon taken from me. [*Taking his purse out of his pocket and presenting it to Scapin.*] Here, go thy ways, redeem my son.

Scapin. [*Holding out his hand.*] Yes, sir.

Géronte. [*Holding the purse fast, which he pretends to be going to give Scapin.*] But tell this Turk he is a villain.

Scapin. [*Holding his hand out again.*] Yes.

Géronte. A scoundrel.

Scapin. [*Keeping his hand held out.*] Yes.

Géronte. A man of no faith, a robber.

Scapin. Let me alone.

Géronte. That he extorts five hundred crowns from me against all right and reason.

Scapin. Yes.

Géronte. That I don't give 'em to him, either dying or living.

Scapin. Very well.

Géronte. And that if ever I catch him, I'll have my revenge of him.

Scapin. Yes.

Géronte. [*Putting his purse in his pocket again, and going.*] Go, go quick, and fetch back my son.

Scapin. [*Running after Géronte.*] Hola! sir!

Géronte. What?

Scapin. Where is the money then?

Géronte. Did I not give it thee?

Scapin. No truly; you put it into your pocket again.

Géronte. Alas! Grief disturbs my senses.

Scapin. I plainly see it does.

Géronte. What the deuce had he to do in that galley? Cursed galley! The devil take this traitor of a Turk!

Scapin. [*Alone.*] He can't digest the five hundred crowns I have wrested from him; but he's not quit with me yet; I'll make him pay, in other sort of coin, for the slander he has put upon me with his son.

Scene XII

Octavio, Leander, Scapin.

Octavio. Well, Scapin, hast thou succeeded for me in thy enterprise?

Leander. Hast thou done anything to rescue my amour from the difficulty it labours under?

Scapin. [*To Octavio.*] There are the two hundred pistoles I have got out of your father.

Octavio. What joy dost thou give me!

Scapin. [*To Leander.*] As for you, I could do nothing.

Leander. [*Offering to go.*] Then must I go die; I have nothing to do with life, if I am deprived of Zerbinetta.

Scapin. Soho! Soho there! Softly. How plaguy quick you go!

Leander. [*Returning.*]   What wouldst have me done with?

Scapin.   Go, I've here what will do your business.

Leander.   You have restored life to me.

Scapin.   But on condition that you allow me a little vengeance upon your father, for the trick he has played me.

Leander.   Everything you please.

Scapin.   You promise me before witness?

Leander.   Yes.

Scapin.   Hold, there are five hundred crowns.

Leander.   Let us be gone quickly, and purchase the dear creature I adore.

ACT III

SCENE I

Zerbinetta, Hiacintha, Scapin, Silvester.

Silvester.   Yes, your lovers have agreed betwixt themselves, that you should be together; and we acquit ourselves of the order they have given us.

Hiacintha. [*To Zerbinetta.*]   Such an order has nothing in it but what is very agreeable to me.   I receive with joy a companion of this kind; and it shall not be my fault if the friendship betwixt the persons we love, does not diffuse itself to us two.

Zerbinetta.   I accept the proposal, and am not a person who gives way when I am attacked with friendship.

Scapin.   And when you are attacked with love?

Zerbinetta.   As to love, that's another affair; one runs a little more risk there, and I am not so courageous in that.

Scapin.   I think you are at present, against my master; and what he has just done for you should give you courage to answer his passion in a proper manner.

Zerbinetta.   I trust him as yet but upon his good behaviour; and what he has now done is not sufficient entirely to convince me.   I am of a gay humour, and laugh for ever; but for all my laughing, I am serious upon certain subjects; and your master mistakes himself if he thinks his having bought me is sufficient to make me absolutely his own.   It will cost him something else besides money; and to answer his passion in the manner he wishes, he must plight me his faith, which is to be seasoned with certain ceremonies thought necessary upon these occasions.

Scapin. That's what he designs too. He makes no pretensions t'ye but in sober sadness, and with all honour; had he had any other thought, I should not have been one to have meddled in the affair.

Zerbinetta. That's what I would believe, because you tell me so; but, on the father's part, I foresee some impediments.

Scapin. We shall find means of accommodating matters.

Hiacintha. [*To Zerbinetta.*] The resemblance of our fortunes ought also to contribute to the growth of our friendship; we have both the same alarms, and are exposed to the same misfortune.

Zerbinetta. You have, at least, this advantage, that you know who gave you birth; and that the countenance of your relations, whom you can discover, is capable of adjusting everything, can ensure your happiness, and command an assent to a marriage already solemnised. But for my part, I meet with no relief from what I am, and am in a condition that cannot mollify the temper of a father who regards nothing but wealth.

Hiacintha. But you have this advantage, at least, that they don't tempt your lover with another match.

Zerbinetta. A change of inclination is not what one has most to fear in a lover. One may naturally enough believe one's merit sufficient to maintain one's conquest; and what I look upon as most formidable in these sort of affairs, is the paternal power, with which merit is of no consequence at all.

Hiacintha. Alas! Why must our just inclinations be crossed? How delightful a thing it is to love, when there is no obstacle to those amiable chains with which two hearts are united together!

Scapin. You're under a mistake; tranquillity in love is a disagreeable calm. A happiness entirely uniform grows tedious to us; there must be ups and downs in life; and difficulties mixed with our affairs awake our ardours, and augment our pleasures.

Zerbinetta. Pray, Scapin, give us a short account, which they say is so diverting, of the stratagem you invented to get money from your covetous old fellow? You know 'tis not labour lost to tell me a story, and that I sufficiently reward it by the joy it gives me.

Scapin. Here is Silvester will acquit himself in that as well as myself. I have a certain pretty vengeance in my head, that I am about to relish the pleasure of.

Silvester. But why wo't contrive to bring these scurvy affairs upon thee, out of mere wantonness?

Scapin. I take pleasure in attempting hazardous enterprises.

Silvester. I've told thee already thou'dst quit the design thou hast in hand, wouldst thou be ruled by me.

Scapin. Yes; but I shall be ruled by myself.

Silvester. What a deuce art going to amuse thyself about?

Scapin. What a deuce art thou in pain about?

Silvester. Why this, that I see you're going to run the risk of a shower of blows, without any manner of necessity.

Scapin. Well, 'tis at the expense of my own back, and not of thine.

Silvester. 'Tis very true, you're master of your own shoulders, and may dispose of 'em as you please.

Scapin. These sort of perils never stopped me, and I hate your dastardly spirits who dare not attempt anything, because they too well foresee the consequences of things.

Zerbinetta. [*To Scapin.*] We shall want your assistance.

Scapin. Go, I shall be with you again by and by. It shall never be said that they've brought me with impunity to betray myself, and discover secrets it had been well nobody had known.

Scene II

Géronte, Scapin.

Géronte. Well, Scapin, how goes the affair of my son?

Scapin. Your son is safe, sir; but you yourself, at this very time, run the greatest danger in the world, and I'd give a good deal you were at home.

Géronte. Why, how so?

Scapin. The moment I'm speaking, they are seeking everywhere to murder you.

Géronte. Me?

Scapin. Yes.

Géronte. Who, pray?

Scapin. The brother of the person Octavio has married. He thinks the design you have of placing your daughter in the room of his sister, is the strongest inducement to dissolve the marriage; and with this thought he has peremptorily resolved to discharge his vexation upon you, and take away your life to revenge his honour. All his friends, who are gentlemen of the blade, are in search for you, and demand tidings of you everywhere. I

myself saw, here and there, some soldiers of his company, who
examine people they meet with, and have seized by files all the
avenues to your house.   So that you can't go home; you can't
take a step to right or left, without falling into their hands.

Géronte.   My dear Scapin, what shall I do?

Scapin.   I don't know, sir, 'tis a strange affair.   I tremble
for you from head to foot, and——stay.   [*Pretends to go to the
farther part of the stage, to see whether anybody is there.*]

Géronte. [*Trembling.*]   Heh?

Scapin. [*Coming back again.*]   No, no, no, 'tis nothing.

Géronte.   Canst thou find no way to put me out of my pain?

Scapin.   I have one in my thoughts; but I should run the
risk of being knocked o' the head myself.

Géronte.   Ah, Scapin, show thyself a faithful servant.   Don't
abandon me, I beseech thee.

Scapin.   I will help you; I have such an affection for you,
that I can't leave you without assistance.

Géronte.   You shall be rewarded for it, I assure you; I promise
you this coat, when I have worn it a little.

Scapin.   Stay.   Here's a thing I have thought of very
apropos to save you; you must get into this sack, and——

Géronte. [*Fancying he sees somebody.*]   Oh!

Scapin.   No, no, no, no, 'tis nobody.   I say, you must get
in here, and take care not to stir in the least.   I shall take you
upon my back, as if it were a bundle of something, and so I can
carry you through your enemies quite to your own house; when
we are once there, we can barricade ourselves, and send for a
body of men strong enough to withstand the violence.

Géronte.   The invention is good.

Scapin.   The best in the world.   You shall see.   [*Aside.*]
You shall pay for your tricks.

Géronte.   Eh?

Scapin.   I say, your enemies will be finely tricked.   Get
you in quite to the bottom, and take care above all things not
to show yourself, and not to stir; whatever may happen.

Géronte.   Let me alone.   I shall be still.

Scapin.   Hide yourself.   Here's a bully in quest of you.
[*In a feigned voice.*]   Fat, me not 'ave de pleasure to kill dis
Géronte, and vil nobody in sharity mak me know vere is he?
[*To Géronte with his usual voice.*]   Don't ye stir.   Begar, me
sal find him, if he ide himself at the centre of de eart.   [*To
Géronte with his natural tone.*]   Don't show yourself.   O dere!
You man vid de sack!   Sire, me give you one ginè you vill sow

me vere be dis Géronte. Do you want Signor Géronte? Yes,
pardi me vant him. And what for, sir? Vat far? Yes,
begar, me tresh him to death vid one cudgel. Oh! sir, cudgelling is not for such gentlemen as he, he is not a man to be treated
in that manner. Vo? dat ninny Géronte, dat rascal, dat scoundrel? Signor Géronte, sir, is neither ninny, nor rascal, nor
scoundrel; and you ought, if you please, to speak in another
manner. How, you treat me vid dat insolence? I defend, as I
ought to do, a man of honour who is abused. Vat? you be one
friend of Géronte? Yes, sir, I am. Hah! begar, you be one
of his friends, me be glad of it. [*Striking the sack several times.*]
Dere, me give dat for him. [*Crying out as if he had received the
blows of the cudgel.*] Oh! oh! oh! oh! oh! sir. Oh! oh! softly,
sir. Oh! gently. Oh! oh! oh! Begone, carry dat to him from
me. Farevel. Pox take the Gascon. Oh!
    Géronte. [*Thrusting his head out of the sack.*] Oh! Scapin, I
can endure it no longer.
    Scapin. Oh! sir, I'm beat to mummy, my shoulders pain
me horribly.
    Géronte. How so? 'Twas on my shoulders the blows
were laid.
    Scapin. No, indeed, sir, they were laid on my back.
    Géronte. What dost mean? I felt the strokes pretty plainly,
and feel 'em plainly still.
    Scapin. No, 'twas only the end of the stick, I tell you, that
reached your shoulders.
    Géronte. You should have retired then, at a little farther
distance, to spare me.——
    Scapin. [*Making Géronte go into the sack again.*] Take care.
Here's another of 'em, who has the appearance of a stranger.
Begar, me skip aboute like a marsh-hare, and me no find dis
devilish Géronte all dis day. Lie snug. You, sir, dere you tell
me, if you please, wether you no see dis Géronte me seek for?
No, sir, I don't know where Géronte is. Tell me in a good sadness, me have no great matter vid him; me only vant to give
him one litel regale of one dozain blows o'er de back vid one
cudgel, and tree or four trusts through de guts vid my sword.
I do assure you, sir, I don't know where he is. Me fancy me
see someting move in dat sack. Pardon me, sir. Dere be some
merry story vidin dere. None at all, sir. Me ave one grand
inclinationg to vip my sword tro dat sack. Oh! sir, take care
what you do. You sow me vat dat be. Softly, sir. How
softly? You have nothing to do, to see what I carry. And me

vill see, so me vill. You shan't see. Hey! hey! vat nonsense
is dis! They are goods that belong to me. Sow me den, me
tell dee. I won't do it. You von't do it? No. Me give dee
one bastonnade upon de shoulders. I don't value it. Ha!
you be one droll. [*Beating the sack, and crying out as if he had
received the blows.*] Oh! oh! oh! oh! sir, oh! oh! oh! oh! Fare
de vell. Dis be one litel lesson for teash dee to speak insolantely.
Plague take the jabbering rascal. Oh!

Géronte. [*Popping his head out of the sack.*] Oh! I am mauled
to death.

Scapin. Oh! I am killed.

Géronte. Why the deuce must they lay me o'er the back?

Scapin. [*Thrusting his head into the sack again.*] Take care,
here's half a dozen soldiers all together. [*Counterfeiting the
voice of several persons.*] Come, let us endeavour to find out
this Géronte, let us search everywhere. Let us not be sparing
of our steps. Let's run the whole town over. Forget no place.
Visit everywhere. Ferret every quarter. Where shall we go?
Let us turn this way. No, here. To the left. To the right.
No, no. Yes. Hide yourself well. So ho! my comrades, here's
his valet——Come, rascal, you must inform us where your
master is. Nay, gentlemen, don't abuse me. Come, tell us
where he is. Speak. Make haste, let's have done. Dispatch
quick. Immediately. Nay, gentlemen, softly. [*Géronte steals
his head out of the sack, and discovers Scapin's roguery.*] If thou
dost not find us out thy master immediately, we shall rain an
inundation of blows upon thee. I choose rather to suffer everything than discover my master. We shall beat out thy brains.
Do what you please. Dost itch for a beating? What, wouldst
feel it a little? There——Oh!

   [*Just as he is going to strike, Géronte gets out of the sack, and
            Scapin runs off.*]

Géronte. [*Alone.*] Oh! scoundrel. Oh! traitor. Oh! villain.
What, assassinate me after this manner?

Scene III

Zerbinetta, Géronte.

Zerbinetta. [*Laughing, and not perceiving Géronte.*] Ha, ha!
I must take a little air.

Géronte. [*Aside, not seeing Zerbinetta.*] I'll swear thou shalt
pay for this.

Zerbinetta. [*Not seeing Géronte.*] Ha, ha, ha, ha! a droll story, a most excellent dupe of an old fellow.

Géronte. There's no joke in this, and you have no business to laugh at it.

Zerbinetta. How? what d'ye mean, sir?

Géronte. I mean that you ought not to make a jest of me.

Zerbinetta. Of you?

Géronte. Yes.

Zerbinetta. Why? who intends to make a jest of you?

Géronte. Why d'ye come here to laugh at me, to my face?

Zerbinetta. This has no regard to you, I was laughing to myself at a story that has just been told me, and the pleasantest that ever was heard. I don't know whether 'tis because I am interested in the thing; but I never knew anything so droll as a trick that has lately been played by a son upon his father, to cheat him of his money.

Géronte. By a son upon his father, to cheat him of his money?

Zerbinetta. Yes. Should you press me ever so little, you'll find me ready enough to tell you the affair; and I've a natural itch of communicating the stories I know.

Géronte. Pray tell me this story.

Zerbinetta. I will readily do it. I shall run no great risk in telling it to you, for 'tis an adventure not long to be kept a secret. Fate would have it that I should fall amongst a gang of those people who are called gipsies, who stroll from province to province, and employ 'emselves in telling o' fortunes, and sometimes in many other things. Arriving at this town, a young gentleman saw me, and conceived a passion for me. From that moment he was always after me, and was presently, as all other young fellows are, who think they have nothing to do but speak, and that upon the least word they say to us, the business is done. But he met with a pride and disdain that made him correct a little his former thoughts. He discovered his passion to the people whose hands I was in, and found them disposed to resign me to him, on payment of a certain sum. But the mischief of the affair was, that my spark was in that condition which we very often observe the generality of sons are, that is to say, he was a little bare of money. He has a father, who, though he is rich, is an arrant curmudgeon, a most sordid mortal. Stay, can't I remember his name? Heh! help me out a little. Can't you name me a person in this town who is noted for being avaricious to the utmost degree?

Géronte. No.

Zerbinetta. There is a ron in his name——ronte. Or——
Oronte. No. Ge—— Géronte; yes Géronte; the same; this
is my hunks, I ha' found him out; 'tis this same stingy mortal
I'm speaking of. To come to our story, our people have determined to-day to leave this town, and my lover was going to
lose me for want of money, had he not been relieved by the
industry of a servant he has, to get it out of his father. As to
the name of the servant, I know it wondrous well. His name
is Scapin; and 'tis an incomparable fellow, and merits all the
praises one can bestow on him.

Géronte. [*Aside.*] Oh! rascal as thou art!

Zerbinetta. This is the stratagem therefore he made use of
to catch his dupe. Ha, ha, ha, ha! I can't remember it but
I must laugh from my very heart, ha, ha, ha! He goes and finds
out this covetous cur, ha, ha, ha! and tells him, that walking
upon the quay with his son, ha, ha! they saw a Turkish galley
which they were invited aboard of. That a young Turk had
given 'em a collation there, ha! That while they were eating,
the galley put to sea; and that the Turk had sent him ashore
alone in the skiff, with orders to tell the father of his master, that
he would carry his son to Algiers, if he did not immediately
send him five hundred crowns. Ha, ha, ha! Behold my miser,
my sordid wretch, under the most furious pangs; and the
tenderness he had for his son, occasioned a strange combat with
his avarice. The five hundred crowns they demand of him,
are to him five hundred stabs with a poniard given him. Ha,
ha, ha! He could not resolve to tear this sum from his entrails,
and the pain he suffers, makes him find a hundred ridiculous
ways of getting his son again. Ha, ha, ha! He'll send a
warrant after the Turkish galley when got to sea. Ha, ha, ha!
He solicits his valet to go offer himself in the place of his son,
till such time as he has raised the money that he had no mind
to give. Ha, ha, ha! To make up the five hundred crowns, he
abandons five or six old suits not worth thirty. Ha, ha, ha!
The valet at every turn lets him see the impertinence of his
propositions, and every reflection is accompanied in a dolorous
manner with a, But what the deuce had he to do in that galley?
Oh, cursed galley! Traitor of a Turk! In short, after many
windings and turnings, after having a long while sighed and
groaned——But methinks you don't laugh at my story. What
say ye to it?

Géronte. I say the young fellow is a rascal, an insolent blockhead, who shall be punished by his father for the trick he has

played him. That the gipsy is an inconsiderate, impertinent hussy, to abuse a man of honour, who will teach her to come here and debauch people's children. And that the valet is a villain, who shall be sent to the gallows, by Géronte, before to-morrow morning.

<h2 style="text-align:center">Scene IV</h2>

Zerbinetta, Silvester.

Silvester. Why do you go out? Are you well aware that you have just been talking to your lover's father?

Zerbinetta. I began to doubt it; I addressed myself to him, without thinking of it, to tell him his own story.

Silvester. What, his own story?

Zerbinetta. Yes, I was quite full of it, and longed to be quit of it again. But what does it signify? So much the worse for him. I don't see that matters can either be better or worse to us.

Silvester. You had a great desire to be babbling; they must have a good deal of tongue who can't keep their own affairs secret.

Zerbinetta. Wouldn't he been told it by somebody else?

<h2 style="text-align:center">Scene V</h2>

Argante, Zerbinetta, Silvester.

Argante. Soho! Silvester.

Silvester. [*To Zerbinetta.*] Get you within doors again. Here's my master calls me.

<h2 style="text-align:center">Scene VI</h2>

Argante, Silvester.

Argante. What, have you agreed together, rascal, have you agreed together, Scapin, you and my son, to cheat me, and d'ye think I shall bear it?

Silvester. Troth, sir, if Scapin cheats you, I wash my hands of it; and I do assure you, I neither meddle nor make in it.

Argante. We shall see that, rascal, we shall see that; I shan't suffer myself to be made a dupe of.

SCENE VII

Géronte, Argante, Silvester.

Géronte. Ah! Signor Argante, you see me oppressed with misfortunes.

Argante. You see me too under a horrible oppression.

Géronte. That villain of a Scapin, by a piece of roguery, has got five hundred crowns out o' me.

Argante. That same villain of a Scapin, by a piece of roguery also, has got two hundred pistoles out of me.

Géronte. He did not content himself with cheating me of the five hundred crowns; he has treated me in a manner I am ashamed to mention. But he shall pay for't.

Argante. I'll have satisfaction of him for the trick he has played me.

Géronte. I intend to take an exemplary vengeance of him.

Silvester. [*Aside.*] Would to Heaven I had not had my share in all this!

Géronte. But still this is not all, Signor Argante; one misfortune is always the forerunner of another. I pleased myself to-day with the hope of having my daughter, in whom I placed all my consolation; and I have just now been informed by my man, that she set out a great while ago from Tarentum, and they believe she there perished in the vessel that she embarked aboard.

Argante. But why, pray, did you keep her at Tarentum, and not give yourself the pleasure of having her with you?

Géronte. I had my reasons for that, and the interests of my family have hitherto obliged me to keep this second marriage a great secret. But whom do I see?

SCENE VIII

Argante, Géronte, Nerina, Silvester.

Géronte. What, are you there, nurse?

Nerina. [*Falling on her knees.*] Oh! Signor Pandolph, that—

Géronte. Call me Géronte, and use that name no longer. The reasons have ceased which obliged me to take it amongst you at Tarentum.

Nerina. Alas! What troubles and uneasinesses has this change of name occasioned us, in the pains we have taken to find you out here.

Géronte. Where's my daughter, and her mother?

Nerina. Your daughter, sir, is not far off. But before I let you see her, I must ask your pardon for having married her, in the abandoned condition we were both in, for want of meeting with you.

Géronte. My daughter married?

Nerina. Yes, sir.

Géronte. And to whom?

Nerina. To a young gentleman named Octavio, son of one Signor Argante.

Géronte. Oh, Heavens!

Argante. What an accident!

Géronte. Show us; show us quickly where she is.

Nerina. You need only go into that house.

Géronte. Go, lead the way. Follow me, follow me, Signor Argante.

Silvester. [*Alone.*] What a surprising adventure is this!

SCENE IX

Scapin, Silvester.

Scapin. Well, Silvester, what are our folks a-doing?

Silvester. I have two things to inform you of. One is, that the affair of Octavio is accommodated. Our Hiacintha is found to be daughter to Signor Géronte; and chance has performed what the prudence of the fathers had concerted. The other piece of news is, that the two old gentlemen threaten thee in a most horrible manner, and especially Géronte.

Scapin. That's nothing. Threatenings never did me any harm; they are clouds which pass very high over our heads.

Silvester. Take care o' thyself. The sons may very likely be reconciled to the fathers, and thou left in the lurch.

Scapin. Let me alone, I shall find way to appease their wrath, and——

Silvester. Retire, here they're a-coming out.

SCENE X

Géronte, Argante, Hiacintha, Zerbinetta, Nerina, Silvester.

Géronte. Come, daughter, go home with me. My joy had been complete could I have seen your mother with you.

Argante. Here comes Octavio, quite apropos.

SCENE XI

Argante, Géronte, Octavio, Hiacintha, Zerbinetta, Nerina, Silvester.

Argante.   Come, son, come and rejoice with us at the happy adventure of your marriage. Heaven——

Octavio.   No, father, all your propositions of marriage will signify nothing. I ought to take off the mask with you, and you have been told of my engagement.

Argante.   Yes, but you don't know——

Octavio.   I know all I need know.

Argante.   I would tell you that the daughter of Géronte——

Octavio.   The daughter of Géronte shall never be anything to me.

Argante.   'Tis she——

Octavio. [*To Géronte.*]   No, sir, I ask your pardon; my resolution is fixed.

Silvester. [*To Octavio.*]   Hear——

Octavio.   No, hold thy tongue; I'll hear nothing.

Argante. [*To Octavio.*]   Your wife——

Octavio.   No, I tell you, father, I'd rather die than quit my lovely Hiacintha. Yes, all you do signifies nothing. [*Crossing the stage to Hiacintha.*]   This is she to whom my faith is engaged; I will love her for life, and won't have any other wife.

Argante.   Lack-a-day, 'tis her we give you. What a hair-brains 'tis! Always true to his point.

Hiacintha. [*Pointing to Géronte.*]   Yes, Octavio, this is my father whom I have found, and now we are out of pain.

Géronte.   Let us go to my house, we shall discourse matters over better there than here.

Hiacintha. [*Pointing to Zerbinetta.*]   Ah! father, I beg it as a favour of you, that I mayn't be parted from the amiable person you see here. She has merit that will make you conceive an esteem for her when you come to know it.

Géronte.   Would you have me keep a person in my house whom your brother is in love with; and who told me, just now to my face, a thousand foolish things of myself?

Zerbinetta.   Sir, I beg you would excuse me. I should not have spoken in that manner, had I known it was you; and I knew you only by report.

Géronte.   How, only by report?

Hiacintha.   Father, the passion my brother entertains for her has nothing criminal in it; and I answer for her virtue.

Géronte. A pretty fancy indeed. Would they not have me marry my son to her? A wench that nobody knows, and by profession a stroller?

Scene XII

Argante, Géronte, Leander, Octavio, Hiacintha, Zerbinetta, Nerina, Silvester.

Leander. Don't complain, father, that I love a person who is unknown, without birth, or portion. The people I purchased her of have just discovered to me that she was of this city, and of a worthy family; that they stole her at the age of four years; and here is a bracelet they gave me, that may help us to find her parents.

Argante. Alas! By this bracelet, it must be my daughter, that I lost at the age you speak of.

Géronte. Your daughter?

Argante. Yes, and I see all the features in her that can give me assurance of it. My dear child——

Hiacintha. Heavens! What extraordinary adventures!

Scene XIII

Argante, Géronte, Leander, Octavio, Hiacintha, Zerbinetta, Nerina, Silvester, Carlos.

Carlos. Ah! gentlemen, a strange accident has happened.

Géronte. What?

Carlos. The poor Scapin——

Géronte. 'Tis a villain that I'll have hanged.

Carlos. Alas! sir, you need be in no pain about that. Passing by a new building, a stone-cutter's hammer fell upon his head, which has fractured the skull, and laid his brains bare. He's a-dying, and desired to be brought hither, that he might speak with you before he dies.

Argante. Where is he?

Carlos. Here he is.

Scene XIV

Argante, Géronte, Leander, Octavio, Hiacintha, Zerbinetta, Nerina, Scapin, Silvester, Carlos.

Scapin. [*Carried by two men, and his head wrapped round with linen, as if he had been wounded.*] Oh! oh! gentlemen, you see

me. . . . Oh! you see me in a strange condition. . . . Oh!
I was not willing to die without asking pardon of all persons
that I may have ever offended. Oh! yes, gentlemen, before I
give up my last breath, I conjure you from my heart, to pardon
me whatever I have done to you; and principally Signor Argante
and Signor Géronte. Oh!

Argante. For my part, I pardon thee; go, die in peace.

Scapin. 'Tis you, sir, whom I have most offended by the
blows of a cudgel that——

Géronte. Speak no more of it, I pardon thee too.

Scapin. 'Twas a very great rashness in me, to cudgel——

Géronte. Let us drop that.

Scapin. Now I am dying, it gives me inconceivable sorrow
that I should cudgel——

Géronte. Lack-a-day! Hold thy tongue.

Scapin. Those unhappy blows with a cudgel that I——

Géronte. Hold thy tongue, I say; I forget all.

Scapin. Alas! What goodness! But is it from the heart,
sir, that you pardon me the cudgelling that——

Géronte. Pho! Yes. Let us talk no more of it; I pardon
thee, that's enough.

Scapin. Ah! sir, how am I refreshed by that word!

Géronte. Yes; but I pardon you on condition that you die.

Scapin. How, sir?

Géronte. I revoke my word, if you recover.

Scapin. Oh! oh! My weakness seizes me again.

Argante. Signor Géronte, in favour of our mirth, you must
pardon him without condition.

Géronte. Be it so.

Argante. Come, let us go to supper, that we may relish our
pleasure more.

Scapin. And as to me, carry me to the lower end of the
table, that I may wait my fate.

THE HYPOCHONDRIACK

(A COMEDY)

THE HYPOCHONDRIACK, *a Comedy of Three Acts in Prose, acted at Paris, at the Theatre of the Palace-Royal, the 10th of February,* 1673

The Hypochondriack was the last of Molière's productions. In the part of Belina, we find a character which is unhappily too common in life, and 'tis with the highest pleasure that we see the sensible Angelica, forgetting the concerns of her love, and giving up herself to grief and sorrow upon her imagining her father was dead. The physicians are not at all spared in this piece, for Molière was not contented with only laughing at them here, but in the part of Beraldo attacks the very foundation of their art, whilst in the part of the Hypochondriack, he ridicules the most universal foible of mankind, the restless love of life and the over and above care to preserve it.

ACTORS

ARGAN, *the hypochondriack.*
BELINA, *second wife to Argan.*
ANGELICA, *daughter to Argan.*
LOUISON, *younger daughter, sister to Angelica.*
BERALDO, *Argan's brother.*
CLEANTHES, *in love with Angelica.*
MR. DIAFOIRUS, *a physician.*
THOMAS DIAFOIRUS, *son of Mr. Diafoirus.*
MR. PURGON, *a physician.*
MR. FLEURANT, *an apothecary.*
MR. BONNEFOY, *a notary.*
TOINET, *servant to Argan.*

SCENE: *Paris.*

ACT I

SCENE I

Scene : Argan's Chamber.

Argan. [*Sitting with a table before him, casting up his apothecary's bills with counters.*] Three and two make five, and five makes ten, and ten makes twenty. Three and two make five. Item, the twenty-fourth, a little insinuative, preparative and emollient clyster to mollify, moisten, and refresh his worship's bowels. What pleases me in Mr. Fleurant my apothecary, is, that his bills are always extremely civil. His worship's bowels, thirty sous. Ay, but Mr. Fleurant being civil isn't all, you ought to be reasonable too, and not fleece your patients. Thirty sous for a clyster! Your servant, I have told you of this already. You have charged me in your other bills but twenty sous, and twenty sous in the language of an apothecary is as much as to say ten sous; there they are, ten sous. Item, the said day, a good detersive clyster composed of double catholicum, rhubarb, *mel rosatum*, etc., according to prescription, to scour, wash and cleanse his honour's abdomen, thirty sous; with your leave ten sous. Item, the said day at night, an hepatic, soporific, and somniferous julep, composed to make his honour sleep, thirty-five sous; I don't complain of that, for it made me sleep well. Ten, fifteen, sixteen, seventeen sous, six deniers. Item, the twenty-fifth, a good purgative and corroborative medicine composed of *cassia recens* with *senna levantina*, etc., according to the prescription of Mr. Purgon to expel and evacuate his honour's choler, four livres. How! Mr. Fleurant, you jest sure, you should treat your patients with some humanity. Mr. Purgon did not prescribe you to set down four livres; put down, put down three livres if you please—fifty sous.——Item, the said day, an anodyne and astringent potion to make his honour sleep, thirty sous. Good ——fifteen sous. Item, the twenty-sixth, a carminative clyster to expel his honour's wind, thirty sous. Ten sous, Mr. Fleurant. Item, his honour's clyster repeated at night as before,

415

thirty sous. Ten sous, Mr. Fleurant. Item, the twenty-seventh, a good medicine composed to dissipate and drive out his honour's ill humours, three livres. Good, fifty sous; I'm glad you are reasonable. Item, the twenty-eighth, a dose of clarified, dulcified milk, to sweeten, lenify, temper and refresh his honour's blood, twenty sous. Good, ten sous. Item, a cordial preservative potion, composed of twelve grains of bezoar, syrup of lemons, pomegranates, etc., according to prescription, five livres. Oh! Mr. Fleurant, softly, if you please, if you use people in this manner, one would be sick no longer, content yourself with four livres; sixty sous. Three and two make five, and five makes ten, and ten makes twenty. Sixty-three livres, four sous and six deniers. So then in this month I have taken one, two, three, four, five, six, seven, eight purges; and one, two, three, four, five, six, seven, eight, nine, ten, eleven, twelve clysters; and the last month there were twelve purges, and twenty clysters. I don't wonder if I am not so well this month as the last. I shall tell Mr. Purgon of it, that he may set this matter to rights. Here, take me away all these things. There's nobody there, 'tis in vain to speak, I'm always left alone; there's no way to keep 'em here. [*He rings a bell.*] They don't hear; my bell's not loud enough. [*Rings.*] No. [*Rings again.*] They are deaf. Toinet! [*Making as much noise with his bell as possible.*] Just as if I did not ring at all. Jade! Slut! [*Finding he still rings in vain.*] I'm mad. Drelin, drelin, drelin, the deuce take the carrion. Is it possible they should leave a poor sick creature in this manner! Drelin, drelin, drelin, oh! lamentable! Drelin, drelin, drelin. Oh! Heavens, they'll let me die here. Drelin, drelin, drelin.

Scene II

Toinet, Argan.

Toinet. [*Entering.*] Here I am.

Argan. Oh, ye jade! O carrion!

Toinet. [*Pretending to have hurt her head.*] The deuce take your impatience, you hurry one so much that I've knocked my head against the window-shutter.

Argan. [*Angrily.*] Ah! baggage——

Toinet. [*Interrupting him.*] Oh!

Argan. 'Tis a——

Toinet. Oh!

Argan. 'Tis an hour——

Toinet. Oh!

Argan. Thou hast left me——

Toinet. Oh!

Argan. Hold your tongue, you slut, that I may scold thee.

Toinet. Very well, i'faith, I like that, after what I've done to myself.

Argan. Thou hast made me bawl my throat sore, gipsy.

Toinet. And you have made me break my head, one's as good as t'other; so we are quit, with your leave.

Argan. How, hussy——

Toinet. If you scold, I'll cry.

Argan. To leave me, you jade——

Toinet. [*Still interrupting him.*] Oh!

Argan. Impudence! thou wouldst——

Toinet. Oh!

Argan. What! must not I have the pleasure of scolding her neither?

Toinet. Have your pennyworth of scolding with all my heart.

Argan. You hinder me from it, hussy, by interrupting me at every turn.

Toinet. If you have the pleasure of scolding, I must on my part, have the pleasure of crying: everyone to his fancy is but reasonable. Oh!

Argan. Come, I must pass over this. Take me away this thing, minx, take me away this thing. [*Rising out of his chair.*] Has my clyster worked well to-day?

Toinet. Your clyster!

Argan. Yes, have I voided much bilious matter?

Toinet. I'faith, I don't trouble myself about those matters. 'Tis for Mr. Fleurant to have his nose in 'em, since he has the profit of 'em.

Argan. Take care to get me some broth ready, for the other I'm to take by and by.

Toinet. This Mr. Fleurant and Mr. Purgon divert themselves finely with your carcass; they have a rare milch-cow of you. I would fain ask 'em what distemper you have, that you must take so much physic.

Argan. Hold your tongue, ignorance, 'tisn't for you to control the decrees of the faculty. Bring my daughter Angelica to me, I have something to say to her.

Toinet. Here she comes of herself; she has guessed your intention.

Scene III

Angelica, Toinet, Argan.

Argan. Come hither Angelica, you come opportunely, I want to speak with you.

Angelica. I am ready to hear you, sir.

Argan. Stay. [*To Toinet.*] Give me my cane, I'll come again presently.

Toinet. Go quick, sir, go. Mr. Fleurant finds us in business.

Scene IV

Angelica, Toinet.

Angelica. Toinet.

Toinet. Well.

Angelica. Look upon me a little.

Toinet. Well, I do look upon you.

Angelica. Toinet.

Toinet. Well, what would you have with Toinet?

Angelica. Don't you guess who I would speak of?

Toinet. I much suspect of our young lover; for 'tis on him that our conversation has entirely turned for these six days past, and you're not well unless you are talking of him every moment.

Angelica. Since you know that, why are not you the first then to talk of him to me, and spare me the pains of forcing you on this discourse?

Toinet. You don't give me time to do it; you have such a care about that matter, that 'tis difficult to be beforehand with you.

Angelica. I own to thee that I am never weary of talking of him to thee, and that my heart eagerly takes advantage of every moment to disclose itself to thee. But tell me, dost thou condemn, Toinet, the sentiments I have for him?

Toinet. Far from it.

Angelica. Am I in the wrong to abandon myself to these soft impressions?

Toinet. I don't say that.

Angelica. And wouldst thou have me insensible to the tender protestations of that ardent passion he expresses for me?

Toinet. Heaven forbid!

Angelica. Tell me a little, dost not thou perceive as well as I something of Providence, some act of destiny in the unexpected adventure of our acquaintance?

Toinet.   Yes.

Angelica.   Dost not thou think that action of engaging in my defence, without knowing me, was perfectly gallant?

Toinet.   Ay.

Angelica.   That 'twas impossible to make a more generous use of it?

Toinet.   Agreed.

Angelica.   And that he did all this with the best grace in the world?

Toinet.   Oh, yes.

Angelica.   Dost not thou think, Toinet, that he's well made in his person?

Toinet.   Certainly.

Angelica.   That he has the best air in the world?

Toinet.   Undoubtedly.

Angelica.   That his discourse, as well as actions, has something noble in it?

Toinet.   That's sure.

Angelica.   That never anything was heard more affectionate than all that he says to me?

Toinet.   'Tis true.

Angelica.   And that there's nothing more vexatious than the restraint I'm kept under, which hinders all communication of the soft transports of that mutual ardour which Heaven inspires us with?

Toinet.   You're in the right.

Angelica.   But, dear Toinet, dost thou think he loves me so much as he tells me?

Toinet.   Um——Those kind o' things are sometimes not absolutely to be trusted to. The show of love is very much like the reality; and I have seen notable actors of that part.

Angelica.   Ah! Toinet, what sayest thou? Alas! in the manner he speaks, is it really possible that he should not tell me the truth?

Toinet.   Be it as it will, you'll shortly be made clear in that point; and the resolution which he wrote you yesterday he had taken to ask you in marriage, is a ready way to discover to you if he spoke truth or not. That will be a thorough proof of it.

Angelica.   Ah! Toinet, if this man deceives me, I'll never believe a man as long as I live.

Toinet.   Here's your father come back.

Scene V

Argan, Angelica, Toinet.

Argan. [*Sitting down.*] So, daughter, I'm going to tell you a piece of news, which you little expect perhaps. You are asked of me in marriage. How's this? You laugh. That's pleasant enough, ah! that word marriage. There's nothing so merry to young girls. Ah, nature! nature! for what I can see then, child, I have no occasion to ask you if you are willing to be married.

Angelica. 'Tis my duty, sir, to do whatever you shall please to enjoin me.

Argan. I'm glad to have such a dutiful daughter; the thing is fixed then, and I have promised you.

Angelica. 'Tis for me, sir, blindly to follow all your resolutions.

Argan. My wife, your stepmother, had a desire I should make a nun of you, and your little sister Louison likewise; and has always persisted in it.

Toinet. [*Aside.*] The sly beast had her reasons for it.

Argan. She would not consent to this match, but I have carried it, and my word is given.

Angelica. Ah! sir, how much am I obliged to you for all your goodness!

Toinet. Troth, I take this well of you now, this is the wisest action you ever did in your life.

Argan. I have not yet seen the person, but they tell me I shall be satisfied with him, and thou too.

Angelica. Most certainly, sir.

Argan. How! hast thou seen him?

Angelica. Since your consent authorises me to open my heart to you, I'll not conceal from you, that chance brought us acquainted about six days since, and that the request which has been made to you, is the effect of an inclination which we conceived for one another at first sight.

Argan. I was not told of that, but I'm very glad of it, and 'tis so much the better that things go in that manner. They say that he's a jolly, well-made young fellow.

Angelica. True, sir.

Argan. Well shaped.

Angelica. Without doubt.

Argan. Agreeable in his person.

Angelica. Most certainly.

Argan. Of a good countenance.

Angelica. Extremely good

Argan. Discreet, and well born.

Angelica. Perfectly.

Argan. Very genteel.

Angelica. The most genteel in the world.

Argan. Speaks Latin and Greek well.

Angelica. I don't know that.

Argan. And will be admitted doctor in three days' time.

Angelica. He, sir!

Argan. Yes. Has not he told thee so?

Angelica. No indeed. Who told you so?

Argan. Mr. Purgon.

Angelica. Does Mr. Purgon know him?

Argan. A fine question! He must needs know him since he's his nephew.

Angelica. Cleanthes Mr. Purgon's nephew!

Argan. What Cleanthes? We are speaking of the person you are asked for in marriage.

Angelica. Well, ay.

Argan. Very well, and that's the nephew of Mr. Purgon, who is the son of his brother-in-law, the physician Mr. Diafoirus; and this son's name is Thomas Diafoirus, not Cleanthes; and Mr. Purgon, Mr. Fleurant, and I, concluded the match this morning, and to-morrow this intended son-in-law is to be brought to me by his father. What's the matter? you look quite astonished.

Angelica. 'Tis because I find, sir, that you have been speaking of one person, and I understood another.

Toinet. What, sir, would you entertain so burlesque a design? And with so much wealth as you have, would you marry your daughter to a physician?

Argan. Yes. What business have you, hussy, to concern yourself, impudence as thou art?

Toinet. Good now, softly, sir, you fly immediately to in-vectives. Can't we reason together without falling into a passion? Come, let's talk in cool blood. What is your reason, pray, for such a marriage?

Argan. My reason is, that seeing myself infirm, and sick as I am, I would procure me a son-in-law, and relations physicians, in order to depend on good assistance against my distemper, and to have in my family sources of remedies which are necessary for me, and to be myself at consultations and prescriptions.

Toinet. Very well, that's giving a reason, and there's a pleasure in answering one another calmly. But, sir, lay your hand on your heart. Are you really sick?

Argon. How, jade, am I sick? am I sick, impudence?

Toinet. Well, yes, sir, you are sick, let us have no quarrel about that. Yes, you are very sick, I agree to't, and more sick than you think; that's over. But your daughter is to marry a husband for herself, and not being sick, it isn't necessary to give her a physician.

Argan. 'Tis for my sake that I give her this physician, and a girl of good-nature should be overjoyed to marry for the benefit of her father's health.

Toinet. Lookee, sir, will you let me as a friend give you a piece of advice?

Argan. What's that advice?

Toinet. Not to think of this match.

Argan. And the reason, pray?

Toinet. The reason's this, that your daughter won't consent to it.

Argan. She won't consent to it?

Toinet. No.

Argan. My daughter?

Toinet. Your daughter. She'll tell you that she has nothing to do with Mr. Diafoirus, nor with his son, Thomas Diafoirus, nor all the Diafoirus's in the world.

Argan. But I have something to do with 'em. Besides, the match is more advantageous than you think for. Mr. Diafoirus has only this son to inherit all he has, and moreover, Mr. Purgon, who has neither wife nor children, gives him all his estate in favour of this marriage, and Mr. Purgon is a man that hath a good eight thousand livres a year.

Toinet. He must have killed a world of people to become so rich.

Argan. Eight thousand livres a year is something, without reckoning the father's estate.

Toinet. All this, sir, is fair and fine. But I still return to the same story. I advise you between ourselves to choose another husband for her, for she's not made to be Madame Diafoirus.

Argan. But I'll have it be so.

Toinet. Oh! fie, don't say that.

Argan. How! not say that?

Toinet. No.

Argan. And why shall I not say it?

Toinet. They'll say you don't know what you talk of.

Argan. They may say what they please; but I tell you, I'll have her make good the promise I have given.

Toinet. No, I am sure that she'll not do it.

Argan. I'll force her to it then.

Toinet. She'll not do it, I tell ye.

Argan. She shall do it, or I'll put her into a convent.

Toinet. You?

Argan. I.

Toinet. Good!

Argan. How, good?

Toinet. You shall not put her into a convent.

Argan. I shall not put her into a convent?

Toinet. No.

Argan. No!

Toinet. No.

Argan. Hey-day, this is pleasant enough; I shall not put my daughter into a convent, if I please?

Toinet. No, I tell you.

Argan. Who shall hinder me from it?

Toinet. Yourself.

Argan. Myself?

Toinet. Yes, you would not have the heart.

Argan. I shall.

Toinet. You jest.

Argan. I don't jest.

Toinet. Fatherly tenderness will hinder you.

Argan. It won't hinder me.

Toinet. A little tear or two, her arms thrown about your neck, a Dear papa pronounced tenderly, will be enough to move you.

Argan. All that will do nothing.

Toinet. Yes, yes.

Argan. I tell ye that I won't 'bate an inch on't.

Toinet. You trifle.

Argan. You shall not say that I trifle.

Toinet. Lack-a-day, I know you, you are good-natured.

Argan. [*Angrily.*] I am not good-natured, I'm ill-natured when I please.

Toinet. Softly, sir, you don't remember that you are sick.

Argan. I command her absolutely to prepare to take the husband I speak of.

Toinet. And I absolutely forbid her to do it.

Argan. Whereabouts are we then? and what boldness is this for a slut of a servant to talk at this rate before her master?

Toinet. When a master does not consider what he does, a sensible servant is in the right to inform him better.

Argan. [*Running after Toinet.*] Ah! insolence, I'll knock thee down.

Toinet. [*Running from him and putting the chair between her and him.*] 'Tis my duty to oppose anything that would disgrace you.

Argan. [*Running after her in a passion round the chair with his cane in his hand.*] Come here, come here, that I may teach thee how to speak.

Toinet. [*Saving herself on the opposite side of the chair to where Argan is.*] I interest myself as I ought, to hinder you from doing such a foolish thing.

Argan. Jade!

Toinet. No, I'll never consent to this match.

Argan. Baggage!

Toinet. I'll not have her marry your Thomas Diafoirus.

Argan. Carrion!

Toinet. And she'll obey me sooner than you.

Argan. Angelica, won't you lay hold of that slut for me?

Angelica. Alas, sir, don't make yourself sick.

Argan. If thou dost not lay hold of her for me, I'll refuse thee my blessing.

Toinet. And I'll disinherit her, if she does obey you.

Argan. [*Throwing himself in his chair.*] Oh! oh! I can bear it no longer. This is enough to kill me.

SCENE VI

Belina, Argan.

Argan. Ah! wife, come hither.

Belina. What's the matter, my poor spouse?

Argan. Come hither to my assistance.

Belina. What is it then that's the matter, my dear child?

Argan. My love.

Belina. My soul.

Argan. They have been putting me in a passion.

Belina. Alas! my poor little love! and how then, my soul?

Argan. Your slut Toinet is grown more insolent than ever.

Belina.   Don't put yourself in a passion then.

Argan.   She has made me mad, my life.

Belina.   Softly, my child.

Argan.   She has been thwarting me this hour about things that I'm resolved to do.

Belina.   There, there, softly.

Argan.   And has had the impudence to tell me that I'm not sick.

Belina.   She's an impertinent gipsy.

Argan.   You know, my heart, how the matter is.

Belina.   Yes, my heart, she's in the wrong.

Argan.   My love, that slut will kill me.

Belina.   Oh so, oh so!

Argan.   She's the cause of all the choler I breed.

Belina.   Don't fret yourself so much.

Argan.   And I have bid you, I know not how many times, turn her away from me.

Belina.   Alas, child, there are no servants, men or women, who have not their faults. We are sometimes forced to bear with their bad qualities for the sake of their good ones. This wench is dexterous, careful, diligent, and above all honest; and you know that at present there's need of great precaution with regard to those we take. Harkee, Toinet.

Scene VII

Argan, Belina, Toinet.

Toinet.   Madam.

Belina.   What's the reason that you put my dear in this passion?

Toinet.   [*In a soft tone.*]   I, madam? Alas! I don't know what you mean, I think of nothing but to please my master in everything.

Argan.   Ah! Traitress!

Toinet.   He told us that he intended to give his daughter in marriage to the son of Mr. Diafoirus; I answered him that I thought the match was very advantageous for her; but believed he would do better to put her into a convent.

Belina.   There's no great harm in that, and I think she's in the right.

Argan.   Ah! my love, dost thou believe her? she's a wicked jade. She said a hundred insolent things to me.

Belina. Very well, I believe you, my soul. Come, recover yourself. Harkee, Toinet, if you vex my jewel ever again, I'll turn you out of doors. So, give me his fur cloak, and the pillows that I may set him easy in his chair. You are I don't know how. Pull your nightcap well over your ears; there's nothing gives people so much cold, as letting the air in at their ears.

Argan. Ah! my life, I'm vastly obliged to you for all the care you take of me.

Belina. [*Adjusting the pillows which she puts round him.*] Raise yourself up that I may put this under you. Let us put this to keep you up, and this on the other side. Let's place this behind your back, and this other to support your head.

Toinet. [*Clapping a pillow hard on his head.*] And this to keep you from the damp.

Argan. [*Rising up in a passion, and throwing all the pillows after Toinet as she runs away.*] Ah! jade, thou wouldst stifle me.

Scene VIII

Argan, Belina.

Belina. Oh so, oh so! What's the matter then?

Argan. [*Throwing himself into his chair.*] Oh! ah! oh! I can hold it no longer.

Belina. Why do you fly into such passions? she meant to do well.

Argan. You don't know, my love, the malice of that baggage. Oh! she has put me beside myself; and there'll be need of more than eight doses of physic, and twelve clysters to set all this to rights again.

Belina. So, so, my little dearie, pacify yourself a little.

Argan. My life, you are all my comfort.

Belina. Poor little child.

Argan. That I may endeavour to requite the love you have for me, as I told you, my heart, I'll make my will.

Belina. Ah! my soul, don't talk of that, pray now, I can't bear the thought of it; the very word of will makes me leap for grief.

Argan. I desired you to speak of it to your notary.

Belina. He's within there, I brought him with me.

Argan. Let him come here then, my love.

Belina. Alas! my soul, when one loves a husband well, one's scarce in a condition to think of these things.

Scene IX

Mr. Bonnefoy, Belina, Argan.

Argan. Come hither, Mr. Bonnefoy, come hither. Take a chair pray. My wife has told me, sir, that you are a very honest man, and altogether one of her friends; and I have ordered her to speak to you about a will.

Belina. Alas! I'm not capable of speaking about those things.

Mr. Bonnefoy. She has unfolded your intentions to me, sir, and what you design for her; and I have to tell you upon that subject, that you cannot give your wife anything by will.

Argan. But why so?

Mr. Bonnefoy. Custom is against it. If you were in a country of statute-law, it might be done; but at Paris, and in countries for the most part governed by custom, 'tis what can't be; and the disposition would be null. All the advantage that a man and woman joined by wedlock can give each to the other is by mutual gift during life; moreover there must be no children, either of the two conjuncts, or of one of them, at the decease of the first that dies.

Argan. Then 'tis a very impertinent custom that a husband can't leave anything to a wife, by whom he's tenderly beloved, and who takes so much care of him. I should desire to consult my counsellor to see what I could do.

Mr. Bonnefoy. 'Tis not to counsel that you must apply, for they are commonly severe in these points, and imagine it a great crime to dispose of anything contrary to law. They are difficult people, and are ignorant of the by-ways of conscience. There are other persons to consult who are much fitter to accommodate you; who have expedients of passing gently over the law, and of making that just which is not allowed; who know how to smooth the difficulties of an affair, and to find means of eluding custom by some indirect advantage. Without that where should we always be? There must be a facility in things, otherwise we should do nothing, and I would not give a sou for our business.

Argan. My wife indeed told me, sir, that you were a very skilful and a very honest man. How then can I do, pray, to give her my estate, and to deprive my children of it?

Mr. Bonnefoy. How can you do? You must secretly choose an intimate friend of your wife's, to whom you may bequeath in due form by your will, all that you can, and this friend shall afterwards give up all to her. You may further sign a great many bonds, without suspicion, payable to several creditors, who shall lend their names to your wife, and shall put into her hands a declaration, that what they had done in it was only to serve her. You may likewise in your lifetime put into her hands ready money, or bills which you may have payable to the bearer.

Belina. Alas! you must not torment yourself with all these things. If I should lose you, child, I'll stay no longer in the world.

Argan. My soul!

Belina. Yes, my dear, if I'm unfortunate enough to lose you—

Argan. My dear wife!

Belina. Life will be no longer anything to me.

Argan. My love!

Belina. And I'll follow you, to let you see the tenderness I have for you.

Argan. My life, you break my heart; be comforted, I beg of thee.

Mr. Bonnefoy. These tears are unseasonable, and things are not yet come to that.

Belina. Ah! sir, you don't know what 'tis to have a husband that one tenderly loves.

Argan. All the concern I shall have, if I die, my soul, is that I never had a child by thee. Mr. Purgon told me that he'd make me able to get one.

Mr. Bonnefoy. That may come still.

Argan. I must make my will then, my love, after the manner the gentleman says; but by way of precaution I'll put into your hands twenty thousand livres in gold, which I have in the ceiling of my alcove, and two notes payable to the bearer, which are due to me, one from Mr. Damon, and the other from Gérante.

Belina. No, no, I'll have none of it. Ah!——how much do you say that there is in your alcove?

Argan. Twenty thousand livres, my love.

Belina. Don't speak to me of riches, I beseech ye. Ah!—— how much are the two notes for?

Argan. They are my life, one for four thousand livres, and the other for six.

Belina. All the wealth in the world, my soul, is nothing to me in comparison of thee.

Mr. Bonnefoy. [*To Argan.*] Would you have us proceed to make the will?

Argan.   Yes, sir, but we shall be better in my little closet.
My love, lead me pray.

Belina.   Come, my poor dear child.

SCENE X

Angelica, Toinet.

Toinet.   They are got with a scrivener there, and I heard
'em talk of a will.   Your stepmother does not sleep, and 'tis
certainly some contrivance against your interest that she's
pushing your father upon.

Angelica.   Let him dispose of his estate as he pleases, provided he does not dispose of my heart.   Thou seest, Toinet, the
violent designs they have against it.   Don't abandon me, I
beseech thee, in the extremity I'm in.

Toinet.   I abandon you!   I'll die sooner.   Your stepmother
in vain makes me her confidante, and strives to bring me into
her interest; I never had any inclination for her, and have been
always of your side.   Let me alone, I'll make use of everything
to serve you; but to serve you more effectually I'll change my
battery, conceal the zeal I have for you, and pretend to enter
into the sentiments of your father and stepmother.

Angelica.   Endeavour, I conjure thee, to give Cleanthes
notice of the marriage they have concluded on.

Toinet.   I have nobody to employ in that office but the old
usurer Polichinello, my lover, and 'twill cost me some kind
words to have him do't, which I'll willingly disburse for you.
To-day 'tis too late, but very early to-morrow I'll send to seek
for him, and he'll be overjoyed to——

Belina.   [*In the house.*]   Toinet.

Toinet.   [*To Angelica.*]   I'm called.   Good night.   Rely upon
me.

ACT II

SCENE I

Toinet, Cleanthes.

Toinet.   [*Not knowing Cleanthes.*]   What do you want, sir?

Cleanthes.   What do I want?

Toinet.   Ah, hah! is it you? surprising! what come you to
do here?

Cleanthes. To know my destiny; to speak to the amiable Angelica, consult the sentiments of her heart; and demand of her, what her resolutions are in respect to the fatal marriage they have given me intelligence of.

Toinet. Yes, but Angelica is not to be spoken with thus point blank; there must be intrigue to manage that point, and you have been told under how strict a guard she is kept. That they allow her not to stir abroad, or speak to anybody, and that 'twas the curiosity of an old aunt only, which favoured us with the liberty of going to that play, which gave birth to your passion; and we are very much upon our guard lest we speak of that adventure.

Cleanthes. Accordingly I come not here as Cleanthes, and under the appearance of her lover, but as a friend of her music-master, who has given me leave to say that he sent me in his room.

Toinet. Here's her father. Retire a little, and let me tell him you are there.

Scene II

Argan, Toinet.

Argan. [*Thinking himself alone, and not seeing Toinet.*] Mr. Purgon told me I should walk in my chamber twelve times to and again in a morning; but I forgot to ask him, whether it should be longways or broadways.

Toinet. Sir, there is one——

Argan. Speak low, hussy, thou hast just split my brains, and thou never considerest that sick folks should not be spoken so loud to.

Toinet. I would tell you, sir——

Argan. Speak low, I say.

Toinet. Sir——   [*She makes as if she spoke.*

Argan. Hey?

Toinet. I tell you that——[*She still makes as if she spoke again.*]

Argan. What is it you tell me?

Toinet. [*Aloud.*] I tell you here is a man wants to speak with you.

Argan. Let him come.

[*Toinet beckons to Cleanthes to come near.*

Scene III

Argan, Cleanthes, Toinet.

Cleanthes.   Sir——

Toinet. [*To Cleanthes.*] Don't speak so loud, for fear of splitting my master's brains.

Cleanthes. Sir, I am exceedingly glad to find you up, and to see that you are better.

Toinet. [*Pretending to be in a passion.*] How better? 'tis false, my master is always ill.

Cleanthes. I had heard the gentleman was better, and I perceive he looks well.

Toinet. What d'ye mean with your Looks well? He looks very ill, and they are impertinent people who told you he was better. He never was so ill in his life.

Argan. She's in the right on't.

Toinet. He walks, sleeps, eats, and drinks like other folks; but that does not hinder him from being sick.

Argan. That's true.

Cleanthes. Sir, I am heartily sorry for it. I come from the young lady your daughter's music-master. He was obliged to go into the country for a few days; and, as I am one of his intimate friends, he sent me in his place, to go on with her lessons, for fear, that if they were discontinued, she might forget what she has already learnt.

Argan. Very well. [*To Toinet.*] Call Angelica.

Toinet. I fancy, sir, it would be better to show the gentleman to her chamber.

Argan. No. Bid her come hither.

Toinet. He can't teach her her lesson as he should do, if they are not by themselves.

Argan. Yes, yes.

Toinet. Sir, 'twill only stun you, and you had need to have nothing to disturb you, or split your brains, in the condition you are.

Argan. No, no, I love music, and I shall be glad to——hoh! here she comes. [*To Toinet.*] Do you go see if my wife be dressed.

Scene IV

Argan, Angelica, Cleanthes.

Argan. Come, daughter; your music-master is gone into the country, and here's a person he has sent to teach you in his place.

Angelica. [*Knowing Cleanthes.*]   Oh, Heavens!

Argan.   What's the matter?   Whence this surprise?

Angelica.   'Tis——

Argan.   What?   Who disturbs you in this manner?

Angelica.   'Tis a surprising accident, sir, that I meet with here.

Argan.   How?

Angelica.   I dreamt last night that I was in the greatest distress in the world, and that a person exactly like this gentleman, offered himself to me, of whom I demanded succour, and he presently freed me from the trouble I was in; and my surprise was very great to see unexpectedly, upon my coming in here, what I had in idea all night.

Cleanthes.   'Tis no small happiness to have a place in your thoughts, whether sleeping or waking; and my good fortune would be undoubtedly very great, were you in any trouble from which you should judge me worthy to deliver you; and there is nothing I would not do to——

SCENE V

Argan, Angelica, Cleanthes, Toinet.

Toinet. [*To Argan.*]   Troth, sir, I'm o' your side now, and unsay all that I said yesterday.   Here are Mr. Diafoirus the father, and Mr. Diafoirus the son, come to visit you.   How rarely will you be hope up with a son-in-law!   You will see one of the best made young fellows in the world, and the wittiest too. He spoke but two words, and I was in ecstasy at 'em, and your daughter will be charmed with him.

Argan. [*To Cleanthes, who makes as if he were going.*]   Don't go, sir; I am upon marrying my daughter, and the person they have brought hither is her intended husband, whom she has not as yet seen.

Cleanthes.   'Tis doing me a great deal of honour, sir, to permit me to be witness of so agreeable an interview.

Argan.   He is son to an eminent physician, and the marriage will be performed in four days.

Cleanthes.   Very well.

Argan.   Please to inform her music-master of it, that he may be at the wedding.

Cleanthes.   I'll not fail to do it.

Argan.   I invite you to it likewise.

Cleanthes.   You do me a great deal of honour.

Argan.   Come, place yourselves in order, here they are.

SCENE VI

Mr. Diafoirus, Thomas Diafoirus, Argan, Angelica, Cleanthes, Toinet, Lackeys.

Argan. [*Putting his hand to his cap without taking it off.*] Mr. Purgon, sir, has forbid me being uncovered. You are of the faculty: you know the consequences.

Mr. Diafoirus. We are in all our visits to bring relief to our patients, and not to bring any inconvenience upon 'em.

[*Argan and Mr. Diafoirus speak at the same time.*

Argan. I receive, sir,
Mr. Diafoirus. We come here, sir,
Argan. With a great deal of joy,
Mr. Diafoirus. My son Thomas, and I,
Argan. The honour you do me,
Mr. Diafoirus. To declare to you, sir,
Argan. And I could have wished,
Mr. Diafoirus. The pleasure we receive,
Argan. To have been able to have gone to you,
Mr. Diafoirus. From the favour you do us,
Argan. To assure you,
Mr. Diafoirus. So kindly to admit us,
Argan. But you know, sir,
Mr. Diafoirus. To the honour, sir,
Argan. What it is to be a poor sick creature,
Mr. Diafoirus. Of your alliance,
Argan. Who can do no more,
Mr. Diafoirus. And to assure you,
Argan. Than to tell you here,
Mr. Diafoirus. That in affairs depending on our faculty,
Argan. That he will seek all opportunities,
Mr. Diafoirus. As also in all others,
Argan. To make you sensible, sir,
Mr. Diafoirus. We shall ever be ready, sir,
Argan. That he is entirely at your service.

Mr. Diafoirus. To testify our zeal for you——[*To his son.*] Come, Thomas, advance, make your compliments.

Thomas Diafoirus. [*To Mr. Diafoirus.*] Should not I begin with the father?

Mr. Diafoirus. Yes.

Thomas Diafoirus. [*To Argan.*] Sir, I come to salute, recognise, cherish, and revere in you a second father; but a second father, to whom, I'll be bold to say, I am more indebted than to my first. The first begat me; but you have adopted me. He received me through necessity; but you have accepted me through favour. What I have from him, is the operation of his body, what I have from you, is the operation of your will; and by how much the mental faculties are superior to the corporeal, by so much am I more indebted to you, and by so much do I hold, as more precious, this future filiation, for which I this day come to pay you beforehand, the most humble and most respectful homage.

Toinet. Prosperity to the colleges, which turn us out such ingenious persons.

Thomas Diafoirus. [*To Mr. Diafoirus.*] Was that well done, father?

Mr. Diafoirus. Optimè.

Argan. [*To Angelica.*] Come, pay your respects to the gentleman.

Thomas Diafoirus. [*To Mr. Diafoirus.*] Shall I kiss her?

Mr. Diafoirus. Yes, yes.

Thomas Diafoirus. [*To Angelica.*] Madam, 'tis with justice that Heaven has granted you the name of stepmother, since one——

Argan. [*To Thomas Diafoirus.*] 'Tis not my wife, 'tis my daughter you are speaking to.

Thomas Diafoirus. Where is she then?

Argan. She's a-coming.

Thomas Diafoirus. Shall I wait, father, till she comes?

Mr. Diafoirus. Always make your compliment to the young lady.

Thomas Diafoirus. Madam, just in the same manner as the statue of Memnon gave an harmonious sound, when it was illuminated by the rays of the sun: so, in like manner, do I feel myself animated with a sweet transport at the appearance of the sun of your beauty. And as the naturalists remark that the flower named the Heliotrope, turns, without ceasing, towards that star of day: so shall my heart, henceforth for ever, turn towards the resplendent stars of your adorable eyes, as to its proper pole. Permit me then, madam, now to pay, at the altar of your charms, the offering of that heart, which breathes not after, nor is ambitious of any other glory than that of being till death, madam, your most humble, most obedient, and most faithful servant, and husband.

Toinet. See what it is to study, one learns to say fine things.

Argan. [*To Cleanthes.*] Heh! What say you to that?

Cleanthes. That the gentleman does wonders, and that if he is as good a physician as he is an orator, it would be a great pleasure to be one of his patients.

Toinet. Certainly. It will be a wonderful thing, if he per forms as fine cures, as he makes fine speeches.

Argan. Here, my chair quickly, and chairs for everybody. Sit you there, daughter. [*To Mr. Diafoirus.*] You see, sir, that all the world admires your son, and I think you very happy in such a young man.

Mr. Diafoirus. Sir, 'tis not because I am his father, but I can say I have reason to be satisfied in him, and that all who see him, speak of him as a youth who has no harm in him. He never had a very lively imagination, nor that sparkling wit which one observes in some others; but it was that, I always looked upon, as a happy presage of his judgment, a quality requisite for the exercise of our art. When he was a little one, he was never what one may call roguish, or waggish. One might always see him mild, peaceable, and taciturn, never uttering a word, and never playing at any of those little games, that we call children's-play. They had all the difficulty in the world to teach him to read, and he was nine years old before he knew his letters. Good, says I within myself; trees slow of growth, are those which bear the best fruit. One writes upon the marble with much more difficulty than one does upon the sand; but things are much longer preserved there, and that slowness of apprehension, that heaviness of imagination, is a mark of a future good judgment. When I sent him to college he was hard put to't; but he bore up obstinately against all difficulties, and his tutors always praised him to me for his assiduity and his pains. In short, by mere dint of hammering, he gloriously attained to be a licentiate; and I can say without vanity, that from the time he took his Bachelor of Physic's degree, there is no candidate that has made more noise than he in all the disputes of the schools. He has rendered himself formidable there, and not an act passes but he argues to the last extremity on the side of the contrary proposition. He is firm in a dispute, strenuous as a Turk in his principles; and pursues an argument to the farthest recesses of logic. But what pleases me above all things in him, in which he follows my example, is that he is blindly attached to the opinions of the ancients, and that he would never comprehend nor hear the reasons and experiments of the pretended discoveries of our age, concerning the circulation of the blood, and other opinions of the same stamp.

Thomas Diafoirus. [*Taking a large thesis out of his pocket rolled up, which he presents to Angelica.*] I have supported a thesis against the circulators, which, with the gentleman's permission, [*Bowing to Argan.*] I make bold to present to the young lady, as a homage I owe her of the first-fruits of my genius.

Angelica. Sir, 'tis a useless piece of goods for me, and I am not skilled in those sort of things.

Toinet. [*Taking the thesis.*] Give it me, give it me, 'tis always worth taking for the picture, it will serve to adorn our garret.

Thomas Diafoirus. And with the gentleman's permission also, I invite you to come and see one of these days, for your diversion, the dissection of a woman, upon which I am to read lectures.

Toinet. The diversion will be agreeable. There are some gentlemen give their mistresses a play, but to give a dissection, is something more gallant.

Mr. Diafoirus. As to the rest, for what concerns the requisite qualities for marriage and propagation, I do assure you that according to the rules of us doctors, he is just such as one could wish. That he possesses in a laudable degree the prolific virtue, and that he is of a temperament proper to beget, and procreate well-conditioned children.

Argan. Is it not your intention, sir, to push his interest at court, and procure for him a physician's place there?

Mr. Diafoirus. To speak frankly to you, our profession amongst your great people never appeared to me agreeable, and I always found it would be much better for us to continue amongst the commonalty. The public business is commodious. You are accountable to nobody for your actions, and provided one does but follow the beaten track of the rules of art, one gives one's self no manner of trouble about what may be the event. But what is vexatious among your great people is, that when they happen to be sick, they absolutely expect their physicians should cure them.

Toinet. That's a good jest indeed, and they are very impertinent to expect that you gentlemen should cure 'em: you don't attend them for that purpose; you only go to take your fees, and prescribe remedies, 'tis their business to cure themselves if they can.

Mr. Diafoirus. That's true. We are only obliged to treat people according to form.

Argan. [*To Cleanthes.*]   Sir, pray let my daughter sing before the company.

Cleanthes.   I waited for your orders, sir, and propose to divert the company, by singing along with miss, a scene of a little opera lately composed. [*To Angelica, giving her a paper.*]   There's your part.

Angelica.   I?

Cleanthes. [*Low to Angelica.*]   Pray don't refuse, but permit me to let you into the design of the scene we are going to sing aloud. [*Aloud.*]   I have no voice for singing; but 'tis sufficient in this case if I make myself understood, you will have the goodness to excuse me, on account of the necessity I am under, to make the young lady sing.

Argan.   Are the verses pretty?

Cleanthes.   'Tis properly an extempore opera, and what you are to hear sung, is no more than numbered prose, or a kind of irregular verse, such as passion and necessity might suggest to two persons, who say things out of their own head, and speak off-hand.

Argan.   Very well. Let's hear.

Cleanthes.   The subject of the scene is this. A shepherd was attentive to the beauties of a public entertainment, which was but just begun, when his attention was interrupted by a noise, on one side of him. He turns to look, and sees a brutish clown, with insolent words abusing a shepherdess. Immediately he espoused the interest of a sex to which all men owe homage; and having chastised the churl for his insolence, he comes to the shepherdess, and sees a young creature, who, from two of the finest eyes he had ever seen, was shedding tears, which he thought the most beautiful in the world. Alas! says he within himself, could anyone be capable of insulting a person so amiable? And what inhuman, what barbarous creature would not be touched with such tears? He was solicitous to stop those tears, which he thought so beautiful; and the lovely shepherdess took care at the same time, to thank him for the slight service he had done; but in a manner so charming, so tender, so passionate, that the shepherd could not resist it, but every word, every look was a flaming shaft, which he found pierced him to the heart. Is there anything, said he, can possibly deserve the lovely expressions of such an acknowledgment? And what would one not do, what service, what dangers would one not be delighted to go through, to attract but one moment the moving tenderness of so grateful a mind? The whole diversion passes without his attending to it in the least; but he complains 'tis too short, because the conclusion of it separates him from his adorable shepherdess, and from this first view, from this first moment he carried along with him all the violence of a passion of many years. He immediately suffered all the miseries of absence, and was tormented that he could no longer see what he saw for so short a time. He does everything possible to regain that sight, the dear idea of which he has in his mind by night and by day; but the great constraint under which his shepherdess is kept, deprives him of all opportunity. The violence of his passion makes him resolve to demand the adorable beauty in marriage, without whom he can no longer live, and he obtained her permission for this, by a letter which he had the dexterity to have conveyed to her hands. But at the same time he has advice that the father of this fair one has concluded a marriage with another, and that all things are disposing for celebration of the ceremony. Judge what a cruel stroke to the heart of the melancholy shepherd. See him overwhelmed with mortal sorrow. He cannot support the horrible idea of seeing all that he loves in the arms of another, and his passion being desperate makes him introduce himself into the house of his shepherdess to learn her sentiments, and know from her what destiny he is to resolve upon. He there meets with preparations for everything he fears; he there sees the unworthy rival, which the caprice of a father opposes to the tendernesses of his love. He sees this ridiculous rival, near the lovely shepherdess, triumphing, as if the conquest were sure, and this sight fills him with indignation, which he has the utmost difficulty to master. He casts a mournful look on her he adores, and both his respect for her, and the presence of her father, prevent his saying anything to her but by the eyes. But at last, he breaks through all restraint, and the transport of his passion makes him express himself in this manner. [*He sings.*]

> Fair Phyllis, 'tis too much to bear,
> Break cruel silence; and your thoughts declare.
> Tell me at once my destiny,
> Shall I live, or must I die?

Angelica. [*Singing.*]

> With sad, dejected looks, O Thyrsis, see
> Poor Phyllis dread th' ill-fated wedding-day;
> Sighing, she lifts her eyes to Heaven and thee,
> And needs she more to say?

Argan.   Hey, hey! I didn't know my daughter was **such a** mistress of the art, to sing at sight without hesitating.

Cleanthes.

> Alas! my Phyllis fair,
> Can the enamoured Thyrsis be so blest,
> Your favour in the least to share,
> And find a place within that lovely breast?

Angelica.

> In this extreme, if I confess my love,
> Not modesty itself can disapprove,
> Yes, Thyrsis, thee I love.

Cleanthes.

> Oh! Sound enchanting to the ear!
> Did I dream, or did I hear?
> Repeat it, Phyllis, and all doubt remove.

Angelica.

> Yes, Thyrsis, thee I love.

Cleanthes.

> Once more, my Phyllis.

Angelica.

> Thee I love.

Cleanthes.

> A thousand times repeat, nor ever weary prove.

Angelica.

> I love, I love,
> Yes, Thyrsis, thee I love.

Cleanthes.

> Ye monarchs of the earth, ye pow'rs divine,
> Can you compare your happiness to mine?
> But, Phyllis, there's a thought
> Does my transporting joy abate,
> A rival——

Angelica.

> I, more than death, the monster hate,
> And if his presence tortures you,
> It does no less to Phyllis too.

Cleanthes.

> If with the match a father's power,
> Would force you to comply.

Angelica.

> I'd rather, rather die than give consent,
> Much rather, rather die.

Argan. And what says the father to all this?

Cleanthes. He says nothing.

Argan. That same father was a blockhead of a father, to suffer all these foolish things, without saying anything.

Cleanthes. [*Continuing to sing.*] Ah! my love——

Argan. No, no, enough of it. This play is of very bad example. The shepherd Thyrsis is an impertinent puppy, and the shepherdess Phyllis, an impudent baggage, to speak in this manner before a father. [*To Angelica.*] Show me the paper. Ha, ha! Where are the words then that you spoke? There's nothing writ here but the music.

Cleanthes. Why, don't you know, sir, that they have found out an invention lately, of writing the words in the very notes themselves?

Argan. Very well. I'm your servant, sir; adieu! We could very well have spared your impertinent opera.

Cleanthes. I thought to divert you.

Argan. Impertinence never diverts. Hah! here's my wife.

SCENE VII

Belina, Argan, Angelica, Mr. Diafoirus, Thomas Diafoirus, Toinet.

Argan. Here's Mr. Diafoirus's son, my love.

Thomas Diafoirus. Madam, 'tis with justice that Heaven has granted you the name of mother-in-law, since one sees in your face——

Belina. Sir, I am very glad I came here apropos, that I might have the honour of seeing you.

Thomas Diafoirus. Since one sees in your face——Since one sees in your face——Madam, you interrupted me in the middle of my period, and that has disturbed my memory.

Mr. Diafoirus. Reserve that, Thomas, for another time.

Argan. I wish you had been here just now, dearie.

Toinet. Oh, madam, you have lost a great deal by not being here at the Second father, at the Statue of Memnon and the Flower named the Heliotrope.

Argan. Come, daughter, join hands with the gentleman, and plight him your troth, as your husband.

Angelica. Sir.

Argan. Hey, sir! What means this?

Angelica. For goodness' sake, don't hurry things too fast. Give us time at least to know one another, and to find the growth of that inclination in each for the other, which is so necessary to form a perfect union.

Thomas Diafoirus. As for me, madam, mine is grown already, I have no need to stay any longer.

Angelica. If you are so forward, sir, it is not so with me, and I confess to you that your merit has not as yet made impression enough upon my mind.

Argan. Hoh! well, well, that will have leisure enough to be made, when you are married together.

Angelica. Ah! father, pray give me time. Marriage is a chain that should never be imposed by force upon a heart, and if the gentleman is a man of honour, he should never accept a person, who must be his by constraint.

Thomas Diafoirus. Nego consequentiam, madam; and I may be a man of honour, and yet accept you from the hands of your father.

Angelica. To offer violence is but a very ill way to make you beloved by anyone.

Thomas Diafoirus. We read in the ancients, madam, that their custom was to carry off the young women they were going to marry, by force from their father's house, that it might not seem to be by their consent, that they flew into the arms of a man.

Angelica. The ancients, sir, are the ancients, and we are moderns. Such grimaces are not necessary in our age, and when a marriage pleases us, we know very well how to go to it, without anybody's dragging us. Have patience; if you love me, sir, you ought to like everything I like.

Thomas Diafoirus. Yes, madam, as far as the interests of my love exclusively.

Angelica. But the great sign of love is, to submit to the will of her one loves.

Thomas Diafoirus. Distinguo, madam. In what regards not the possession of her, *concedo*; but in what regards that, *nego*.

Toinet. 'Tis in vain to reason. The gentleman is come fire-new from college, and he'll always be too hard for you. Why should you resist so much, and refuse the glory of being tacked to the body of the faculty?

Belina. She has some other inclination in her head perhaps.

Angelica. If I had, madam, it should be such as reason and honour might allow me.

Argan. Hey-day! I act a pleasant part here.

Belina. If I were as you, child, I would not at all force her to marry, and I know very well what I would do.

Angelica. I know, madam, what you mean, and the kindness you have for me: but perhaps your counsels mayn't be lucky enough to be put into execution.

Belina. That's because very wise and very good children like you, scorn to be obedient and submissive to the will of their fathers. That was held a virtue in times of yore.

Angelica. The duty of a daughter has bounds, madam, and neither reason nor law extend it to all sorts of things.

Belina. That's as much as to say you have no aversion to matrimony; but you've a mind to choose a husband to your own fancy.

Angelica. If my father won't give me a husband to my liking, I shall conjure him, at least, not to force me to marry one I can't love.

Argan. Gentlemen, I beg your pardon for all this.

Angelica. Everybody to their own end in marrying. For my part who would not marry a husband but really to love him, and who intend to be entirely attached to him for life, I confess to you I use some precaution in the affair. There are some persons who take husbands only to set themselves free from the restraint of their parents, and to put themselves in a condition of doing whatever they please. There are others, madam, who make marriage a commerce of pure interest; who only marry to get a jointure, to enrich themselves by those they marry; and run without scruple from husband to husband, to engross to themselves their spoils. Those people in good truth don't stand much upon ceremonies, and have little regard to the person of the man.

Belina. You are in a mighty vein of reasoning to-day, and I would fain know what you mean by that.

Angelica. I, madam, what should I mean but what I say?

Belina. You are such a simpleton, my dear, that there's no enduring you any longer.

Angelica. You would be glad, madam, to oblige me to give you some impertinent answer; but I tell you beforehand, you shan't have that advantage.

Belina. Your insolence is not to be equalled.

Angelica. No, madam, your talking is in vain.

Belina.   You have a ridiculous pride, an impertinent presumption which makes you the scorn of all the world.

Angelica.   All this will do no good, madam. I shall be discreet in spite of you, and to take away from you all hope of succeeding in what you want to be at, I shall get out of your sight.

SCENE VIII

Argan, Belina, Mr. Diafoirus, Thomas Diafoirus, Toinet.

Argan.   [*To Angelica who goes out.*] Harkee, there's no medium in the case.   You've your choice to marry in four days' time, either this gentleman, or a convent.   [*To Belina.*]   Don't give yourself any uneasiness, I'll bring her to good order.

Belina.   I'm sorry to leave you, my child, but I have an affair in the city, which can't be dispensed with.   I shall come back again presently.

Argan.   Go, love, and call upon your lawyer, that you may bid him hasten you know what.

Belina.   B'y, my little dearie.

Argan.   B'y, jewel.

SCENE IX

Argan, Mr. Diafoirus, Thomas Diafoirus, Toinet.

Argan.   This woman loves me——'Tis not credible how much.

Mr. Diafoirus.   We shall take our leave of you, sir.

Argan.   Pray, sir, tell me a little how I am.

Mr. Diafoirus. [*Feeling his pulse.*] Here, Thomas, take the gentleman's other arm, to see whether you can form a good judgment of his pulse.   *Quid dicis?*

Thomas Diafoirus.   Dico, that the gentleman's pulse, is the pulse of a man who is not well.

Mr. Diafoirus.   Good.

Thomas Diafoirus.   That 'tis hardish, not to say hard.

Mr. Diafoirus.   Very well.

Thomas Diafoirus.   Recoiling.

Mr. Diafoirus.   Bene.

Thomas Diafoirus.   And even a little frisking.

Mr. Diafoirus.   Optimè.

Thomas Diafoirus.   Which shows an intemperature in the *parenchyma splenicum,* that is to say, the spleen.

Mr. Diafoirus.   Very well.

Argan. No, Dr. Purgon says, 'tis my liver that's bad.

Mr. Diafoirus. Why yes, he who says *parenchyma*, means both one and t'other, because of the strict sympathy they have together, by means of the *vas breve* of the *pylorus*, and sometimes the *meatus cholidici*. He orders you, doubtless, to eat roast meat.

Argan. No, nothing but boiled.

Mr. Diafoirus. Ay, yes, roast, boiled, the same thing. He orders you very prudently, and you can't be in better hands.

Argan. Sir, how many corns of salt should one put in an egg?

Mr. Diafoirus. Six, eight, ten, by even numbers; as in medicines, by odd numbers.

Argan. Sir, your very humble servant.

SCENE X

Belina, Argan.

Belina. I come, child, before I go abroad, to inform you of a thing, which you must take care of. As I passed by Angelica's chamber-door, I saw a young fellow with her, who immediately made his escape as soon as he saw me.

Argan. A young fellow with my daughter?

Belina. Yes. Your little daughter Louison was with 'em, who can give you tidings of 'em.

Argan. Send her hither, lovey; send her hither. [*Alone.*] Oh! the impudent baggage! I am no longer astonished at her obstinacy.

SCENE XI

Argan, Louison.

Louison. What do you want, papa? My mamma told me, that you want to speak with me.

Argan. Yes, come hither. Come nearer. Turn you. Look up. Look upon me. Heh?

Louison. What, papa?

Argan. So.

Louison. What?

Argan. Have you nothing to tell me?

Louison. To divert you, I'll tell you, if you please, the story of the ass's skin, or the fable of the crow and the fox, which they taught me t'other day.

Argan. That's not what I want.

Louison. What then?

Argan. O ye cunning hussy, you know very well what I mean.

Louison. Pardon me, papa.

Argan. Is it thus you obey me?

Louison. How?

Argan. Did not I charge you to come immediately and tell me all that you see?

Louison. Yes, papa.

Argan. Have you done so?

Louison. Yes, papa, I am come to tell you all that I have seen.

Argan. And have you seen nothing to-day?

Louison. No, papa.

Argan. No?

Louison. No, papa.

Argan. Indeed?

Louison. Indeed.

Argan. Hoh! very well, I'll make you see something.

Louison. [*Seeing Argan take a rod.*] Ah! papa.

Argan. Ha, hah! you little hypocrite, you don't tell me you saw a man in your sister's chamber.

Louison. [*Crying.*] Papa.

Argan. [*Taking her by the arm.*] Here's something will teach you to lie.

Louison. [*Falling down on her knees.*] Ah, papa, pray forgive me. 'Twas because my sister had bid me not to tell it you; but I'm going to tell you all.

Argan. You must, first of all, have the rod, for having told a lie. After that we shall consider of the rest.

Louison. Forgive me, papa.

Argan. No, no.

Louison. My dear papa, don't whip me.

Argan. You shall be whipped.

Louison. For Heaven's sake, papa, don't whip me.

Argan. [*Going to whip her.*] Come, come.

Louison. Oh! papa, you have hurt me. Hold, I'm dead.

[*She feigns herself dead.*

Argan. Hola, what's the meaning of this? Louison, Louison. Oh! bless me! Louison. Ah! my child. Oh! wretched me!— My poor child's dead. What have I done, wretch! Oh! villainous rod! A curse on all rods! Oh! my dear child; my poor little Louison.

Louison. So, so, papa, don't cry so, I'm not quite dead.

Argan. D'ye see the cunning baggage? Oh! come, come, I pardon you for this time, provided you'll really tell me all.

Louison. Ho! yes, papa.

Argan. Take special care you do however, for here's my little finger knows all, and will tell me if you lie.

Louison. But, papa, don't tell my sister, that I told you.

Argan. No, no.

Louison. [*After seeing if anybody listened.*] Why, papa, there came a man into my sister's chamber when I was there.

Argan. Well?

Louison. I asked him what he wanted, and he told me he was her music-master.

Argan. [*Aside.*] Um, um. There's the business. [*To Louison.*] Well?

Louison. Afterwards my sister came.

Argan. Well?

Louison. She said to him, Begone, begone, begone, for goodness' sake! Begone, you make me in pain.

Argan. Very well?

Louison. And he wouldn't go.

Argan. What did he say to her?

Louison. He said, I don't know how many things.

Argan. But what was it?

Louison. He told her this, and that, and t'other, how he loved her dearly, and that she was the prettiest creature in the world.

Argan. And then?

Louison. And then he fell down on his knees to her.

Argan. And then?

Louison. And then he kissed her hand.

Argan. And then?

Louison. And then my mamma came to the door, and he ran away.

Argan. Was there nothing else?

Louison. No, papa.

Argan. My little finger however mutters something besides. [*Putting his finger to his ear.*] Stay. Eh? ha, hah! Ay? Hoh, hoh! here's my little finger tells me something that you saw, and that you have not told me.

Louison. Oh! papa. Your little finger is a fibber.

Argan. Have a care.

Louison. No, papa, don't believe it, it fibs, I assure you.

Argan. Hoh! well, well, we shall see that. Go your way,

and be sure you observe everything, go. [*Alone.*] Well! I've
no more children. Oh! what perplexity of affairs! I have not
leisure so much as to mind my illness. In good truth, I can hold
out no longer. [*Falls down into his chair.*

SCENE XII

Beraldo, Argan.

Beraldo. Well, brother, what's the matter, how do you do?
Argan. Ah, brother, very ill.
Beraldo. How, very ill?
Argan. Yes. I am so very feeble, 'tis incredible.
Beraldo. That's a sad thing indeed.
Argan. I haven't even the strength to be able to speak.
Beraldo. I came here, brother, to propose a match for my
niece Angelica.
Argan. [*Speaking with great fury, and starting out of his chair.*]
Brother, don't speak to me about that base slut. She's an idle,
impertinent, impudent baggage, and I'll put her in a convent,
before she's two days older.
Beraldo. Hoh! 'tis mighty well. I'm very glad your strength
returns to you a little, and that my visit does you good. Well,
come, we'll talk of business by and by. I've brought you an
entertainment here, that will dissipate your melancholy, and
dispose you better for what we are to talk about. They are
gipsies, dressed in Moorish habits, who perform some dances,
mixed with songs, that I'm sure you will be pleased with, and
this will be much better for you than one of Mr. Purgon's
prescriptions. Let's go.

ACT III

SCENE I

Beraldo, Argan, Toinet.

Beraldo. Well, brother, what say you of this? Is not this
well worth a dose of cassia?
Toinet. Ho! good cassia is an excellent thing.
Beraldo. So, shall we talk a little together?
Argan. A little patience, brother, I return presently.

Toinet. Hold, sir; you don't remember that you can't walk without your cane.

Argan. You are in the right.

Scene II

Beraldo, Toinet.

Toinet. Pray, sir, don't abandon the interest of your niece.

Beraldo. I'll try every way to obtain for her what she wishes.

Toinet. We must absolutely prevent this extravagant match, which he has got in his head, and I've thought with myself, it would be a good job, if we could introduce here a physician into our post, to disgust him with his Mr. Purgon, and cry down his conduct. But as we have nobody at hand to do it, I have resolved to play a trick of my own head.

Beraldo. How?

Toinet. 'Tis a whimsical fancy. It may be more fortunate perhaps than prudent. Let me alone with it; do you act your own part. Here's our man.

Scene III

Argan, Beraldo.

Beraldo. Will you suffer me, brother, to desire above all things, that you'll not put yourself into any heat in our conversation.

Argan. Done.

Beraldo. That you'd answer without any eagerness to the things I may say to you.

Argan. Yes.

Beraldo. And that we may reason together upon the business we have to talk of, with a mind free from all passion.

Argan. Lack-a-day yes. What a deal of preamble!

Beraldo. Whence comes it, brother, that having the estate which you have, and having no children but one daughter —for I don't reckon your little one—whence comes it, I say, that you talk of putting her into a convent?

Argan. Whence comes it, brother, that I am master of my family, but to do what I think fit?

Beraldo. Your wife does not fail advising you to get rid thus of your daughters; and I don't doubt, but that, through a spirit of charity, she would be overjoyed to see 'em both good nuns.

Argan. Oh! you are thereabouts. My poor wife is at once brought in play. 'Tis she does all the mischief, and all the world will have it so of her.

Beraldo. No, brother, let's let that alone; she's a woman who has the best intentions in the world for your family, and who is free from all kind of interest; who has a marvellous tenderness for you, and shows an affection and kindness for your children which is inconceivable, that's certain. We'll not talk of that, but return to your daughter. With what intention, brother, would you give her in marriage to the son of a physician?

Argan. With an intention, brother, to give myself such a son-in-law as I want.

Beraldo. That's no concern, brother, of your daughter's, and there's a more suitable match offered for her.

Argan. Yes, but this, brother, is more suitable to me.

Beraldo. But ought the husband she takes, to be for you, or for herself, brother?

Argan. It ought, brother, to be both for herself, and for me, and I will bring into my family people that I have need of.

Beraldo. By the same reason, if your little girl was big enough, you'd marry her to an apothecary.

Argan. Why not?

Beraldo. Is it possible you should always be so infatuated with your apothecaries and doctors, and resolve to be sick in spite of mankind and nature?

Argan. What do you mean, brother?

Beraldo. I mean, brother, that I don't see any man who's less sick than yourself, and I would not desire a better constitution than yours. 'Tis a great mark that you are well, and have a habit of body perfectly well established, that with all the pains you have taken, you've not been able yet to spoil the goodness of your constitution, and that you are not destroyed by all the medicines they have made you take.

Argan. But do you know, brother, 'tis that which preserves me, and that Mr. Purgon says, I should go off, if he was only three days without taking care of me.

Beraldo. If you don't take care of yourself, he'll take so much care of you, that he'll send you into the other world.

Argan. But let us reason a little, brother. You have no faith then in physic?

Beraldo. No, brother, and I don't find 'tis necessary to salvation, to have faith in't.

Argan. What! don't you think a thing true which has been

established through all the world, and which all ages have revered?

Beraldo. Far from thinking it true, I look on't, between us, as one of the greatest follies which prevails amongst men; and, to consider things philosophically, I don't know a more pleasant piece of mummery; I don't see anything more ridiculous, than for one man to undertake to cure another.

Argan. Why won't you allow, brother, that one man may cure another?

Beraldo. For this reason, brother, because the springs of our machines are hitherto mysteries that men scarce can see into; and because nature has thrown before our eyes too thick a veil to know anything of the matter.

Argan. The physicians know nothing then in your opinion?

Beraldo. True, brother. They understand for the most part polite literature; can talk good Latin, know how to call all distempers in Greek, to define, and to distinguish 'em; but for what belongs to the curing of 'em, that's what they don't know at all.

Argan. But nevertheless you must agree, that in this matter physicians know more than other people.

Beraldo. They know, brother, what I have told you, which won't cure any great matter; and all the excellency of their art consists in a pompous nonsense, in a specious babbling, which gives you words instead of reasons, and promises instead of effects.

Argan. But in short, brother, there are people as wise and as learned as yourself; and we see that in sickness all the world have recourse to physicians.

Beraldo. That's a mark of human weakness, and not of the truth of their art.

Argan. But physicians themselves must needs believe in the truth of their art, since they make use of it themselves.

Beraldo. That's because there are some amongst 'em, who are themselves in the popular error by which they profit, and there are others who make a profit of it without being in it. Your Mr. Purgon, for example, knows no artifice; he's a thorough physician, from head to foot. One that believes in his rules, more than in all the demonstrations of the mathematics, and who would think it a crime but to be willing to examine 'em; who sees nothing obscure in physic, nothing dubious, nothing difficult, and who with an impetuosity of prepossession, an obstinacy of assurance, and a brutality void of common sense and reason, bleeds and purges at haphazard, and hesitates at nothing. He means no ill in all that he does for you, 'tis with the best principle in the world, that he will dispatch you, and he'll do no more in killing you, than what he has done to his wife and children, and what upon occasion he would do to himself.

Argan. That's because you have a spite against him, brother. But in short, let's come to fact. What must we do then, when we are sick?

Beraldo. Nothing, brother.

Argan. Nothing?

Beraldo. Nothing. We must only keep ourselves quiet. Nature herself, when we'll let her alone, will gently deliver herself from the disorder she's fallen into. 'Tis our inquietude, 'tis our impatience which spoils all, and almost all men die of their physic, and not of their diseases.

Argan. But you must allow, brother, that we may assist this nature by certain things.

Beraldo. Lack-a-day, brother, these are mere notions which we love to feed ourselves with; and at all times some fine imaginations have crept in amongst men which we are apt to believe because they flatter us, and that 'twere to be wished they were true. When a physician talks to you of assisting, succouring and supporting nature, of removing from her what's hurtful, and giving her what's defective, of re-establishing her, and restoring her to a full exercise of her functions; when he talks to you of rectifying the blood, refreshing the bowels, and the brain, correcting the spleen, restoring the lungs, fortifying the heart, re-establishing and preserving the natural heat, and of having secrets to lengthen out life for a long term of years; he repeats to you exactly the romance of physic. But when you come to the truth and experience of it, you find nothing of all this, and 'tis like those fine dreams which leave you nothing upon waking but the regret of having believed 'em.

Argan. That's to say, that all the knowledge of the world is shut up in your head; and you pretend to know more on't than all the great physicians of our age.

Beraldo. In talk, and in things, your great physicians are two sorts of people. Hear 'em talk, they are the most skilful persons in the world. See 'em act, and they're the most ignorant of all men.

Argan. Lack-a-day! You are a grand doctor, by what I see, and I heartily wish that some one of those gentlemen were here to pay off your arguments, and check your prating.

Beraldo. I, brother, I don't make it my business to attack the faculty, and everyone at their perils and fortune, may believe whatever they please. What I say of it is only amongst ourselves, and I could wish to have been able to deliver you a little out of the error you are in, and, to divert you, could carry you to see one of Molière's comedies upon this subject.

Argan. Your Molière with his comedies is a fine impertinent fellow, and I think him mighty pleasant to pretend to bring on the stage such worthy persons as the physicians.

Beraldo. 'Tisn't the physicians that he exposes, but the ridiculousness of physic.

Argan. 'Tis mighty proper for him to pretend to control the faculty; a fine simpleton, a pretty impertinent creature, to make a jest of consultations and prescriptions, to attack the body of physicians, and to bring on his stage such venerable persons as those gentlemen.

Beraldo. What would you have him bring there, but the different professions of men? They bring there every day princes and kings, who are of as good a family as the physicians.

Argan. Now by all that's terrible, if I was a physician I would be revenged of his impertinence, and, when he was sick, let him die without relief. He should say and do in vain, I would not prescribe him the least bleeding, the least small clyster, and would say to him, Perish, perish, 'twill teach you another time to make a jest of the faculty.

Beraldo. You are in a great passion at him.

Argan. Yes, he's a foolish fellow; and if the physicians are wise, they'll do what I say.

Beraldo. He'll be still wiser than your physicians. For he'll not ask 'em for any assistance.

Argan. So much the worse for him, if he has not recourse to remedies.

Beraldo. He has his reasons for not intending it, and he thinks that 'tis not proper but for vigorous and robust people, and those who have strength left to bear the physic with the disease; but for him, he has but just strength to bear his illness.

Argan. Very foolish reasons, those! Hold, brother, let us talk no more of that man, for it raises my choler, and you'll bring my distemper on me.

Beraldo. With all my heart, brother; and to change the discourse, I must tell you, that for a little repugnance which your daughter has discovered to you, you ought not to take the violent resolution of putting her into a convent, that in choice of a son-in-law, you should not blindly follow a passion that transports you, and that you ought in this matter to accommodate yourself a little to the inclination of your child, since 'tis for all her life, and since the whole happiness of a married state depends on it.

Scene IV

Mr. Fleurant (with a syringe in his hand), Argan, Beraldo.

Argan.   Oh! brother, with your leave.

Beraldo.   How, what would you do?

Argan.   Take this little clyster here, 'twill be soon done.

Beraldo.   You are in jest sure. Can't you be one moment without a clyster or a purge? Send it back till some other time, and take a little rest.

Argan.   This evening, Mr. Fleurant, or to-morrow morning.

Mr. Fleurant. [*To Beraldo.*] For what reason do you pretend to oppose the prescriptions of the faculty, and to hinder the gentleman from taking my clyster? You are very pleasant to have this boldness!

Beraldo.   Begone, sir, we see well enough that you have not been accustomed to speak to people's faces.

Mr. Fleurant.   You ought not to make a jest of physic in this manner, and to make me lose my time. I'm not come here but on a good prescription, and I'll go tell Mr. Purgon how I've been hindered from executing his orders, and from performing my function. You'll see, you'll see——

Scene V

Argan, Beraldo.

Argan.   Brother, you'll be the cause here of some misfortune.

Beraldo.   The great misfortune of not taking a clyster which Mr. Purgon had prescribed! Once more, brother, is it possible that there should be no way of curing you of the disease of the doctor, and will you all your lifetime lie buried in their drugs?

Argan.   Ah, brother, you talk of it like a man that's in health; but if you were in my place, you'd soon change your language. 'Tis easy to talk against physic, when one's in full health.

Beraldo.   But what distemper have you?

Argan.   You'll make me mad. I wish that you had my distemper, to see if you would prate thus. Ah! here's Mr. Purgon.

SCENE VI

Mr. Purgon, Argan, Beraldo, Toinet.

Mr. Purgon. I have just now heard very pleasant news below at the door. That you make a jest of my prescriptions here, and refuse to take the remedy which I ordered.

Argan. Sir, 'twas not——

Mr. Purgon. 'Tis a great insolence, a strange rebellion of a patient against his physician.

Toinet. That's horrible.

Mr. Purgon. A clyster which I had taken the pleasure to compose myself.

Argan. 'Twas not I——

Mr. Purgon. Invented, and made up according to all the rules of art.

Toinet. He was in the wrong.

Mr. Purgon. And which would have produced a marvellous effect on the bowels.

Argan. My brother——

Mr. Purgon. To send it back with contempt!

Argan. [*Pointing to Beraldo.*] 'Tis he——

Mr. Purgon. 'Tis an exorbitant action.

Toinet. True.

Mr. Purgon. An enormous outrage against the profession.

Argan. [*Pointing to Beraldo.*] He is the cause——

Mr. Purgon. A crime of high treason against the faculty, which can't be enough punished.

Toinet. You're in the right.

Mr. Purgon. I declare to you that I break off all commerce with you.

Argan. 'Tis my brother——

Mr. Purgon. That I'll have no more alliance with you.

Toinet. You'll do well.

Mr. Purgon. And to end all union with you, there's the deed of gift which I made to my nephew in favour of the marriage.

Argan. 'Tis my brother that has done all the mischief.

Mr. Purgon. To condemn my clyster?

Argan. Let it be brought, I'll take it directly.

Mr. Purgon. I should have delivered you from your malady before 'twas long.

Toinet. He doesn't deserve it.

Mr. Purgon. I was going to cleanse your body, and to have discharged it entirely of all its ill humours.

Argan. Ah, brother!

Mr. Purgon. And I wanted no more than a dozen purges, to have gone to the bottom with you.

Toinet. He's unworthy of your care.

Mr. Purgon. But since you were not willing to be cured by my hands,

Argan. 'Tisn't my fault.

Mr. Purgon. Since you have forsaken the obedience which a man owes to his physician,

Toinet. That cries for vengeance.

Mr. Purgon. Since you have declared yourself rebellious to the remedies I've prescribed you,

Argan. Ah, not at all.

Mr. Purgon. I must tell you that I abandon you to your evil constitution, to the intemperature of your bowels, the corruption of your blood, the acrimony of your bile, and the feculency of your humours.

Toinet. 'Tis very well done.

Argan. Oh! Heavens!

Mr. Purgon. And my will is that within four days' time, you enter on an incurable state.

Argan. Ah! mercy!

Mr. Purgon. That you fall into a bradypepsia.

Argan. Mr. Purgon!

Mr. Purgon. From a bradypepsia into a dyspepsia.

Argan. Mr. Purgon!

Mr. Purgon. From a dyspepsia into an apepsia.

Argan. Mr. Purgon!

Mr. Purgon. From an apepsia into a lienteria.

Argan. Mr. Purgon!

Mr. Purgon. From a lienteria into a dissenteria.

Argan. Mr. Purgon!

Mr. Purgon. From a dissenteria into a dropsy.

Argan. Mr. Purgon!

Mr. Purgon. And from a dropsy into a privation of life where your folly will bring you.

SCENE VII

Argan, Beraldo.

Argan. Ah! Heavens, I'm dead! Brother, you have undone me.

Beraldo. Why? what's the matter?

Argan. I can hold no longer. I feel already that the faculty is taking its revenge.

Beraldo. Faith, brother, you're a simpleton, and I would not for a great deal that you should be seen doing what you do. Pray feel your own pulse a little, come to yourself again, and don't give up so much to your imagination.

Argan. You see, brother, the strange diseases he threatened me with.

Beraldo. What a simple man you are!

Argan. He said I should become incurable within four days' time.

Beraldo. And what does it signify what he said? Is't an oracle that has spoken to you? to hear you one would think that Mr. Purgon held in his hands the thread of your days, and by supreme authority could prolong it to you, or cut it short as he pleased. Consider that the principles of your life are in yourself, and that the anger of Mr. Purgon is as incapable of killing you, as his remedies are of keeping you alive. Here's an opportunity, if you have a mind to it, to get rid o' the doctors, or if you were born not to be able to live without 'em, it is easy to have another of 'em, with whom, brother, you may run a little less risk.

Argan. Ah! brother, he knew all my constitution, and the way to govern me——

Beraldo. I must confess to you, that you are a man of great prepossession, and that you see things with strange eyes.

SCENE VIII

Argan, Beraldo, Toinet.

Toinet. [*To Argan.*] Sir, there's a doctor desires to see you.

Argan. What doctor?

Toinet. A doctor of physic.

Argan. I ask thee who he is.

Toinet. I don't know him, but he's as like me as two drops of water, and if I wasn't sure that my mother was an honest woman, I should say, that this was some little brother she had given me since my father's death.

Argan. Let him come in.

Scene IX

Argan, Beraldo.

Beraldo. You are served to your wish. One doctor leaves you, another offers himself.

Argan. I much fear if you be not the cause of some misfortune.

Beraldo. Again! are you always upon that?

Argan. See how I have at heart all those distempers that I don't know, those——

Scene X

Argan, Beraldo, Toinet (dressed as a physician).

Toinet. Permit me, sir, to make you a visit, and to offer you my small services for all the bleedings and purgations you shall have occasion for.

Argan. Sir, I'm very much obliged to you. [*To Beraldo.*] By my troth, Toinet herself!

Toinet. I beg you to excuse me, sir, I had forgotten to give my servant a message, I'll return immediately.

Scene XI

Argan, Beraldo.

Argan. Hah! would not you say that 'tis verily Toinet?

Beraldo. 'Tis true that the likeness is very great. But this is not the first time we've seen these sort of things, and histories are full of these sports of nature.

Argan. For my part, I am astonished at it, and——

Scene XII

Argan, Beraldo, Toinet.

Toinet. What d'ye want, sir?
Argan. What?
Toinet. Did you not call me?
Argan. I? no.

Toinet.   My ears must have tingled then.

Argan.   Stay a little here, and see how much this doctor is like thee.

Toinet.   Yes truly, I have other business below, and I've seen him enough.

SCENE XIII

Argan, Beraldo.

Argan.   If I hadn't seen 'em both together, I should have believed 'twas but one.

Beraldo.   I have read surprising things of these kind of resemblances, and we have seen of 'em in our times, where all the world have been deceived.

Argan.   For my part I should have been deceived by this, and should have sworn 'twas the same person.

SCENE XIV

Argan, Beraldo, Toinet (in a physician's habit).

Toinet.   Sir, I ask pardon with all my heart.

Argan. [*Aside to Beraldo.*]   This is wonderful!

Toinet.   Pray, sir, don't take amiss the curiosity I had to see such an illustrious patient as you are; your reputation, which reaches everywhere, may excuse the liberty I've taken.

Argan.   Sir, I'm your servant.

Toinet.   I see, sir, that you look earnestly at me.   What age d'ye really think I am?

Argan.   I think that you may be twenty-six, or twenty-seven at most.

Toinet.   Ha, ha, ha, ha, ha!   I'm fourscore and ten.

Argan.   Fourscore and ten!

Toinet.   Yes.   You see an effect of the secrets of my art, to preserve me thus fresh and vigorous.

Argan.   By my troth, a fine youthful old fellow for one of fourscore and ten.

Toinet.   I'm an itinerant physician, that go from town to town, province to province, kingdom to kingdom, to seek out famous matter for my capacity, to find patients worthy of employing myself on, capable of exercising the great and fine secrets which I've discovered in medicine.   I disdain to amuse myself with the little fry of common diseases, with the trifles of rheumatisms and defluxions, agues, vapours, and megrims. I would have diseases of importance, good continual fevers, with a disordered brain, good purple fevers, good plagues, good confirmed dropsies, good pleurisies, with inflammations of the lungs, this is what pleases me, this is what I triumph in; and I wish, sir, that you had all the diseases I've just now mentioned, that you were abandoned by all the physicians, despaired of, at the point of death, that I might demonstrate to you the excellency of my remedies, and the desire I have to do you service.

Argan. I'm obliged to you, sir, for the kind wishes you have for me.

Toinet. Let's feel your pulse. Come then beat as you should. Aha! I shall make you go as you ought. Ho! this pulse plays the impertinent; I perceive you don't know me yet. Who is your physician?

Argan. Mr. Purgon.

Toinet. That man's not written in my table-book amongst the great physicians. What does he say you are ill of?

Argan. He says that 'tis the liver, and others say that 'tis the spleen.

Toinet. They are all blockheads, 'tis your lungs that you are ill of.

Argan. Lungs?

Toinet. Yes, what do you feel?

Argan. I feel from time to time pains in my head.

Toinet. The lungs exactly.

Argan. I seem sometimes to have a mist before my eyes.

Toinet. The lungs.

Argan. I have sometimes a pain at the heart.

Toinet. The lungs.

Argan. I sometimes feel a weariness in all my limbs.

Toinet. The lungs.

Argan. And sometimes I'm taken with pains in my belly, as if 'twas the colic.

Toinet. The lungs. You have an appetite to what you eat?

Argan. Yes, sir.

Toinet. The lungs. You love to drink a little wine?

Argan. Yes, sir.

Toinet. The lungs. You take a little nap after repast, and are glad to sleep.

Argan. Yes, sir.

Toinet. The lungs, the lungs I tell you. What does your physician order you for your food?

Argan. He orders me soup.

Toinet. Ignorant!

Argan. Fowl.

Toinet. Ignorant!

Argan. Veal.

Toinet. Ignorant!

Argan. Broth.

Toinet. Ignorant!

Argan. New-laid eggs.

Toinet. Ignorant!

Argan. And a few prunes at night to relax the belly.

Toinet. Ignorant!

Argan. And above all to drink my wine well diluted.

Toinet. *Ignorantus, ignoranta, ignorantum.* You must drink your wine unmixed; and to thicken your blood which is too thin, you must eat good fat beef, good fat pork, good Dutch cheese, good rice gruel, and chestnuts and wafers, to thicken and conglutinate. Your doctor's an ass. I'll send you one of my own choice, and will come to see you from time to time, as long as I stay in this town.

Argan. You will very much oblige me.

Toinet. What the deuce do you do with this arm?

Argan. How?

Toinet. Here's an arm I'd have cut off immediately, if I were as you.

Argan. And why?

Toinet. Don't you see that it attracts all the nourishment to itself, and hinders this side from growing?

Argan. Yes, but I have occasion for my arm.

Toinet. You've a right eye there too that I would have plucked out, if I were in your place.

Argan. Pluck out an eye?

Toinet. Don't you find it incommodes the other, and robs it of all its nourishment? Believe me, have it plucked out as soon as possible, you'll see the clearer with the left eye.

Argan. There needs no hurry in this affair.

Toinet. Farewell. I'm sorry to quit you so soon, but I must be present at a grand consultation we are to have about a man who died yesterday.

Argan. About a man who died yesterday?

Toinet. Yes, to consider, and see what ought to have been done to have cured him. Your humble servant.

Argan. You know that sick folk are excused from ceremony.

Scene XV

Argan, Beraldo.

Beraldo. Truly, this doctor seems to be a very skilful man.
Argan. Yes; but goes a little of the fastest.
Beraldo. All your great physicians do so.
Argan. To cut off my arm, and pluck out my eye, that the other may be better? I'd much rather that it should not be quite so well. A pretty operation, truly, to make me at once both blind and lame.

Scene XVI

Argan, Beraldo, Toinet.

Toinet. [*Pretending to speak to somebody.*] Come, come, I'm your humble servant for that. I am not in a merry humour.
Argan. What's the matter?
Toinet. Your physician, troth, wants to feel my pulse.
Argan. Look you there, at fourscore and ten years of age.
Beraldo. Well, come, brother, since your Mr. Purgon has quarrelled with you, won't you give me leave to speak of the match, which is proposed for my niece?
Argan. No, brother, I'll put her in a convent, since she opposed my inclinations. I see plainly there's some intrigue in the case, and I have discovered a certain secret interview, which they don't know I have discovered.
Beraldo. Well, brother, allowing there were some little inclination, would that be so criminal, and can anything be offensive to you, when all this tends only to what is very honest, as matrimony?
Argan. Be it what it will, brother, she shall be a nun, that I'm determined upon.
Beraldo. You will very much please a certain person.
Argan. I understand you. We are always harping upon that string, and my wife sticks greatly in your stomach.
Beraldo. Well, yes, brother, since I must speak frankly, 'tis your wife that I mean; and I can no more endure the infatuation you are under in respect to her, than I can your infatuation in respect to physic, nor to see you run headlong into every snare she lays for you.
Toinet. Ah, sir, don't talk of madam, she's a woman of whom there's nothing to be said; a woman without artifice, and who loves my master, who loves him——one can't express it.

Argan.   Ask her but how fond she is of me.

Toinet.   'Tis true.

Argan.   What uneasiness my sickness gives her.

Toinet.   Most assuredly.

Argan.   And the care, and the pains she takes about me.

Toinet.   'Tis certain. [*To Beraldo.*] Have you a mind I should convince you, and show you presently how madam loves my master? [*To Argan.*] Sir, let me undeceive him, and deliver him from his mistake.

Argan.   How?

Toinet.   My mistress is just returned. Clap yourself down in this chair, stretched out at your full length, and feign yourself dead. You'll see the sorrow she'll be in, when I tell her the news.

Argan.   I'll do it.

Toinet.   Yes, but don't let her continue long in despair, for she may perhaps die by it.

Argan.   Let me alone.

Toinet. [*To Beraldo.*]   Hide you yourself in this corner.

Scene XVII

Argan, Toinet.

Argan.   Is there not some danger in counterfeiting death?

Toinet.   No, no. What danger can there be? Only stretch yourself out there. 'Twill be a great pleasure to confound your brother. Here's my mistress. Steady as you are.

Scene XVIII

Belina, Argan (stretched out in his chair), Toinet.

Toinet. [*Pretending not to see Belina.*]   Oh! Heavens! oh, wretched! what a strange accident!

Belina.   What ails you, Toinet?

Toinet.   Ah, madam!

Belina.   What's the matter?

Toinet.   Your husband's dead.

Belina.   My husband dead?

Toinet.   Alas! yes. The poor soul is defunct.

Belina.   Certainly?

Toinet.   Certainly. Nobody knows of this accident as yet, I was here all alone with him. He just now departed in my arms. Here, see him laid at his full length in this chair.

Belina. Heaven be praised. Here I am delivered from a grievous burden. What a fool art thou, Toinet, to be so afflicted at his death!

Toinet. I thought, madam, that we should cry.

Belina. Go, go, 'tis not worth while. What loss is there of him, and what good did he do upon earth? A wretch troublesome to all the world, a filthy, nauseous fellow, never without a clyster, or a dose of physic in his guts; always snivelling, coughing, or spitting; a stupid, tedious, ill-natured creature; for ever fatiguing people, and scolding, night and day, at his maids and his footmen.

Toinet. A fine funeral oration!

Belina. You must help me, Toinet, to execute my design, and you may depend upon it, in serving me, your recompense is sure. Since, by good luck, nobody is yet acquainted with the affair, let us carry him to his bed, and keep his death a secret till I have accomplished my business. There are some papers, and there is some money, that I have a mind to seize on, and it is not just that I should have passed the prime of my years with him, without any manner of advantage. Come, Toinet, let us first of all take all his keys.

Argan. [*Starting up hastily.*] Softly.

Belina. Ah!

Argan. Ay, mistress wife, is it thus you love me?

Toinet. Ah, hah! the defunct is not dead.

Argan. [*To Belina who makes off.*] I'm very glad to see your love, and to have heard the fine panegyric you made upon me. 'Tis a wholesome piece of advice, which will make me wise for the future, and prevent me doing a good many things.

SCENE XIX

Beraldo (coming out of the place where he was hid), Argan, Toinet.

Beraldo. Well, brother, you see how 'tis.

Toinet. In good truth, I could never have believed it. But I hear your daughter; place yourself as you were, and let us see in what manner she will receive your death. 'Tis a thing which 'twill not be at all amiss to try, and since your hand is in, you'll know, by this means, the sentiments your family has for you.

[*Beraldo conceals himself again.*

SCENE XX

Argan, Angelica, Toinet.

Toinet. [*Pretending not to see Angelica.*] Oh, Heaven! Ah! sad accident! Unhappy day!

Angelica. What ails you, Toinet, and what d'ye cry for?

Toinet. Alas! I've melancholy news to tell you.

Angelica. Eh? What?

Toinet. Your father's dead.

Angelica. My father dead, Toinet?

Toinet. Yes, you see him there, he died this moment of a fainting fit that took him.

Angelica. Oh, Heaven! what a misfortune! what a cruel stroke! Alas! must I lose my father, the only thing I had left in the world! And must I also, to increase my despair, lose him at a time when he was angry with me! What will become of me, unhappy wretch? And what consolation can I find after so great a loss?

SCENE XXI

Argan, Angelica, Cleanthes, Toinet.

Cleanthes. What's the matter with you, fair Angelica? And what misfortune do you weep for?

Angelica. I weep for everything I could lose most dear and precious in life. I weep for the death of my father.

Cleanthes. Heavens! what an accident! how unexpected a stroke! Alas! after the demand I had conjured your uncle to make of you in marriage, I was coming to present myself to him, to endeavour by my respects and entreaties to incline his heart to grant you to my wishes.

Angelica. Ah! Cleanthes, let us talk no more of it. Let us here leave off all thoughts of marriage. After the death of my father, I'll have nothing more to do with the world, I renounce it for ever. Yes, my dear father, if I have lately opposed your inclinations, I will follow one of your intentions at least, and make amends, by that, [*Kneeling.*] for the concern I accuse myself of having given you. Permit me, father, now to give you my promise of it, and to embrace you, to witness to you my resentment.

Argan. [*Embracing Angelica.*] Oh! my child!

Angelica. Hah!

Argan. Come, be not frighted, I am not dead. Come, thou art my true flesh and blood, my real daughter, and I am charmed that I have discovered thy good nature.

Scene XXII

Argan, Beraldo, Angelica, Cleanthes, Toinet.

Angelica. Ah! what an agreeable surprise! Since, by extreme good fortune, Heaven restores you, sir, to my wishes, permit me here to throw myself at your feet, to implore one favour of you. If you are not favourable to the inclination of my heart, if you refuse me Cleanthes for a husband; I conjure you at least, not to force me to marry another. This is all the favour I ask of you.

Cleanthes. [*Throwing himself at Argan's feet.*] Ah! sir, allow yourself to be touched with her entreaties and mine; and show not yourself averse to the mutual ardours of so agreeable a passion.

Beraldo. Brother, can you withstand this?

Toinet. Can you be insensible, sir, of so much love?

Argan. Let him turn physician, I consent to the marriage. [*To Cleanthes.*] Yes, sir, turn physician, and I give you my daughter.

Cleanthes. Most willingly. If it only sticks at that, sir, to become your son-in-law, I'll be a physician, and even an apothecary, if you please. That's no such a business, I should do much more to obtain the fair Angelica.

Beraldo. But, brother, a thought's come into my head. Turn a physician yourself. The conveniency will be much greater, to have all that you want within yourself.

Toinet. That's true. That's the true way to cure yourself presently; and there's no distemper so daring, as to meddle with the person of a physician.

Argan. I fancy, brother, you banter me. Am I of an age to study?

Beraldo. Pshaw, study! why, you are learned enough; there are a great many among 'em, who are not better skilled than yourself.

Argan. But one should know how to speak Latin well, to know the distempers, and the remedies proper to apply to 'em.

Beraldo. You'll learn all that by putting on the robe and cap of a physician, and you will afterwards be more skilful than you'd wish to be.

Argan. What! do people understand how to discourse upon distempers, when they have on that habit?

Beraldo. Yes. You have nothing to do, but to talk, with a gown and cap any stuff becomes learned, and nonsense becomes sense.

Toinet. Hold, sir, were there no more than your beard, that goes a great way already; a beard makes more than half in the composition of a doctor.

Cleanthes. I'm ready at worst, to do everything.

Beraldo. [*To Argan.*] Will you have the thing done immediately?

Argan. How, immediately?

Beraldo. Yes, and in your own house?

Argan. In my own house?

Beraldo. Yes, I know a body of physicians, my friends, who will come instantly and perform the ceremony in your hall. 'Twill cost you nothing.

Argan. But what shall I say, what shall I answer?

Beraldo. They'll instruct you in a few words, and they'll give you in writing, what you are to say. Go dress yourself in a decent manner, I'll go send for 'em.

Argan. With all my heart, let's see this.

Scene XXIII

Beraldo, Angelica, Cleanthes, Toinet.

Cleanthes. What's your intention, and what d'ye mean by this body of your friends——

Toinet. What's your design?

Beraldo. To divert ourselves a little this evening. The players have made an interlude of a doctor's admission with dances and music, I desire we may take the diversion of it together, and that my brother may act the principal character in it.

Angelica. But, uncle, methinks you play upon my father a little too much.

Beraldo. But niece, this is not so much playing on him, as giving into his fancies. We may each of us take a part in it ourselves, and so perform the comedy to one another. The carnival bears us out in this. Let's go quickly to get everything ready.

Cleanthes. [*To Angelica.*] Do you consent to it?

Angelica. Yes, since my uncle conducts us.

INTERLUDE

First Entry

Upholsterers come in dancing to prepare the hall, and place the benches to music.

Second Entry

A cavalcade of physicians to the sound of instruments.

Persons bearing clyster-pipes which represent maces, enter first. After them come the apothecaries with their mortars, surgeons and doctors two by two, who place themselves on each side the stage, whilst the president ascends a chair, which is placed in the midd'e, and Argan who is to be admitted a doctor of physic, places himself on a low stool at the foot of the president's chair.

Præses. Sçavantissimi doctores,
Medicinæ professores,
Qui hic assemblati estis;
Et vos altri messiores,
Sententiarum facultatis
Fideles executores;
Chirurgiani and apothicari,
Atque tota compania aussi,
Salus, honor, and argentum,
Atque bonum appetitum.
Non possum, docti confreri,
In me satis admirari,
Qualis bona inventio,
Est medici professio;
How rare and choice a thing is ista
Medicina benedicta,
Quæ suo nomine solo
Marveloso miraculo
Since si longo tempore;
Has made in clover vivere
So many people omni genere.

 Per totam terram videmus
Grandam vogam ubi sumus;
Et quod grandes and petiti
Sunt de nobis infatuti:

Totus mundus currens ad nostros remedios,
Nos regardat sicut deos,
Et nostris præscriptionibus
Principes and reges subjectos videtis.

'Tis therefore nostra sapientia,
Bonus sensus atque prudentia,
Strongly for to travaillare,
A nos bene conservare
In tali credito, voga and honore;
Et take care à non recevere
In nostro docto corpore
Quam personas capabiles,
Et totas dignas fillire
Has plaças honorabiles.

For that nunc convocati estis,
Et credo quod findebitis
Dignam matieram medici,
In sçavanti homine that there you see;
Whom in thingis omnibus
Dono ad interrogandum,
Et à bottom examinandum
Vestris capacitatibus.

First Doctor. Si mihi licentiam dat dominus præses,
Et tanti docti doctores,
Et assistantes illustres,
Learnidissimo bacheliere
Quem estimo and honoro,
Demandabo causam and rationem, quare
Opium facit dormire.

Argan. Mihi à docto doctore
Demandatur causam and rationem, quare
Opium facit dormire.
To which respondeo,
Quia est in eo
Virtus dormitiva,
Cujus est natura
Sensus stupifire.

Chorus. Bene, bene, bene, bene respondere,
Dignus, dignus est intrare
In nostro docto corpore.
Bene, bene respondere.

Second Doctor.

> Cum permissione domini præsidis,
> Doctissimæ facultatis,
> Et totius his nostris actis
> Companiæ assistantis,
> Demandabo tibi, docte bacheliere
> Quæ sunt remedia,
> Quæ in maladia
> Called hydropisia
> Convenit facere?

Argan.

> Clisterium donare,
> Postea bleedare,
> Afterwards purgare.

Chorus.

> Bene, bene, bene, bene respondere,
> Dignus, dignus est intrare
> In nostro docto corpore.

Third Doctor.

> Si bonum semblatur domine præsidi,
> Doctissimæ facultati
> Et companiæ præsenti,
> Demandabo tibi, docte bacheliere,
> Quæ remedia eticis,
> Pulmonicis atque asmaticis
> Do you think à propos facere.

Argan.

> Clisterium donare,
> Postea bleedare,
> Afterwards purgare.

Chorus.

> Bene, bene, bene, bene respondere:
> Dignus, dignus est intrare
> In nostro docto corpore.

Fourth Doctor.

> Super illas maladias,
> Doctus bachelierus dixit maravillas:
> But if I do not tease and fret dominum præsidem,
> Doctissimam facultatem,
> Et totam honorabilem
> Companiam hearkennantem;
> Faciam illi unam quæstionem.
> Last night patientus unus
> Chanced to fall in meas manus:

> Habet grandam fiévram cum redoublamentis
> Grandum dolorem capitis,
> Et grandum malum in his si-de,
> Cum granda difficultate
> Et pena respirare.
> Be pleased then to tell me,
> Docte bacheliere,
> Quid illi facere.

Argan.   Clisterium donare,
Postea bleedare,
Afterwards purgare.

Fifth Doctor. But if maladia
Opiniatria
Non vult se curire,
Quid illi facere?

Argan.   Clisterium donare,
Postea bleedare,
Afterwards purgare.
Rebleedare, repurgare, and reclysterisare.

Chorus.   Bene, bene, bene, bene respondere:
Dignus, dignus est intrare
In nostro docto corpore.

The President. [*To Argan.*]
Juras keepare statuta
Per facultatem præscripta,
Cum sensu and jugeamento?

Argan.   Juro.
The President.
To be in omnibus
Consultationibus
Ancieni aviso;
Aut bono,
Aut baddo?

Argan.   Juro.
The President.
That thou'lt never te servire
De remediis aucunis,
Than only those doctæ facultatis;
Should the patient burst-O
Et mori de suo malo?

Argan.   Juro.

The President.

Ego cum isto boneto
Venerablili and docto,
Dono tibi and concedo
Virtutem and powerantiam,
Medicandi,
Purgandi,
Bleedandi,
Prickandi,
Cuttandi,
Slashandi,
Et occidendi
Impune per totam terram.

THIRD ENTRY

The surgeons and apothecaries do reverence with music to Argan.

Argan.   Grandes doctores doctrinæ,
Of rhubarbe and of séné:
'Twou'd be in me without doubt one thinga folla,
Inepta and ridicula,
If I should m'engageare
Vobis loüangeas donare,
Et pretendebam addare
Des lumieras au soleillo,
Et des étoilas au cielo,
Des ondas à l'oceano,
Et des rosas to the springo.
Agree that in one wordo
Pro toto remercimento
Rendam gratiam corpori tam docto.
Vobis, vobis debeo
More than to nature, and than to patri meo;
Natura and pater meus
Hominem me habent factum:
But vos me, that which is plus,
Avetis factum medicum.
Honor, favor, and gratia,
Qui in hoc corde que voilà,
Imprimant ressentimenta
Qui dureront in sæcula.

Chorus.   Vivat, vivat, vivat, vivat, for ever vivat
               Novus doctor, qui tam bene speakat,
               Mille, mille annis, and manget and bibat,
               Et bleedet and killat.

Fourth Entry

All the surgeons and apothecaries dance to the sound of the instruments and voices, and clapping of hands, and apothecaries' mortars.

First Surgeon.
               May he see doctas
               Suas præscriptionas
               Omnium chirurgorum,
               Et apotiquarum
               Fillire shopas.

Chorus.   Vivat, vivat, vivat, for ever vivat
               Novus doctor, qui tam bene speakat,
               Mille, mille annis, and manget and bibat,
               Et bleedet and killat.

Second Surgeon.
               May all his anni
               Be to him boni
               Et favorabiles,
               Et n'habere jamais
               Quàm plaguas, poxas,
               Fiévras, pluresias
               Bloody fluxies and dissenterias.

Chorus.   Vivat, vivat, vivat, vivat, for ever vivat
               Novus doctor, qui tam bene speakat,
               Mille, mille annis, and manget and bibat,
               Et bleedet and killat.

Fifth and Last Entry

While the chorus is singing, the doctors, surgeons, and apothecaries go out all according to their several ranks, with the same ceremony they entered.

www.ingramcontent.com/pod-product-compliance
Lightning Source LLC
Chambersburg PA
CBHW031141050726
47495CB00018B/260